FIFTH IN THE IMMORTALS OF INDRIELL SERIES

BETRAYAL

MELISSA A. CRAVEN

PRAISE FOR IMMORTALS OF INDRIELL

2016 RONE Award Winner – Best Book Cover
2016 YA Books Central Finalist for Best Indie
2015 Dante Rossetti YA Awards Finalist
2015 International Book Awards Finalist
2015 USA Best Book Awards Finalist

"I loved that Emerge wasn't the usual vampires, shape shifters and werewolves but an entirely new concept." Amazon reviewer ★★★★★

"Just when you think Allie's journey is coming to an end... Craven shows you just how wrong you were. You should NOT miss the end of this book." Amazon reviewer ★★★★★

"Craven has skillfully developed an Urban Fantasy set in a real life, believable context. I can almost believe this ancient race of Immortals actually lives among us." Hub Pages Reviewer ★★★★★

"Emerge is a story that begins as a single snowflake and ends in an avalanche. Craven has put together a story that unfolds again and again, revealing characters of unusual depth." Amazon Reviewer ★★★★★

"Craven has a talent for keeping her reader's attention as she reveals Allie's story, layer by interesting layer. And when you get to the last page, you're left wanting more!" Amazon Reviewer ★★★★★

"The immortal characters all have a special gift, but so does the author. Craven's is a superpower that we can all benefit from: storytelling." Amazon Reviewer ★★★★★

Betrayal: Immortals of Indriell Book 5

By: Melissa A. Craven

Midnight Hour Studio INC

Atlanta, Georgia

For more information contact: Hello@Melissaacraven.com or visit the author's website at **Melissaacraven.com**

*Previously published as Emerge: The Betrayal (Immortals of Indriell Book 5) © May 1, 2019

Cover design by: Daqri Combs: Covers by Combs

Edited by: Rebecca Jaycox

Interior design by: @BooklyStyle

ASIN: eBook B08Q6HC4YW

First Edition for Print by Midnight Hour Studio: December 10, 2020

Printed in the United States of America

In Betrayal, find out what happened during the time Allie and Aidan were apart. And then download your free copy of Scholar to discover everything there is to know about the Immortals of Indriell.

Visit **bit.ly/ScholarOffer** to download now

For the amazing and talented Michelle Lynn
My soon-to-be co-writer and author bestie

Your enthusiasm and support mean the world to me

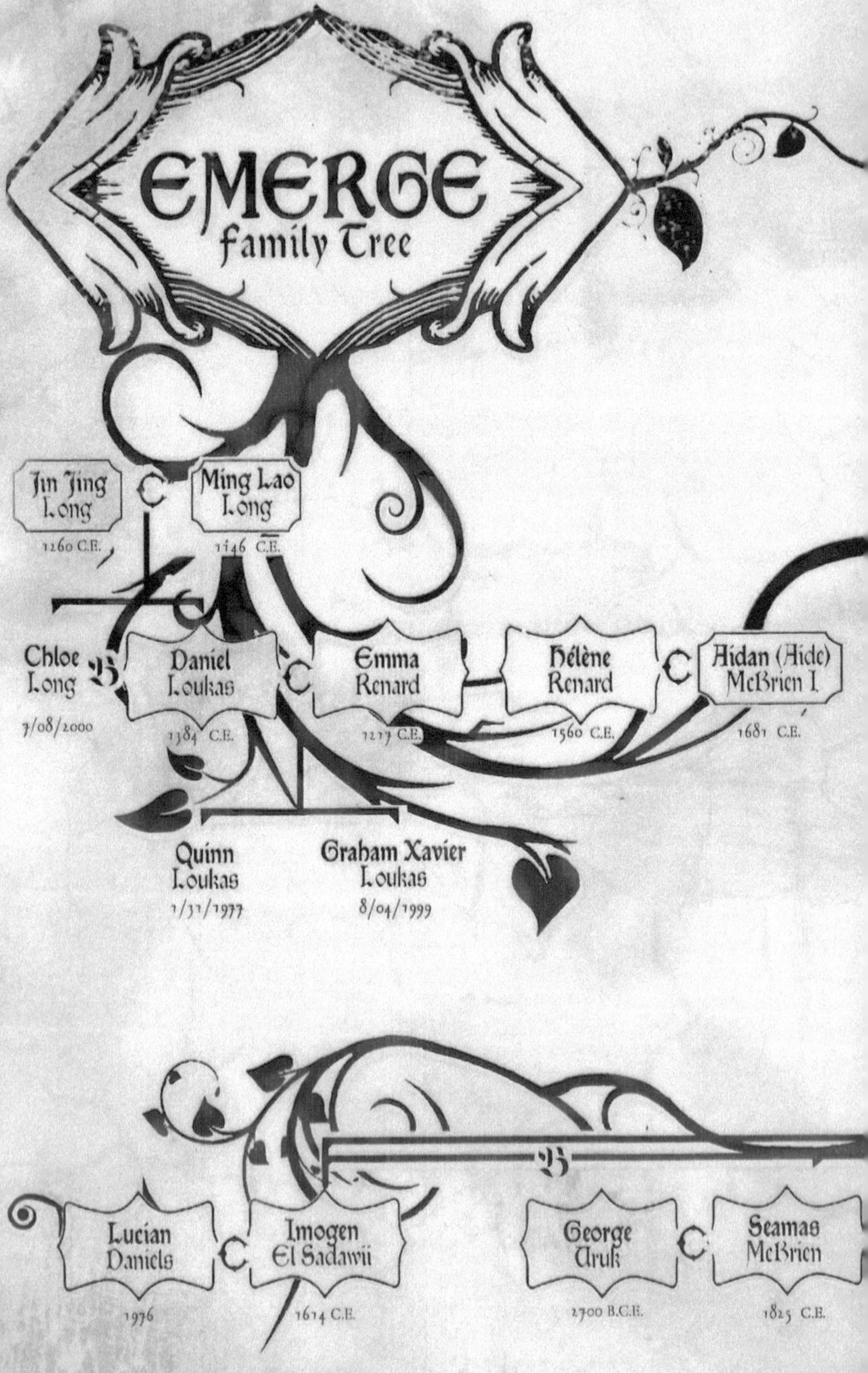

EMERGE
Family Tree

Jin Jing Long
1260 C.E.

Ming Lao Long
1146 C.E.

Chloe Long
7/08/2000

Daniel Loukas
1384 C.E.

Emma Renard
1217 C.E.

Hélène Renard
1560 C.E.

Aidan (Aide) McBrien I.
1681 C.E.

Quinn Loukas
1/31/1977

Graham Xavier Loukas
8/04/1999

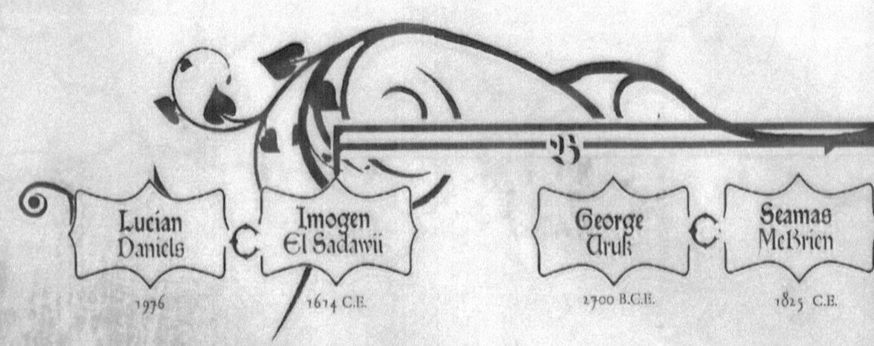

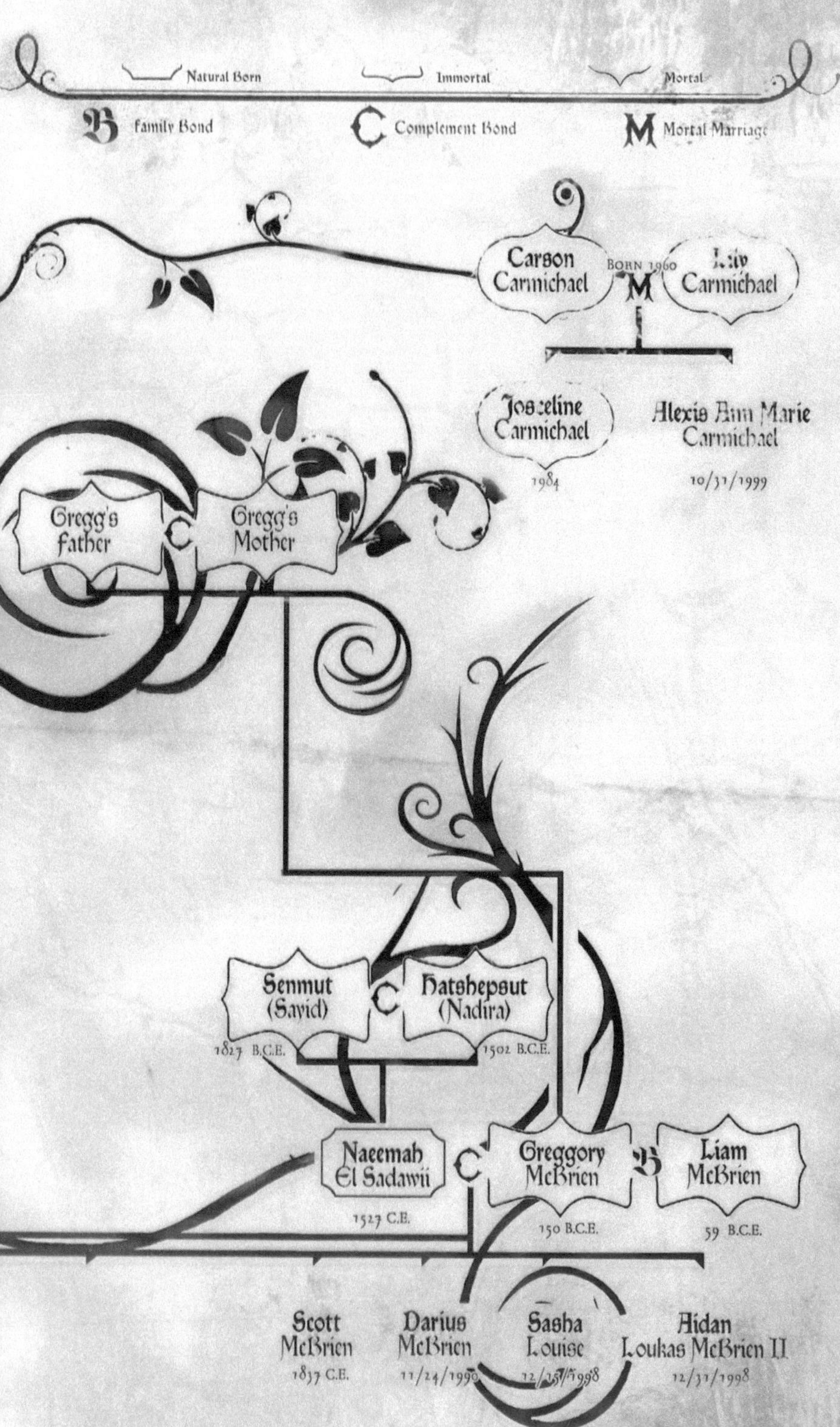

Natural Born
Immortal
Mortal
B family Bond
C Complement Bond
M Mortal Marriage
Carson Carmichael
Born 1960
M
Liv Carmichael
Josceline Carmichael
1984
Alexis Ann Marie Carmichael
10/31/1999
Gregg's Father
C
Gregg's Mother
Senmut (Sayid)
1823 B.C.E.
C
Hatshepsut (Nadira)
1502 B.C.E.
Naeemah El Sadawii
1523 C.E.
C
Greggory McBrien
150 B.C.E.
B
Liam McBrien
59 B.C.E.
Scott McBrien
1837 C.E.
Darius McBrien
11/24/1990
Sasha Louise
12/25/1998
Aidan Loukas McBrien II
12/31/1998

Immortals Of Indriell Series Timeline

Nov. 2016

July 2016

April 2016

Aug. 2015

April 2016

Mar. 2016

Oct. 2015

June 2015

June 2015

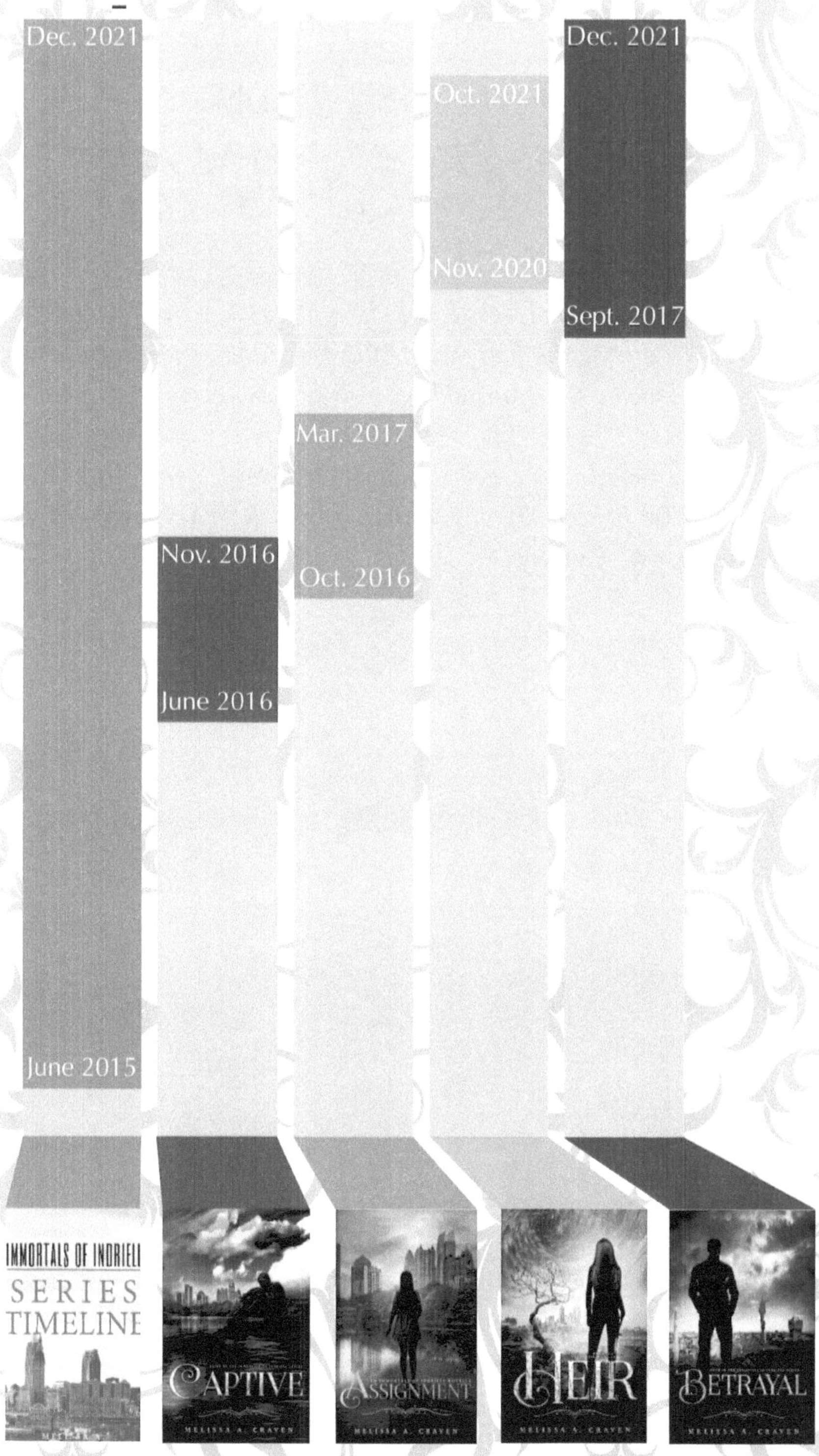

Dec. 2021

June 2015

Nov. 2016

June 2016

Mar. 2017

Oct. 2016

Oct. 2021

Nov. 2020

Dec. 2021

Sept. 2017

Note to the Reader

Betrayal takes place between Judgment (book 2) and Heir (Book 4) during the four years Allie and Aidan spent apart. I've included a timeline guide as well as a character chart for reference.

And I'm always eagerly available to answer questions in my private Facebook group, ***Fantasy Book Warriors*** *—* **Melissa A. Craven**

Cast List For Betrayal

Alexis (Allie) Carmichael – Child of prophecy and adopted daughter of mortal parents, Lily and Carson Carmichael

Aidan McBrien – Adopted son of Greggory McBrien and Naeemah El Sadawii, arguably the most powerful Immortal of his generation.

Darius McBrien – Syntrophos to Allie Carmichael and brother to Aidan McBrien.

Greyson Hauser – Naomi's father and Allie's Art professor/boss.

Pilar – Teacher at the Milan Initiative

Kassandre – Allie's natural mother. Syntrophos to Greggory McBrien. Also served as Chief Justice of the International Senate

Ashar/Navid – Allie's natural father. A dream walker, also known as Navid. Served as Chief Justice of the International Senate

Alísun – Allie's ancient grandmother and last queen of Indriell. Was captive of Marcus Servius for almost two-thousand years

Alexander – Allie's ancient grandfather. Also known as the Scholar

Marcus Servius – Also known as the ancient Lord Teigan and Senator Robert Sinclair. Livia's "adopted" father. Leader of the Coalition and owner of Soma

Porcia – Livia's adopted mother and wife to Marcus

Servius (Porcia and Marcus have never completed the Complement bond)

Livia McBrien – Allie's natural sister. Also known as Alivia. Former leader of Soma, "adopted" daughter of Marcus Servius and Complement to Liam McBrien.

Naomi Hauser – Friend to Aidan McBrien and daughter of Greyson Hauser, long time friend of the McBrien family

Emma Renard—Mentor to Allie Carmichael. Complement to Daniel Loukas. Mother to Quinn, Graham and Parker Loukas

Quinn Loukas – Syntrophos to Sasha El Sadawii and a dream walker

Syntrophos pairs

Alexis Carmichael and Darius McBrien
Sasha McBrien and Quinn Loukas
Greggory McBrien and the ancient, Kassandre

Aidan's Syntrophos Army

Aidan McBrien and Naomi Hauser
Neela and Ivy
Ezra and Wes
Samantha and Bennett
Rowan and Spenser
Gemma and Ruthie
Ace and Lola

Syntrophos leaders of the Milan Initiative

Cleo and Genevieve

Dream walkers

Quinn Loukas
Navid
Brecken
Raina
Brigs
Danica
Hale
Scarlett
Silver
Dominic
Rocco
Maddox
Max

PART I
FOUR YEARS AGO...

CHAPTER 1

Aidan | Rural New York | The New Moon

"She's dead?" Aidan blinked the soot from his eyes, turning his back on the burning orchard and the sight of Ming Lao, lying so still among the ashes. Chloe's heartbreaking wails cut right through him.

"But Jin will survive." Allie choked on the words, so certain of her visions that had brought them all this way to save his parents from a similar fate.

"He'll wish he hadn't," Darius added.

The three ran along the path through the woods taking them from the apple orchard to the main gates. The battle grew distant behind them.

"What's next?" Aidan looked to Allie for answers. She was exhausted and terrified, but she was in control and the power of her visions danced like green fire in her eyes. She knew what to do and Aidan trusted her with his life and the lives of everyone he loved.

"We have to find your mom." Allie took off like a huntress, stalking her prey. Aidan and Darius followed close behind. The bond his brother now shared with Allie clung to them with a cloying sweet scent. A spike of fear and jealousy coursed through Aidan's veins, distracting him from the fight. Allie had him blocked from her thoughts tonight. She wanted to protect him from her evolving visions, but it left him feeling alienated and uncertain.

When they reached the sloping green lawns, Allie stopped along the tree line where his family continued to battle their unknown enemy.

The fires burned out of control here. Churning black smoke filled the sky as the clang of weapons crashed like thunder. Allie stepped from Aidan's side, long enough to grasp Naeemah's wrist, wrenching her away from a blow that would have taken her out of the fight.

His mother turned, eyes widening in fear when she saw Aidan in the thick of it when he was supposed to be safe at home. Allie had insisted that he and the others needed to be here to help change the outcome of her vision and that was all the motivation he'd needed.

"What are you doing here?" Naeemah raged at them.

"Emma needs you. They have Quinn. Go now, please." Allie sobbed, shoving his mother toward the path.

"Come with me, both of you." Her gift commanded them to obey.

"No!" Allie's voice boomed with a command of her own, breaking whatever influence his mother's gift might have had over them. "We are needed here."

With a nod, Naeemah turned and fled along the path back to the orchard, but someone followed her. Aidan glanced over his shoulder at Allie. She stood with his father, uncle and brother. She was safe for the moment.

Without another thought, Aidan charged after his mother, stalking the man who pursued her. Drawing his sword, Aidan attacked, taking the enemy by surprise. The man turned, lifting his weapon to meet Aidan's blade. He was strong. Powerful. An evil glint lit his eyes.

"You'll do nicely." He took another step toward Aidan, tossing his dagger from hand to hand. "I'll take you back to my dungeon at Soma. Your buddy Quinn's no fun anymore."

Aidan grinned, spreading his arms wide. "Well, come at me, Bro." He raced back toward the gates, his assailant hot on his heels. He intended to lead the man back to where Allie and his father were just a moment ago, but his opponent was faster than Aidan anticipated. Aidan whirled around, raising his blade just in time to avoid losing his head. His attacker wielded a sword and dagger now and Aidan had to move quickly, meeting each blow with a practiced hand. He could feel it coming on. He was falling into the zone where nothing else existed but the fight. Aidan's last clear thought was he'd done the one thing he promised Allie he wouldn't do. He'd left her side.

"You're strong," the man said, sizing Aidan up. "But I'm stronger."

Aidan paid him no mind. He moved from one sword form to the next, blocking, attacking and retreating. He was methodical. Like a machine, but he was barely holding his own against a man with centuries more experience. Time and again, the man's sword bit into Aidan's flesh, drawing blood and gore from his body, like a lion toying with his kill.

The blood red moon broke through the clouds, bathing the sloping lawn with light as Aidan continued fighting a losing battle. It didn't occur to him to call for help, so entrenched in the zone he was.

An ear-splitting shriek echoed along the path to the orchard, but Aidan barely registered the sound. Something else tugged at the corners of his mind, pulling his attention away from his opponent, gradually freeing him from the dark cloud of his mind.

Rage.

White-hot rage flashed through him like a bolt of electricity, but the emotion didn't belong to him.

Then he saw her, standing in the moonlight, as beautiful as she was terrifying in her fury. This girl who was everything to him.

The chaos of battle stilled, all sound muffled to a low hush. His attacker gone. Aidan stood in the light of the blood red moon with Allie. She was the only one who mattered. The only one who would ever matter. Unadulterated joy like he'd never before experienced erupted within his soul, casting a golden green light around them. She truly was everything. *His* everything. How could he have not known the moment he first laid eyes on her—this thing he knew with such certainty now? He was finally whole in the knowledge that Allie was his other half—his equal in power—his best friend and his Complement.

A sob caught in his throat. *I will never lose her.* The rush of clarity hit him with a force he couldn't have imagined. Love for this beautiful, outlandish and often infuriating girl bloomed in his chest. The fear he'd carried with him every day since the moment Aidan knew he loved Allie, vanished. For so long he'd feared that one day he would lose her to some other man in some distant future. A man who was meant to be her partner. Now he knew, *he* was that man. They would have their time and it no longer mattered when that might be. Today. Tomorrow, or years from now, they would share lifetimes of happiness and sorrow together.

Aidan fell to his knees, overwhelmed.

"Aidan!" Her desperate scream sounded in the distance.

He frowned, letting his gaze fall from her to his father, struggling to break away from Liam's hold.

"Aidan!" His father's voice broke through the stillness.

Pain lanced through Aidan's body.

A hand gripped the back of his skull as Aidan's power surged in his chest.

"No," he whispered. His attacker hadn't vanished at all. Aidan gazed down at the source of his agony, frowning at the dagger buried to the hilt in his side. Pain wasn't a new experience for Aidan. He endured the physical pain of others every day of his life. This he could overcome.

But this wasn't just physical pain. Aidan's power burned hot like liquid fire in his chest, just out of reach. Aidan couldn't protect himself. His attacker had him right where he wanted him, clutching the fragile strands of Aidan's healing gift, taking it for his own.

"No." He couldn't fathom a life without healing. It would ruin him. Aidan sought Allie's face. If he lost his ability to heal—lost his ability to fight at her side as her equal, would she still love him? Could he be enough? Or would he always hold her back?

Her rage surged within him again, giving him strength. She was fighting her anger, refusing to let it win.

Let it go, Allie. He took a shuddering breath as she threw her head back, her fists clenched at her sides. An otherworldly screech ripped from her throat. Blood oozed from her nose and eyes and her hands dripped crimson drops onto the grass at her feet. She was glorious in her wrath. An ethereal green glow surrounded her as she unleashed her judgment.

Aidan coughed; blood oozing from his mouth. His injuries were deep, but he couldn't take his eyes off Allie.

Her raptor gaze zeroed in on the man who held Aidan's future in his hands. Allie eyes filled with blood and she roared in outrage. Her anger hit him like a shock wave, but Aidan only felt the intensity of her love, and the euphoric realization he saw reflected in her gaze. She knew ... Allie knew they were Complements.

Golden green light flashed across the sky and dead silence fell around those who'd witnessed Allie's judgment. The strength drained from his attacker's grip and he slumped to the ground beside Aidan. In the moment before his father's arms wrapped around him, dragging him to safety, Aidan realized what she'd done. For him. The man before him now was mortal. Allie had stripped him of his immortality to save Aidan from a life without the ability that defined him.

The girl he loved had just saved his life.

As her frightened eyes met his, he poured all the love he had for her into that gaze, willing her to understand she was still the same Allie he'd always loved. He saw the way his father looked at her, shocked and afraid of what she'd just done. This terrifying gift of hers would carry a heavy weight. Aidan needed her to know she was not evil.

A sob tore from her throat and Aidan wanted nothing more than to comfort her, but his legs wouldn't obey him. His vision grew dark as his blood continued to seep into the ground beneath him.

"Come Aidan," Gregg lifted him onto his feet. "I've got you." He draped Aidan's arm around his shoulder.

"Allie," Aidan said, willing his father to take him to her. The forest swirled around him and he feared he wouldn't remain conscious much longer.

"Aye, she's okay, son. She just needs a moment." Gregg guided him back down the pathway to the orchard.

Allie's sorrowful wails pierced Aidan's heart and her raw screams echoed in the growing darkness. "Please, Dad?" He coughed, wincing at the coppery taste of blood on his lips.

"Liam will see to her. We must go, you're in bad shape, son. Stay with me." But Aidan couldn't fight it any more. His last conscious thought was of Allie. His Complement.

Fresh tears burned Aidan's eyes. He couldn't take much more of this. He was so sure of it that night in the orchard. So certain that Allie had experienced the same revelation. It was a devastating blow when he'd realized that same night, she still had no idea they were Complements. Now, barely a week later and Aidan knew he couldn't live like this. He was a selfish asshole, but he couldn't live with the pain of her not knowing. Allie was currently dealing with the enormity of her new judgment gift as well as her confusing relationship with Darius. She needed Aidan to be in her corner right now. But Aidan didn't have the strength to sit back and watch the way she lit up whenever Darius was around. The agony of his jealousy would destroy them. Hiding it would destroy him.

Aidan paced the hallway outside Emma's office in the underground, working up the courage to knock. It wasn't fair to bother her when her family was dealing with Ming Lao's death and Quinn's return.

"Are you going to wear a hole in the floor?" Emma opened the door, her tired eyes filling with concern as Aidan furiously wiped his eyes. "Come in." She held the door open for him.

"I'm sorry. I know you're busy. I can come back."

"Oh you poor thing. How long have you known?" She pulled him into the room and guided him to a chair.

"A week." He sighed, relieved her gift could sense why he was there.

"You should have come to me right away." She took the seat opposite him.

"It only just occurred to me an hour ago that you've known all along. I forgot your gift allows you to see the Complement bond even before it forms."

"It's no picnic keeping so many secrets. Part of me is thrilled you finally know because I can't imagine two people more perfect for each other than you and Allie. But with the whole Syntrophos thing happening with Darius, you must be dying inside."

"I can't take it, Emma." Aidan's eyes burned and his throat tightened. "How is anyone supposed to do this?" He scrubbed a hand over his face. "It's only been a few days and I already know I can't keep this up. I know this monumental, life-altering thing about the girl I'm going to spend the rest of my life with. And I can't tell her."

"Of course you can't. You know very well if she's not ready to see it, she's not ready to hear it either. Telling her will only cause you more pain, and it will drive a wedge between you."

"I would never cheat her out of such an amazing moment." To tell a Complement before they were ready to see it on their own was the ultimate betrayal. He wouldn't do that to Allie.

"When did you see it?" Emma asked.

"In the middle of the battle," Aidan said. "While I was getting my ass handed to me, I was caught up in the most incredible moment of my life." Aidan smiled at the memory. "And I thought I saw the same realization come over her."

"I'm so sorry, Aidan." Emma reached for his hand.

"I don't know what to do." Aidan squeezed Emma's hand, grateful for her support.

"You're going to have to leave. You need time to come to terms with what you know."

Aidan shook his head. "No. I can't leave her."

"Aidan, you are only seventeen years old."

"Almost eighteen," he mumbled, staring down at his lap.

"And Allie just turned seventeen a month ago. It could take her years to catch up to you. You are not equipped to handle this on your own. And that's okay." She leaned forward, tilting his chin up to meet her gaze. "Immortals hundreds of years older than you have struggled with the physical and emotional pain of such a secret. As much as you love Allie, you have to take care of yourself right now. And that means taking some time away from her."

"It's the worst thing I could do to her. Do you know why it took her so long to admit she loves me?"

"Because she's the most stubborn young woman on the planet?" Emma smiled.

"Truth." Aidan returned her smile. "But she's also scared. When she first came to Kelleys Island neither of us knew what it was like to have a real friend. For the first time we each had a person who wasn't intimidated by our power or felt the natural inclination to defer to us. We finally had a chance to just be ourselves, together. She's resisted loving me all this time because she was so scared we were going to ruin that friendship. That somehow, by loving me she was going to lose me. We are finally in a good place, Emma. We're together and happy, despite all the shitty things happening around us. If I leave, she's going to think her fears were right all along."

"Maybe they were," Emma said. "She's clairvoyant, Aidan. It's entirely possible that in some way her gift warned her this would happen."

"I can't leave her. I can't." Just the thought of not seeing her every day had his heart racing in his chest.

"But you can't be with her either. It will destroy you, watching her go about her life, believing she's nothing more than your high school sweetheart and Darius is her lifelong Syntrophos. And what happens if you inadvertently force it on her before she is ready?"

"Can that really happen by accident?" Aidan's eyes widened in alarm. To force a Complement bond when one partner wasn't ready was akin to rape. He'd never forgive himself.

"You're young. You're both Unproven. You're in an intimate relationship with your girlfriend you happen to share a telepathic connection with. It's highly possible you could subconsciously coerce her. It's time you learn how to block Allie fully from your mind. For both your sakes.

Aidan's shoulders slumped in defeat. "Where would I even go?"

"Don't you have a standing offer at the Cologne Conservatory of Music in Germany?"

"Yes, but Mom and Dad want me to go to Oberlin right here at home."

"They have a preparatory program for high school students, don't they?"

Aidan nodded. "They do."

"So why not go there for a few months? Do you really think Allie wouldn't be thrilled for you to take such a once in a lifetime opportunity? That she wouldn't support you?"

"Well, yeah, she would understand." The tension in Aidan's body began to relax.

"I'm not telling you to break up with her," Emma said. "Just put a little distance between you for now and give yourself the distraction of music to occupy your mind for a time.

You just need a little break to prepare for what living with Allie not knowing will mean for you."

"I think ... I could live with that. But what about my parents? They've always been dead set against me leaving for school abroad. They'd never consider letting me leave before I even graduate."

"You've got more than enough on your plate, Aidan. You let me handle your parents," Emma said, a smile playing at the corner of her mouth.

PART II
TEN MONTHS LATER

Chapter 2

Allie | Cleveland | September

"Your freshman students are a terrifying bunch of idiots." Allie dropped a pile of art history papers on the side table beside her chair and stretched her limbs after a long night of grading.

"Seriously, Allie?" Greyson darted back into the hall.

"Oops." She caught a glimpse of his naked back as he ducked into his bedroom, clutching the towel at his waist.

"You stayed all night? Again?" He called down the hallway.

"Didn't think you'd mind." Allie thumbed through Greyson's lecture notes for his morning classes, making sure they were in order before placing them in his briefcase.

"Of course I mind." Greyson shuffled back into his living room, now fully dressed and drying his long hair with the towel he'd had loosely draped around his hips just a moment before. "You're my intern, you shouldn't spend so much time at my house."

"It's quiet here. I get more done." Allie shrugged. "I thought about crashing in Naomi's room, but I doubt your daughter would be too happy about that. I guess I lost track of time grading this epic stupidity."

Greyson sighed as he walked to the kitchen on bare feet. "Don't ever become a professor, Allie. Your students will hate you." He fussed around in the kitchen, returning with a cup of hot tea for two. "I'd offer you a biscotti, but you ate all of my cookies. Again."

She shot him a scathing look, setting the non-coffee aside. "Sorry, I haven't had a decent snack in weeks. Naeemah hasn't gotten to your house yet."

"Is that why you're always here? Better snacks?" Greyson flipped through the pile of papers. "Man, you are way harsh. These students aren't art history majors, Allie. Survey of Art History is supposed to be an easy class." He frowned at the big red F on the top paper. "Let my mortal students get their feet wet before you murder them in a sea of red ink. And why are you grading freshman papers anyway? You *are* a freshman."

"Did I mention they were idiots? Anyone could grade that garbage."

"Come on, this one can't be that bad." He leaned over her shoulder, pointing to the girl's name on the top. "She had a decent contribution to the last lecture."

"Are you kidding? I was there; she's the worst of the bunch. Half that class is in love with you, and that's the only reason you have more students than the other art history professors combined."

"Ouch, and here I thought it was because I'm a damn good teacher." He bopped her over the head with the stack of papers, as he sat down on the couch opposite her.

"You are. You can't help it you have nothing to work with in this class."

"Go home, Allie. You have to stop spending the night. It's not good for my reputation."

"Whatever. No one cares what I do. I'm just a freshman intern." Greyson created the position for her when she'd landed a coveted spot in his summer accelerated program that ultimately earned Allie a scholarship to Cleveland Institute of Art.

"He's right, Red," Darius said as he came through the front door bearing coffee and donuts. "It is *not* okay to spend the night at your professor's house. People will talk."

"About what?" She frowned at him as he waggled his eyebrows. "Ew, gross. That's disgusting, Greyson's a million years old."

"I have shoes older than you, but again, ouch. I'll have you know appropriately aged women find me very attractive," Greyson said, lacing up his boots. "But even they don't spend the night at my house."

Allie made retching noises. "Ugh, can we stop talking about Greyson's sex life now? No one in their right mind is going to think we're together. That's insane."

"Stop. Spending. The night. Here." Darius tossed a duffle bag in her lap. "I brought your clothes. Go get ready for class. Sasha's meeting us for breakfast in twenty minutes."

"I gotta shower first." Allie grabbed a donut raced into Greyson's room.

"Allie, I have a guest bathroom," Greyson growled.

"I like your shampoo. I'll be quick, promise."

"You're going to get me fired." Greyson said, a note of humor in his voice.

"It's your fault for making her an intern," Darius said.

"I heard that!" Allie leaned back into the hall. "Greyson, don't forget you have that faculty meeting at ten."

"What faculty meeting?"

"The one about the fall bronze casting pour. Remember we talked about setting up a Japanese *anagama* kiln and getting the whole university involved. You're running the meeting."

"That's today?"

"I made notes for you. They're in your bag."

"Right. That's why I hired you."

Chapter 3

Aidan | Cologne, Germany | September

"That sounded like a third grader picking up a violin for the first time." Wendy stared at Aidan with her bow poised over her cello. She was the epitome of a classically trained musician. Always had been, even when they were students at Cliffton Academy together a lifetime ago.

"Sorry, my head's not in it today." The vibration of the strings under his fingers felt slightly off, not enough for most people to notice, but Wendy wasn't most people. She had nearly two years of concentrated study on him now.

"You don't get to have days like that here," she said.

She was right. As a student of the Cologne Conservatory of Music, Aidan needed to be perfect. This was his dream, after all. Since he was a child prodigy, he'd wanted to attend one of the great European academies of music, but his parents wanted him to attend Oberlin Conservatory of Music back home in Ohio—also an incredible school for a budding musician. Once upon a time, Aidan had wanted anything but that—until Allie came into his life. Now, he wanted nothing more than to get back home to be with her. The last ten months had completely changed his perspective.

Knowing he would spend the rest of his life with Allie was a comfort to him now, but those first few days after the realization were the worst moments of his life. He'd spent the summer at the conservatory, but ultimately decided he needed more time, taking one more semester abroad to get his head on straight. Aidan loved every minute of his educational experience here, but living on the other side of the world was torture. Now, with only two months left, Aidan was finally ready to face a life of loving Allie in whatever way he could. She would see him for what he truly was when she was ready.

"Start again," Wendy said. "Get your mind off your distractions and back on *Thaïs: Méditation.*"

"Sorry, I've got this." Aidan adjusted the strings of his practice violin. He preferred playing his Stradivarius. This one was fine, better than most, but he couldn't waltz into school as an eighteen-year-old freshman with a genuine, privately owned Stradivarius that probably belonged in a museum somewhere.

"When is your next rehearsal with your quartet?" Wendy asked. In high school, she was the most gifted cellist he'd ever met, but her time here had turned her into one of the finest musicians at their school. And she'd made the time to mentor him, knowing he planned to transfer at the end of the semester. Most wouldn't waste their time. He was lucky to have her.

"Tomorrow evening." Aidan said. "And I'm not ready."

"You'll be ready. It's a rehearsal but it's important. You need to be thinking about the final symphony this semester. I don't need to tell you how stressful it is to compete at this level for a spot in the final production."

"It's two months away, Wendy. I can do this."

"You're overthinking it. Your technique is perfect when you aren't trying too hard so get your shit together, McBrien."

"You're right. One more time." Aidan nodded for her to begin. Lifting bow to stings, Aidan closed his eyes and thought of Allie, letting muscle memory take over. Missing her had become a constant, like breathing. When he'd left almost ten months ago, they'd planned for Allie to spend the summer in Germany. Then Allie was invited to join the summer program at the Cleveland Institute of Art, and he knew how much she'd wanted to go. It was a rare opportunity for a recent high school graduate and it ultimately earned her a full ride to CIA. Logically, he knew it was good for them both to pursue the things they loved, but on days like today, it just didn't seem worth it.

"That's it," Wendy praised, as she followed him through the difficult piece. "You nailed it that time."

"Thanks." Aidan smiled, letting the music flow from his fingertips. He'd missed playing with Wendy. She was one of the rare few musicians who genuinely challenged him.

"Thinking about her again?" Wendy teased, putting her bow away. She had her own quartet rehearsal to get to.

"One of these days, you two have to meet," Aidan said. "I have a feeling you'd be instant friends, ganging up on me together."

"She's your muse. Think about her when you play and you'll be brilliant." She packed up her cello and turned to go. "Oh great, your other girlfriend is here." She nodded toward the back of the practice room where Naomi waited. "That one definitely doesn't like me."

"Naomi's protective. We've been friend's since I was a kid, but she's not great with people." Aidan gave a gruff laugh. "She and Allie are like oil and water."

"So, have you decided to stay yet?" Wendy asked the same question every time they met.

"You know, Oberlin is also one of the finest conservatories in the world." Aidan gave her his standard answer.

"It's all right." She wrinkled her nose. "But they don't have me. You can't leave. You haven't even experienced the real thing yet. That day camp program you did this summer was child's play. You need to get your shit together and commit to at least a full year here before it's too late."

"I couldn't agree more," Naomi said, as she stood with arms crossed and look on her face that said they weren't through with this tired argument.

"I know it sounds crazy, but this is my decision. And I'm ready to go home."

"I don't think I like your girl too much for letting you do this," Wendy said, as she turned to leave.

"Allie knows my mind, and she knows this is my decision to make. She's not asking me to come home. If anything, she's on your side." Aidan smirked at the annoyed look on Naomi's face.

"Same time next week. Don't flake out on your practice time this weekend." Wendy marched across the room, lugging her cello case over her shoulder.

"I never flake out," Aidan called to her retreating figure.

"I'm liking her a lot more than I did," Naomi said, a wry smile lifting the corner of her mouth.

"Well, that's something, I guess." Aidan sighed.

"Let's go get food. You have to be starving by now."

"I'll eat at home. I need to practice tonight."

"You have all night for that. We're going to the Belgian Quarter where we're going to drink strong German beer and order lots of great food. You need a night away from this music nonsense."

"It's not nonsense, Naomi." Aidan rolled his eyes, flinching when she slipped her hand into his as they headed across the campus to her car. It bothered him, the natural intimacy he still shared with Naomi. It was the ultimate betrayal of Allie, but at the same time, he was torn. He didn't want to hurt Naomi's feelings. He'd always cared for her and always would. Once upon a time, he thought they had a real chance at a relationship. But that was before Allie. Aidan waited a moment before he pulled his hand free of hers. He pretended not to see the hurt look on her face.

Great, now I feel even worse.

"You work harder at this than you do with training. It worries me, Aidan. You can't let music come first. You are the most powerful Immortal of your generation, and you're in danger of losing control."

"I'm maintaining," Aidan insisted. He trained as often as his demanding schedule allowed, but she was right. It wasn't nearly enough.

"You are eighteen years old, you cannot afford to stay stagnant and maintain. You have to keep pushing yourself, or you're going to wake up one day, and your power is going to surprise you with something you aren't prepared for."

"I know, you're right. But it's only a few more months. Once we're back home, I'll get my shit together."

Naomi shook her head, her mouth set in a tight line like she held something back.

"Go on. Say it," Aidan said. "I know when you're stewing about something, so you might as well tell me off about whatever it is I've done this time. And then we can go get food." He shoved his violin in the backseat of her tiny German auto and slammed the door.

"Fine." Naomi slid into the driver's seat. "Buckle up.

We'll talk when we get to the restaurant. I need a minute to figure out how to say this nicely."

"You don't do nice."

"I know." She turned to eye him as she made her way along the congested streets of old Cologne, heading toward the Belgian Quarter. "That should tell you how serious this is." She squeezed the steering wheel with a white knuckled grip. "Have you even been to the Quarter or any of the museums?"

Her question surprised him. "No, but—"

"Have you tried to experience this wonderful city at all? I don't think you've stepped foot off campus since you've been here."

"I'm not here to sightsee, Naomi. I'm here to soak up as much experience as I can before I go back home."

"You should be doing both. In fact..." She turned down a side street. "We're going for a quick tour. I promise it won't take long.

Aidan didn't argue. He gazed out the window as they approached the Hohenzollern Bridge stretching across the Rhine River. She had a point. The city was gorgeous, but he hadn't given it much notice.

"We're taking the footpath across." Naomi zipped into a nearby parking lot. "The bridge has the best views of the city."

"I don't have much time for this, Naomi. But I do want to see it. Let's not cross the whole way. Then you can show me the Belgian Quarter and we can talk over dinner. But then I *have* to get home to practice. Deal?"

"Deal." She hopped out of the car, her excitement overpowering her irritation.

Aidan followed Naomi to the towering arched bridge. It reminded him of the Detroit Superior Bridge back home, but a much more European version of it. And it was three times the length.

"The Cologne Cathedral is beautiful isn't it?" Naomi pointed to the opposite bank in the distance. "It's gothic, obviously, but the spires and flying buttresses are just breathtaking. The original structure dates back to the thirteenth century."

"Allie would love this." He winced at the look on Naomi's face. But the way Naomi talked about art and architecture always reminded him of Allie. They shared a common love of the subject.

"Did you know the Cologne Cathedral has the highest gothic vaults in the world? You should visit the interior. It's like nothing you've ever seen."

"Before we leave for home, I want to see it," Aidan said, pausing to take selfie with the cathedral in the background to send Allie. "And then you can show me what a gothic vault is and explain exactly what a flying buttress is while you're at it."

"Didn't you pay attention in Liam's ancient history class last year? I gave several guest lectures on Gothic and Romanesque architecture."

Aidan shrugged, giving her a sheepish smile. "Sorry, I've never been the best student when it comes to studying these things from a text book. I'm much better in person. Promise." Aidan resisted the urge to take her hand as they walked along the footpath over the Rhine. He didn't want to feel that kind of intimacy with Naomi anymore. It wasn't fair to her or Allie, but it still hit him from time to time. Somehow, even though he knew without a doubt Allie was his Complement, he still had strong feelings for Naomi. Feelings he didn't understand or want.

"What in the world is that?" Aidan pointed at the rusted

grating along the walkway. "Are those padlocks?" They were everywhere, attached to the bridge wherever there was space available.

"They're love-locks," Naomi said simply.

"What's a love-lock?"

"Lovers stroll along the bridge at night to watch the city lights. It's romantic. Couples place a padlock here and throw the key into the Rhine as a symbol of the permanence of their love."

"That's ... sweet." Aidan smiled at the thought of Allie's reaction. She would think it was super cheesy, but she'd secretly love it. He took another picture to show her with a promise they would come here someday to do the love-lock thing together.

Aidan noticed the wistful look crossing Naomi's face. His healing gift sensed the cloud of depression closing in on her. She wanted to share that kind of love with someone so much it was painful. For all her tough demeanor, Naomi was a sensitive person who felt more than most would ever know.

"Dinner?" She turned to him with a forced smile.

"I'm starving."

"I know a great little pub you'll love." She didn't talk much on the drive into the Quarter, but Naomi pointed out all the sites and insisted he had to visit the Ludwig Museum with her soon.

Naomi's gruff demeanor returned as she slid into a parking spot right in front of an old pub.

"Let's sit outside. It's not too crowded, so if I get shouty, we won't have to worry about too many ears hearing things they shouldn't." She held the wrought-iron gate open for him.

Open cafes and pubs lined the streets of the *Belgisches Viertel*—the Belgian Quarter, but the one Naomi chose was different. The alley between the buildings had been transformed into a garden complete with ivy creeping up the cracked brick walls.

"Go on. Get a seat and order some Kölsch."

"What's Kölsch?"

"Seriously, you've been here for months and you've never had Kölsch? It's a pale beer somewhere between ale and a lager. You'll love it."

Aidan gave the waiter a sympathetic smile when Naomi told him to keep the drinks coming and not bother them otherwise. She also ordered Bavarian beer pork shanks and schnitzel for two.

"So what's on your mind? I know that look. You're like a dog with a bone, so out with it." Aidan sat back in his chair, taking a long gulp of the ice-cold beer. It was an unusually warm day, but for the first time in weeks, Aidan relaxed, letting the tension ease from his shoulders. Naomi was right; he needed to take a moment to appreciate where he was.

"You're a stupid boy. That's what's going on."

"Okay." He chuckled. "Why is that?"

"I've watched you since we arrived. You're throwing everything you've got into these few months."

"That's kind of the whole point, Naomi. It's what's expected."

"That's not it. You're trying to make this one semester count as the real thing when it's not. This school was on your bucket list, Aidan. And you're giving it up, just like that?"

"How many times do I have to say it? Oberlin is just as prestigious as any other top conservatory."

"But it's not what you wanted. You're giving up your dreams for a girl."

Aidan glanced down at his beer. "That's not fair." He couldn't explain it. The way it crushed his spirit to be so far away from the girl he loved. How the separation was constantly on his mind.

"No, it's not. It's not fair to you." Naomi reached for his hand. "You know how I feel about Allie, but I know you're in love and you have blinders up with her." She shook her head. "Doesn't she realize what you're giving up just to be near her?"

"Well, Allie happens to believe me when I tell her I'm ready to go home. If you remember, she sees into my mind. She knows better than anyone how I feel about being this far away from her. It's true. I once wanted this education more than I wanted air in my lungs. But things have changed. Music will always be important to me, but it is no longer the most important part of my life. I would think, as my friend, you'd be happy for me."

"I am," she said reluctantly. "It's just difficult to watch you give up something that was once the only thing you ever wanted for yourself. You don't see it, Aidan. You are such a selfless person, always looking out for those you love and rarely taking anything for yourself."

"I'm not giving it up. I'm just altering my dream to include the girl I love. She would do the same for me in a heartbeat, without even thinking about it."

"Would she?" Naomi scowled as the waiter brought their food and darted away as fast as he could.

"I see her thoughts, too, Naomi. I know the real Allie. You have nothing to fear about her taking advantage of me. I can see it when she worries she's pulling me away from a school I love. I can feel it when she misses me so much she cries herself to sleep. And I can see her feelings about you. How she doesn't really care for you either, but yet she tries to understand the version of you I know and love. I know her mind, Naomi. She wants this for me as much as you do, but she knows how ... lackluster all this is without her to share it with."

"But you love it here. I can see it in your face every time you pick up that violin."

"I do. I won't deny that. But I love her so much more."

"If she loves you as much as you say she does, then she wouldn't stand in your way if you really wanted to stay here."

"Of course, she wouldn't."

"I want you to do one thing for me, Aidan. Just think about it. For one moment, think about what it would be like to stay in Cologne and finish your degree here."

"It would be wonderful. I'm not denying that. I would love to be right here at the heartbeat of the classical music world, learning from the greatest musicians of our time."

"Then why not do it? And don't tell me it's because you want to be with Allie. I want to know what you would do if you weren't making such an important decision about your life based on proximity to your girlfriend."

"When you say it like that, it sounds ridiculous." Aidan sipped the last of his warm beer as the waiter brought them another round.

"It is ridiculous, but what would you do if she wasn't in the picture?"

"I'd be here. No doubt about it." Aidan crossed his arms over his chest. He was over this tired argument. He could put an end to it right now and just tell her what Allie truly meant to him. Once she understood Allie was it for him, she'd stop the endless questions. But the idea of telling Naomi something so deeply personal about Allie—something Allie didn't even know about herself—just felt wrong.

"You're Immortal, Aidan. Your life with Allie can wait."

"Music can wait, too. I can always come here another time. Maybe after Allie is Proven, we'll come here together."

When it's safer for her to be out in the world. But Naomi didn't know just how dangerous it was for Allie. Allie was an unknown. The child of prophecy and a direct descendant of the royals of Indriell. Her identity needed to remain a carefully guarded secret. Kelleys Island was still the safest place for her. Hell, it wasn't exactly smart for him to be living abroad either. Aidan was also a powerful unknown.

"If you wait too long, you'll never be able to come back, Aidan. Not in the way you want to be here. We both know in a few more years, you'll have nothing to left to learn here. You have to do this while you still have something to learn from these mortals. You've got one chance to reach your true potential musically. Before you know it, that chance will vanish forever. Does Allie know that?"

"No." Aidan sighed, hating that yet again, Naomi had a point.

"So she thinks you can just go to Oberlin now and in a few decades you can come back here and do it all over again? Do you think she'll ever forgive you when she finds out that won't happen?"

"Probably not." Aidan hung his head.

"Then what are you going to do about it?"

"I'll talk to her. I won't change my mind, but you're right. She needs to know what this really means."

"I guess that's something." Naomi leaned back in her seat, slicing off a hunk of pork with a smile. "She's going to tear your face off isn't she?"

"Probably." Aidan set his fork down, not really hungry anymore. "Do you know what it's like?" He shook his head. "To miss someone so much you'd go to the ends of the earth just to be with them?"

"I do." Naomi glanced down at her plate. "Why do you think I'm here?"

Chapter 4

Allie | Cleveland | October

"Ouch." Allie waved her hand in the air to dispel the sting of hot wax on her thumb.

How many times are you going to do that? Aidan's thoughts were still hazy with sleep. It was early morning in Germany and the middle of the night for Allie. *Do you have any idea what it's like to wake up from a sound sleep thinking you've set yourself on fire?*

Sorry. Allie tapped the surface of her wax sculpture with the hot needle of her wood-burning tool. *I didn't mean to disturb you.* She usually kept better track of the time for both of them. It was hard work, trying not to interrupt Aidan at important moments with the six-hour time difference to consider. Since he'd left for school, they'd honed their ability to shut each other out to perfection. Now their thoughts only mingled when they wanted them to.

I'm never sad about losing a little sleep if it means I get to talk to you. What are you making, babe? And why hot wax? You trying to tell me you're into that?

You wish. She snorted. She loved flirty, sleepy Aidan the most. *It's a model of a dragon for a bronze casting.*

So, you're making a bronze sculpture with wax? Why? Their mental connection allowed her to see the adorable frown creasing his brow, and she wanted to run her fingers through his sleep-tousled hair. In moments like this, their telepathic link made the miles disappear, allowing them to really see each other in their mind's eye.

Well, I'm making it out of wax first, putting all the detail into each scale and claw. And then I'll spend at least two weeks dipping it in slurry—a thin plaster kind of mixture to build up a shell around it until every nook and cranny is covered in a thick casing of hard plaster. But before I do that, I have to create vents using tubes of wax.

Sounds like a lot of work. When does the bronze part happen?

It is a crap ton of work. Allie tapped the hot needle to the wax one more time to get the last of her dragon scales just right. *When the whole thing is covered in plaster with tons of vents and openings, it will go in the kiln to melt the wax.*

So, you're going to destroy what you're making now? How does that even make sense?

The wax is just a tool to build the plaster mold. Once all the wax drains out of the mold and the vent tubes, it goes back into the kiln to harden the shell and clean out any residual wax. Then it get's buried in sand while the bronze is melting in the crucible. Once the bronze is hot lava ready, it takes several people to carry the crucible and pour the liquid bronze into the molds.

Oh, I get it, the bronze takes place of the wax and you're left with a dragon. But if the wax runs out when it's first fired, how does the bronze not run out, too?

That's why it's buried in sand. Allie turned her wood burner off. *The sand keeps the metal inside the mold until it hardens and cools. Then we dig it up.*

And then you just crack it out of the mold and it's done?

I wish. Allie laughed. *I'll have to beat the hell out of this thing to get it out of the mold. I'm kind of looking forward to that part. After all the hours of backbreaking work to get this thing cast, it still won't be done. I'll have to scrub all the plaster off with rough steel wool and cut the bronze tubes from the vents. Then I have to grind those spots down until they're smooth. And then I might finally finish the damn thing.*

Allie and power tools? Aidan rolled onto his side. *That sounds like a terrifying combination.*

I am not a spaz, Aidan Loukas. At least not when it comes to art. I've used a grinder before, thank you very much.

I'm glad I'm a music major. It's hard work, but it will never require the use of power tools.

Don't you have that piece due today? Allie asked.

Yeah, I'm not happy with it, though. I'm not sure I achieved the assignment.

Are you ever going to let me hear it?

Sure, let me get my violin. He groaned as he rolled out of bed.

Fitzy's going to kill you for playing at six in the morning.

My brother's getting used to the noise at all hours of the day and night. He goes around mumbling about "creatives" like it's an expletive.

Let's hear it then. I'm sure it's better than you think.

Shouldn't you be in bed, baby? It's late, and I can feel you're tired.

I am exhausted. I don't know how mortals survive college without cracking.

Well, most people don't do double majors in fine art and art history. Go get in bed, and I'll play for you.

Allie tiptoed into her room, careful not to make too much noise to wake Darius. When they first moved into their little cottage near campus, Liam and Darius remodeled the master bedroom into a Syntrophos suite. They had their own individual spaces but never closed the sliding doors between their rooms. Neither one of them liked to be apart.

"I'm wide awake, Red," Darius said.

He was in bed reading. "Can't sleep?"

"Not until you do, apparently. It feels weird falling asleep alone, even when you're just in the other room."

"I'm headed to bed now," she whispered. "Night, Darius."

It's super weird you two are sharing a room. I would be totally jealous if I didn't know anything about Syntrophos. Not that I'm not jealous. I still am, but I get it. Sort of. I'm trying, anyway.

I know it's difficult, Aidan. But I love you for trying so hard.

Love you, too, babe. Now listen and tell me if I've butchered this piece beyond repair.

Allie climbed into her bed, letting the muscles of her neck and back relax from the tension of the last hours bent over her sculpture. As Aidan began to play, she smiled. She would recognize the voice of his violin in a crowd of violinists. It was distinctly his, and it was her favorite sound in the whole world.

She listened, letting the music wash over her, hearing the tone of his violin and the emotions he poured into it in a way only he could do. Aidan always left a piece of himself in the music he played. The melody was familiar but with an unfamiliar twist. It lulled her into a tranquil state of mind. She would sleep well tonight.

So what do you think? he asked when he'd finished.

It's beautiful as always.

I think you're biased, baby. You have no idea how fierce the competition is here.

I have an idea. She thought of the insane level of talent surrounding her as an art student at one of the best art schools in the country. She couldn't imagine what it would be like at the level Aidan was competing.

Put your critical ears on. You have such a great ear for music without the complication of all the technical BS to cloud your judgment. Your opinion is important.

It's Dvorák, but not in the traditional sense. It sounds like Humoresque, but it's almost like there's a touch of Coldplay in there, too. Am I losing it? That can't be right. A frown creased her forehead.

Yes, you totally got it. His grin was infectious. *This is for my modern music class. We're supposed to create an arrangement of a masterpiece from the Romance period with a subtle contemporary influence, and this whole time I've felt like I've butchered Dvorák beyond repair.*

You nailed the assignment, Aidan. It's perfect, so stop obsessing and go wow your peers with your mad skills.

Aidan snorted. *You're adorable, Lex. I always thought conservatory would be a breeze because I'm so far ahead of my mortal peers. But they make me work for it. There is some amazing talent here.*

Aidan ... When are you coming home? And that was the bad thing about their telepathic link. She couldn't always filter her thoughts. *Never mind me,* she rushed to say. *You know I just miss you.* She tried so hard not to make him feel guilty for staying in Germany longer than expected. It was selfish of her to begrudge him anything he wanted for himself and his music.

I'll be there for Christmas, Lex. I promise.

I don't mean to pester you. I'm so happy seeing you live your dream. You deserve this time, Aidan.

I miss you, Allie. More than you could possibly know. I do love it here, but I'm so ready to come home.

Allie constantly worried about him. When Aidan left, her clairvoyance had reared its ugly head, telling her this separation would last years, not months. It was ludicrous. Her gift was rarely so cut and dry; Allie refused to believe it would actually happen. Not when there wasn't a single piece of evidence telling her things were headed that way. She could see his mind. He was just as homesick for her as she was for him. Still, the idea that some unseen force might keep them apart made her a panicky mess inside. A mess she tried to shield him from.

Aidan simply would not do that to her. Not after all they'd been through. Her gift was wrong.

Then why didn't he come home at the end of summer like he promised? She cringed at the errant thought. *Sorry, I didn't mean that either.* When he'd told her he wanted to stay for just one more semester, Allie had fully supported his decision, but it scared her.

It's okay, Lex. I'll be home before you know it, and then you can help me find a place near Oberlin that's not too far from your school.

You can totally move in with me and Dare. Quinn, Sasha and Santi are all down for it.

Well, those three make it work, but me, you, and Darius will need to take it slow considering your reaction every time we're all in the same room together.

You're probably right. Before Aidan left, she tended to leave the room whenever the three of them were alone. But that was months ago. She understood her relationship with Darius so much more now. *It helps now that I know not to feel guilty for my bond with Darius. It's not romantic. He's just my ride or die guy.*

Nice way to put it.

I know this isn't easy. Allie winced, hoping she hadn't screwed up yet another attempt to explain to Aidan how she felt about his brother.

I'm trying. He sighed. *It's just ... I know you love me, but I want to be your ride or die guy.*

You're my, I can't live without you guy.

Okay, say more things like that. His smile warmed her insides and she knew they'd be okay. *Good night, baby, sweet dreams.*

Love you. Have a good day. Allie rolled over and closed her eyes with a smile. At least they had this.

"Can we go to sleep now?" Darius asked through a yawn.

"Sorry, er ... phone call's over, night, Dare. Love you." Humming the last few bars of Aidan's song, Allie fell asleep, content and confident in their love despite the physical distance between them.

Chapter 5

Aidan | Cologne, Germany | October

Aidan's head snapped back with a painful crunch of Naomi's fist to his jaw.

"Seriously?" He glared at her, spitting blood on the floor of the gym he shared with Naomi and his brother, Scott. "That was a cheap shot."

"Sorry," she mumbled, looking anything but contrite.

"What's gotten into you lately?" Naomi had been on a tear since their lunch nearly a month ago.

"Nothing," Naomi insisted, taking her stance on the mat. They were sparring as a warm up for their training with Scott later in the afternoon before Aidan's evening rehearsals.

"It's obviously not nothing, Naomi. I know when something's bothering you." Aidan took his position across the mat, crouching in a defensive pose.

Naomi came at him like a freight train, slamming into his chest and wrapping her arms around him in a vise grip. She had him down on the mat again in seconds.

"You've been pissy ever since I told you I'm leaving after this semester." He broke her hold and grappled with her across the mat until he had the upper hand. "I know you think I should stay permanently, but I've made my decision."

"You still haven't told her the truth." She shoved him hard, sweeping her leg under his and flipping him onto his back. "I'll support your decision when you start acting like an adult and be honest with your girlfriend about what this decision of yours means. I'm not letting you give up your one chance at this school so easily. Not for her."

"Fine." Aidan slapped the mat and relaxed the tension in his arms. Naomi did the same, rolling onto her back with a thud. "I will tell Allie everything. But it's a conversation I want to have with her in person. I will tell her what it means to give up Germany, knowing I'll probably never have this experience again, but I'm also telling her I do not want this anymore. I know you don't understand, but it's the right decision for Allie and me. I'm going home after the final symphony."

"I still have six weeks to change your mind." Naomi shot to her feet, a scowl plastered on her face.

"Why do you hate her so much?" Aidan snapped. "What did Allie ever do to you?" Aidan had never wanted to get in the middle of Allie and Naomi's angst, but he couldn't understand why they'd hated each other on sight. Neither of them had ever given the other a chance. It made his life a living hell. "I need you to get past this petty bullshit, Naomi."

"Petty?" she snarled. "That girl ... never mind. Let's just spar, I'm in the mood to kick your ass."

"Clearly." Aidan rubbed his jaw where a bruise was forming.

"Don't be a baby, you'll heal before your rehearsal tonight."

"Finish your thought, Naomi." Aidan stood, relaxing his stance. "Let's hear what's so bad about Allie. Tell me what awful things she's done to make you hate her so much before you ever even met her. Let's get it all out, so we can move past it."

"You don't want to hear it." She shook her head, pacing to the other side of the gym for a bottle of water. It was just a pretense to put some distance between them. That was Naomi's tell. Whenever things got a little too real, she left.

"You're not running away from this conversation. Not this time."

"Fine." She whirled around, her clear blue eyes filled with emotions he'd never seen in her before. "I thought you of all people would get it, but you will always be blind where she's concerned."

"All right," Aidan said in a softer tone. "Tell me what bothers you about Allie and my relationship with her. I mean ... you and I have a history ... but you walked away from me, remember?" And despite his love for Allie, it still hurt, the way Naomi ended things with him and then flaunted her new relationship with Liam. Aidan ran his hand through his hair in frustration. As much as he didn't want to admit it, he still had feelings for Naomi and it killed him to see her so hurt.

"We both know I walked away before I could get hurt. Again," Naomi said, her tone defeated.

There wasn't much Aidan could say to that. As much as he cared for her, it was always Allie and always would be. "You left me to be with Liam. Do you know how screwed up that is, to get dumped for your two thousand year old uncle?"

"It was never like that with Liam. We were just friends. I flirted, he thought it was cute, but he refused to take it any further. That was it. The only bonus for me was it made you jealous and Allie insane with anger."

"So all that crap senior year was just a way to mess with Allie?"

"You have no idea what it's been like since she came into the picture." She hung her head. "You're right, it is petty bullshit, but it still hurts."

"Why don't you tell me?" Aidan said, forcing himself to be patient. She was entitled to feel her feelings, as much as he might not understand them.

"I have so many reasons to hate her." She stood, fists clenched and eyes bright with anger. "The little golden girl of Kelleys Island."

"Golden girl?" Aidan wanted to laugh but thought better of it. Naomi believed in whatever was bothering her. She meant the world to him—even when she was being a brat, and he needed to try to see her point of view. "Okay, tell me. I'm listening." He folded his arms across his chest, taking a moment to strengthen the block in his mind that kept his thoughts from waking Allie. She didn't need to hear this.

"Do you have any idea what it's like to come in second place with literally everyone in your life? And you want to know who's first? Go on, take a guess?"

"Allie? That's not—"

"Oh, yes, it's true," she spat. "I know you love me in your own way, but it doesn't hold a candle to what you feel for Allie. Second place." She started pacing across the small room; the light streaming in through the high clerestory windows caught the golden undertones of her hair. She was beautiful, but she was broody and angry and he knew how that felt more than anyone.

"Liam does care for me. At one point, it seemed like we were heading toward something real, despite the age difference holding him back. Then he bonded with his little redheaded sister, and he's been distracted ever since. Second.

Place. I used to babysit for Kahlynn all the time. I love that little girl, but she prefers Auntie Allie now and I hardly ever see her even when I'm home."

"She's Kahlynn's aunt. Of course they're close but that doesn't mean Kahlynn doesn't love you too."

Naomi shrugged, sinking back down to the matt to sit across from him. "Darius and I have been on and off again since middle school. We suck at relationships, but we've always been close. Allie shows up and forges a Syntrophos bond with him, and he barely notices me anymore. Second place.

"When Allie arrived, my whole world changed. I grew up with your family, but I was always on the outside looking in. Always wanting to be part of the group but I never had a place. And she just waltzed in and took her place."

Aidan scooted across the mat to sit next to Naomi. He didn't have the words to make her feel better, but he needed her to know she was important. Without a word, he draped his arm around her.

"And Quinn was captured because of her. We finally got him back and we lost Imogen—*my* mentor because of Allie. Imogen and Lucien have been at Soma since the battle and we're no closer to bringing them home than we were when they were first taken. Not to mention what happened with Ming Lao and her parents. Allie got them killed, Aidan. And now Chloe and Jin are an absolute wreck."

"None of that is her fault," Aidan interjected, his temper rising. Naomi had a point in some ways, but she'd crossed a line in blaming Allie for the battle last winter. "She didn't willfully cause those things, and she fought like hell to keep them from happening at all."

"None of it would have happened if she never showed up," Naomi snapped, and Aidan fought to keep his own emotions in check. Some deep and hidden part of his soul fractured under the pressure of loving two women who seemed to naturally oppose one another.

Love? I don't love Naomi. He wasn't sure he could ever attribute what he had once felt for Naomi as love. The feelings he still harbored for her didn't make any sense.

"You have your father, Naomi. A father who loves you more than you give him credit."

"Don't get me started on Dad."

"Greyson loves you. His world revolves around you, but you don't let him get close enough to see it."

"I know he loves me. But do you know what it's like to live in the shadow of your own mother? A mother you've never met or bonded with? I will always be second best to Isebeau Hauser. And I hate myself for being jealous of her. But it looks like these days I'm coming in *third* with my father."

"I don't even know how to respond to that," Aidan said.

"I called Dad last night. Guess who answered the phone in my own house?"

"Allie." Aidan closed his eyes. She was Greyson's new intern, but what was she doing at his house, answering his phone?

"Apparently, she's helping Dad with his lesson plans for the semester and feels comfortable enough to answer my damn phone in my damn house while *my* damn father is cooking *her* dinner!"

"I do see your point there, Naomi. I'm so sorry." Aidan pulled her into his arms before he could think better of it.

"And Naeemah," Naomi whispered. "She hates me."

"She doesn't hate you. Mom's just overprotective of her McBrien boys. You know we're all momma's boys."

"Did you know she's the only mother I've ever known?" Naomi laid her head on his shoulder.

"She cares for you in her own way," Aidan assured her.

"Did you know ... when I was nine, I bonded with her?"

Aidan leaned back to look at her with a frown. "You have a mother bond with her?"

"It's not reciprocated." She cast her eyes down in embarrassment. "It's okay. She doesn't know—no one does. But she knows how it feels to have a bond with someone who doesn't return it."

"What do you mean?"

"I overheard her talking with your father once. She bonded Allie as her daughter, but Allie hasn't returned it. She has a mother of her own." Naomi pulled away from him. "Second place." A note of contempt crept into her voice.

Aidan's heart ached for Naomi and all the hurt she'd experienced in her young life. "I'm so sorry." He sat beside her, his arm around her waist and her head resting on his shoulder. He wanted to convey the depth of his feelings for her through his healing touch.

"Don't." She pulled away from the warmth of his power. "Not like that." She stood, crossing the room to gather her things. "Scott will be here soon so I'm going to head out."

"Don't go." Aidan followed her. "I'm sorry ... I don't have the words to tell you how I feel about you, Naomi. All I can say is, I love you as much as I love Allie, just in a different way. You are no less important to me than she is."

"Bullshit," she scoffed, folding her arms over her chest. "I see the way you look at her."

"I can't help that," Aidan said, wishing he knew how to fix this.

"It's not that I'm jealous or in love with you that way. I know we don't make as much sense as you and Allie." Naomi uncrossed her arms. "I guess I don't have the words either. I just … it kills me to see you giving up everything for her when I don't think she realizes what she's asking you to do."

"She's not asking me, Naomi. She's never asked me to give up anything. Since the beginning, Allie has been my biggest supporter for even coming here in the first place. Allie and I are together, and this is a decision we have made as a couple. I need you to hear me this time, Naomi. My education will not suffer because I've decided to attend Oberlin instead."

"I just want you to be absolutely certain." Naomi sighed, finally relenting.

Aidan hugged her close, his heart clenching in agony for her pain. Naomi was a dark horse. Depression affected Immortal minds as much, if not more, than it did with mortals. The crush of loneliness and the monotony of the years were sometimes more than some could bear. With Naomi, it was a constant battle, and Aidan wanted so much to help her. Little more than a year ago, he'd discovered he could lift the cloud of depression from her mind with his healing touch, but only for a short while. She'd found it worse when the clouds descended again, so she decided she preferred to stay as she was without his help. Aidan had worked tirelessly to hone that aspect of his healing gift. He hoped he could offer her a longer reprieve in the future.

"Let me help you, Naomi?" he whispered as he held her.

"It's okay, Aidan. I can handle it." She hugged him tight, neither willing to let go just yet. "Just being with you helps more than you could know."

Warmth stirred in his chest, vibrating outward, filling him with a sense of peace and something else he couldn't define in words.

"I said I was fine. You don't need to make me feel better."

"I'm not doing anything. At least not on purpose," he said. "I don't know what this is."

Naomi tilted her head back, gazing into his eyes with a question on her face. Her eyes went wide, and her breath caught in her throat.

Aidan's own chest constricted, as if a tight band cut off his lungs. He couldn't take a full breath. Their arms wrapped around each other, locking them in a painful embrace.

"Is this ... is your gift progressing?" Naomi struggled to get the words out.

Aidan stared into her eyes, mesmerized. "I don't think this is me." His feelings for her crashed around in his mind, as if everything he knew about Naomi restructured in the span of a moment. His thoughts and feelings evolved to a higher level of understanding his brain couldn't even fathom before. "This is us." He stared down at her, pressing his head against her forehead.

"What is this, Aidan?" He could see the same realizations forming in her mind. Her heart pounded against his chest as he held her tighter, wanting to be close to her.

"Do you have any idea how much I need you, Naomi?" he murmured against her hair. "I can always count on you to be completely honest with me. You're always looking out for my best interest, even when my focus is somewhere else, you remind me to be true to myself."

"Are we ... bonding?" Naomi gasped, struggling to catch her breath.

"I think so."

"But how?"

He saw it the moment her heart stopped beating. It was the same moment his own stilled in his chest.

Golden fire blazed hot around them, like a cage of light separating them from the rest of the world. For that moment, it was only Aidan and Naomi. Nothing else mattered.

Aidan fell to his knees with a sob, pulling Naomi down with him. Both gulped great gasps of air into their lungs. Aidan never tasted anything so sweet. It was like taking a breath for the first time.

His heart leaped at the sight of Naomi's smile, his pulse racing at a hypnotic speed. He thought his heart might burst right out of his body, so strong was the force of his new heart-beat. But it wasn't alone. His pulse was strong, but so was Naomi's, thumping like an echo right alongside his.

"I know what this is," he whispered, closing his eyes as his perspective changed in an instant.

"I've never felt anything like this," Naomi said. "It's so powerful." She looked at him, her gaze uncertain.

Aidan lifted his hands to cup her beautiful face. "Is this what it's like for Darius and Allie?" Part of him wanted to tear his brother's face off for daring to care for Allie the way he now cared for Naomi—and he was fully aware of how big of a hypocrite that made him—but the other part of him finally understood what they were going through. "You are a part of me, Naomi. You're my Syntrophos."

"Syntrophos." She tested the word on her tongue. "Are you sure?"

"Yes. I saw it happen to Allie and Darius. He once described the feeling to me. He wanted me to know how much he cares for Allie, but he made a mess of explaining it." Aidan could laugh at the memory now, but at the time, he'd struggled not to kick his brother's ass for falling in love with his girlfriend. He got it now. No one had invented words to describe what he felt for Naomi. There was no question Allie was the love of his life, and that would never change, but in a way, Naomi was the second love of his life and his best friend. It was the best he could come up with, but that still didn't do justice to his feelings for either woman. This almost spiritual love for Naomi existed on a whole different plain than any he'd experienced before. It was friendship, but more. It was family, but more. It was ... transcendent.

"This is permanent?" Her eyes grew soft, and he felt the tension leaving her body.

"Yes," was all he could say.

"You're mine this way? Forever?"

"Yes, Naomi. I am your Syntrophos. I really don't know exactly what that means yet, but I do know you own a piece of my heart forever."

The smile lighting her face took his breath. "Aidan," she whispered, letting her fingers trail through his hair in an intimate gesture. "I don't know if I've ever felt like I belonged with anyone. This is so new. I can hardly fathom it. For the first time in my life ... I feel whole. Like I'm finally ... enough."

"You were always enough, Naomi." He held her tight, hoping she never felt lost or alone ever again.

Allie | Kelleys Island | October

“Hey, Chloe, you ready to work?” Allie gave her friend her best “I’m so excited to be here” smile. But inside, Allie was a nervous wreck. Since the death of her mother, Chloe was a different person.

Chloe was still mourning.

Chloe was trying to figure out how to go on without Ming Lao.

But the new Chloe was mean. Really mean.

“Whatever.” Chloe stalked across Aidan’s office. He’d left it for Allie’s use while he was at school. “Can we just spar today? I’m in the mood to kick something, so it might as well be your ass.”

Allie winced, trying her best not to let Chloe’s venom get to her. Her friend was in pain. But Chloe didn’t want sympathy. That was the best way to piss her off. Chloe wanted revenge.

“We can in a bit. Let’s have a chat first,” Allie said, hesitating. Gregg had told her to keep trying, and Allie was in it for the long haul. She would be there for Chloe no matter what. Even if that was the last thing Chloe wanted. Allie wasn't backing away.

"What do we possibly have to talk about?" Chloe leaned her head back against the chair in front of Aidan's desk. "You want to fix me. I can see it with my gift. You're trying to decide which approach to take." She leaned forward. "How about we go with neither and call it a day?"

"I'm your friend, Chloe. I care," Allie said softly.

"Then say what you have to say and then let's get to work."

"I don't pretend to know how you feel, Chlo. Losing your mom like that. But one of these days, I will lose the only mother I've ever known—"

"You're joking, right?" Chloe sat up and laughed in her face. "You think you can compare losing a mortal mother to what happened to *my* mother? That was a stupid thing to say ... even for you."

Ouch. "I know it's not the same. You lost your mother in a violent way. I wasn't trying to compare, I—"

"My mother died in battle protecting her family. It's how she would have wanted to go," Chloe said, her smoky quartz eyes flashing an angry green. "Your *mortal* mother has been dying since the day she was born," Chloe hissed. "She has always been mortal. You have never expected to have your mother by your side for eternity. You haven't lived your whole life knowing she would always be a constant. That you would have both your parents *forever*. Now, I'm left with a gaping hole in my world, and a broken father who can't get out of bed. Do not pretend to compare your world to mine. You have no idea what it's like. To be stuck in this place where every goddamned corner reminds me of her and everything I've lost. You are not close with your mother the way I was."

"I used to be," Allie said firmly. "Before my Awakening, my parents were my entire world. But bit-by-bit, I've had to put some distance between my mortal family and myself. It's safer for them that way." Allie leaned forward, resting her hands on the smooth leather surface of Aidan's desk. "You know who helped me through that? Your mother. She taught me it was okay to make myself a priority. That if they knew what I faced, they would want me to focus on my training. Ming Lao taught me how to do what I needed to do and still keep my relationships with my mortal family without cutting them out of my life completely." Allie sat back in her chair, staring at the high ceilings. "I never would have had the strength to do that if not for your mother. I can't imagine how much you're hurting, Chloe, but if she were here right now, she would give you the same advice. Ming Lao would want you taking care of yourself and she wouldn't want the hate you have for Livia to destroy the daughter she raised. She went down that road herself, Chlo, she wouldn't want it for you."

"Pretty words from someone who knew my mother for little more than a year. You can try to be sympathetic. You can try to help, but I. Don't. Want it. Especially from you. You still have your family, and you will have time to come to terms with their natural deaths. What happened to my mother wasn't natural. It was pure evil. And that ... *monster* you're holding in the crypt? Your *sister* is responsible. As long as she is here, safe and sound in her luxury, white-collar prison, then you and I are not friends."

"She's Gregg's prisoner, not mine. I don't want Livia here any more than you do." Having Livia so close was like a thorn in Allie's side. She couldn't forget she was there and she couldn't do anything about it.

"Then why do you visit her?" Chloe slammed her fist

down on the desk between them. "That woman murdered my mother with her abomination of a gift. I don't care if she's your sister, I will never forgive her."

"No one is asking you to forgive her." Allie walked around to the front of the desk to face Chloe. "She might be my sister by blood, but, Chloe, you are more my sister than she will ever be." Allie knelt in front of her friend. "I will never forgive her for what she did to Ming Lao and Jin Jing. For what she's taken from you. I visit her because I want answers." That was only part of it. She did want answers, but Allie was also drawn to her sister—her clairvoyance craved Livia's presence. As much as Allie resisted it, she couldn't stay away from Livia's cell.

"Why is she still here? Why haven't we turned her over to the Senate? She should pay for her crimes."

"I agree, but I don't think we can release her, Chloe. Navid and my grandparents are convinced she can be rehabilitated ... and I think there's more going on with Livia than we know. I'm still trying to figure that out."

"I can't do this, Allie." Chloe rested her head against her knees, pulling them tight against her chest. A warm glow surrounded her, and Chloe's breath came in a rapid, panicked rush. "I can't *breathe* with her here. Knowing she's down there in the crypt so near the family she slaughtered, it keeps it all fresh in my mind." Chloe threw her head back; a baleful tear tinged with blood trailed down Chloe's cheek.

"It's okay, Chloe. I'm here." Allie crouched by her side. "Just breathe. Don't suppress your power, just let it come." Allie tried to take her hand but Chloe shoved her away.

Allie watched as Chloe's shoulders trembled and her hands shook, fighting back the inevitable.

"Let her come to you, Chloe. She just wants to help."

"No, it's too much," Chloe whispered, squeezing her eyes

shut. But the warm glow swirled around her, taking on a familiar form. It was beautiful and so very sad at the same time.

The spectral golden dragon lay curled at Chloe's feet. Although made of mist and power and light, it moved like a living, breathing being.

"She was supposed to be my final gift to my mother," Chloe cried, refusing to meet her dragon's eyes. "A guardian to always be with her."

But the vapor-like dragons Chloe created as a monument to her fallen family had taken on a life of their own. The two she'd made for her late grandparents still lay deep within the crypt, standing watch over them as Chloe had intended. But the one she'd made for her mother refused to leave her side. It came to her when she was in pain. And it had her mother's obsidian eyes.

"She's still here with you, Chloe," Allie said. "She wants you to move on."

"That *thing* is not my mother. It does not hold her spirit. It's a result of an irresponsible use of my power. I didn't know what I was doing, but I wanted to leave my mother with a noble tribute."

"I don't know what happened when you brought this beautiful creature into existence, but whatever she is, she's watching over you," Allie said, as the small dragon sat beside Chloe like a sentry. "If a piece of your mother is within her, then you might find her a comfort one day."

Chloe opened her eyes, taking one look at the shifting, swirling substance that made up her dragon, and she bolted.

With a deep sigh, Allie rested her head back against her seat, watching the dragon with the sad eyes approached her. She pressed her cold scales against Allie's cheek. She could feel Ming Lao's presence in the dragon.

"I won't stop trying," Allie whispered.

The noble dragon bowed her head and faded to nothing.

She wasn't sure any of them would ever be able to look the creature in the eyes and not think of Ming Lao. Allie just hoped one day Chloe could think of her mother with love and bittersweet memories and not feel her death all over again. But Allie wasn't sure that day would ever come.

CHAPTER 7

Aidan | Cologne, Germany | October

"I don't want to tell anyone," Naomi said, staring at the ceiling above the sofa in Aidan's room. "I'm not ready to share our bond with the world."

"Neither am I." Aidan came to sit beside her. He couldn't get enough of being near her. For months, he'd resisted his lingering feelings for Naomi, thinking the worst of himself and now those feelings finally made sense. "I'm not ready for that drama yet."

"Yeah, I bet you're not looking forward to telling Allie," she snapped.

He arched a brow at her. "You're mad at me for agreeing with you?" Allie wasn't going to be happy about his new relationship with Naomi. He could hear it now. *Literally, Aidan, anyone but Naomi.* But Allie knew what having a Syntrophos was like. She knew he didn't have a choice and she would accept his relationship with Naomi just as he had accepted her relationship with Darius—begrudgingly and in time.

"Sorry." She winced. "I'm going to need some time to get used to the idea of sharing you with her. I'm experiencing lots of possessive thoughts."

"And I'm just now realizing how much restraint my brother has shown since he bonded with my girlfriend." He moved to drape his arm around Naomi. "But something tells me Darius is going to be furious with me for bonding with you." He laughed at the thought of his brother's face when they broke the news. There were just too many feelings tied up in a snarled mess between the four of them.

"It's not like any of us had a choice."

"True. But ... three Syntrophos pairs in one family?" Although Quinn and Sasha seemed to have mastered the bond already.

"It's her," Naomi said.

"It's not Allie's fault." Aidan sighed. "Naomi." He sat up and turned to face her. "I will never survive this relationship if you don't stop blaming Allie for everything. It's tearing me apart."

"No, Aidan. I'm sorry, that's not what I meant." She sat up on the edge of her seat beside him. "I don't know what it is about Allie, but she's ... special." Naomi said the word like a curse. "And don't you ever tell her I said that. I know I have to learn to like her."

"That's asking a lot right now." Aidan smirked. "I'd be thrilled if you guys just stopped actively hating each other. Allie *is* special." Naomi didn't know how right she was. "You've met her grandparents." It was impossible to meet Alísun and not immediately know she was their rightful queen and her husband, Alexander, was the legendary scholar.

"Yeah, I know she's some kind of *princess* we have to protect." Naomi rolled her eyes.

"And there's a lot more about that I'm not able to tell you." Naomi didn't need to know Allie was the fulfillment of prophecy. After she'd bonded with Darius, Allie said she was "gathering her equals," just as the prophecy said she would. He laughed at the very idea of Allie gathering Naomi close for any reason.

"What's so funny?"

"I'm so screwed." His shoulders shook with laughter, but it wasn't funny. Not really. He had no idea how he would ever be enough for both Naomi and Allie. How could he navigate the dangerous waters between two such strong-willed women? They were like oil and water, his Complement and Syntrophos. Allie was the sun, and Naomi was the moon. And there he was, a lone star stuck in the middle, unable to give either of them up.

"I will learn to get along with her for your sake. As long as she can respect our connection."

"She has her own bond with Darius. She'll understand. Give her some time to ... absorb the blow."

"This is going to get messy, isn't it? Three Syntrophos pairs and this weird overlap between ours and Allie's? Are you sure you have to date her?" A flicker of irritation shone in her eyes.

"It's not just dating, Naomi." What he had with Allie was permanent, and he wanted to share that knowledge with Naomi, but he didn't feel like he had the right to tell her. Not when Allie didn't know and the two were at such odds. Aidan had no idea how this would ever work. Already the panic began to rise in his chest just thinking about it. Panic that would only escalate once they were home in a few short weeks.

A sense of dread hit him in the gut. *We can't go home. Not yet.* The realization shattered Aidan's heart all over again and he was caught up in the agony of those first few days after he'd recognized his Complement. He needed more time with Naomi, learning to understand their bond and what that might mean for their training. Allie and Darius deserved the same, and the ten months they'd had just wasn't enough. No matter how much he and Allie wanted to be together now, it wasn't what any of them needed. He had to think of what their Syntrophos needed. Allie and Aidan had the rest of their lives to be together. But right now, they needed to work on their relationships with their Syntrophos if they ever wanted a future where the four of them could get along.

"Hey." Naomi took his hand. "You're shaking, Aidan. Just breathe." She rubbed a soothing hand across his back. "I'm so sorry. We'll figure it out. I'll do whatever I can to make this easier for you."

Easier for me? Why was it her job to make it easier for him? When would it be her turn? Naomi already felt like second place, even before their bond. *I have to show her how important she is. For once, she needs to come first.*

Aidan held her hand, taking a deep, calming breath as an easy silence fell between them. His thoughts drifted to Allie and Darius. He remembered how torn Allie was between wanting to be with him, but also wanting to be with Darius to explore their strange bond. Aidan was only just now realizing how impossible that situation was for her.

He gazed at Naomi, thinking he'd need a lifetime with her to truly understand what lay between them. A few months was not the answer. He prayed Allie would understand the rash decision he was about to make and hoped she could forgive him for making it for them.

"Let's stay," Aidan said, squeezing Naomi's hand.

"What? I thought we already decided to stay in tonight," Naomi said. "I ordered take out. It should be here soon."

"No, I mean Germany. Let's stay."

She titled her head. "How long?"

"Three more years should do it. I'll get my degree from

the Cologne Conservatory of Music, just like I always wanted, and you and I will have that time together to explore our bond. We'll go home at Christmas and explain the situation to our families in person. And to Allie."

"She'll think you're choosing me over her. Are you prepared for that?"

"I want you to come first this time, Naomi. Allie knows how much I love her." They would make it work. More visits. More time together in the dreamworld. They had more options at their disposal than most people in long distance relationships had.

"Are ... are you sure?" She turned toward him with a hesitant smile.

"No." He returned her smile. "Not at all. But all four of us deserve a chance to explore these bonds before we venture into other relationships. We can visit Allie and Darius and take our time testing the waters with all of us together. And eventually, we'll figure it out."

Aidan wasn't sure about his quick decision. The thought of three more years without Allie tore him up inside. But Allie was in a good place. She had Darius, all the training she needed and she was busy with schoolwork she loved. Allie was strong and independent; she would be okay without him for a little while longer. Right now, Naomi needed him, and he'd do anything in the world to keep that incredible smile on her face. Happiness shone in her eyes, transforming her face. Seeing Naomi with such joy lighting her up ... it breathed new life into him, like her happiness was also his.

And maybe ... after a few years apart, Allie would be ready to truly see him and they could be together for the rest of their lives.

"How do we hide this?" Naomi asked, settling on the mat in front of the floor to ceiling windows of their home gym. "Fitzy's going to know the second he sees us."

"We have to suppress the bond," Aidan said. "I was there when Allie and Darius had to learn. It's simple enough, and they managed it on the first try, but we have to be careful to maintain focus on masking our bond at all times."

"And why do we have to hide it?"

Aidan sat on the floor opposite her. "People fear the Syntrophos bond. They either believe we're a myth or we've died out, and it's best to let them think that since the bond makes us more powerful." Aidan reached for her hands, relaxing into their shared meditation pose. Fitzy would be home soon, so they had to master this quickly.

"Okay, let's do this." Naomi took a deep breath, closing her eyes.

"We need to reach a meditative state together, focusing all our energies on our shared bond." Aidan shut his eyes, clearing his mind of all distractions. They sat together, perfectly in sync. As Aidan took a breath in, Naomi exhaled. With their minds clear, they focused on the link binding their lives together forever.

Aidan reached inside himself, searching for Naomi's bond residing within. He found it easily. She was like a bright flame of fierce loyalty burning hot within his core. An intense desire to protect that flame washed over him. Like it was his responsibility to nurture that spark, coaxing it into a blazing hot inferno only he had the privilege of seeing.

With a trembling realization, Aidan understood this flame was a piece of Naomi's soul inside him, bared to him and only him. Guarding their bond was his most sacred duty. To fail her wasn't an option.

"We've got this," Naomi whispered, opening her eyes.

"We need to split our concentration so a portion of our consciousness remains focused on our bond at all times. An easy thing for almost any Immortal to do, but an essential tool for Syntrophos pairs to protect each other so other Immortals can't sense the Syntrophos bond."

"I won't fail you," Naomi said, her blue eyes blazing into his brown ones.

"Nor I you." Aidan gave her hands a gentle squeeze. Nothing would stop him from protecting his Syntrophos. But they needed guidance. They would have to tell Fitzy soon, but he wanted to keep Naomi to himself for just a little longer. Long enough to break the news to Allie in person.

CHAPTER 8

Allie | Kelleys Island | November

Allie headed down to the crypt after another pointless training session with Chloe. As usual, Allie left her friend feeling like the biggest ass in the world for trying to help—and for being Livia's sister. The compulsion to visit Livia was strong. Allie couldn't seem to stay away, even though it never ended well. Her gift demanded these visits and wouldn't let Allie rest until she did her sisterly duty.

But Allie had Liam to consider. Liam was Allie's brother through their Immortal bond. And Livia was her sister through blood. Liam and Livia were Complements—Livia just didn't know it yet.

Liam deserves so much better.

Two thousand years of waiting and Liam got the short end of the stick. Allie would never forget the look on his face the night he'd told her Livia was his Complement. He was equal parts overjoyed and devastated. Livia was not the woman he'd been waiting for all his life. But she was here now and on some level, Allie knew he wanted to find the good in her, buried under all that bad.

As much as Allie hated the things her sister had done,

there was something strange simmering beneath Livia's outward armor. The things Allie's gift told her about Livia's character didn't match her behavior and Allie was determined to break through her sister's barriers to find the real woman beneath the hard surface. Allie didn't have to like her, but she wasn't doing this for Livia or herself. She was doing this for Liam, and also for Navid. He was desperate for a chance to know his eldest daughter and he was convinced Allie and Livia would become friends eventually. Allie couldn't see that happening, but she hoped they could at least be civil for Navid's sake. That was the hope Allie carried with her during her often-tempestuous visits with her sister. A sister she didn't think she could ever like, much less forgive.

Livia had been a prisoner of the McBriens' since Quinn's return nearly a year ago and they still didn't know what to do with her. They couldn't let her go back to her father, or to Soma, even though Livia showed no interest in returning to either. Allie wanted to let the Senate have her; if only to give Chloe and Jin some peace of mind. But true justice wasn't always on the Senate's agenda. Gregg and Navid believed that turning Livia over to their government would be like placing a weapon of mass destruction into the wrong hands.

Too bad they were probably right.

But they couldn't keep Livia behind bars forever. Allie's grandparents wanted Livia to earn their trust and eventually her freedom, but Allie wasn't going to let that happen any time soon. She would never trust the woman who'd done such horrifying things to her friends.

For now, Livia spent her days inside her high-class prison cell in the underground. She had everything she could possibly need with every comfort and amenity at her disposal, including supervised visits with Navid in the Yard.

Their father was the only one who could really talk to

Livia. Since learning he was her father—her real father—Livia had let her walls down with Navid more than with anyone else.

That thought sent a wave of jealousy through Allie, making her want to turn back and leave Livia to her solitude, but her gift wouldn't let her rest until she visited. Allie slowed her pace as she reached the massive door leading to the underground prison cells where Livia resided. The green aura of her gift lit the way, pulling her reluctantly toward her sister.

"She's coming, try to be nice this time," Liam said, his voice carrying down the long hall.

"I don't know why she tries so hard. I'm not worth it." Allie could hear the self-loathing in her sister's voice. She rarely saw Livia in a vulnerable moment. To hear such doubt coming from her gave Allie pause.

She almost sounds remorseful. Allie didn't know what to do with that. She wanted to cling to her hate and just leave, but her gift wouldn't allow it.

"Fine, I'm going, I'm going," Allie muttered, fully aware how strange it was to talk to her gift.

"She cares about you in her own way," Liam said.

Well, I wouldn't say that. Allie vowed to have another conversation with her brother. She didn't need him filling Livia's head with blatant lies.

"You are her flesh and blood, and you've been through things she can't understand," he continued. "She's trying to get to know the real you, and you need to let her."

"She doesn't need to know the real me. She's better off thinking of me as an enemy like everyone else."

"Just try to have an actual conversation with your little sister. Just this once."

Allie peeked around the corner of her sister's cell, not

wanting to interrupt them. It would kill Liam to know she'd heard their hushed conversation.

"Hey, Livia," Allie said with as much enthusiasm as she could muster. Allie tried to present a cheery front when visiting her sister, hiding the fact that she really hated these visits.

But maybe Liam was right, and they both needed to give each other a real chance. Allie thought she could do that much for her brother. The animosity between them was eating at him, but as her gaze landed on her sister's hateful face, anger and betrayal gnawed at Allie's insides.

"You're like clockwork," Livia said with a sneer, taking a step away from Liam. "You show up every other day no matter how many times I tell you to leave me alone." She crossed to the far side of her cell to pour herself a drink.

"That's right. Go ahead, booze it up." Allie was used to seeing her sister with a glass of whisky in hand. But Allie did a double take when she saw Livia furiously dunking a tea bag instead.

"Retract the claws, both of you," Liam said, leaning against the kitchen counter and crossing his arms. "I'm sick of playing referee. Now sit down, do yourselves a favor and actually talk to each other. You might be surprised how much you two have in common."

Allie glared at her brother, curling her fists at her side.

"That's right, you two even give me the same look when you're pissed."

Allie glanced at her sister to see her relax her fists as well.

"Whatever." Allie flopped onto the suede sofa at the center of the room. She really couldn't call it a cell, except for the bars blocking her sister from leaving. Everything else was beautiful. And white. So much white, right down to the silk rug at her feet. The walls and floor were rough-cut stone, but

Livia had transformed the cave-like room into something out of a design magazine. There was even a crystal chandelier hanging overhead.

"I'll just leave you two to your visit." Liam shoved off the counter with a sigh. "I'll come back this evening."

"Bring some Scotch with you when you come. My tea is rather weak without it."

"We talked about not drinking for a while, Liv." Liam stepped behind her. "Just try it for a few days at least."

"Fine." Livia relented. "Bring chocolate instead." She set the teapot back on the bar cart with a thud.

Allie didn't miss the smile on Liam's face, or the way his hand lingered at the small of Livia's back before he turned to leave, dropping a quick kiss on Allie's forehead. She knew they were Complements, but Allie had not expected the surge of anger and betrayal she felt at the sight of this small affection. Liam was supposed to be on her side. It was ridiculous: they were Complements, she should be happy for him. As much as she struggled to picture it, at some point they would be a complete family, with Liam's daughter, Kahlynn. Allie was fiercely protective of her niece and couldn't imagine a world where Livia became her mother.

Allie swallowed hard, her throat tightening as she saw Liam's future with his little family—a future without her in it.

Allie had two choices: she could continue hating her sister, and then watch Livia and Liam create a life together without her, or she could stop doing this just for Liam and Navid, and do it for herself as well. She'd seen a version of that future during her Awakening. Although she didn't understand it at the time, she'd seen a world where Allie and her sister loved each other. But could she really make the effort, knowing what Livia had done to Chloe and her family? Did she really want a future where the three of them, and Kahlynn, could be a real family?

"Want some tea?" Livia offered with a sigh. "It's Chamomile with citrus. It's supposed to be *calming*."

"Sure, thanks," Allie said, smoothing her hand over the soft suede cushion beside her. "How do you keep all this white stuff clean down here in the dungeon?"

"I'm a stickler for cleanliness." Livia stood with her back to Allie, making a second cup of tea.

"We're definitely different there, I can't keep a white shirt clean."

"When I was a child, my father would punish me for the slightest speck of dust or dirt on my clothes or belongings. I suppose that's where I get it. I like white because it shows everything and I can be sure my things are clean at a glance."

Did she just open up to me? Maybe she was trying for Liam's sake too.

"I can see it on your face, you know." Livia handed Allie her cup of steaming hot Chamomile.

"What?" Allie asked.

"I don't deserve Liam's kindness. I agree with you. I don't, but I do appreciate it." She took the seat opposite Allie, placing her mug on the acrylic coffee table between them.

"Everyone deserves kindness," Allie said. "Particularly when there are others who aren't quite ready to give it." This was the first real exchange they'd had. It felt weird, but Allie dropped the facade she usually kept firmly in place when visiting Livia.

"Why are you here, Allie?" Livia took a sip of her tea. "Why do you insist on coming here, acting like you're happy to see me when you obviously hate me?"

"Honestly ... I don't know." Allie sipped from her own

mug. "Every few days I just find myself coming down here, like an impulse I can't ignore."

"Your clairvoyance guides you?"

Allie's shoulders tensed. "How did you kn—"

"Relax." Livia lifted a hand. "No one told me. It's a logical conclusion given our mother's gifts and what happened when I came for you last year. You were prepared for my attack."

"I did see it coming," Allie relented. "Not that it did much good." Allie absently dunked her tea bag. "And now my gift wants me to be here, so I'm here." She shrugged. "You're my sister. I don't have to forgive you or like you, but we are flesh and blood, and I have precious little of that in my life. I don't know, maybe we owe it to Navid to stop this bullshit head butting and try to be real for once. How about we try that today, and if we both hate it, then we can go back to thinly veiled hostility and fake smiles. Deal?"

"All right, then. What do you want to talk about?" Livia crossed her arms over her middle in a protective gesture.

"I don't know, just tell me something about you I don't know." Allie didn't really care what they talked about. She didn't think there was anything Livia could say to change her opinions of her sister.

"Fine, I'll play your game," Livia agreed. "Once upon a time, I had a father I loved very much. I was Daddy's little girl, and he would do anything for me. I was a sensitive girl, and I loved my family, but I knew nothing of my father's evil side back then. And then one day, I had an Awakening, and not long after my powers began to emerge. I was no longer just his little girl—I was Daddy's secret weapon. I used to think he changed, but I know now he just stopped pretending to be my father. He had plans for me. He trained me day and night, turning me into a warrior. When I was a young woman, all I wanted was his approval. Until the thought of his approval disgusted me as I began to question his motives. I didn't like the things he asked me to do, or the ways he expected me to use my abilities. That was when he started abusing my mother. Not always physically. His brand of abuse was more emotional. But she was the woman who raised me and loved me no matter what I could or couldn't do. She became his prisoner long before I realized it. It wasn't until he started using her to bend me to his will that I saw my mother had always been a prisoner in her own home. So, I had to do whatever my father wanted, or my mother suffered the consequences. There was never a question of whether I was going to be a good person or bad person. There was no question of whether I agreed with his agenda and his ways of achieving his goals. None of that mattered to me or to him. The only thing that ever mattered to me was my mother's safety and comfort. So, I did whatever Marcus wanted. He didn't even notice when I stopped seeking his approval. He no longer saw me as a cherished daughter. I was just his right hand, his secret weapon and his dutiful dog. Since then, I've had little motivation to do anything other than what was expected of me to keep my mother safe and happy. End of story."

"That's horrible," Allie said. She couldn't imagine living her life with such fear. "I'm sorry you've experienced that kind of abuse from a man who called himself your father." Allie leaned forward, setting her mug on the table. "I just don't think I could ever justify sacrificing so many people for my mother's safety. I love her more than anything in this world, but she wouldn't want me to become that person just for her."

Livia stood, taking their empty mugs to the sink in the tiny kitchen across the room.

"It's different when your mother is the only person you have ever been able to trust; when the one who causes her pain is the one who should care for her more than life itself."

"I can't put myself in your shoes, Livia. I just can't wrap my mind around your decisions. Especially that night. You murdered Chloe's mother right in front of her." Allie kept her voice even, just stating the facts.

"Not that it matters now, but at the time, I didn't think I had a choice," Livia said, her back to Allie as she rinsed the mugs in the sink and placed them in the dishwasher. Apparently, her sister was the kind of neat freak who washed the dishes before she washed the dishes. "I thought I was fighting for my life. If I had known you guys were going to put me in white-collar prison with bubble baths and handsome jailers, I probably would have come willingly."

"We always have a choice, Livia. We choose life and we accept the consequences of our actions, even if that means we lose our freedom in the process."

"I lost my freedom anyway." Livia returned to her seat across from Allie.

"Maybe you haven't," Allie said. "You're away from your father now. You don't have to bend to his every wish anymore. Grandmother Alísun said your mother has finally escaped your father's grasp, and now you have, too. If what you say is true, that's more freedom than you've ever had. You have a chance at a fresh start. It's up to you what you do with it." Allie watched as Livia considered her words.

The first time Allie really looked at her sister after the night of the battle, the things her gift told her didn't match what her eyes saw. Allie could read a person's true character, and at the time, she'd thought she was mistaken. She let her gift examine her sister now, and she saw goodness there. At Livia's core, she was everything her behavior said she wasn't. She was loyal, strong, and she loved fiercely. Allie wanted to believe Livia could be that person, but she needed to see the evidence of it.

Livia sat across from Allie, her spine stiff. "Yes, my mother is safe now, and there is no need to go back. But what makes you think you can change me? Or that I even want to change?"

"I can't. That's not my job. I just know this hard and hateful woman you present is not you. My gift tells me that much, but I'm beginning to wonder if you even realize it. You've been his creature for so long maybe you don't know yourself as well as you think do. I can imagine what your life has been like up to this point but you have a chance to change that."

Livia snorted. "You will never know what it's like to be me, to face the things I've had to face. To do the things I've had to do. You don't even realize it, do you?"

"Realize what?" Allie said with a sigh.

"Kassandre and Ashar *allowed* Marcus to abduct me when I was four years old. They *allowed* it!" Livia slammed her fist on the acrylic coffee table causing a crack to split the surface. "Our mother saw everything, and together our parents orchestrated every moment of our lives. They pushed me to become this woman I don't even recognize. While they gave their golden child a cushy life with loving parents and friends and everything you could possibly need, leaving me stranded in a living hell. So don't sit there and think you can *imagine* what my life has been like because you haven't suffered. You don't know what suffering is."

"Cushy life?" Allie tilted her head in confusion. "Golden child? Is that what you think? That our parents somehow favored me over you?" Allie felt the slightest twinge of sympathy for her sister. A crack in the armor of her hatred.

Livia stood, her hands clasped behind her as she paced. Resentment burned in her silvery eyes. "Every decision they made for *my* life was so you would live to fulfill some ancient prophecy."

"Livia, no." Allie shook her head. "You've spent enough time with Navid now to know that's not true. I know I haven't experienced the same horrors as you, and I never pretended to, but you don't know shit about my life. Our parents manipulated every moment of *both* our lives. I grew up alone and lonely, constantly on the move and thinking the entire world hated me. I'm not stupid, I know that is nothing compared to what you've been through, but it's not nothing to me. They didn't choose me over you. As much as I've hated them for it, our parents gave us the only chance they believed we had. They gave us the best life they could to bring us here, to this moment, where we can be in the same room with each other and have an actual conversation. I don't know what their end game was, but I do know Navid would never choose me over you."

"You've known him all your life?" Livia's voice held a note of jealousy. One of the few emotions Allie had seen her display.

"I knew him only as a close family friend until I learned the truth last year. I'm still getting to know Navid as my father, but I can tell you he is the most honorable, kind man you will ever meet."

Livia nodded as if she agreed. "So what now?" She frowned. "You still hate me. And I'm not sure I even like you. But we're sisters and I think we both care deeply for our father."

"I can't forgive you for what you did to Chloe and her family. I can't betray her like that."

"I can live with that," Livia said. "It's the least I deserve for destroying a family."

Allie was surprised by Livia's admission of guilt and her remorse seemed genuine. She didn't know what to do with that or this visit. She was prepared to hate Livia forever. But that was before she got a glimpse at the real Livia.

"So, maybe let's let the past stay in the past," Allie finally said. "Decisions were made for us, but we are here now and I say it's time we both look toward a future of our own making. If that includes a future where we are friends ... I guess we will have to wait and see what happens.

"You're different today." Livia smiled—like a genuine smile. "You've got backbone." She gave a nod. "I prefer this Allie. This girl makes more sense than that sugary sweet girl you've been trotting through here for the last year. In case you haven't noticed, I don't respond to nice. But I can respect a girl not afraid to say what she means."

Allie shrugged. "How about let's not be fake anymore? I don't like the bitchy I-hate-everyone, Livia. I think I prefer the stone-cold-honest Livia instead."

"Sounds like we have a truce," Livia said.

Allie just didn't know what that meant.

Allie left her sister feeling confused. She still hated her for destroying Chloe's family, but after today, she got a glimpse of the real woman behind the armor, and Allie's resolve started to crumble.

"Doesn't matter," Allie muttered. "She's still the reason Ming Lao's gone." Chloe was more of a sister than Livia would ever be. Allie's loyalty would always lie with Chloe. But as Allie made her way through the crypt, she couldn't shake the feeling that she wanted this chance to get to know Livia, if only to make room in her life for her brother's Complement.

Allie headed past the cell Quinn and Santi lived in for a short time. After they returned from their captivity, they spent a few weeks behind bars, just to be sure their bond with Soma was truly broken. Allie would never forget that night, nearly a year ago. Her life had changed forever in the span of a few moments. After her judgment gift manifested, and she'd stripped Aidan's attacker of his immortality, Allie was afraid she would hurt her friends and family. But her gift hadn't resurfaced since then. She could feel it, flickering just under the surface of her temper, but she had it under control. It was a lot like her ability to lend strength to others. There was no "practicing" involved. It came to her when she needed it. She was still learning to trust in her power and in her own control of that power, but for the moment, she was confident she wouldn't hurt anyone she loved. It just didn't sit well with her that her friends didn't know what she was capable of. Gregg and Liam insisted the fewer who knew about it, the better, so Allie kept it to herself. Even from Aidan. She didn't want him to know. She feared he would never look at her the same way again if he knew what she'd done to save him that night.

Allie stepped through the doorway of the underground prison and ran right into her grandparents.

"Allie-girl, hello," her grandfather, Alexander, said. His bright smile and quick wit always set Allie at ease. She'd only known him for a short while, but she loved him already.

"Hi Grandpa Alex," she said.

"We were just taking a tour of this ... er ... lovely dungeon."

"Allie, dear." Her frigid, queenly grandmother gave a curt

nod. "It is good to hear you and Livia have been talking. You've made progress today."

"Oh, you heard all that, did you?" Allie murmured, casting her gaze down to her feet. Her grandmother scared the bejesus out of her.

"Darling, eavesdropping is rude," Alexander whisper-shouted.

"It was your idea," her frosty grandmother replied.

"Yes, but we weren't supposed to get caught." Alexander slowly shook his head and smiled.

Allie hid her laughter. Despite her reservations with her grandmother—the legend, and all-powerful, last Immortal Queen of Indriell—her grandparents together were a riot.

"We didn't mean to invade your privacy, Allie-girl," Alexander said. "I know we're hovering, but we are just so anxious to be part of both our granddaughters' lives."

"It's called helicopter parenting," Allie said and immediately regretted it.

"What's a helicopter?" Alísun asked.

"You've flown in planes, darling. A helicopter is just smaller ... and it hovers." Alexander guided her back to the stairs.

"Oh, I get it," Alísun said. "We won't hover, dear. At least we will try not to. But we do need to stay informed with everything you're dealing with, Alexis."

"You're doing it again, my darling," Alexander said. "How about a cup of tea with your old grandparents?" he asked, as they returned upstairs to the common room. "We promise we won't pry."

"That sounds nice," Allie said. About as nice as a visit to the dentist.

"I'm coming up," Aidan called from the trail below.

Allie waited impatiently as he scaled the rope ladder to her tree house high among the branches. With their busy schedules, their dreams didn't mingle as often as either of them would like and she was eager to get her arms around him.

"I missed you." She rushed into his arms, inhaling his familiar earthy scent. It wasn't the same as being together in the waking world, but they lived for these shared moments in the dreamworld.

Allie laid her head against his chest as he buried his nose in her hair.

"I miss you every moment of every day," Aidan whispered, running a hand across her back.

Allie tilted her head back to meet his lips in a hungry kiss. She slid her hands up his chest to run her fingers through his silky hair. Her pulse pounded and her power churned hot in her chest as Aidan's hands came to rest gently on her hips.

There are definitely perks to this telepathy thing.

Aidan chuckled, breaking their kiss and pressing his forehead to hers. His rapid breath warm against her face. *Once upon a time, that so wasn't the case.*

"We've come a long way since that first night in the dreamworld." Allie smiled up at him. During her busy days with school and training she thought of him often, but these precious moments in the dreamworld reminded her of how much she missed having Aidan in her daily life.

"The tree house is starting to look fancy." Aidan gazed around the yurt-style room at all the new changes she'd made since the last time he was here. "Like a cozy little retreat just for us."

"My favorite house growing up was the tree house in the

Amazon rainforest. I only got to stay there on weekends, but it was so epic, I wanted share it with you."

"How do you make it stay here? Everything we imagine disappears once we leave," Aidan said, taking her hand as he walked around the circular room.

"Navid's been helping me. I create things, and he makes it permanent with his dream walker mojo."

"It's beautiful." With its thatched roof and open windows draped with soft white fabric billowing in the breeze, it reminded Allie of some of the best moments of her childhood.

An enormous tree trunk ran through the center of the room, its branches held the structure steady, like a giant hand. Comfortable chairs waited for them near the open windows, and a canopy bed draped in a pale blue silk fabric rested against the wall behind them. It was the perfect oasis away from their demanding school schedules.

"I needed this." Aidan heaved a sigh of relief, as he sat back in the wide bamboo lounge, pulling Allie down on his lap.

"Me too. Today was weird." She leaned against him, relishing the moment knowing it wouldn't last long.

"Weird how?" He leaned his head back with his eyes closed, his hand snaking out to take hers, pressing a kiss to her fingertips.

"I had a real conversation with Livia." Allie rested her head against his chest, relaxing as the tension of the afternoon finally left her.

"Really? How did that go?"

"I don't really know."

"Want to talk about it?"

"Not really." She squeezed his hand. "It was just strange.

Everything is strange right now." She sighed, gazing out across the jungle of her dreamscape.

"Yeah, tell me about it," Aidan said with a frustrated sigh. She knew his noises as well as her own, something was troubling him.

"Everything all right with you?" Allie lifted her head to meet his gaze.

"Things are just ... weird." He gave her a hesitant smile that sent a pang of worry through her.

"Want to talk about it?"

"Not really." He smiled, but it didn't reach his eyes

"I miss you, Aidan."

"I miss you so much, Allie. You have no idea." He held her even tighter.

"I can't wait until you're home next semester." She didn't like the way the color drained from his face at the mention of his homecoming. *Has he changed his mind?*

"May I join you?" Navid's voice echoed from the sky like a soft breeze.

"Of course," Aidan called, looking relieved for the interruption. Allie's heart plummeted to her toes, worried there was something Aidan wasn't saying.

"Hello up there." Navid appeared along the trail below.

"Come on up," Allie said. "I've been working on the interior, come see."

Navid climbed the ladder to join them.

"Aidan, always nice to see you," Navid said. "How is school?"

"Busy. I love it." He stood to greet her father.

"I see you've added some furniture." He eyed the bed with a scowl. "I like the drapes and the white lights around the ceiling. Care to make any of it permanent?"

"Yes, please," Allie said.

Allie watched the flash of green fire in his eyes, the telltale sign of his power, as he circled the room, making Allie's finishing touches permanent fixtures of her dreamscape.

"Navid." Allie rolled her eyes when the bed vanished, and a hard bench stood in its place. "That was for me." She gestured at the books stacked on the nightstand. "I spend a lot of time here, relaxing and reading."

"You have a nice chair for that. But how about a swing down below?" He gave her a mischievous smile.

"As long as it's comfortable, Dad." Allie tried to hide her smile. "You sound just like my ... other dad."

"That's why I chose him." Navid reached to tuck an errant curl behind her ear. "He's a good man who has adored you since the moment he laid eyes on you. I wanted you to have a good father figure."

"Now I have two." Allie leaned against Navid, draping her arm over his shoulder.

"I'll be waking up soon," Aidan said. "Time to go."

"I hate that we only overlap for such a short time. I wish I could enter the dreamworld when I'm awake like Navid can."

"I could teach you if you really wanted to learn. It won't come without sacrifice, though," Navid said.

"That would be amazing." Allie beamed at Aidan.

He returned her enthusiasm with a broad smile. "That would give us a lot more time together. You know I miss you like crazy." He glanced down at her.

"Me too." She leaned into him for another hug.

"Good night, Allie. Love you."

"Love you, too."

"A moment, Aidan?" Navid asked, a serious tone entered his voice. "I have a favor to ask."

"Uh, sure." Aidan shrugged and followed Navid back

down the ladder. "Sweet dreams, Allie." He winked as he disappeared down below.

Allie watched as the two walked along the pathway through the jungle, lost in their own conversation. She wasn't sure she liked it. Judging by the look on Aidan's face, he didn't either. He looked upset. Maybe even a little angry.

She loved Navid, but dad talks with her boyfriend were definitely Carson's territory.

A moment later, Navid vanished, and Aidan turned to wave as he faded back into the waking world.

"What was that all about?" Allie recreated a mental image of the bed she'd chosen for her tree house, bringing it into existence again. She flopped down onto the heavenly soft mattress and reached for one of her books. But she couldn't relax.

Cold dread crept up her spine. Something was on Aidan's mind. Something he wasn't telling her.

Aidan | Cologne, Germany | November

"Excellent," Wendy praised. "You're kicking ass, my friend. I'm so glad you decided to stay. I knew you couldn't leave. Certainly not to go home and chase some tail."

Aidan stopped playing, dropping his bow at his side. "Never speak that way about Allie again." He glowered at his mortal friend. "Leaving her was the hardest thing I've ever done, and I'm still not convinced I made the right decision."

"You're still not thinking about going home are you?" Wendy frowned.

"No." Aidan flipped through his sheet music for their next piece. He loved practicing with Wendy, but she was pushing too far into his personal life.

"You haven't told her yet?" Her eyes widened in disbelief. "You are going to end up in the dog house if you don't come clean soon."

"I will. I just need to do it in person over Christmas break."

"Bad idea. A lot can happen in a few weeks. If she finds out you're stringing her along, she's going to flip her shit.

Long distance doesn't work, Aidan. Do both of you a favor and just rip the Band Aid off already."

"It's not like that with her," Aidan said. "She isn't just some high school girlfriend I haven't had the balls to break up with yet." But there were no words a mortal like Wendy could understand that would explain how deeply Aidan loved Allie. "Let's just practice." He lifted his bow to his instrument and began to play the first few notes of *Mendelssohn's Violin Concerto in E Minor*.

"Tell her," Wendy insisted. "Tell her now."

Aidan walked through the quad later that evening after his quartet rehearsals ran late. He normally called Naomi and waited for her to pick him up, but tonight he was anxious to see her and didn't want to wait, it was faster just to walk home. The cold air made his breath come out in puffs of white fog. Shoving his free hand deeper into his pocket, he quickened his pace. Aidan loved every minute of his life here in Cologne. The music. The creativity and camaraderie among students talented enough to truly push his limits. The musical side of Aidan was thrilled about staying. But he wasn't looking forward to telling Allie. It would break her heart—hell, she probably already saw it coming. But if he knew her as well as he thought he did, then she loved him enough to give him this, and she would understand about Naomi and his need to give their Syntrophos bond the time it deserved.

Or she's going to think I'm trying to break up with her? Ever since he'd bonded with Naomi, Aidan had kept his thoughts closely guarded to protect Allie's feelings. It wasn't that he had bonded with a Syntrophos—Allie wouldn't have a problem with that. It was that his Syntrophos was Naomi and that Allie would have to share him with her for the rest of their lives.

That, and I'm a coward. But until he saw Allie face to face, he had to keep his new bond a secret from everyone. Allie deserved to be the first to know.

Aidan shook himself out of his thoughts. Something wasn't right. He stared around the quiet campus. Moonlight shone brightly over the quad but the shadows seemed to cling to Aidan. The fresh fallen snow crunched under his boots, but his Immortal ears picked up another sound. The hairs on the back of his neck prickled with awareness. He quickened his step, cursing himself for allowing the Immortals following him to get so close. He knew better than to let his guard down.

"Aidan McBrien"? The voice rang out in the darkness.

I am such an idiot. He should have waited for Naomi. That was why she was in Cologne in the first place, to be another set of eyes and ears watching over him. Aidan wasn't even properly armed. He reached for the dagger concealed at his waist, as he slowly turned around.

"Not to worry, son," the second Immortal said, her accent distinctly American. "We're here on Senate business. We just need to ask you a few questions." The man's polite tone did nothing to ease his fear as two red dots came to rest over Aidan's chest. Both agents held their magnetized weapons at the ready.

This is bad. Aidan was an unknown Immortal and had never registered with the Senate. The fact that these officers knew his name meant he was out of time, and things were about to get real.

"I think maybe you have me confused with someone else." Aidan held his hands up, giving them an affable smile.

"I'm Darius McBrien. I do have an uncle by the name of Aidan. Perhaps I can arrange a meeting."

"Nice try, kid. If you'll come with us, I'm sure we can clear up this matter quickly." The woman stepped forward, lowering her weapon, and Aidan took a few steps back, preparing to make a run for it.

"Let's not do this the hard way, son," the good cop said, his voice meant to be friendly and reassuring, but the dot on Aidan's chest said he would shoot if Aidan made another move. "We'll give your guardian a call when we get to the local precinct. But for now, we have to arrest you."

"On what charges? You have the wrong guy." Aidan stood still, taking stock of his situation. The quad was completely deserted at this hour. Among the unnatural shadows, it was likely no one would see or hear it if shots were fired. No witnesses would see them drag Aidan to their waiting car. Panic gripped Aidan in its clutches as the shadows darkened and swept across the quad.

"Your brother, Darius McBrien, is currently in Cleveland Ohio, enrolled as a student at the Cleveland Institute of Art. He is also nine years your senior."

"Your information is wrong," Aidan insisted, clutching his knife in desperation. He could not let this happen. Aidan blinked furiously trying to make his brain work, but something about the darkness left him disoriented.

"Don't make us shoot you, *sohn*," good cop said in his clipped German accent.

Aidan eyed the shadows creeping closer, taking a hesitant step back.

"Not another step," the woman said as she directed the shadows to envelop Aidan. Her gift dulled his senses and slowed his thoughts. His grip loosened around his dagger and Aidan dropped his only protection into the snow.

Fire! Aidan remembered too late. He could do something with fire. He looked down at his hands, hoping to find the answers there. His shoulders slumped in defeat. There was no way out of this. He couldn't string two coherent thoughts together.

"I'm Lieutenant Sinclair, and this is my partner, Lieutenant Schreiber," bad cop said, as she placed a pair of slim magnetic cuffs around Aidan's wrists and patted him down for concealed weapons. She also relieved him of his phone, violin case and the knife he'd dropped. "The Senate has charged you with failure to register your identity and your abilities as our law demands of all its Immortal citizens." She tucked his belongings into his violin case, tossing the knife on top of his instrument.

Aidan grasped at the power slowly slipping away from him as the magnetic force took effect. Coupled with Sinclair's darkness, Aidan found himself confused, weaponless and powerless, and he was going to jail. He glanced around, desperate for help as they marched him across the campus to a waiting car.

Dad is going to flip.

"Watch your head," Lieutenant Schreiber said as they shoved him into the backseat.

"Where are we going?" Aidan demanded. "I'd like to ask my ... my brother to join me. He's my guardian while I'm at school." Aidan shook his head, trying to clear the shadows from his mind but they clung to him like honey.

"This is just a routine questioning. Nothing official. No need to drag your brother out of bed this late."

"You can't question me without my guardian present," Aidan insisted. "I know my rights."

"You are not a registered citizen. You have no rights. But

if you cooperate, you may have a phone call once we get to the precinct."

Aidan stared out the window into the dark night, his heart hammering in his chest. He was in way over his head this time.

"Where are you taking me?" Aidan demanded. Once the agents had him safely restrained, the confusion lifted from his mind replaced with a delayed sense of panic. If he had any hope of getting out of this, he needed a plan. Quick.

"We told you twice already, the local precinct," Lieutenant Sinclair said.

"Then why are we leaving the city?"

"This is Eastern Europe, son," Schreiber said. "It's not like the States. Immortals have to keep a lower profile this close to Coalition territory." The Coalition headquarters were in Vienna, Austria, less than ten hours from Cologne.

"Our offices are on the outskirts of the city," Sinclair supplied. "We'll be there soon."

"I should call my brother to meet us there."

"You'll get your phone call once you're booked."

"Senate law says *any* Unproven Immortal has the right to have a parent or guardian present before questioning," Aidan said, desperate to get in touch with Scott as soon as possible.

"You are in Germany," Schreiber said. "A long way from America."

"Senate law is the same world-wide. You claim I am not a registered citizen, but in this case, that doesn't even matter. I'm only eighteen." They didn't need to know he was mere weeks away from his nineteenth birthday.

"For someone who has spent his whole life hiding from

the Senate, you sure know an awful lot about our laws."

Sinclair turned in her seat to face him. "Maybe you've forgotten, but that law is subjective to the situation and is left to the arresting officers to determine."

She had him there.

"Keep that in mind and if you cooperate, maybe we can talk about that phone call," Lieutenant Schreiber added.

Defeated, Aidan sat back against the leather seat, wondering if he could make a run for it once they stopped. But that idea came to a crashing halt when they approached the gates of what looked like the mansion of a foreign consulate. Armed guards patrolled the perimeter of the tall iron fence. Running was not an option. He would have to wait for Liam and his tracking gift to figure out he wasn't where he was supposed to be.

Why wasn't I paying attention? Aidan wanted to punch something. If he'd seen it coming a moment sooner he could have at least tried to reach Allie through their connection.

The guards waved them through the gates, and Aidan willed his heart to stop thundering in his chest. He could not afford to be the scared eighteen-year-old kid he suddenly felt like. He needed to be the confident, powerful Immortal he'd trained all his life to be.

Lieutenant Schreiber drove down the winding lane lined with trees and topiary shrubs trimmed in exotic shapes and sizes around fountains and garden sculptures. They rounded to the back of the rambling brick mansion and down a steep, snow-covered hill to a utilitarian building obscured in the shadows.

The jail.

"Out," Sinclair barked as she opened the rear door for Aidan. "And don't try anything stupid."

Aidan didn't know what to expect when he stepped

through the front door, but the bustle of activity was a surprise. It was well past midnight, but the precinct was alive with officers blaring out orders.

"This way." Sinclair guided Aidan to a dark, quiet room where she removed his handcuffs, replacing them with a more potent magnetic collar.

"Strip." Schreiber barked as Sinclair left the room, closing the door behind her.

Aidan stared at his surroundings, at the camera equipment and stark white walls. "Excuse me?" Aidan thrust a nervous hand through his hair.

"Remove your clothes, *sohn*. Every stitch."

"No thanks." Aidan stood, his back ramrod straight. "It's rather cold in here."

"Don't waste my time. If you want to call your brother, we have to book you. And to book you, we need photographs."

"So take a mug shot."

"This isn't a simple mortal arrest with mug shots and fingerprints," Schreiber said patiently. "You are not registered and we have no record of your abilities. We will start with photos of your identifying features, but before this night is over, you will be a registered Immortal citizen one way or another. Now strip."

Aidan fumbled with the buttons of his coat.

Schreiber snapped his fingers. "Don't make a meal of it. I don't have all night."

"Sorry, I don't make a habit of undressing in front of strange men." Aidan reluctantly slipped his sweatshirt over his head, letting it fall to the floor with his coat.

As Schreiber took pictures of his face, Aidan shivered, partly from the temperature of the room and partly from humiliation. The lieutenant took pictures of Aidan's tattoos and other identifying marks on his body, including close ups of his eyes and hair. He even recorded Aidan's measurements and scribbled notes in a file.

"Get dressed," Schreiber finally said, taking a seat to watch Aidan dress.

Aidan's face burned with anger and embarrassment as he struggled into his jeans, feeling violated. He just wanted to go home and forget this ever happened.

"My phone call?" Aidan crossed his arms over his chest, trying to rub some feeling back into them.

"Soon," Lieutenant Schreiber said, guiding him to another room across the hall. Sinclair waited with a slice of pizza and a coke for Aidan.

He refused to touch it.

"Let's get the paperwork out of the way, and then you can call your brother," Sinclair said. "Full name?" She sat poised with an iPad to take his answers.

"Aidan McBrien."

"Full name, Aidan. Middle names, etc."

"Aidan McBrien."

"Don't you have an uncle of that same name?"

"I do."

"So you are Aidan McBrien II?" She looked up expectantly. "Is there a middle name?"

Aidan sat back with his hands in his in his lap and his mouth shut. They would have to work a lot harder if they expected him to talk.

"Answer the question."

He shrugged. "After I talk to my brother, you can have all the answers you want."

"Age?" She moved on to the next line of her form.

Aidan smirked. "Lady, if you think I'm going to willingly offer you information about myself without my legal guardian present, you are sorely mistaken." This couldn't just be about his status as an unknown. They were stalling for time, and Aidan worried this was going to snowball into something way worse if he didn't get his phone soon.

"Abilities?" she continued.

"Does anyone actually answer that question?"

"We have ways to force the answers, I assure you."

"I'm sure you do. But this could all go a lot easier on both sides if you would just let me call my brother. He will answer your questions after we've consulted with our family's attorney."

"So, we're doing this the hard way, then." She lifted a device from her belt. "One tap of this to your collar and you'll be spilling your mother's secret recipes along with anything else we want to know."

"Clearly, you've never met my mother." Aidan laughed, knowing it would only piss her off more. Aidan schooled his features as she stood and walked to his side of the table. He really didn't want to find out what that thing would do to him.

"Sinclair," Schreiber said as he returned to the room. "A word?"

"Still with the good cop, bad cop?" Aidan chuckled to cover his sigh of relief.

"We'll be right back." Lieutenant Sinclair left with her partner.

Aidan ran a hand through his sweaty hair. He was a confident guy with a lot more experience than most kids his age, but this was more than he could handle on his own. He desperately needed his brother, but if he had to face whatever torture Sinclair threatened him with, he would.

"Looks like a change of plans, *sohn*." Lieutenant Schreiber returned alone.

"Is my brother here?" Maybe Liam was already aware of his situation.

"No. You still have some questions to answer first."

"So, what's this new development?" Aidan rested his elbows on the table, rubbing a hand over his face.

"Whenever we make an arrest, the basic information gets logged into the system. We don't have you booked yet, but your name and charges are in the system, along with a brief description of your level of power and general description."

"Let me guess, someone higher up wants to talk to me?"

"The Senate is sending representatives to question you. You can either let us finish booking you so we can call your brother, or you can wait and let the Senate reps deal with you. I can assure you, they will not be the easier choice here. If you were my *sohn*, I'd tell you to do whatever it took to make that call to your brother."

"But to do that, I have to spill my guts about my family and my abilities?"

"Yes."

"Then you are a very different father than the one who raised me. Nothing you can do will make me talk without family present."

"Perhaps a night in a cell will change your mind."

Lieutenant Sinclair stepped into the room through a door on the opposite wall. "Let's go." She held the door open for him.

"A night alone isn't going to change anything." Aidan followed her down the long, dark hallway.

"Stand still," she barked.

Aidan flinched as she reached for his collar. His heart landed somewhere in the vicinity of his toes when he realized her hand was empty of the torture device.

"Relax, I'm taking it off for the night."

Then tension in his arms relaxed. Maybe once the magnetic influence wore off, he could get a message to Allie.

"Inside." Sinclair pointed to the cell, the bars humming with magnetic energy.

Nope, still screwed.

"Any chance I could just stay in the interrogation room?" Aidan suggested.

"None."

Aidan closed his eyes and stepped into the closet-sized cell. A wave of lethargy hit him like a bucket of ice over his head.

"This is the real thing, Aidan. The cuffs and collars will separate you from your power, but a cell like this … it will torment you. Take some time to think about spending all your days in this room. And maybe in a day or two, you'll be more willing to answer a few simple questions." She slammed the cell bars closed, leaving him in total darkness.

Weakness overwhelmed him, and Aidan's legs gave out. Crashing onto the cold concrete floor, he shivered. No amount of training had prepared him for this experience. It wasn't just the separation from his power; it was the fear. Five minutes in this room and he was as weak as a kitten. In two days he'd be worthless. As a strong, powerful Immortal, Aidan didn't do weak. It wasn't something he knew how to deal with.

Two days in here and he'd be ready to crack. Hell, he was nearly there now.

After an hour, Aidan shivered in a pool of his own sweat. In a moment of desperation, he searched for his bond with Naomi but came up empty. He couldn't feel the warmth of their bond anymore and that terrified him more than anything else. She would sense something was wrong.

Stay out of it, Naomi. He willed her to hear him. The last thing he needed was his Syntrophos showing up here demanding answers when no one was supposed to know he was here. Aidan needed his brother Scott, but Naomi had to stay away. It was too dangerous. If the Senate found out about their bond, they would never know another moment's peace.

After three hours in the cramped cell, Aidan was desperate for the escape of sleep, but the room wasn't long enough for him to lie down. He could only curl into a ball, clutching his knees to his chest to conserve his body heat, but even that was exhausting.

When Aidan lost track of time, he couldn't trust what he would do once they let him out. He wasn't strong enough to face this alone.

"I just want to go home," he whispered into the darkness.

Chapter 10

Allie | The Dreamworld | November

"I see the bed is back." Navid narrowed his eyes at Allie, a playful smile on his lips. He made a habit of visiting her dreamscape just before dawn and she looked forward to his visits.

"I like to read in bed." Allie sat up, returning her father's smile with a roll of her eyes.

"As long as there's no hanky-panky going on, I suppose it can stay."

"Hanky-panky?" Allie's laughter rang out across the early dawn morning. "No hanky-panky is happening anywhere near the dreamworld. That's too creepy for me."

"And that is enough of that conversation." Navid sat on the bed beside her. "I've brought Livia with me, if you don't mind inviting her in."

Allie gazed across her dreamscape, expecting to see her sister waiting on the path below. "She's still in her cell though, right?" It made her uneasy to think of her sister free from the magnetic cell keeping her under control.

"She is in the Yard with me," Navid said. "She cannot

enter the dreamworld from her cell. She needs to touch her power to do so."

"I see. You've been spending time with her here? Probably a lot of time." Allie hated the twinge of jealousy she felt at the idea Navid might prefer his other daughter.

"It is a reprieve for her, and it gives us time to get to know each other. I have known you your whole life, but my eldest is a stranger to me."

"But I haven't known you my whole life," Allie said. "Not the real you."

"I look forward to the day when we all know each other so well, we're sick of the sight of each other." Navid smiled. "Do not worry, I have much love for both of my beautiful daughters.

"So if she's out there waiting to come in, does that mean she's a dreamwalker?"

"No, but she is my daughter and has an affinity for the dreamworld just as you do."

"Right ... but how is she out there if you're not with her?"

"Quinn is waiting with her. We have come to talk to you about an important matter."

"She ... um. She hasn't, like, latched onto his gift again?"

"No nothing like that. Believe it or not, it is quite painful for her to do that. She hopes to never use that gift again."

"How can she walk with Quinn? I thought I could only travel this world with you because you're my father."

"So did I, but we've done some experimenting, and it seems you can travel with any of my allies in this world."

"Allies? This sounds serious."

"It is. That's why we are here."

"How do I let them into my dreamscape?"

"Invite them."

Allie stood and crossed the room to the largest open

window. "Quinn and Livia, please come in," Allie called into the lingering darkness. "Feels a bit like inviting vampires inside my house," she muttered, as she conjured up two more chairs for her guests.

"Your sister is not a vampire." Navid chuckled. He helped her arrange the four chairs around a smoldering fire pit.

"Nice touch. That won't burn the place down, will it?" Allie asked. "My tree house is highly flammable."

"It won't if you don't want it to. Care to make it permanent?"

"Yes, please."

"You have the entire dreamworld at your fingertips, and you decide the best use of it is a tree house?" Quinn stepped off the ladder, shaking his head.

"Hey now, don't be hating on my dreamscape." Allie narrowed her eyes at him.

"You can do literally anything you want here, and you made a reading nook?" He eyed her bookshelves and mounds of books on her nightstand.

"My life is exciting enough. When I come here, I want to relax."

"Whatever, you did the same thing," Livia said. "Except yours is a castle, not a tree house, and you gave yourself a whole library."

"It's for research," Quinn said, shoving her playfully. "And it was there when I found the castle."

Of all the people affected by Livia's actions, Quinn had the most reason to hate her, but over the last year, he'd found a way to forgive her. They weren't exactly friends, but he seemed to understand her better than most.

"What's going on?" Allie frowned. "And what's this about a castle?"

"We're at war, Allie, and we're here to recruit you," Quinn said, taking a seat and leaning back with his arms crossed behind his head. "No way to sugar coat it, that's why we're here."

"War?" Allie sat down with the others, keeping a careful eye on Livia. It was unnerving to see her walking around freely without a collar restraining her power.

"It's been brewing for some time," Navid said.

"How can I help? Surely, other walkers would be more useful than me." Allie glanced at her sister who sat quietly listening to Quinn and Navid explain the situation.

"That's the problem," Quinn said. "Walkers are disappearing left and right."

"At first it was the old ones, like me," Navid said. "I thought they were going to ground to ride out the controversy in solitude, but I was wrong."

"Now it's the younger and weaker walkers disappearing," Quinn added. "The few walkers we trust are staying in the old fortress. We're banding together, joining forces to go against Brecken."

"Who is Brecken?" Allie asked.

"He is a young and powerful dream walker," Navid said. "Probably the most powerful ever born. The only one who can rival him is Quinn."

"So this Brecken guy is capturing the missing walkers? Can't they just ... wake up?"

"He is strong, Allie," Navid said. "Strong enough to keep them here against their will."

"So, they can't wake up in their physical bodies?"

"Brecken is keeping them somewhere between sleep and awake," Quinn said. "When they're awake, it's like they're sleep walking. Alert to their surroundings and interacting in their lives, but not fully present."

"Left in that state long enough, a walker could go mad—even in the waking world," Navid added.

"Are there enough of you to oppose him?" Allie asked.

"No. That's why we need you and Livia," Quinn said. "You two are rare, natural children of a powerful dream walker. You can travel the world of dreams with an escort, but you cannot fight this war with us."

"Then what *can* we do?" Allie asked.

"There are ways you can help us distract our enemies. Brecken's walkers are powerful. Much more than they should be," Navid said. "He promises them more power and more time in the dreamworld. We don't know how, but he delivers on that promise."

"They torment dreamers, feeding off their fear to make them stronger," Quinn added. "That's where you two come in." He leaned forward, resting his elbows on his knees. "We battled with Brecken's crew recently, and it didn't go well. We lost a few of our best crew because we were fighting our enemy while also trying to protect the dreamers Brecken uses to strengthen his walkers. It's our duty to protect dreamers, but he uses them to slow us down. We can't afford to let that happen again. Next time we face him, we hope you two can protect the dreamers so we can focus on the fight. We will teach you how to guide the innocent dreamers back to their own dreamscapes."

"Won't Brecken's people just target us?" Livia asked.

"That's the beauty of this plan." Quinn grinned, his teeth gleaming white against his dark skin. "Since you are not walkers, they can't touch you," Quinn said. "Brecken won't be able to influence you as a dreamer or as a walker."

"So he can't harm us at all?" Allie asked.

"He cannot touch a hair on your head," Navid said. "If he tries, you will simply wake up and leave Brecken and the dreamworld behind. He cannot keep you there. Otherwise, I would never ask this of my daughters."

"But there's a lot you need to know before we can proceed," Quinn said.

"Yes, the dreamworld is a fluid place," Navid continued. "It reacts to the walkers who take command, traveling this world and shaping it to fit their needs. We are kings here, with everything we could ever want right at our fingertips. It's a seductive power that slowly drives us insane if we are not careful to mind our thresholds. I can safely stay in the dreamworld for three hours without a break. I can go a little longer than that if I take much longer breaks between my visits here. Most walkers have a threshold much shorter than mine. Quinn can stay here for several hours without a negative effect. In that way, he is one of the strongest walkers I have ever known. You and Livia are anomalies. You are here as dreamers, but you remain cognizant of what happens here. You have an infinite threshold we can use to our advantage."

"And how will we protect these dreamers?" Allie asked, glancing at her sister who remained impassive. Livia already knew all of this, which meant Allie was the last to know. She wasn't sure how she felt about that.

"We will train you," Quinn said. "But you will not be directly involved in the battle. Only a walker can face another walker."

"Remind me what Allie-rule number one is?" Navid interjected.

Allie rolled her eyes. "Stay in my dreamscape. Don't ever leave my dreamscape, under any circumstances, and don't listen to the dreamers whispering in the winds."

"Very good. Now here is Allie-rule number two of the dreamworld," Navid said. "Do not engage with a walker you do not trust. Ever. You *will* lose. Period."

"Why are they *Allie*-rules," Allie muttered. "Shouldn't they be Allie/Livia-rules?"

"I'm older and wiser. I don't need to be constantly reminded of what I can and can't do in these circumstances." Livia's severe tone pissed Allie off, but when she glanced at her sister, she saw a shadow of a smile and realized Livia was trying to be funny.

"Hey, I can follow directions." Allie nudged Livia's shoulder. "Most of the time."

"We can't break the rules this time," Quinn said. "Brecken is changing the way this world works. He bends the entire dreamworld, morphing it into something the old ones can't even recognize."

"Here, our only limitation is our imagination," Navid said. "Most walkers are not armed with a multitude of gifts in the waking world. For those like myself, Quinn and Brecken, being a walker is just one of many gifts, marking us as the most powerful Immortals of this realm. One of Brecken's strongest gifts is his imagination."

"The things that guy comes up with..." Quinn shook his head. "He's really messed up."

"His walkers make such rapid fire changes during battle, only a skilled dream walker could keep up with them," Navid said.

"One moment, you're facing a pack of rabid wolves, and in the next instant, you're free falling off a cliff into a bottomless pit," Quinn said. "You have to think fast to counteract the imagination of the one you're facing. And it's like they know all your worst fears and use them to torture you."

"Just like a boggart?" Allie chimed in.

"Exactly," Navid said.

"You read the books?" Allie sat up straight, grinning at her father.

"I knew you loved them, so I read them years ago."

"A boggart?" Livia frowned.

"You know, like in Harry Potter when Professor Lupin teaches Harry how to face the Dementors. He uses a boggart to train him because they turn into your worst fear."

"Dementors? What is she talking about?" Livia asked, eyebrows raising.

"It's one of her coping mechanisms." Quinn scratched his head. "Whenever she's trying to wrap her mind around something new, she compares it to Harry Potter. I don't know why, but it helps her."

"The boy wizard," Allie said, scowling at her sister. "He saved wizard-kind from the dark lord."

"O-kay, if you say so," Livia said, looking uncomfortable. Allie imagined her sister didn't have much experience with the simple joy of escaping her world through the pages of a book.

"I swear, one of these days, I'm locking everyone in the underground until you read all seven books and watch all eight movies." Allie slumped back in her seat.

"There are movies?" Navid asked.

"We seem to have gotten off subject," Livia said, trying to suppress her smile. "I'm sure Allie is as anxious as I am to begin training and learn more about your strategies."

"Right." Navid cleared his throat. "Our goal is to free the walkers trapped in Brecken's prison worlds and end the torment of innocent dreamers. But before we can face Brecken again, you and Livia must learn how to enter the dreamworld while your bodies remain awake."

"That sounds difficult." Allie frowned.

"It will be, so we need to get to work on this soon."

Allie nodded. "All right then, I'm in. Let's do this."

CHAPTER

11

Aidan | Cologne, Germany | November

"One more time," Lieutenant Sinclair demanded. "Why haven't you registered with the Senate?"

"I've told you." Aidan slumped in his chair back in the interrogation room. "I won't answer your questions without my legal guardian present." After two days in the magnetized cell separated from his power and his strength, Aidan almost wept when Lieutenant Schreiber brought him out and fed him a breakfast of Brötchen and Schwarzwaelderschinken—a kind of German smoked ham. He felt stronger already, but Aidan had never experienced fear like that. He could not go back into that cell. Ever.

"You don't have to tell me your private details. I've spoken with the Senate officials waiting to see you, and we just need you to provide a logical reason for why you and your entire family have failed to enlighten the Senate of your existence. Answer this one question, and we can finish booking you, and you may call your brother."

Aidan sat, staring at the edge of the table in front of him, refusing to answer, but terrified they would throw him back in that cell again if he didn't.

"Give the kid a break. He's scared," Lieutenant Schreiber said, looking like he was tired of this game as well. "Look, we can sense how powerful you are. Off the record, I can't really blame you for trying to fly under the radar, but we have to take your statement, and your refusal is only going to last so long before this gets much worse. I'm going to call your brother so he'll be here when you're ready."

Aidan gave him the number, doubtful if he'd actually call, but grateful for the gesture.

"Answer the question and your brother will be waiting for you when you're done." Schreiber left them alone, making Aidan wary of what would come next with bad cop Sinclair.

"I can make you talk." Sinclair sat on the edge of the table in front of him, a hateful sneer on her leathery face.

"I'm sure you can, Lieutenant. I'm sure you could use your considerable talents and that torture device you keep waving at me to make me spill my guts. But I am also sure you'd have a hard time justifying your actions against an Unproven, impressionable, young, and defenseless Immortal boy."

"Cut the crap. We both know you're more powerful than most Proven Immortals. The law would be on my side."

"Would it?" Aidan raised his brow in question. "Which of us do you think the Senate would find more useful? Me, arguably the most powerful Immortal of my generation—whom you've denied his legal rights? Or some beat cop who bumbled her way into my path?"

"The young man has a point," a smooth, cultured voice interjected. "This whole situation is well above your pay grade, Lieutenant."

Aidan eyed the new Immortal standing in the doorway. A beautiful Spanish woman. Powerful and intimidating.

Another good cop? Or is this the part where I should pee myself?

"Leave us," the woman said, causing Sinclair to flee the room at the authority ringing in her voice.

Right, pee myself. This was probably not a good development.

"I am Cleo." She offered an elegant hand to him as she took her seat.

Aidan didn't know if she meant him to shake it or kiss it. He opted for a quick handshake.

"Do you know why I am here?" she asked, folding her hands in her lap.

"Not at all," he lied. He could make all sorts of guesses about this woman, but he still wasn't offering up any information until his brother arrived to take him home.

"The local authorities received some intel about you anonymously. Where you'd likely be, and since you are not registered with the Senate as you should be, that gave them enough cause for your arrest."

"And a reason to hold me long enough for you to get here," Aidan said. That was why they wouldn't let him call Scott.

"Very good, you learn quickly." She pressed her full lips into a thin smile. "That bodes well for our future relationship.

"So I'm guessing this anonymous intel came from you, but where did you hear about me?" Aidan tapped his fingers on the stainless steel table, trying to maintain his composure when he really felt like screaming.

"That's not important."

"Maybe not to you." Just as Lieutenant Schreiber said, Aidan had spent his life flying under the radar. He didn't know many Immortals outside his family and the ones he did know, he trusted implicitly. So where was she getting her information?

"Aidan Loukas McBrien, you are a hard one to track." Cleo leaned forward, her smooth as silk voice hypnotizing.

"What of it?" Aidan shrugged. "I'm nobody. Just an American kid going to university in Cologne."

"And I'm just a scientist looking for a new lab rat." Her laughter was like music, but her words set Aidan on edge.

"You're not from the Senate, are you?" The color drained form Aidan's face. This was bad before, but it just got a whole lot worse.

"Not directly. But that's not important, either. I'll admit the information I received on you was impressive, enough to bring me here to investigate. We are always looking for powerful young Immortals to mentor."

"I have a mentor, thanks."

"A mentor who can't seem to get out of bed these days," Cleo murmured. "It's a shame, what happened to Jin Jing and Ming Lao Long. She was a brilliant woman, and no Immortal should be left to suffer a life without his Complement."

"How do you know these things?" Aidan asked, surprised he was able to control his voice, let alone not lose his shit right there. He was ten seconds away from asking for his mom.

"I have sources." She sat back in her seat and crossed her legs, giving him a guarded look. "I find there is much more here than I anticipated. Much more than was promised."

"Promised?" That one word spoke volumes. Betrayal. Someone close to Aidan had brought this woman searching for him. Aidan crossed his arms over his chest to hide his trembling hands. He'd always thought his training had prepared him to handle anything but there was only so much his father could teach him in theory. In reality, he was scared out of his mind and needed to gain control of this situation if he was going to survive.

"Give me your hand." Cleo placed hers palm up on the table between them.

"Nope." Aidan tucked his hands under his arms. "Not going to happen, lady."

"It won't hurt ... much." A flash of power lit her dark eyes.

"I'd like to call my brother *now*. I'm allowed a phone call, and I demand to speak to him."

"He's been here since yesterday afternoon." She gave a thoughtless wave toward the waiting room. "Would you like to see him?"

"Finally." Aidan scooted his chair back to stand.

"You can stay right there." She reached behind her placing a hand on the wall. The drywall vanished. Aidan could now see the waiting room, but his irate brother and Syntrophos couldn't see him.

"I need to speak with my brother, now." Scott McBrien ran his hands through his normally tidy hair. "You can't keep him like this. I am his legal guardian while he is in school. He's just a kid."

"Take a seat, Mr. McBrien. We will call you when we have more information. Your brother isn't in the system yet, so it seems he hasn't been booked," Lieutenant Sinclair said with all the sincerity of a lump of coal.

"You've had him for more than two days!" Naomi looked like she hadn't slept or changed clothes in all that time. "Just let me talk to him."

"Let me check his status and see if I can locate him." Sinclair hid her smirk.

"Locate my ass!" Scott slammed his fist on the counter. "This building is smaller than my house; he can't be far."

"He isn't," Naomi insisted. "My bond tells me he's right

behind that wall." Naomi took a menacing step toward Lieutenant Sinclair like she meant to tear her limb from limb.

Naomi, shut up. Aidan groaned.

"Sit down now, young lady." The officer pointed to the waiting room chairs. "Like I said, I'll check on what's holding him up." Lieutenant Sinclair left poor Fitzy and Naomi standing in the waiting room. Aidan watched as his brother snapped up his phone, probably calling their father.

"You want to talk to them, I can make that happen." Cleo's hand dropped from the wall as her tone took on a mesmerizing quality, soothing and tranquil. Aidan's pulse slowed and the tension in his body relaxed. "I can make this whole nightmare go away. Place your hands on the table. Now, Aidan."

She clasped her hands around his. Aidan hadn't even realized he'd complied with her demand. He was a fly in her trap. He couldn't look away from those fathomless eyes. Iridescent pearl, they called to him.

"Very good."

Aidan winced at the sharp bite of her ability, raking through his chest like a talon. She laid him bare.

"So many secrets for one so young," she whispered in a rasping voice, making his head spin. She was so beautiful, he wanted to sink into her eyes and forget all his troubles.

Taking a page from Allie's book, Aidan shoved everything he knew of Allie and Naomi into a box in his mind, focusing on guarding those secrets to the detriment of all others.

She pushed her way into Aidan's mind, the talons of her gift scraping and clawing at the box holding his most dangerous secrets. But Aidan refused to let her in, resisting her with a will she couldn't break.

He gasped when she finally released him, pulling a great

gulp of air into his lungs. Aidan shuddered at the lingering touch of her gift, like a taint of tar on his soul.

Cleo stood, gliding out of the room without a word. She returned a moment later with a can of Coke and a protein bar.

"Eat." It wasn't a request, and Aidan had little inclination to resist her. After his time in the cell, he was weak and starving, and whatever she'd done to him left him exhausted.

"My ability tells me much about you, young Aidan." She took the seat opposite him again. "But you guard your closest secrets with a will even I can't break. You are quite the find. Even for one so young, I can't imagine what knowledge you have, coming from the family you do."

"What do you want from me?" Aidan said in a weary voice, shoving the protein bar into his mouth with little interest in the taste.

"Let's start with the bond that young woman spoke of. Her little slip has me even more intrigued."

"She's my sister. We have a close bond." Aidan shrugged, hoping she would buy it.

"Too easy. You have two sisters. Imogen and Sasha El Sadawii. That young woman in the waiting room is Naomi Hauser, daughter of Greyson Hauser."

"It's a recent bond. We've always been close like family."

"We both know family bonds don't work that way. Particularly with someone you've been intimate with before."

"Jeez, lady, where are you getting your information?" How could she possibly know such private details of his life? Someone betrayed him, but Aidan racked his brain and couldn't think of a single person who would do such a thing.

"If she isn't your sister, then what bond could she possibly be speaking of? You aren't Complements. I could sense it if you were. So what are you hiding, Aidan? I've used my gift to tell me all sorts of delicious details about you, but you guard her and one other like they're the Hope Diamond."

"It's nothing you would understand," Aidan said desperately.

"I can make all of this nonsense about your failure to register vanish in an instant." She snapped her fingers. "I can send you home with Naomi and your brother today."

"And what do you want in return for such a huge favor?"

"You come work for me in Milan."

"Can't do it. I'm here on a student visa. I can visit most of Europe, but I have to live in Germany while I attend school."

"You think I don't know your student visa is a forgery your brother, Darius, created? You think something so trivial is going to stop this? This is happening, Aidan. It's best if you jump on board."

"Then why don't you stop beating around the bush, and tell me what *this* is? You want me to cooperate then give me a reason. Otherwise, you can put me back in that cell or send me home."

"Very well." Cleo leaned back in her chair, folding her hands in her lap. "This is how things are going to work from now on. As far as your family is concerned, you will receive a slap on the wrist and community service for your failure to register. You will continue pursuing your education. For now."

"And what will this *community service* entail?" Aidan asked, mimicking her posture.

"Each week, you will teach one of my students."

"Teach?" Aidan frowned. "That's it?"

"For now."

"Darlin', I'm afraid you're going to have to be much more specific." Aidan flashed a menacing grin. "If you expect me to fall in line, you're going to have to divulge all the details. No more of this 'for now' bullshit."

"Fine. You will teach a class of powerful and talented young Immortals who have not had access to the kind of training you've had. Each week, you will train one on one until you've met with each student individually. Then we will require you to visit our facilities in Milan, Italy, to continue training these gifted students. Think of us as a boarding school for elite young Immortals. Once a month, you will spend four days with us." The rest of your time, you may continue with your life as usual."

"Not going to happen, lady." Aidan stubbornly resisted.

"We will work around your school schedule as best we can, but we hope in time, you will see your work with the Milan Initiative as priority."

"Do you have any idea how hard I've worked to get here? Or how demanding my academic schedule is?" Aidan laughed. "I don't get one day off, much less four."

"You will find a way to make it work. If that means taking fewer classes, you will adjust your schedule accordingly."

"That's not possible. The program isn't designed for part-time students."

"Perhaps you need further motivation." Cleo clapped her hands once. "Ready?"

The most beautiful woman Aidan had ever seen stepped into the room. She was tall with sleek dark hair to her waist, full lips, and perfectly sculpted brows. Her copper skin glowed like silk in the sun. But what terrified Aidan the most was the unseen. These two women were Syntrophos. And they weren't even bothering to hide it.

"Bring her in," Cleo said.

"No." Aidan shot to his feet when he realized they had Naomi. "Leave her out of this."

"Naomi, good of you to join us," Cleo said as her Syntrophos shoved Naomi into a chair beside Aidan, the slim collar at her throat matching the one he wore. "Your father and I go way back, but I didn't know about this little detail."

"You don't know anything," Naomi spat.

"Oh, but sweetheart, you're the one who told us," Cleo said. "The moment you showed your cards, we had you. We knew Aidan was exactly the kind of powerful young Immortal we've been looking for but *this*. This is pure gold."

They knew Naomi was his Syntrophos. They were swimming in the deep end now, and Aidan found himself wishing for his dad like a little boy.

"Now, what we want to know," the dark haired Syntrophos said, leaning in with a menacing scowl, "is how you're masking your bond so well?" Both women waited as the seconds ticked by.

"Don't know what you're talking about." Naomi crossed her arms in defiance.

"Genevieve, why don't you catch our new friends up to speed?" Cleo asked.

"Let's make this short and sweet, shall we?" Genevieve said. "You two will be working with the Milan Initiative. You will help train others like us."

"There is no *us*." Aidan scowled. "You leave Naomi out of this."

"I am sorry to be such a brute, I really am," Cleo said. "But this is too important. We need you *both* on board with the Milan Initiative. This is non-negotiable."

"I'm not down for that," Naomi said bravely, but Aidan's bond told him she was scared out of her mind.

"You will or Governor Naeemah El Sadawii, Greggory McBrien and Greyson Hauser will suffer the consequences of their actions." Genevieve slammed her fist on the table, her nose an inch from Aidan's. "Failure to register an Immortal child is a severe crime, but withholding an important tool such as yourselves is a felony. Naeemah and Greggory will lose their position as Governor and will serve time for their transgressions along with Greyson Hauser. The Senate deserved the right to train you as they saw fit. Your parents took it upon themselves to bar them from that right."

"This is serious, Aidan," Cleo said, "but it doesn't have to be."

"I know a bluff when I hear one." But he wasn't so sure about that. These women were not Senate sycophants. They were powerful, both in their nature, their bond and their positions within this Milan Initiative—whatever that was. They probably could follow through on their threats.

"We know everything, Aidan." Cleo lit a cigarette, inhaling deeply. "Greggory and Naeemah are harboring another young unknown—a powerful little redhead who means a great deal to you. If your own parents aren't incentive enough, perhaps the safety of Ms. Alexis Carmichael will give you the final, necessary ... nudge."

"And what is it you think you know about her?" Aidan's blood ran cold at the mere mention of his Complement's name. He exchanged a quick glance with Naomi. With a nod, she recognized his need to protect Allie. She might not like Allie very much, but she knew enough about her to know her identity needed to be guarded carefully. These women knew far too much already.

"She is your equal," Genevieve said triumphantly. "She's nearly as powerful as you are, and the two of you together will become one of the Senate's greatest tools. Some day. That could be right now, or it could be after she is Proven. It's up to you."

"And?" Aidan pushed. "If you expect me to yield to your

threats, I want to know what you're *actually* threatening. How do I know you won't do the same thing to her tomorrow?"

"Her abilities are questionable. The Chief Justice would be very interested in her clairvoyance ... and her recent developments."

Aidan sucked in a deep breath, fear lancing through him like an electric jolt.

"But we're more interested in you and Naomi. The warrior bond you share trumps a talented clairvoyant as far as we are concerned. Alexis is nothing to us." She shrugged her shoulders.

Aidan tried to hide his relief. They didn't know as much about Allie as they thought they did.

"And if I still refuse your ... offer?"

"Then we hand Alexis to the Chief Justice along with your parents and your eldest siblings who knowingly withheld your existence from your government. We'll start with your bother, Scott McBrien." She gestured toward the waiting room where Scott likely still paced.

Aidan couldn't refuse. He couldn't risk letting them get their hands on Allie. Couldn't risk his entire family's freedom for his own safety. "And if I cooperate, you will leave her alone? My family too?"

"You have our word," Cleo said. "And I promise our word means a lot more than the word of the International Senate who won't be far behind us with an offer not half as pleasing.

With a last look at Naomi, Aidan nodded. "Name your terms and we will decide if we accept."

"You will each teach a class as I have described. Aidan, you can do so from Cologne for now. In time, when your family has learned to accept your new role, you will come join Naomi and the rest of us in Milan. However, your involvement in the Milan Initiative must remain a secret from your families. The moment you tell your family, the deal is off."

Aidan suspected as much. They wanted to separate him from everyone he loved. Slowly, so they wouldn't notice until it was too late.

"And what exactly is the Milan Initiative and their agenda?" Naomi asked. "I want to know what we're contributing to."

"We are a top secret, privately funded boarding school for select student who possess the bond. We do not answer to the International Senate. Our duty is to explore this extraordinary bond that links us as warriors."

"For what purpose?" Aidan asked.

"To aid the Immortal population and protect these highly valuable pairs from those who would use them for personal gain."

"You're building an army," Aidan said.

"Our goal is to protect this bond and those who have it. We study the connection seeking to understand it and train those who have it. That is all."

"I don't believe you." Aidan ran his hands through his dirty hair in frustration. "What is your end game? What do you hope to accomplish with this army you want us to train?"

"As a group, you will eventually work with the Senate, but not for them. That is all I can tell you now," Cleo said, her tone indicating this discussion was closed.

"So, you want me to teach here, but you expect Naomi to leave?" Aidan asked.

"Yes, Naomi will reside in Milan at the school with us," Cleo announced. "She will teach a class of her own."

"That's not going to happen," Aidan refused. "She will

stay with me in Cologne, or we have no deal. There is no need to drag her into this too."

"Naomi will have the freedom to come and go as she pleases. She will have her pick of housing. You both will earn a respectable salary and all your needs will be met, but Naomi is our insurance policy, a way to guarantee you actually hold up your end of the bargain."

"You don't need Naomi for that. I will do as you say so long as the people I love are safe. And that includes Naomi."

"Then we have no deal. Perhaps Ms. Carmichael will prove to be a suitable backup?"

"No!" Aidan shot to his feet, his chair clattering against the concrete floor behind him. "Don't make me choose between Naomi and my family." His voice broke. "You have no idea what you're asking." He raked his hands through his hair. "I just ... I want to go home." He was so tired and his nerves were shot. Aidan was at his breaking point and they knew it.

"Aidan," Naomi said softly. "I know you need to do this for your family. They are my family too. I will go with them."

"Naomi, no." Aidan's heart ripped apart inside his chest. He could not choose one over the other. Allie and Naomi each held a piece of him. He could not betray Allie to keep Naomi with him, and he couldn't allow them to take his Syntrophos to protect his Complement. There was no answer to this situation. "This is bullshit!" Aidan roared, kicking his chair across the room. "Don't make me sacrifice one of the most important people in my life for this. You win." He fell to his knees. "I'll do whatever you ask of me, but don't take Naomi's freedom for my mistakes."

"Your reaction right now is precisely why we need you, Aidan." Cleo crouched beside him. "Both of you." She looked from Aidan to Naomi. "Our students desperately need guidance to deal with these warring emotions they don't understand."

"Naomi will be treated well," Genevieve added. "And she will teach our youngest pair."

"Youngest?" Naomi asked.

"They are just seventeen years old. Two precocious girls who desperately need good teachers. They live in a state-of-the-art training facility near the Lake Maggiore region just north of Milan. For the last year, their lives have been ... clinical, and they need more guidance than we can currently give them."

"I'll go." Naomi turned her exotic blue eyes to Aidan, and he saw something there he hadn't seen before.

He narrowed his eyes at her in question and she gave a slight nod. He didn't know if she'd known it for a while or she only just now suspected it, but Naomi knew Allie was his Complement and they had to tread carefully here. It was one thing to manipulate Aidan with the well being of his Syntrophos, but he shuddered to think what they could make him do using both Allie and Naomi's safety against him.

"Come sit with me, Aidan." Naomi reached to pull him up off the floor. "We have more negotiating to do before you can go home."

Aidan reluctantly stood, letting her guide him back to his chair.

"Right ... so, what if I can't give you four days a month every month?" He scratched at the dark stubble along his jaw.

"We will give you time to make the decision to leave school on your own terms. We are confident you will make the right choice," Cleo said.

"And if I don't? If I decide to stay in Cologne?"

"You won't. But on the off chance you do want to stay in

school, we will support that. It will just mean your time with us will be much longer."

"And what will I be teaching these kids?"

"For starters, you're going to show us how to hide the bond," Genevieve interjected.

"Yes, you will teach us that and our students everything you know of this bond," Cleo added.

"You don't even know what it's called?" Naomi asked.

"We call it a warrior union," Cleo said evenly, "but enlighten us if you know the true name for such a bond."

"Not yet," Aidan resisted. "I know precious little about this bond. I can teach you what I know in an hour or two, but I am no expert."

"Remember, we were interested in you before we learned of Naomi," Cleo said. "The fact that you share this bond with her is a pleasant surprise, but it is not the only reason we want you to join us."

"You could find anyone capable of training a group of young Immortals. Why me?" Aidan asked

"Greggory McBrien is an ancient warrior. His son will have much to teach our students. Most of them have had little to no training. They will respond better to one of their own generation. Someone who understands their gifts. We've been looking for someone like you for quite some time now, Aidan, but you exceed our wildest expectations."

"How long must I endure this ... position?" Aidan asked, resigned that this was happening.

"Indefinitely," Genevieve said.

"You want me to sign my life away, with no end in sight?" Aidan closed his eyes, trying to make sense of this madness. He just wanted to go home and pretend none of this happened, but Cleo had an answer for everything. She cut him off at every angle. There was no way out of this.

Gregg would want his son to tell him everything—to let him handle this for Aidan, but Aidan wasn't sure he could risk his family, Allie and Naomi to save his own neck. He was going to have to do this, and hope Liam could track them with his gift and get them out of this mess someday. But at the back of his mind, Aidan thought about the kids on the other end of this nightmare. Who was looking out for them? Surely, they were prisoners too.

This is just another Soma. A Soma for Syntrophos. And he had to willingly walk through the front door without an escape plan.

"Let's start with five years," Cleo offered. "At that time, we will reevaluate the situation."

"That's a long time," Naomi said. "How about one year?"

"Three years," Cleo countered.

Naomi crossed her arms, giving Aidan a reluctant nod.

"Fine. We have a deal," Aidan said. "As long as Alexis, Naomi and the rest of my family are safe, I will cooperate. But the minute that changes, we're out."

"Very well, we will start immediately," Cleo said with a satisfied smile. "Naomi will leave with us tonight. Aidan will return home with his brother and smooth things over with his family. Next week, Genevieve and one of our staff will escort our first student to Cologne for training."

"And don't think that your Uncle Liam will be able to track you, either. We have safeguards in place to negate abilities like his," Genevieve said.

"Of course, you do. But my brother, Scott will not accept such a radical change in my schedule," Aidan said.

"You will attribute your frequent trips to your community service," Cleo said.

"He will insist on coming with me; that's why he's here. My family will *never* allow me to travel alone."

"We will send our own escorts to retrieve you," Genevieve said. "That should be enough to appease your family."

"You don't know my family."

"We are done here." Genevieve slid a form across the table. "Sign it."

"Not until I read it," Aidan insisted.

"Fine." Cleo puffed on her cigarette.

It was a simple contract for a minimum of three years of service to be reevaluated with a new contract at the end of this one. A single sheet of paper outlined all they had discussed, including a substantial salary for his service. Naomi had the same deal with a similar contract.

Aidan studied the simple form once more, desperately trying to find a way out of signing it.

"It is just a formality." Cleo said. "You belong with us, Aidan McBrien. Sign on the dotted line and your contribution to the Initiative will mean something. Your work will be fulfilling and your family will not suffer. Alexis will not suffer."

Aidan glanced at Naomi, hoping she had thought of something he hadn't.

"We don't have a choice, Aidan. It's better this way than whatever they have behind door number two. You know that scenario won't look half as appealing as this." She held up her contract.

"Your partner is right," Cleo said. "Sign it."

"Pen?" Aidan relented. Naomi was right—there was no real choice here. In reality, what they offered was no different than what the Senate had offered his sisters. Sasha had to jump whenever they decided she needed additional specialized training. And Imogen had it even worse. For years, she'd worked for the Senate whether she wanted to or not. As long as she cooperated, she got to keep her normal life with her family and her husband. If she ever tried to leave, the reality of her service to the Senate would rear its ugly head. But that was before she'd become a prisoner of Soma. Now, she worked for a new master, against her old one. Aidan was a pawn in a game of power, just like both his sisters were. For all the power he was born with, it didn't matter. It couldn't save him now. He was naive to ever think it wouldn't go this way. Since the moment of his birth, Aidan was headed for a moment just like this.

"No pens." Genevieve handed him a dagger. "You will sign in blood."

"That's not gross or extreme at all." Naomi sliced her palm open with the dagger. Dipping the tip of the knife in her blood, she signed her life away. For him, making the final decision so he wouldn't have to.

Chapter 12

Allie | The Dreamworld | November

"Allie, you're never going to get this right if you don't chill." Quinn came up behind her, straightening her shoulders, and pressing his large hand against her diaphragm to correct her breathing. "Relax. This is the easy part."

Allie darted a glare at Livia, who sat peacefully on the grassy lawn in the Yard, already in a deep meditative state.

"I'm nervous. What if I can't do it?" Allie bit her lip, trying to find a peaceful thought to focus on, so she could relax her body and expand her consciousness. Apparently, Livia could do that on command.

"You can do this, Allie." Navid took her hand in his. "It took Livia several attempts, too," he added in a whisper.

"Sure, maybe the seventh time is the charm," she muttered.

"Stop trying to compete with your sister and focus on all the dreamers you'll be able to help once you can enter the dreamworld at will. How much you'll be able to help us fight this war. Use that thought as your motivation."

"That's it," Quinn said in his deep, mellow voice. "Breathe and release."

"Focus," Navid echoed his student's tone. A student who had quickly become the teacher.

With a deep breath, Allie let her thoughts drift to the war in the dreamworld and the unrest between the dream walkers and those defenseless dreamers who needed her help.

"Very good, sweetheart," Navid murmured. "Now, take my hand and follow me."

Allie nodded, squeezing her father's hand. She was still nervous, but he needed her to do this. With her eyes closed, she followed, feeling the subtle pull of Navid's presence like an anchor dragging her to the bottom of the ocean.

Allie was weightless, floating in a peaceful state. The feeling was almost euphoric, like she hadn't a care in the world. And then she fell flat on her face, the taste of dirt in her mouth.

"Easy now," Navid said. "Give yourself a minute to adjust.

Allie glanced up, the dreamworld whirling around her like a kaleidoscope of colors and images. Sweat slid down her back, and her palms grew slick against the grass beneath her.

"Yep, she's going to blow." Quinn took a step back.

Allie tried to stand, intent on telling him off, but he was right. In the next instant, Allie projectile hurled the entire contents of her stomach onto the ground.

"Nice range." Quinn gave her a wink.

"Shut up or I'll aim for your fancy boots next time." Allie trembled as she wiped her mouth and stood on shaky legs. "Ugh, I feel like I just apparated for the first time." She shuddered, taking in great gulps of air.

"What?" Livia frowned.

"Potter again?" Quinn asked and Navid nodded.

"It will pass in a moment or two." Navid handed Allie any icy bottle of water. She held it to her forehead and the nape of her neck before chugging the most perfect, thirst-quenching water she'd ever had. She eyed her father with a questioning glance.

"A walker talent." He shrugged. "In time you learn to enhance the things you create with your mind."

"I'm going to need to taste your cheesecake before we leave. And it won't count against my diet if it's in the dreamworld," Allie said.

"Feeling better, are we?" He chuckled.

"If she's talking about food, she's fine," Quinn said.

"Okay, so I'm here." Allie looked around shaking her arms and legs to work out the kinks. "Whoa this is really weird. I didn't think I'd be so aware of my physical body back in the Yard." She swayed on her feet. It was like being in two places at once. She was aware of her corporeal state in the waking world and yet her presence in the dreamworld felt just as physical. It was like seeing double and it left her nauseated.

"It's a strange sensation that will pass once you become accustomed to traveling the world of dreams," Navid said. "But never forget, no matter how real it feels, everything that happens here takes place in your mind." He tapped her temple for emphasis. "The things you experience here cannot affect your physical body."

"So if I get shot here, what happens?"

"You wake up without injury," he explained.

"Normally," Quinn interjected. "Sometimes walkers can experience real physical consequences. But we're pretty certain that can't happen with you and Liv."

"Pretty certain? I don't like the sound of *pretty certain*."

"I guess we'll have to wait and see." Quinn grinned and moved along the path ahead of her.

"So, what now? Whose dreamscape are we in?" Allie fell in step beside Navid.

"We are in the dreamworld proper," Navid said. "Most walkers have their own dreamscapes just like yours, but we are not confined to that space the way you and Livia are.

"Come on, we have the whole of the dreamworld to wander and explore." Quinn flashed an impish grin, beckoning her to follow him along a well-worn path, seemingly in the middle of nowhere. "We have so much to show you and so many people for you to meet before we have to leave."

"How long do we have?"

"About an hour this time," Navid said. "In the future, Quinn and I will stagger our arrivals to give you both more time here."

"Couldn't we stay with the other walkers?" Allie asked. She wasn't limited by a threshold like the dream walkers were.

"Possibly, but at this point, the only walker I trust with my daughters' safety is Quinn."

Allie darted a look around, taking in the lovely forest of white birch trees to the right of their path with a riot of vibrant leaves in shades of purple she'd never seen before. To their left, a sweeping meadow with rolling hills stretched into the distance, the green, green grass dotted with exotic flowers. The murmur of the leaves in the wind grew into a rush of white noise.

"Dreamers, right?" Livia said, looking to Navid in question.

"Yes, their voices can grow quite loud outside your dreamscape."

"Where are they coming from?" Livia asked, gazing into the distance, a look of longing on her face.

"Their call is persuasive." He took Livia's hand. "You

must ignore the whispers while you travel with us. Dreamers can lure you away and it will be very easy for you two to get lost here if you lose focus."

"Right." Livia shook herself to break the spell the dreamers cast.

"Where are they?" Allie asked.

"They sound close, but this world doesn't operate in simple terms of distance. This part of the dreamworld belongs to the walkers. Dreamers rarely come here, but they are all around us."

"We are safe here, Allie," Quinn assured her. "I found this place months ago, just after Santi and I returned home."

"It's beautiful." Allie gave a shiver of foreboding, forcing herself to ignore the whispers on the wind. "It's so old. Ancient, like it has a life of its own." She barely registered the Sherpa lined sweater she now wore at the mere thought of how cold she was. Pulling it tightly around her, she followed Quinn into the forest, the fall leaves crunching under her feet.

"This place is the heart of the dreamworld, Allie," Navid said, walking beside her. "And it hasn't been seen in centuries. Not until it revealed itself to Quinn."

"Revealed itself?" She glanced at her friend. Quinn had experienced a lot of heartache in the last two years. He'd gone through hell at Livia's hand, but he'd found it within himself to leave it in the past. He wasn't the same guy she remembered. He seemed older and more focused. And now, here he was in his element. Confidence oozed from his aura.

"Watch up ahead." Quinn pointed to a pair of rusting gates in complete disrepair. "You'll get your first glimpse there."

"Of what?" She picked up her pace, responding to his

eagerness. Like he was returning home and was excited to show her everything about this part of his life.

"The Commander's Keep," he said with a wink. "You're going to love it."

Allie followed as the incline increased, and the path widened where the overgrown stood wide open for anyone to enter.

"The gates used to be functional," Quinn began, "but a previous commander expanded the boundaries of the keep, so the gate and surrounding walls are just relics. I protect our borders now, using my invisibility gift. Brecken and his people have been scouring the dreamworld for the keep, but they don't know I've had it shielded for more than a year. This is where the remaining walkers are gathering to fight, and he doesn't even know it."

"Wow." Allie stepped past him to get her first look. "Quinn, you have a castle."

"It needs a fair bit of work, but yeah." Quinn's eyes crinkled with his smile. "What do you think?"

It was a wreck, complete with a reeking, swampy moat around the overgrown fortress. Part of the outer stone walls lay broken from some long ago battle. A new wall stood in its place. Crumbling walls remained erect on the grassy knoll by some miracle of dreamworld engineering. A broken turret tower rested in the shallows of the moat, its other half a rambling, twisted stairway reaching aimlessly toward the sky. Three rounded guard towers stood intact, with crenelated walls and brightly colored flags billowing in the breeze. A narrow stone bridge led them to the fortress gatehouse, a broad stone facade barring their entry. Behind the gates, an enormous structure rose from within. Beyond the fortress walls, the keep was a solid slab of stone with intricate statues and relief sculpture adorning its strong facade. This place was old. Allie could feel its lifeline in her bones.

"It's beautiful," she finally spoke. "It feels almost ... sentient."

"It is in a way," Quinn said. "The history and mysteries of the dreamworld are concealed inside the Keep. Come on, I'll give you the tour." Livia and Navid followed behind.

"Quinn!" a feminine voice called to them from the nearest guard tower

"Ah crap." Quinn's face flushed.

"Get your ass in here," the girl on the wall called.

"Well, she sounds lovely." Allie watched the blond woman pace the length of the wall. She moved like a caged panther.

"Who is that with you?" the woman demanded, staring a hole through Allie's chest.

"Okay, I'm scared now," Allie muttered.

"Keep an eye on that one, Allie. That is pure crazy, right there," Livia said.

Most of the woman's silvery blond hair fell in messy braids to her waist, but one side of her head was shaved, revealing tattoos along her skull, flowing from the top of her head to the tips of her fingers. Dressed in ratty camouflaged pants and a leather halter baring her midriff, she looked feral and unkempt.

Quinn snorted. "You have no idea. Raina is ... Raina. Just ... don't mention you saw her to Santi. Or Sasha."

"And why is that?" Allie arched her brow.

"She ahhh ... " Quinn scratched the back of his head. "She's very vocal about ... wanting to have my children."

"What the hell, Quinn?" Allie gaped at the beautiful Immortal woman standing with her hands on her hips, looking like she hadn't bathed recently, yet she somehow made it work.

"Listen." He paused at the middle of the bridge. "Some of the walkers here have been under Brecken's thumb for a long time. And you know what happens when any of us stay here too long, right?"

"You go a little squirrelly?" Allie suggested.

"You could say that," he said, the corner of his mouth lifting in amusement.

"What are you waiting for?" Raina called. "An engraved invitation?"

"She is bad ass," Allie said, admiring the warrior woman.

"Yeah, but don't ever forget, Raina is batshit crazy, and I'm a little scared of her. Just don't tell her I said that."

"And why, exactly, does she want to have your children?"

"She thinks our, uh, *offspring* would be unstoppable with two dream walkers for parents."

"She's probably right," Livia said.

"And the idea that we don't often have natural born children hasn't crossed her mind?" Allie glared at her sister.

"Raina doesn't find that reason enough not to try."

"Has she met Santi and Sasha yet?"

Quinn's smile twisted into a grimace. "Briefly. Santi tolerates her. Sasha, not so much."

"You've got way too many women in your life, Quinn." Livia clapped him on the chest as she walked past them.

"Yeah, that's all probably going to blow up in your face." Allie followed her sister through the creaking gates of the Commander's Keep.

"Sounds about right," Quinn muttered, as he followed.

"So is there a commander in the Commander's Keep?" Allie asked, stepping into the vacant yard behind the wall. The keep rose up before them, casting them in the not quite natural shadows of the dreamworld. These shadows gave her the willies.

"There is now," Navid offered. "For the first time in more than a thousand years."

"But haven't you commanded the dreamworld before?" Allie asked.

"I have been a leader here, yes, but that is not the same as commander."

"What's the difference?" Allie asked.

"A leader is selected out of necessity. We need order among us. We are often an unruly sort, needing the guidance of an alpha, for lack of a better term. Someone to hold us accountable. A long time ago, I was that leader until our numbers dwindled after the Great War. The few dream walkers who remained occupied our own remote corners of the dreamworld and kept to ourselves.

"And a commander?" Allie asked, taking in the once elaborate main hall of the ground floor. Underneath the rubble and grime, the keep was breathtaking.

"A true commander is born, not made. The dreamworld itself recognizes a commander as its master. The last commander faded from this world eons ago, and the world of dreams has not recognized another since."

"Since now?" Allie asked, watching Quinn move about the main level of the keep, showing Livia around.

"The keep does not show itself to just anyone who happens to stumble upon it," Navid replied.

"Quinn?" Allie's eyebrows tried to climb up to her hairline. "He's just a kid. He can't possibly be ready for that."

"He is older and wiser than his twenty years. And ready or not, he was born to be the Commander of the Dreamworld. This mantle weighs heavily on his young shoulders, as I'm sure you can relate."

"Allie," Quinn called from an upstairs landing. "Come up to the third floor, the others are here."

Allie and Navid made their way inside and up the winding stairway past vast rooms and empty halls. All was quiet in the keep, yet the place seemed to thrive with energy.

"The others here ..." Allie wasn't sure how to phrase her question.

"They respect him," Navid replied. "Quinn has earned their loyalty, and he will continue to do so until every last dream walker answers to him."

"And what happens if Brecken and his walkers don't?" Allie lowered her voice.

"As the true commander, once he has restored order to the world of dreams, he will be like a king. Quinn will have the authority and the power to expel those who oppose him from the dreamworld forever. For us, there is no worse fate."

"In here." Navid guided her through an elaborately carved doorway into a lounge room the size of the common room back home. Quinn and Livia stood near the entry talking to a rather handsome looking walker.

Quinn was still the same friend he'd always been, but knowing his fate was so similar to her own—that he carried such enormous responsibility—she felt closer to him somehow.

"Navid caught you up to speed, then?" He stared at her uncertainly.

"Do I have to call you Commander Loukas?" She shot him a playful smile. She knew how important it was she treat him the same as she always had.

"Please don't, Prophecy-girl." He rolled his eyes. "I'm still trying to get used to it from my walkers. "

"Well, I can't think of a better man for the job." Allie hugged him tightly. "I've got your back if you ever need to talk, or if you just need a good freak out with someone who gets it."

"Thank you." Quinn wrapped his huge arms around her. "I'm so glad to have you on our team."

"Uh oh," Livia lowered her voice. "Crazy at ten o'clock. She looks pissed."

"Quinn?" Raina's voice echoed across the room. "Who's that you're hugging?"

Quinn dropped his arms, stepping away from Allie with a 'heaven help me' look on his face.

Raina ran across the room and hurled herself at Quinn, wrapping her arms and legs around him.

"Raina, we've talked about this," Quinn said, his hands hanging at his sides.

"I didn't kiss you this time." She laughed. "You're such a prude." She sandwiched his face between her palms.

"Let's keep working on a reasonable greeting for next time, so Santi doesn't kill me."

"Santi?" Raina frowned. "She can't come here to the keep, so what's it matter? I can be your DW-girl, and she'll never even know."

"Trust me, she'll know." He extricated himself from Raina's clingy grip.

"Who is *she*?" Raina pointed at Allie, her nails long and filed to sharp points like talons.

"This is my good *friend*, Allie. I told you about her and her sister, Livia, last week. Allie's like a sister to me."

"Sister?" Raina cocked her head in a weird, bird-like way, analyzing Allie from head to toe. "She's pretty. I don't like pretty."

And I don't like crazy. Allie took a step closer to Navid, grateful when Livia joined her. This girl was cuckoo for Cocoa Puffs.

"Allie and Livia are Navid's daughters. They are going to help us against Brecken."

"Right, right." She nodded, blinking tears from her eyes and shaking her head in confusion. "I don't like Brecken." Raina hung her head like a sad little girl, and Allie's heart melted. She might be crazy and a bit volatile, but she was just trying to find her way back to herself.

"Raina was Brecken's prisoner for a long time," Navid whispered.

"I can hear you, old man." Raina shot Navid a dirty look. "I'm *not* crazy."

"Of course not, darling." Navid reached for her with a careful hand, like a horse trainer working with a skittish, wild colt. "What did we talk about last night?"

"I'm not crazy. I'm *healing*." She rolled her eyes, lifting her hands in air quotes. "I'm not supposed to say "crazy" anymore."

"That's right. Now, why don't you introduce our guests to the others?"

A bright smile lit Raina's face. "Come with me!" She grabbed Allie and Livia's hands and hauled them farther into the room.

Allie couldn't fathom what Raina had been through as Brecken's captive, but the girl was quickly growing on her. Sasha and Santi might not care for her obvious infatuation with Quinn, but Allie could see through Raina's hard exterior and odd behavior to the injured, but child-like young woman hiding beneath her hard exterior.

"This is Commander Quinn's quarters," she babbled, "but he lets us all hang out in the great room here. The walkers have rooms downstairs. We come and go frequently since we can't always stay for long periods. Especially me. I only get a half hour a day right now, but Mr. Navidie tells me

I can get back to my normal threshold in a few months if I behave myself. I used to be able to stay for nearly two hours at a time." She sighed wistfully.

Raina abruptly changed direction and dragged Allie and Livia over to a fireplace big enough for Allie to do handstands. The smooth stone floor was covered with threadbare rugs while the antique tapestries looked perfectly preserved. Light illuminated the room, but the source was questionable. The light wasn't electric or gas; it was just there. A rough and rowdy crowd of men and women fell silent as Quinn stepped into the room behind Allie.

"Commander," the murmur of respect echoed around the room. At a glance, Allie recognized three kinds of walkers sitting on the couches and chairs around the fireplace. The severe, Navy Seal types with tattoos, dark clothes and cold stares. And those who might appear more at home in a motorcycle club, wearing leather, piercings, and even more tattoos. And only a few like Navid. Older, more reserved, and ready to stand behind their youngest generations, giving guidance where it was needed.

"Everyone, this is Allie and Livia," Raina said, pointing at each of them, mixing them up.

"Allie's the short redhead." Quinn chuckled. "Livia's the one who looks more like Navid in a wig."

"Watch it, *Commander*," Livia murmured as she analyzed each member of the group, sizing them up.

"Right." Raina crossed her arms, so she was pointing at Allie and then Livia. "Allie, Livia, this is everyone." She seemed to lose interest then, and drifted away to sit with her friends.

"So she finally did it," a military type said with a slow clap. "Welcome to the keep." He gave Allie a wink. "I'm Brigs."

"Only took her, what, seven attempts to figure it out?" another added. "Not too shabby since she's not a *real* walker." He stood to shake Allie's hand with his rough, calloused one. "Name's Mac." He nodded, his eyes crinkling as he smiled. "Glad to have you."

"Don't listen to this bunch, Allie. They're lazy assholes sitting around busting each other's balls waiting for their next battle," Quinn said.

"But we're pretty amazing over here," a brunette woman said. She was the least severe looking woman with a glossy, high ponytail and a variety of tiny symbol tattoos around her eyes. "I'm Danica. These are my girls, Hale and Scarlett." She introduced the two women sitting beside her on a large red sofa.

"Name's Sawyer," a tall military type said with a nod.

"Dominic."

"Rocco."

"Maddox."

"Silver."

"We'll never remember all your names, but it's great to meet everyone," Allie said, nudging Livia to say something. The way she stood silently staring at them made Allie nervous, so Livia was probably freaking them all out.

"Yes, right," Livia said, clearing her throat. "Lovely to meet you all."

"So, how are your daughters going to help us in battle?" Silver asked. "It's great they're here, but do they know what they're getting into?" She looked to Navid for answers.

"We know," Livia said. "And we're prepared to do our part the next time you face Brecken."

"We'll take care of the dreamers, so you don't have to worry about their safety," Allie added, not really sure if they were all that worried about the dreamers if she were honest.

"Well, that's something, I suppose," Brigs said. "A worry off Quinn's shoulders at least."

"Just don't get in our way when it matters, and you'll do just fine," Sawyer added.

"How will they train?" Danica asked. "We have to get them prepared for what they'll see. The only way to really do that is to jump in, sink or swim."

"We're going to do a mock battle soon," Quinn said. "Just a quick skirmish to show Allie and Livia what to expect. Do whatever you have to do to make sure you can be here for the skirmish. You're not going to want to miss it." He grinned. "It will be the one and only time I give you all permission to raise hell."

CHAPTER 13

Aidan | Cologne, Germany | November

"How dare you question an underage Immortal without his guardian present!" Scott McBrien roared at Lieutenants Sinclair and Schreiber.

Poor Fitzy. Aidan shook his head, watching his brother behind Cleo's transparent wall. Scott was scruffy, dirty, and decidedly un-Fitzy in his rumpled clothes.

"Mr. McBrien, we are perfectly within our rights to question young Aidan given the charges against him."

"I know the law." Scott slammed his fist down on the table. "He is underage and *nothing* gives you the right to question him without a parent or guardian present. He's just a child."

"An unregistered and very powerful one you and your family have concealed from the Senate. It is within the law to arrest you and every Proven member of your family to pay for this crime."

Scott deflated. "You have no right to hold him like this. Do you have any idea what you've put our family through?"

"Lieutenant Schreiber is going to take you home, Mr. McBrien. We will call you when there is news."

"Like hell. I am not leaving without Aidan and Naomi."

"If you'd just let me talk to him, I could calm him down." Aidan watched with clenched fists as three officers dragged his brother from the precinct and Cleo removed her hand, letting the wall return to its normal state.

"There's still the matter of answering a few questions to satisfy the local authorities," Cleo said. "They still need to finish booking you so your arrest is properly recorded. Then you may go home."

"I'm not telling these idiots anything." Aidan turned to face them, refusing to sit down.

Naomi sat on the tabletop and reached to pull him closer. He went willingly, leaning against the table beside her. "Try to relax, Aidan. You'll be going home soon."

"Yeah," he scoffed. "Without you." He almost choked on that last word. How could he possibly say goodbye to Naomi?

"We'll see each other again soon," she murmured. "It won't be so bad." She tried to smile, but her eyes still reflected her sadness.

"Well, we're certainly not going to tell them the truth," Cleo said. "But we have to give them something."

"We'll fill out the forms for you," Genevieve said, taking the iPad from Cleo.

"Name. Aidan ... Aloysius McBrien II."

"The third," Cleo corrected. "We might as well throw them off as much as possible."

"Aloysius? Really?" Aidan scowled. "That's ridiculous."

"And Loukas isn't?" Genevieve arched a perfectly sculpted brow at him.

"I was named after my uncle and one of my father's best friends."

"Age? They know he's eighteen, but he'll be nineteen in

less than a month. Lets fudge the month of birth so he's slightly younger."

"September thirty-first rather than December? That makes him eight months younger," Cleo suggested.

"Jeez, what don't you know about me?" Aidan shoved his free hand into his pocket, feeling nothing so much as numb at this point. Naomi still sat next to him, clinging to his other hand. He could feel her desperation at the thought of their impending separation.

"Wouldn't you like to know?" Genevieve smirked. Their demeanor had changed the moment they had their signed contracts tucked away. Both women were more at ease. Less formal.

"Abilities. Shoots fire from fingertips. Fast healer. And something completely random ... Let's make him a telepath."

Aidan wasn't going to tell them that was partly true. He was a receptive telepath, but just with Allie. Not that it helped him now. He tugged on the collar still clasped around his throat.

"Ooh, I know, let's give him the ability to manipulate dark matter." Genevieve continued typing her ridiculous responses for his benefit.

"We want to get them off his back, not make them terrified he exists." Cleo reminded her.

"Right. Okay, I've got it." Genevieve started typing again. "Power of persuasion."

"Did you just give him the Jedi mind trick?" Cleo's throaty laugh grated on his nerves.

"His mother and maternal grandfather are precedent with their persuasive abilities. Adopted or natural born, it makes perfect sense he would inherit a portion of their talents."

"Good point." Cleo nodded her approval.

"Do I have any secrets anymore?" Aidan asked, fury churning in his stomach for their blasé attitude toward his situation. "You know the names of my Complement and first child yet?"

"We could probably figure it out." Genevieve grinned.

At least they don't know that much. Aidan relaxed.

"All right you two," Cleo said. "We just need a plausible reason for Aidan's crime and then we can go."

"How about the obvious reason?" Aidan suggested. "Any dumbass in my position would have done the same to save themselves a lifetime of government meddling."

"Good enough for me," Genevieve said, typing his official statement verbatim. "We'll add some brown nosing to it, too. Like now that the cat's out of the bag, I'll register like a good boy and be a model citizen. Yada, yada, yada."

"You know the International Senate is going to start meddling," Aidan said. "They make my sisters' lives a living hell. They'll do the same to me now."

"The International Senate no longer has the security clearance where you're concerned," Cleo said.

"You're officially above their pay grade now," Genevieve added.

"That's not disturbing at all," Naomi muttered.

Aidan was far too tired to even think about what that could mean. "When do we get out of here?"

"I'll take care of that now." Cleo took the iPad with Aidan's statement and returned to the waiting officers.

"You're a good kid, Aidan," Genevieve said. "I'm sorry this had to be such a trying ordeal, but you have my word. You can trust us. And I promise, once you begin working with these kids, you will see how much we need you and Naomi, and you will come willingly."

"There are much better ways to recruit someone than

manipulation and abduction. For that alone, you'll never have my trust."

"We've watched you for a long time, Aidan. Nothing short of this would tear you away from that school. Think of it as a means to an end and one day, you will see the bigger picture."

"All right kid, lets get you booked and out of here," Lieutenant Sinclair said, as she stepped into the room, checking over his farce of a statement. "See how easy that was? You could have saved us all a lot of time if you'd signed the damn statement days ago."

"Easy, sure." He'd only had to sign his life away. For the next three years, Aidan was beholden to the Milan Initiative, and couldn't breathe a word of it to his family or Allie. He was trapped and his whole world was about to crumble.

Weary down to his very bones, Aidan let himself into the backdoor of the townhouse he shared with his brother, Scott. He was sick about the deal he made with Cleo, but he needed a long hot shower and some sleep before he could even think about the ramifications of what he'd agreed to.

"Dad, I don't know what else to do." Scott's voice drifted down the hall from the living room. "I've tried everything. They just aren't playing by the rules. We're coming up on the fourth day, and they still have him in a cell. The best I can tell, Aidan is refusing to answer their questions, so they're saying they can't book him yet, and he doesn't get privileges like lawyers until he's booked."

"It's bullshit. They're breaking the law. I'll go myself in the morning with half the International Senate if I have to."

Aidan was surprised to hear his father's voice in the room and not on the other end of a phone call.

"Da?" All of Aidan's emotions came crashing down around him when he realized his father was just steps away and not on the other side of the ocean. He charged down the hallway and flung his arms around Gregg.

"Aidan?" Gregg held him tight, brushing his hand over the back of Aidan's head, like he wasn't sure he was really there. "Are you all right, son?"

"I'm fine, Da. Just tired, hungry, and really glad to see you." He pressed his face against his father's shoulder, trying to rein in his emotions.

"How are you here?" Scott crossed the room to hug his brother. "I was worried sick. Start saying things."

"It's under control," Aidan said, running a hand through his messy hair. He had to get his game face on if he expected his family to buy the first of his many lies. "It's just like you said. They wouldn't let me call you or a lawyer until I talked. I refused to talk." He shrugged.

"So, how are you here now?" Gregg asked.

"I made a deal." Aidan groaned as he sat down in his favorite armchair. "It's not like I go back to being an unknown. They know who I am now, so no matter what, it's only a matter of time before the Senate comes poking their nose into my life. This way, at least I got to negotiate things on my terms."

"And what are those terms, son?" Gregg crossed his arms over his chest with a look that said he'd undo whatever it was Aidan had agreed to.

"Community service."

"Community service?" Scott echoed. "That's it?"

"That's it. For now anyway." Aidan sighed. "I just have to teach a class once a week."

"What kind of class?" Gregg asked.

"I'll have a group of gifted students who haven't had much training. They'll come to me here in Cologne, so I can stay in school. And after a while, I'll go to them once a month."

"Go them where?" Gregg asked.

"Not sure yet," Aidan hedged.

"What's the catch?" Scott asked.

"They won't press formal charges against the family or pursue an investigation. Which means they won't find out about Allie."

"So you traded yourself?" Fitzy growled. "Stupid, selfless idiot." He flopped onto the sofa across from Aidan.

"Aye, he is that," Gregg agreed. "And no less than I would have done in his shoes."

"We can't let them get their claws into him, Da," Fitzy said. "They'll never stop. We have to get him out of this."

"It was always going to come to this, son," Gregg said. "I had hoped it would come much later, but Aidan's a strong young man with a good head on his shoulders. He negotiated a good deal. I'm proud of you, Aidan. You did the right thing."

"Thank you, Da. And thank you for coming all this way."

"I was on the first plane out of Cleveland the second I heard. Your mother is beside herself."

"I'm surprised she's not here." Nothing would keep Naeemah away when it came to the safety of her children.

"She was attending the North American Assembly for us. I need to get back soon to make an appearance there myself."

"You didn't tell Allie, did you?" Aidan tried to hide the stress in his voice.

"No, I thought it best not to worry her or the rest of the family until there was something to be worried about."

"Good. It's over now so let's not make a big deal about it."

"Is it really over, though?" Scott asked.

"Seems like a done deal, Fitzy." Aidan shrugged, making light of the whole incident.

"Well, before I leave, I want to talk to whomever you made this deal with," Gregg insisted.

Aidan nodded, not sure how he was going to deal with that. "I'll try to get in touch with the Senate rep later today. I have her number." He did have Cleo's phone number. Hopefully she could do her part to set his father at ease. "But first, I'm going to eat everything in sight, and then I'm going to sleep. Then I'm going to figure out how to catch up on schoolwork. I'll have to come up with a really good excuse for my professors."

"You should take a few days off." Scott twisted his hands nervously in his lap. "You look like hell. And where is Naomi?"

"Thanks, Fitzy, I'm fine," Aidan said, but he was anything but fine. "Naomi went home to rest." In truth, they'd already taken Naomi to Milan, but he had to pick up his life as if nothing happened. Like he wasn't missing a piece of himself. He'd have to make an excuse for her absence soon.

"What did they do to you, son?" Gregg asked gently. "They had you for three days in a cell."

"It was a waiting game. They questioned me a lot but I refused to talk without a family member present. And then they brought a Senate rep in to talk to me and she said if I took this deal, they'd leave me alone otherwise. So I gave them a bogus statement and took the deal and that was it."

"I still want to talk to her," Gregg said.

"It's a good deal, Dad. You know as well as I that this is

the best we could hope for now that they know I exist. I don't mind teaching. They're even going to pay me for my time. Let's just think of it as an after school job."

"As long as you're just teaching, there's no sense in rocking the boat," Gregg said. "But there is no way the Senate will be satisfied with community service, not once they realize how powerful you really are. I suppose we will deal with that when the time comes. You might have to go to ground for a while until it blows over."

"You didn't tell them everything, did you?" Fitzy asked.

"Hell no. I faked all my answers. To them, I'm Aidan Aloysius McBrien."

"Aloysius?" Gregg's brow rose.

"The third." Aidan forced a laugh. "I suppose I had some fun with it."

This community service slap on the wrist was too good to be true. But Aidan had to sell his whole family on the idea. They couldn't know what was really going on, or they would fight it. And that would mean bad things for Naomi.

He didn't trust Cleo and Genevieve. They wouldn't hesitate to punish Naomi if he didn't cooperate, and Aidan wouldn't risk her safety any more than he would risk Allie's.

He was trapped and on his own with no way out.

Chapter 14

Allie | The Dreamworld | November

Allie sat on her yoga mat, fidgeting with anticipation and a little dread. She wasn't looking forward to the part where she threw up in front of Commander Quinn's walkers.

"Relax, Allie." Quinn sat down beside her. "This is a huge part of traveling the dreamworld. You have to be in control of your mind and body."

"Yep. I know." Allie's foot tapped against her mat. "Working on it."

"Try a little harder." He pressed his palm against her foot to still her tapping. "We need you to be good at this, Allie."

"Right, so why are we in the Yard and not in our beds?"

"This is dangerous," Santi said, sinking to the ground behind Quinn where Sasha was already seated.

"I thought you said nothing could hurt Allie and Livia in the dreamworld?" Darius sat behind her, trying to keep up with his role in this newest development.

"It's rare, but things can happen in the dreamworld that affect us in the waking world. It's important we have a safe place for our physical bodies to rest, and those we trust to guard us," Quinn added.

"We're here to guard your bodies and bring you back should anything go wrong," Sasha said.

"If Quinn is captured, there is a chance we could bring him back before Brecken has a chance to get him inside one of his prisons," Santi said. "So we wait and watch for any signs of distress."

"Distress? What should I look for?" Darius looked from Sasha to Santi, his hand squeezing the life out of Allie's.

"I'll be fine, Dare," Allie said.

"I don't like this." A worried frown creased his brow.

"That's why we do this in the underground, so Brecken's people can't come after your physical body in the waking world when he knows you're busy in the dreamworld, fighting his walkers," Sasha said. "Allie's a bad ass. She's got this." Sasha winked at Allie. "I just wish I could come with."

"So we're pretty much just watching them sleep?" Darius asked.

"Sorry, you got the boring end of this deal." Allie rolled her neck from side to side, shaking her hands and stretching her back to loosen up.

"But how do I bring her back if it seems like she's in trouble?" Darius asked.

"Slap her, dump water over her head, whatever it takes to jar her out of her dream state," Santi said. "We will guide you while they are gone, Darius, so if you ever need to guard her on your own, you will know what to do."

"Today is about showing Allie and Livia what a real fight in the dreamworld looks like. You're just observing today," Quinn said.

"All right. Let's do this thing." Allie closed her eyes, leaning back against Darius to find a comfortable position, and reached for that state of calm that allowed her to follow

Quinn to the dreamworld where her father and her sister already waited.

"Be careful," Darius whispered in her ear. He hated seeing her go somewhere he could not.

The now familiar tug around her middle launched Allie into the dreamlike, weightless phase she enjoyed. That part felt like flying. This time she landed on her feet, but dizziness took over and she face planted.

"She does the best entries," Brigs said.

"Wait for it." Livia chuckled.

"Oh crap," Allie groaned right before she tossed her breakfast on the hard packed earth beneath her. She rolled over onto her back, clamping her eyes shut to ward off the nausea.

"She's definitely not graceful." Brigs leaned over her with an arrogant smile on his face. "You all right there, slick?"

"Shut your faces," Allie groaned.

"Do it again!" Raina clapped.

"Ugh, when's that going to stop?" Allie glanced up and regretted it immediately. Quinn's entire army of walkers stood in a circle around her, staring.

"I'm thinking that's just you, Red." Quinn leaned down to give her a hand.

"Give me a minute." Allie rested her head back in the grass. "I'm not ready to get off the merry-go-round yet."

"What a wuss." Raina cackled.

"Yep." Allie winced, giving her a thumbs up. Sitting up and blinking at her surroundings, she saw they were in a clearing beside a well-worn path through an ancient forest of redwoods. Enormous trees scraped the sky, obscuring the sun within the depths of the forest. "Where are we?"

"Somewhere safe," Navid said. "We've left the boundaries of the keep, but we're deep within our territory."

"You ready to see the craziest thing you'll ever see?" Quinn hauled her to her feet.

"Sure, lead the way." She took a step forward and wobbled.

"You all right, beautiful?" Brigs reached out to steady her. At least she thought it was Brigs. He was the handsome military type who always had a toothpick in his mouth.

"Yup, I'm good." She laughed nervously. He was looking at her in that 'I want to date you' kind of way, and Allie was never good at dealing with interested boys. She tended to blurt 'I have a boyfriend' before they'd said anything.

"We're good, thanks," Livia said, sweeping past Brigs to give Allie an easy out if she wanted it.

"Thanks," Allie muttered. Livia usually kept her distance, but Allie preferred it if she didn't have to talk to her sister much. Things were weird between them and Allie still didn't trust her.

"You ladies stick with me, and I'll teach you everything you need to know." Brigs winked.

Allie hated winking guys. The McBrien boys were the only ones allowed to wink at her. Anyone else and it was creepy. She smiled at the thought of Aidan's reaction to flirty-boy-Brigs.

"How about you lead the way?" Livia and Allie followed him along the pathway through the forest until they reached a low-lying marshy area beside a raging river.

"All right, everyone," Quinn called to the group. "We've got a short window to do this. Allie, Livia and Navid will go up to the tower to observe while we crack some heads. Let's show them what we're about." He clapped once and everyone fell in line, weapons and gear appearing from nowhere.

"What tower?" Allie glanced around. There was nothing but trees and grass.

"That one." Navid turned her back around to face the river.

"That was *not* there a minute ago."

"Welcome to the dreamworld." His smile was so wide his eyes crinkled at the edges. "It's a dream come true to show my daughters this place. Shall we?" He grasped their hands to travel, and in the next instant, they stood atop the crumbling tower, watching the scene below.

"Uh." Allie leaned over, clutching her stomach. "I might be sick again."

"Deep breaths." Navid clapped her on the back. "You'll get used to traveling with me eventually."

"Why isn't she sick?" Allie shot a dirty look at her sister.

"Stronger constitution, I imagine." Livia shot her a smirk right back.

"No one says that anymore."

"Did you just call me old? Is that the best you've got?"

Navid chuckled. "Stop bickering you two, or I'm going to turn this car around and we're going home."

"Is he being funny?" Livia asked.

"Trying to," Allie said. "He's always trying, but rarely succeeds."

"I've just always wanted to say that." Navid smiled. "It's good to hear you two tease each other. Like real sisters."

A wave of guilt hit Allie in the gut and she didn't miss the way Livia turned away, her shoulders stiffening like she was physically trying to be as hard as stone.

"So, what does a dreamworld battle look like?" Allie asked.

"You're about to find out." Navid pointed to the left side of the field where Quinn stood with four of his walkers and the right side where Brigs waited with five walkers. Raina stood at the middle, holding a red flag.

"Raina's not fighting?"

"Not while she's in recovery. She needs time to heal. She's come a long way already. You should have seen her when she came looking for Quinn."

"I assumed you guys must have rescued her," Allie said.

"No, Raina got away from Brecken on her own, but she was so far gone, she could hardly function. She tracked Quinn for days until she finally found him and collapsed in his arms. He helped her make it back to the waking world, and we tracked her body to a long term Psychiatric facility in New Orleans. We were able to get her out, and she's staying in Cleveland with Brigs and a few other walker friends in recovery. Naeemah and Gregg offered them the apartment Darius and Scott used to share. Raina was a mess those first few days, but Quinn wouldn't leave her until he knew she would be okay. That's why she thinks she's in love with him."

"I wonder what Aidan could do for her?" Allie mused out loud.

"Hadn't thought of that. It might be worth exploring if she's willing."

"But would he have to meet her in person or here?"

"Are we interrupting your chat?" Quinn's head popped over the parapet wall.

"Did you just climb up here?" Allie glanced over the wall to see him hanging on the ledge.

"Shall we get started now?" he asked.

"Yes, oh great Commander Loukas. You have our undivided attention. Proceed with your mock battle."

"Nothing fake about this battle, Red."

Allie gasped as he just let go and fell twenty feet to the ground, landing in a crouch.

Raina raised her flag and gave a warrior cry, and as she dropped it, she vanished back to the waking world.

Quinn made the first move. The ground shook, and Allie clutched at the tower wall to steady herself. In an explosion of dirt and rock, the ground shifted and the river surged across the marshland, separating Quinn's side from Brigs's.

Brigs responded by erecting a bridge over the canal.

The canal widened into a lake, washing the bridge away before Brigs and his team could use it.

Allie was reminded of the games back home but this was way more intense. Quinn was in his element for sure.

Allie saw boats morph from nothing more than the walker's imaginations, as a naval battle took shape below. The lake grew deeper and wider with each passing moment until the tower was an island in the midst of a war zone.

Bombs exploded, cracking into the sides of Brigs's main vessel.

"You sank my battleship!" he cried in outrage, replacing his sinking vessel with a submarine equipped with torpedoes.

"They're so fast!" Allie stared in awe. Everything changed so rapidly, if she blinked, she'd miss something important.

The water receded back to the river, replaced with acres of thick, gloppy mud. Boats vanished in favor of three wheelers and trucks with huge tires.

"Now, they're just goofing off," Navid muttered, shaking his head.

The tide of the mock battle had shifted from trying to kill each other to seeing who could sling the most mud.

"They certainly seem to be having fun," Livia said.

"I see what you mean about us not being able to keep up." Allie winced as Quinn's four-wheeler toppled, and he went flying into the mud. But before he could hit the ground, he conjured a dirt bike and landed, spraying mud and muck all over Brigs's team. He changed the dirt bike for a truck and sped away, laughing like a kid at the pool.

"He's here!" Raina fell into the mud pit, screaming like a banshee, her voice booming across the clearing like a bullhorn. "Brecken is here!" She pointed at the horizon before she vanished again, unable to maintain her presence in the dreamworld.

Allie turned to see a horrific sight. Lines of soldiers as far as she could see marched toward them.

"Oh, my God." Allie squeaked. "We have to get out of here. We're outnumbered."

"It's not as bad as it seems," Navid said. "Quinn can handle it. Raina gave us enough warning to prepare."

"Thirty seconds is enough?" She crouched low, as the first blazing orb flew through the air. "Was that a freaking catapult?" Her eyes grew wide with fear.

"When you're a walker, thirty seconds is plenty long enough." Navid pulled Livia down beside Allie. "And yes, that was a catapult. Remember, he can't harm anyone with his weapons, not in the physical sense. The dreamworld is all about mental manipulation."

"What is this? The Dark Ages?" Livia frowned, peeking between the stones to watch Brecken's sea of soldiers march closer. "Why such a show of force if he can't harm anyone? Is this all just about a bunch of boys playing with their toys?"

"He can still bring great harm to our minds," Navid explained. "Remember, Brecken's ultimate goal here is to capture Quinn and his walkers and trap them in the dreamworld. The show of force is necessary. You're about to see what we're really up against."

Already, Allie struggled to keep up with everything happening on the battlefield. Before, Quinn and his walkers were just fooling around, putting on a show. Now, the clearing was a real war zone, with tanks and soldiers, machine guns right alongside catapults, trebuchets, and battering rams.

"How does he have so many walkers?" Livia asked. "I thought you were a dying breed."

"For a long time, we were. But you need to look through the lens of a dream walker and tell me what you see."

Allie watched the immense forces Brecken came at them with, but something didn't add up.

"They're all the same," Allie finally said. "Like real live GI Joes."

"What's a GI Joe?" Livia asked.

"Toy soldiers," Allie said.

"Except these aren't toys," Navid said.

"They're dreamers." Allie gasped with the realization.

"But why do they all look alike?" Livia asked.

"They all look like Brecken," Navid explained. "The real Brecken is somewhere down there in the middle of a thousand faces."

"So, we can't find him." Allie's shoulders fell.

"Brilliant," Livia murmured, her tone admiring.

"He's the enemy." Allie glared at her sister.

"I didn't say it was good for us. It's just a smart, tactical maneuver we'll have to overcome."

"We have to help those soldiers back to their dreamscapes?" Allie asked.

"One good shove will send them back to the safety of their own dreamscape," Navid explained.

"That's it?" Livia frowned.

"They are programed to fight anyone who interferes."

"Why bother?" Livia asked, looking perplexed.

"Seriously?" Allie shook her head. "Those are innocent mortals out there."

"But they can't like, die here, right? This is just a dream for them?"

"Yes, they are merely dreaming," Navid said. "But Brecken and his walkers feed on their fear to make themselves stronger."

"So we bust our asses to save a bunch of zombie dreamers from a bad dream so Brecken can't syphon their fear? Unless we can remove the vast majority of these dreamers, it seems like a waste of energy to even bother."

"But we will do it because it's the right thing to do," Allie said. But she was kind of wondering the same thing. Part of her wanted to get caught up in the crazy battle her mind couldn't keep up with. Helping the dreamers was the equivalent to being the ball boy at the World Series. They were close to the main event, but their part was rather boring.

"Can you tell who those dreamers are by looking at them?" Navid asked patiently.

"No, they're disguised to look like Brecken," Livia responded.

"Dreamers are an interesting lot. They're all susceptible to the whims of the dream walkers who control this world. Some more than others. Children for instance."

"Are you saying all those soldiers are just kids?" Livia frowned.

"Not one of them will be older than ten and Brecken keeps these same children tethered to him. Whenever they fall asleep, he pulls them in to fight his battles. To them, this battle will be a nightmare that will haunt them forever. Children's minds are different. They experience the dreamworld in a way that makes them more like you two, actually. They are more cognizant of what happens here. Their dreams are hyper-realistic and when they wake, they will not be able to shake this nightmare.

"These mortal children caught up in our nonsense here will develop night terrors, insomnia, hallucinations and even long term depression and anxiety. The longer Brecken keeps them tethered, the more likely they will suffer from mental illness. We recently learned several of Brecken's young dreamers have committed suicide to escape the terrors of their dreams. Those are extreme cases, but many more are growing ill from lack of sleep because they are too afraid to fall asleep. So yes, they can be injured, but in a much less obvious way. The dreamworld is a psychological minefield for dreamers, mortal or Immortal. If you two can save even a single child from that fate, it will be worth it."

"He does that to children on purpose?" Allie glowered at the scene below, wishing she could get her hands on the real Brecken. "He doesn't deserve this power." Her judgment gift thirsted for his immortality and Allie didn't think she'd feel bad about using it on him.

"He might not have a choice, Allie," Livia said softly. "Sometimes, there is more to the bad guy than just his actions. Someone more important is always pulling the strings behind the scenes, and we need to find out who that is. This whole thing has Marcus Servius written all over it. I just don't know what he hopes to gain by having a foothold in this world."

"My thoughts exactly," Navid said.

Now that she knew Navid was her real father, Livia had stopped calling Marcus her father. It was clear to anyone who listened to her talk about Marcus that she hated him and everything he stood for.

So why am I still struggling to forgive her for a past I know she had little control over? Not for the first time, Allie wondered what it would be like to think of Livia as a real sister. But no matter how much Marcus manipulated Livia, in the end she still made terrible choices and Allie wasn't sure she could ever forgive that.

"What are those other towers?" Livia asked, pointing toward Brecken's army.

"Those are prison worlds—very dangerous dreamscapes," Navid said.

Allie peeked over the parapet to see the towers. Across the wide open expanse of the battlefield, dozens of black stone towers appeared, dotting the clearing that was empty only a moment ago.

"I get a hella bad vibe from those things," Allie said.

"Allie and Livia rule number three of the dreamworld," Navid began, "do not, under any circumstances, go anywhere near one of those towers. They have a gravity-like force that will pull you inside, and once you're in there, we might not be able to get you out. Those dreamscapes were designed to trap a walker. I don't know how or if they will affect you, but I'd rather not find out."

"So if you get pulled in, you're stuck in there forever?" Allie asked.

"Forever," Navid said. "Unfortunately, that is what this battle is about. Brecken is here to trap Quinn and his walkers inside his prison world. It's his way of taking leadership of the dreamworld by force. He intends to trample over anyone who stands against him."

"Once inside one of those things, couldn't you just wake up?" Livia asked.

"No." Navid shook his head sadly. "Brecken's towers force his captives into a stasis where they aren't fully asleep or awake. It's only a matter of time before those inside either succumb to the insanity or submit to his rule.

"Stay away from the creepy nightmare towers, check, check," Allie said, a shiver of fear running down her spine.

"Does Quinn have enough walkers to fight this guy? Maybe we should retreat and try again when we have more numbers."

"Quinn has talent on his side. All of those loyal to him are well equipped to handle this fight. And they know to stay far away from the towers. Brecken's walkers are much weaker, and fickle."

Another round of fireballs sailed through the sky.

"Why on earth are they using such old technology?" Livia asked.

Allie glanced over the parapet to see the two sides engaged in a battle straight out of ...

"World of War!" Allie stood up, peering over the wall. Soldiers in fancy armor. Swords from the pages of fantasy novels, even the creepy towers made more sense now. "What the hell is going on down there?"

"Allie, get down." Navid pulled her back behind the parapet. "What have you seen?"

"It's a freaking game. Brecken's turned the dreamworld into like ... a virtual reality video game."

"A game?" Livia sneered. "What's the point of that?"

"I have no idea, but he's read way too many fantasy novels. He's out there playing war games for his own amusement."

"Idiots. Every one of them," Livia muttered, staring down at the rapidly changing carnage below. "Wasting everyone's time with this nonsense."

Allie nodded. "Boys and their stupid toys."

"Well, let's get down there and save some kids," Livia said with a weary sigh.

"Are you sure you're ready for this? It's going to be chaos down there," Navid said. "We should watch for a while before you attempt anything."

"We're ready," Allie took her sister's hand. "Show us what to do."

"Don't worry, Dad," Livia said, taking his hand. "They won't even notice we're here until it's too late. Let them play their war games while we're busy pulling the rug out from under them."

Was that the first time she called him dad? Judging by the proud look on Navid's face, it was. Allie rarely called him that herself, and she'd known Navid her whole life. *But I had a real father.* Carson was her dad in every sense of the word, but Navid was so much more than just her biological father. It still felt like a betrayal to Carson to think of Navid as her dad, too.

With a flash and a wave of nausea, they traveled to the outskirts of the battlefield.

"We'll work from the back this time. At least until you get the hang of it," Navid said, drawing a weapon from thin air. "Choose a soldier and when they aren't looking, grab an arm and shove them toward the river. Some will fight you but most will wander back to the safety of their own dreamscape, eager to be away. Just keep working at it, one by one."

"And if we get them out of here will they be free of Brecken forever?" Allie asked.

"For most it will break the influence he has over them but only for a time," Navid said. He will eventually pull them back. The longer they've been with him, the more difficult it will be to break the ties that bind the dreamers to Brecken."

"Then we need to overthrow this bastard soon," Livia said. Allie found it baffling that someone who once used and abuse children herself could hold such righteous anger on these kid's behalf.

"We need to find a way to get through as many soldiers as

possible," Allie said. "One at a time won't do much good when we have a thousand suffering."

"Let's do what we can today but we have to find a permanent solution to this problem," Livia said.

"Defeat Brecken," Navid said. "That's our end game."

Chapter 15

Aidan | Rhineland, Germany | December

"I hate teaching." Aidan paced across stone pavilion, waiting for his newest student. This was his third training session in his new position with the Milan Initiative and he was just as nervous as the first time.

"Would you sit down already?" Pilar said from her perch on the lounge beside the fire pit. "You're making me crazy." She had been the biggest surprise of all. After Cleo and Genevieve left to return to Milan with Naomi, Aidan hadn't seen either of them, nor had he laid eyes on his Syntrophos in all that time. Pilar was Aidan's babysitter. She escorted him from his home in Cologne to the training facility and back, posing as a Senate official to appease Fitzy. Yet Aidan suspected she was similarly trapped within the Milan Initiative. A strange predicament for a two thousand year old Immortal. Aidan just wasn't sure if he could trust her yet.

He started to ask Pilar about his newest student, but her stony glare shut him up.

"Don't ask again," she said. "Ezra will be down soon."

"Right," he muttered, taking a seat opposite Pilar. Aidan had always thought he hated teaching his friends. Turned out he just hated teaching, period. Sure, he had a lot he could share, but he was a disaster at preparing lessons. It never seemed to go the way he intended, and he often ended up bumbling his way through it. Aidan's foot bounced against his knee as he cast another glance across the pavilion.

"Sit still," Pilar snapped. "Why are you so nervous? He's just a kid."

"Sorry." Aidan stood. "I just really suck at this." Aidan moved to pace the perimeter of the training room, taking laps around the lounge area surrounding the fire pit. It wasn't really a room. Cleo had rented a freaking castle along the Rhine River, just south of the city. Each week, a new student came to stay here over a long weekend to train with Aidan. The grounds were enormous with sweeping, snow-covered lawns and tall trees guarding the property. They had all the privacy they needed. Aidan favored the covered pavilion that must have once served as an outdoor ballroom. Today, it was a training ground for Aidan and his youngest student yet, Ezra, a seventeen-year-old boy from London. His Syntrophos, Wes, was a twenty-year-old college student from New Orleans.

"I happen to think you'd be pretty damn good at this if you'd get out of your head and just go with the flow. You try to plan it like you can teach them a series of lessons like XYZ, but you're not teaching algebra, Aidan. These kids don't need structured lessons. They need someone who recognizes what they need, when they need it, and to sometimes let them set the tone of their lessons."

"You sound like my dad." Aidan smiled. "He always says I overthink this."

"Teaching?"

"Yeah, it was part of my training. Dad always said people would look to me as the enemy or the leader, so I'd better get used to taking charge now. I've spent the last couple of years training some of my younger friends. Even my girlfriend. Though I'm pretty sure I've learned more from her than she has from me."

"See, you're a natural with experience and everything. Perfect guy for the job."

"Right, lucky me." Aidan returned to his seat by the fire. "What's taking this kid so long?"

"We had an intense workout this morning, so I let him shower and primp a little longer than usual."

"I do not primp," Ezra said, thrusting a hand through his carefully styled hair.

Aidan turned to see the skinny boy crossing the pavilion.

"I just like long showers, and I prefer to let my hair dry naturally in front of the fire like a civilized human being." His dark hair fell in a perfect wave over one eye. "Hi, I'm Ezra." He offered his hand to Aidan. His wary green eyes blazed like dark emeralds.

"Nice to meet you." Aidan shook his hand.

"They neglected to tell me my new teacher is a hottie. I might have come willingly if someone bothered to show me pics."

"Okay, then." Aidan laughed, certain his face flushed pink.

"Did I forget to mention Ezra's a flirt?" Pilar said, her lips thinning into an unamused smile.

"I love all people, so don't mind me, I'm harmless," Ezra said.

"Right, that's a line of BS if I ever heard one. I'll let you two get aquatinted." Pilar stood to go. "I'll check back around lunchtime." She headed back toward the house but paused half way across the pavilion. "Ezra, that doesn't mean you get to ask a billion stupid questions to evade anything personal.

You tell Aidan about yourself, so he can get a feel for where you've come from and what you've been through. Don't waste his time."

"Yes, Mom." He rolled his eyes. "She thinks she knows all my tricks but she doesn't."

"You are going to be my most interesting student, aren't you?" Aidan chuckled.

"You'll thank me later."

"Come have a seat by the fire," Aidan offered. "We'll have a chat this morning and spend the afternoon sparring, so I can assess your previous training."

"I'm all yours." Ezra winked, taking the seat opposite Aidan. "You have a girlfriend, don't you? Guys like you always have hot girlfriends. Tell me about her." Ezra crossed his ankle over his knee, smoothing the wrinkles in his dark skinny jeans.

"I do have a girlfriend and she's pretty fantastic."

"Blond, big boobs? Kind of a ditz?"

Aidan nearly choked on his laughter. "Definitely not. And she'd tear your face off if you said that around her. She's a smart redhead with a hell of a temper, and she's as kind as she is beautiful."

"So that's a yes on the big boobs." Ezra smirked.

"The ass is not so bad either." Aidan couldn't stifle his smile. *Allie would adopt this kid as her new bestie in a heartbeat.*

"So, heartbreaker, what brings you to Germany?"

"School."

"Music, right? You play violin?"

"Yep. And that's enough about me. Tell me about your family." Aidan forced himself to stop tapping his foot against the slate floor.'

"Dead," Ezra said, bouncing his knee with a nervous twitch.

"Coalition?"

"Supposedly."

"Why supposedly?" Aidan wasn't fooled by Ezra's nonchalance. He was choosing his words carefully. Already Aidan knew Ezra wasn't here by choice and he didn't trust the Milan Initiative, which meant he could be a potential ally.

"Well, two years ago, I lived in London with my parents, and life was pretty normal. I had a normal Awakening and a few months later, I met Wes. We hit it off right away. One night we were out late and a couple of assholes jumped me. Too many for us to handle alone. They roughed me up pretty bad—I'm a lover not a fighter. Anyway, Wes was freaking out, fussing over me and then it just happened. We bonded just like that. The Milan Initiative came knocking on our door a few weeks later, eager for me and Wes to come train with others like us. My parents weren't down with that and neither was Wes. They wanted me home for another year or two before they felt it was necessary to dive into that kind of training."

"Weeks?" Aidan's brow shot up in surprise. *That's awfully convenient.* "They just showed up out of the blue right after you bonded?" Aidan asked. "How did they even know about you and Wes?"

"Convenient, yeah?"

"A little too convenient," Aidan said without thinking. He shouldn't show his true feelings about the Initiative. He needed to be more careful.

"I've heard stuff about you, you know," Ezra said, lowering his voice.

"Like what?"

"Like you and Naomi don't want to be here any more than the rest of us. Like maybe things happened a certain way to bring you both here too."

Aidan studied Ezra with his gift, feeling for his emotions and current mood. His pulse raced and he was scared despite his outward bravado.

"You can trust me," Ezra said softly. "I can tell you things about the Initiative." Ezra met his gaze, begging for Aidan's trust. "I'm the snoop, so I know things the others don't."

Aidan glanced over his shoulder for Pilar or one of the many guards she traveled with when escorting a student.

"It's okay, Pilar's a friend. They'll leave us alone for a little while." Ezra leaned forward, his elbows on his knees. "We don't get the luxury of privacy very often so I have to take advantage of it when it comes around."

"And how do you know you can trust me?" Aidan said cautiously.

"Naomi told me I could. I've been training with her for a few weeks. I'm her favorite." Ezra shrugged. "She told me to tell you to 'listen to the boy, dinkus.'"

Aidan laughed, his tension melting away. Only Naomi could have sent that message. "She used to call me that when I was five. So tell me what you know." Aidan said, not sure what to make of Ezra.

"Work with me here because it's kinda crazy, and you're probably not going to believe me." Ezra shot a last look over his shoulder, lowering his voice. "They have ways of tracking kids with this bond."

"How?" Aidan lowered his voice, too, eager for anything Ezra could tell him.

"I'm going to sound like a total nutter here, but they use the dreamworld. It's this place ... or realm or something, I don't know how to describe it—"

"I'm up to speed on the dreamworld," Aidan said. For centuries the dreamworld was an obscure place with a dwindling population of dream walkers, most Immortals didn't know of its existence anymore. "They're using a dream walker?"

"Yes." Ezra scooted to the edge of his seat. "See, I knew you'd be my go to guy for this stuff I don't know what to do with. I overheard our evil-lady leaders talking about this dreamworld stuff months ago and it took me a while to make sense of it. They have this guy, Brecken. He's a powerful dream walker, and he knows how to find us in our dreams. In the real world, searching for younger kids with the bond would be an impossible task, but Brecken is like a freaking dog with our scent. But I think it's only young Immortals. It's like it's easier for him to trace the bond when we're Unproven."

"That's why everyone is so young." Aidan drummed his fingers against his knees. "They've streamlined their recruiting process." An anxious tremor raced down Aidan's spine. He did not like this. Not at all. This whole thing reeked of manipulation.

"I heard they had their own dream walker all set to join the team last year, and I guess it fell through. Now, Brecken is off on some other mission, and they're looking for new access to the dreamworld. That's why we haven't had anyone new in a while."

"A new dream walker, huh?" Aidan sat back in his seat. "About a year ago?" Of course, it fell through. Right around the time Quinn escaped Soma. Right after Allie saw his picture on the auction block at Amrita. Someone with the Milan Initiative had tried to buy Quinn. But how could they have known he was a dream walker then? Quinn was just figuring that out for himself.

"You look freaked," Ezra said. "I freaked you out."

"Ezra, I need to know how you have all of this information," Aidan said. "And I need total honesty from you if we're going to be friends."

"It's a talent I have." Ezra's shoulder lifted in a half-shrug. "Think about it, earlier when I showed up did you sense me coming from the McMansion behind us?" He shot a thumb over his shoulder.

"I was distracted, talking to Pilar." Aidan glanced at the distance between the pavilion and the house. A wide, sweeping lawn separated the two structures, but it wasn't so far that Aidan couldn't have sensed the young Immortal coming across the lawn.

"Do you often get so distracted you don't notice other Immortals creeping up behind you?" Ezra gave him a poignant look.

The kid had a point. "No, that never happens, but you were still across the room when you called out your arrival."

"I was there the whole time you were talking to Pilar about being nervous and how you hate teaching, but your dad made it part of your training. I can sneak up on just about anyone and they never notice me. I'm not suppressing my Immortal presence, I'm just sending out a very non-threatening vibe that kinda allows me to hide in plain sight. So, I hear things. I make it a point to hear things. Information is a hot commodity when you're sucked into a game of lies and deceit with no way out."

"And why are you telling me what you know?" Aidan wanted to trust the kid, but he needed to tread carefully here.

"I want to go home. I never wanted to be here, and I don't think half the kids in the Initiative do either."

"Why pin your hopes on me?" Aidan asked.

"Timing," Ezra said with a careless shrug. "I'm taking a leap of faith, hoping you won't disappoint me."

Aidan sat back against his seat, studying Ezra's earnest face. The Initiative was looking for new access to the dreamworld. It was only a matter of time before Cleo or Genevieve figured out Aidan had that kind of access through Allie. Only a matter of time before they pulled her into this mess right along with him.

They're orchestrating these bonds. Aidan wished he could talk to his father about this. Gregg would know if that was even possible. But there had to be a way the Initiative was forcing these bonds to happen to such young kids. It was too convenient for it to happen naturally and for so many when the bond was so rare. *Maybe this Brecken guy can find people with the potential for the Syntrophos bond? Then they bring the two together and force an emotional situation to see what happens.*

"You have a scary look on your face," Ezra said nervously.

"Sorry." Aidan tried to smile his reassurance, but he was freaked out and angry and, like Ezra, he just wanted to go home. "You've shed some light on some very interesting details. You'll let me know if you discover anything more I might want to hear?"

"That's it?" Ezra frowned. "I tell you all the juicy bits and I get nothing in return?"

"We're still building trust, Ezra." Aidan smiled. "If you prove to be trustworthy, I've got your back. If you cross me or Naomi, there will be repercussions." Aidan let the authority of his power color his voice with a threatening tone. He would never hurt the kid, but he needed Ezra to respect him and maybe fear him a little too.

"Whoa." Ezra let out a nervous breath. "You're scary powerful."

"But a good friend to have in your corner," Aidan said.

Ezra nodded. "I'll keep my eyes and ears open for anything you might find of interest. But ..."

"But what?" Aidan asked.

"Can we—Wes and I, um ..."

"Spit it out," Aidan said with a kinder tone.

"Can we count on your protection?"

Aidan's heart wilted at the sincere note of desperation in Ezra's voice. "What are you afraid of?" Aidan asked.

"Everything." Ezra sighed. "You'll see."

"You can count on our friendship," Aidan said. "If you need anything, get to Naomi and she'll get a message to me." Aidan didn't know what he could do for Ezra, but he felt a little less alone, knowing his student didn't trust the Milan Initiative any more than he did. The kid was a good ally.

"So, where does the Coalition come into your sad story?" Aidan asked, not wanting to push their boundaries any further today.

"After we turned them down in the beginning, Cleo and Genevieve left, and we thought that was the end of it. Wes and I were out late one night, like we do ... or did. We came home and found my parents slaughtered in their beds. We've been in Italy ever since. We didn't really have anywhere else to go. The whole thing has always sounded like a means to an end to me. We're here, aren't we? Just like they wanted."

"You think Cleo and Genevieve sent the Coalition to your home? Or was it Pilar?"

"Pilar I'd trust with my life. She's a pawn just like us. But this thing doesn't start and end with Cleo and Genevieve. There are others pulling strings behind the scenes. They talk of their benefactors, but I don't know who that could be."

"I'm sorry to hear about your parents," Aidan said.

"Me too. It was barely a year ago, but it feels like another life."

"You and Wes haven't had much choice in this whole thing, have you?"

"None. I would never go back and change it, but ever since we bonded, our lives haven't been our own."

"Tell me about Wes," Aidan said, trying to steer the conversation to happier topics.

"Wes is great." Ezra's face lit up with a huge smile.

"And how did a kid from London even meet a guy from New Orleans?"

"We met when Wes was doing a study abroad program through his university. He needed an Immortal host family, so he submitted a request through the Senate, and they placed him with us. After we bonded, he decided to stay for a while. He's not as close with his parents as I was with mine. My parents took him in and treated him like another son."

Sounds like an arranged meeting. But Aidan wasn't sure Ezra realized it might have started that far back.

"And you had no idea what this bond was? That must have been difficult." *Jeez, I sound like a freaking shrink.*

"At first, I was convinced we were Complements." Ezra gazed down at his hands in his lap, a flush creeping into his cheeks. "But Wes is straight, so it freaked him out."

"The feelings are confusing, especially at first," Aidan said. "It's a complicated relationship. Even more for you guys, I imagine."

"What did you call it? A Syntro-something?"

"Sin-tro-fus."

"So it's like a real thing, then? It's always been a thing?"

"It's rare, especially in recent centuries, but the Syntrophos have ancient roots. Some say we are the direct descendants of the royal lines of Indriell and its noble houses.

Some say we're the blood of the first Immortals. And some say the Syntrophos bond rises when the world has need of it, which might account for how many of our generation are bonding this way. We have a strong history if you know where to look."

"I've heard things ... speculations." Ezra's hands twisted nervously in his lap

"Like what?"

"One of the girls says that because we have this special bond, we don't get a Complement, too. Like there's no way it would ever work. So, like, this is it for us. This friendship bond and we should make the most of it, if we can."

"I am happy to tell you that is not true," Aidan said, relieved he could at least put Ezra's mind at ease on this issue.

"How do you know?" Relief flooded his face.

"This is between just you and me, okay?" Aidan leaned forward. "I am asking you not to repeat this to anyone other than Wes. I will tell the others when the time is right, but I'd rather keep this from anyone higher up the chain."

"You have my word. I won't repeat anything you say."

"My father shared a Syntrophos bond with a very special woman. She died when I was young, but my father had both a Syntrophos and a Complement, my mother. His Syntrophos was an anchor, who also had a Complement, and together, the three of them were linked through her."

"An anchor?"

"She was the center of the bond, the anchor that held them together. Each Syntrophos has an anchor. Once you have bonded with your Complements, either you or Wes will emerge as the anchor."

Ezra nodded, blowing out a big breath. "That's a relief."

"How long have you been in love with him?" Aidan asked gently.

"With Wes? Is it that obvious?" He cast his eyes down at his lap.

"My gift tells me a little of what you're feeling, so I had some help with that. Most people probably wouldn't' notice."

"He certainly doesn't." Ezra sighed. "I guess I've had a thing for him right from the start." He shrugged. "Can't help it. The heart wants what the heart wants, even though it's never going to happen. I'd give anything to not feel this way."

"It's the bond. It's confusing. You do love him and he loves you. It's just a new kind of love that isn't black and white. It's not a simple friendship, and it's not romantic love either. I'm told time will help. Eventually, it will make sense to you."

"So, you have the hots for Naomi? How's your girlfriend feel about that?"

"Oh, they've hated each other for years. Like full on, claws out, girl-hate." Aidan grimaced, thinking about how Allie would take it when she found out.

"That's got to be entertaining at least. Girls are so weird."

"Tell me about it. I love them both but it tears me up inside. My bond with Naomi is new so we're still figuring it out. I've known her all my life and I've always had feelings for her, but it makes more sense now.

"Does your girlfriend know about the bond?"

"Nope. I'm putting it off because I'm a coward, and it's really something I need to tell her face to face."

Aidan's gift wanted to reach out to Ezra to help sooth his emotions, but that wasn't the answer. "It won't always be this difficult, Ezra."

"You're saying there are other fish in the sea, and I won't always feel like this ... awful, I love him, but I can never have him, stabbed in the gut anguish I feel all the time?"

"You're the dramatic sort, aren't you?" Aidan shook his

head with a smile. "You are going to date tons of guys, and Wes will hate them all, telling you they aren't good enough for you. And you'll hate his girlfriends. But when both sides of the Syntrophos are settled with their own Complements, I'm told they bring the balance needed to the relationship.

"Tons of guys, huh?" He rolled his eyes. "How many gay Immortals my age do you know?"

"I know one." Aidan grinned. "Let's call him." Aidan fished his phone out of his pocket.

"You still have a phone?" Ezra gasped. "How?" He glanced up, eyes wide with wonder.

"I have a very ... influential family who aren't going to take to kindly to me disappearing. I think Cleo intends to pull me away little by little. That's why Naomi is in Italy and I'm here at school. They know I'm not going anywhere without Naomi. So for now, I guess I have some semblance of freedom."

Ezra eyed the phone and Aidan was pretty sure he saw drool.

"You want to call someone?" Aidan asked.

"No." Ezra sighed. "I don't have anyone to call. "But I'd sell Wes for an hour alone with Instagram and a Starbucks."

Aidan laughed. "I'm probably not supposed to do this, but you'll like Graham." He started to dial.

"What, no!" Ezra lunged for the phone. "Are you crazy?"

"I'm doing the stupid straight guy thing where I introduce you to my one gay friend. Like you're perfect for each other because you're both gay, but I'm not an idiot. I just think you two would genuinely hit it off as friends."

"Don't dial that phone, Aidan. I will kill you."

"Too late."

"Oh, my God, who are we Facetiming?" Ezra scooted in close to sit beside Aidan.

"Come on." Aidan held his phone up. "Humor me. I have a point."

"I hate you." Ezra pasted on a smile as Graham finally picked up.

"You better be dying." Graham switched on the light next to his bed. "Someone better be dying or on fire."

"Wake up, sunshine," Aidan said. "I have someone I want you to meet."

"Aidan, it's four in the morning here. You cannot introduce me to cute boys at four in the morning." Graham's wavy dark blond hair stood up on end, and he had pillow marks on his face and chest. "At least not before coffee." He rubbed his eyes.

"You sound like that redhead we all know and love." Aidan wanted to ask how she was doing, but the less Ezra or any of his new students knew about Allie, the better. "Graham, this is Ezra. We've been doing some training together in that class I've been teaching."

"Yeah I heard about your community service, dumbass. How the hell did you get caught?"

"Not paying attention," Aidan said dryly, making light of his run in with the Senate. "Be nice and say hello to my student."

"Hey Ezra." Graham managed a sleepy half smile. "What's up?"

"Hi. Sorry. Apparently, straighty here is trying to prove a point." Ezra's ears turned pink.

"He'll get around to making sense eventually. I usually just go with it. Aidan's a great teacher, even though he thinks he sucks. But when he gets you in the sparring ring, go for his left knee. He's got this trick spot right behind the join—"

"I do not have a trick knee, Graham," Aidan interrupted. "Don't listen to him."

"You call me. I've been sparring with this guy for years. I've got all the secrets."

"I'm going to be the uber stupid, straight guy for one sec, and then we can all pretend like this call never happened," Aidan said.

"Aidan, don't be an idiot." Graham ran his hands through his hair. "Ezra, I apologize for whatever he's about to say."

"I'll be quick. Ezra here is feeling a little down for the lack of eligible gay Immortals his age. And crushing on a certain someone he'd rather not be crushing on."

"Ooh, straight guy crush? Never a good idea." Graham winced. "I've been there man, it's not fun."

"Wait, who did you have a crush on?" Aidan asked.

"Not you." Graham rolled his eyes. "I may have had a thing for Darius once upon a time."

Aidan made retching noises, smiling when Ezra laughed.

"Who is Darius?" Ezra asked.

"My brother, who is far too old for Graham."

"Hey, he's only like ten years older, and I'm sorry, dude, but your brother is adorable. I could totally gross you out and tell you about my current mad crush on Greyson."

"Stop talking, little man." Aidan grimaced. "He's Naomi's father."

"You have no idea. He's so hot, I don't even care how old he is," Graham said.

"Well, I'm pretty sure my sister and my girlfriend agree with you," Aidan said. "But let's get back to the point of my call, so you can get back to sleep."

"Right. Listen, Ezra." Graham sat up against his headboard. "I totally know what it's like to feel like the only gay Immortal teenager in the world. But there are more of us out there than you'd think. There's an online network I can show you. It's not sleazy at all. It's just a really great community that offers the kind of support we all need."

"Like just for Immortals? That would be great, thanks, man."

"And *you* can call me anytime. But Aidan, try to make it after ten am, bro. I need my beauty rest."

"Fine. Go to sleep, little man. Talk to you later."

"Miss you, Aidan. When you coming home?"

"Very soon." Christmas break started next week and he couldn't wait to get home. "Night, Graham."

"Night, Ezra." Graham winked and ended the call.

"I will have dreams about that sleepy smile of his." Ezra sighed.

"That's not really why I called him," Aidan said. "I just wanted you to know there are other people all over the world going through the same thing. Immortal. Mortal. Gay. Straight. Bi. Pan. Trans. Everyone our age has tons of crazy shit we're dealing with. And all we really want is a normal life where we get unlimited screen time, all the iced coffees we want and to fall in love with someone amazing."

"I guess we can't all be as lucky as you and the redhead."

"Yeah. Lucky," Aidan sighed. "I just have to figure out how I'm going to tell her I'm staying in Germany a few years longer than we planned."

"Ouch," Ezra said. "I'm sorry you got caught up in this mess with us."

"I guess we can all probably relate to that 'means to an end' thing when it comes to the Milan Initiative."

"That's the first time I've seen Ezra really laugh in ages," Pilar said after Aidan sent his student back to his rooms for the evening. They'd spent the afternoon sparring and Aidan realized Ezra could barely hold a sword correctly.

"He's a good kid," Aidan said. "But we've got a lot of work to do with him." Aidan returned their equipment to the freestanding shelves along the far end of the pavilion.

"Not everyone comes from a family like yours," Pilar said, helping him gather discarded weapons. "His family is young and, like many Immortal families these days, they don't place as much emphasis on battle training as they probably should. Most of them focus on honing abilities and don't spend nearly enough time teaching their children how to protect themselves. Some don't have the time. Others don't have the resources. You're lucky."

"I didn't think so when I was a kid." Aidan thought of all the years spent training in the underground. He was only a few years older than Ezra, but he had light-years more experience. Aidan watched Pilar out of the corner of his eye. Ezra said she was a friend, but he wasn't sure yet. She was an intimidating woman. And tall, taller than Aidan, and he was creeping up on six and a half feet. She was an Amazon warrior from the ancient Greek city of Themiskyra on the Black Sea of modern day Turkey. Her dusky skin shone like smooth copper and her long dark braids fell to her waist. She was gorgeous, but scary at the same time. Pilar was more than two thousand years old, and she'd studied the Syntrophos bond most of her life. She was fascinated with the bond and probably knew more about it than even Gregg. Aidan had already gathered that she kept most of her knowledge close to the belt. She didn't trust Cleo and Genevieve with her knowledge.

"We'll be leaving in a few hours. I'll escort you home before Ezra and I head back to Italy. I'll be back next week with Wes."

"I'll be leaving for Christmas break next week," Aidan said.

"No you won't," Pilar said.

"I've had plane tickets home for months. If Cleo and Genevieve don't want my mother to rain down the apocalypse on their heads, they better let me go home for a visit. I'll be back when the new semester starts."

"Leave it to those two to not explain things clearly." Pilar's shoulders sagged. "I'm sorry, Aidan, but whatever agreement you have with them, they've sugar coated it. They've given you freedoms they don't give anyone else. Not even me. But make no mistake, you belong to the Initiative. You aren't going anywhere."

"How do they expect me to keep this from my family if I can't ever visit them?"

"They know about your 'community service?'" She said it with a sneer.

"Yes but they'll expect me home next week. My parents are Governor of the Great Lakes Region, if Mom thinks I have community service keeping me here in Germany for the holidays, she's going to pull some strings to get me home. I don't think you understand, people don't tell my mother no."

"Get them to come here for your holiday. The Initiative won't interfere as long as you stay where you are supposed to be and keep your mouth shut. But there is no way you are returning to the States. For any reason."

"This is bullshit." Aidan kicked the marble edge of the fire pit in frustration, raking his hands through his hair. "I want my life back."

"I am afraid neither you nor I have that luxury. Like it or not, we are beholden to the Initiative." Pilar said, her voice low and concerned. "The sooner you learn that lesson, the better."

"It's just ... I had a plan to set my family at ease about all of this and now that's not going to work." Aidan sank down onto the lounge. He had to get home to explain things to Allie. About Naomi, the Initiative, all of it. And now they'd robbed him of that too.

"They know about your connection with her," Pilar said, crouching down beside him. "The girlfriend. Do not bring her here."

Aidan's blood ran cold. "What connection?"

"Cleo has discovered your girl is a telepath with a direct link to your mind. Right now, she believes the distance protects your mind from this girl. She does not see this as a useful tool. Do not give her a reason to think it is."

"Useful? How can sharing a thought with my girlfriend be useful for them." Aidan's hands trembled as he shoved them into his pockets.

"Cut the crap. I knew your father a long time ago and he wouldn't raise a fool. You know exactly what I mean and you need to shut it down while you still can. Cleo doesn't know it yet, but it's only a matter of time before she learns exactly what a telepathic mind can do. You know our gifts are fueled by our power, but those gifts that happen up here." She tapped his forehead. "Abilities that work through the psyche are connected to the power of the dreamworld. You have the link to the dreamworld they're looking for. Don't let them find it. You're strong enough to sever that connection. Do it. If not to protect yourself, do it to protect the girl you love."

"Why are you helping me?" Aidan asked, his face like iron.

"It's not about you." She shook her head. "I can't do anything to help the kids already caught up in the Initiative, but I can make damn sure we don't ruin anymore lives.

CHAPTER 16

Aidan | The Dreamworld | December

"Aidan, I know you love Allie, but if they got their hands on her, you'd never forgive yourself." Naomi sat on his sofa back in his room at the house he shared with Fitzy. This was her first visit since her move to Milan, and he'd missed her so much. After more than a month apart, it hurt to breathe without her.

Aidan lay with his head in her lap, content to be beside her again. "I don't know how to protect her from this."

"Yes, you do. You're just too chicken shit to do it."

Naomi was right.

"If you put it off any longer, a lot of people are going to get hurt."

Aidan glanced up at her. "You really think we can trust Ezra and Pilar?"

"Yes. All the kids hate Cleo and Genevieve. They make a good show of going along with the pretense that the Milan Initiative is just a fancy boarding school for talented kids, but they know they're trapped."

"The last time I saw Navid in the dreamworld, he asked to speak with me privately," Aidan said. "I thought he was going to give me the 'don't hurt my daughter' speech. But he said some things that didn't make much sense at the time—they make more sense now. He told me it was okay to leave her. That it was important for me to go my own way for a time, and I should trust my instincts. That Allie would understand, and we would have our time together. I thought he meant it was okay for me to stay here with you. Like he knew we were about to become Syntrophos."

"He's creepy the way he knows so much about everyone and everything." Naomi shivered. "He's the one who convinced me I should move to Germany with you last year."

"He's not creepy. Navid's Complement is the most powerful clairvoyant to ever live. I imagine they know a lot about all of us."

"It's still creepy. But if he knows so much about you and the things that are happening to us now, then reconsider his words. What would Navid say if he knew your access to the dreamworld through his daughter would ultimately give the Milan Initiative access to the dreamworld and every potential young Syntrophos out there?"

"He would tell me to shut it down," Aidan said. "No matter what."

"Then you know that's what you have to do."

Aidan walked along the pathway leading to Allie's tree house. He always entered her dreamscape this way. Now that she understood the way her dreamscape worked, her connection to the dreamworld was even stronger.

He'd known for a while it was his telepathic connection with Allie that allowed him to come here and maintain his awareness in a way other dreamers couldn't. Without Navid's guidance, they would have made a mess of things. Even now, Aidan felt the pull to wander, the urge to step outside the safety of Allie's dreamscape to explore, but Navid had warned them that it was too dangerous to wander this world alone.

He didn't know how Cleo and Genevieve could expect him to track the young, unsuspecting Immortals who had the potential to become Syntrophos when he was essentially riding Allie's coattails here, but he had a feeling they'd find a way to make it work.

No matter how much he needed this connection to stay close to Allie, it wasn't worth the pain it could cause so many others. And eventually, Allie was going to find out what was happening with him, and she'd stick her nose in it until she was in just as deep as he was. He was torn between duty and love. An impossible choice that was tearing him up inside.

"But if I don't tell her everything, she's going to think I don't trust her." Aidan kicked a stone in his way, wishing he had the right answer that would solve all his problems. Deep down, he just wanted to protect Allie. She was so strong and could handle her own shit, he knew that. But this whole mess was his fault and he didn't want his mistakes to ever touch her.

Aidan walked along the tree-lined pathway, hands shoved in his pocket, avoiding the inevitable. The cherry blossoms were in perfect bloom and a salty, ocean breeze swept through his hair. Lights twinkled in the branches, and white Chinese lanterns lit the way.

He smiled, taking in the romantic setting. She always prepared this pathway for him. Sometimes, it was the same for a while, and then she would change it to something equally spectacular.

"You like?" Allie asked, appearing on the path ahead of him.

"It's beautiful." His gaze heated as he stared at her, drinking her in. She managed to take his breath every time he laid eyes on her. Her beauty was never a question, but she was so much more. As smart and funny as she was, she was also inspiring, spontaneous and full of surprises. "But you always look amazing."

"I meant the lights, but thank you."

"You're wearing a dress." He smiled, his breath catching in his throat. She wore a lacy pink, swishy kind of dress falling down to her ankles. Her gorgeous red hair cascaded down her back with a spray of cherry blossoms tucked behind her ear. A light dusting of freckles dotted the creamy soft swell of her breasts and her strange pale green eyes flashed like gems in the lamplight.

"I am. Don't get used to it." She took his hand as they walked along the lane.

"I like it. But you look just as beautiful in your paint-stained jeans and t-shirts with those badass sai blades at your hips."

"You say all the best words," Allie said, looping her arm through his.

"So what's the occasion?" Aidan gestured at her dress and their surroundings. "You've made the dreamworld match your dress. Everything's pink. You hate pink."

"I don't know. I just like the cherry blossoms. It's the one pink thing I don't hate."

"Are we celebrating something? I don't think I've missed any important anniversaries, have I?" He knew he hadn't. Every milestone he'd experienced with Allie was carved into his memory from the day she ran right into him to the day she finally told him she loved him.

"I've missed you." She shrugged. "We've both been so busy lately; we don't get much time here anymore. You're coming home so soon but I want us to catch up before then." She tugged on his hand with one of her smiles that made him speechless.

"The time difference and cramming for final performances has made it harder. I'm sorry, baby. I miss you, too." Aidan pulled her back in, slipping his arm around her waist. Seeing her in the dreamworld was better than nothing, but it still wasn't the same as sharing a life with her, which was all he really wanted. But it didn't look like that was going to happen anytime soon.

"It won't be once you're home next week. I'm so excited I can hardly focus on school." She pulled him along the pathway, excitement dancing in her eyes.

"We have a swing now," Aidan said, as they approached her tree house.

"Let's sit. I've planned for a beautiful sunset." Allie shoved him into the swing, climbing on top of him to press her lips to his. "Do you know how much I love you, Aidan McBrien?" she murmured, running her fingers through his hair.

He couldn't help it: he kissed her back, letting his hands fall to her waist and pulling her closer. He wanted to stay in this moment with her forever—anything to avoid what he was about to do to them. But he didn't have that luxury, and he couldn't let this go on. He needed to do what he came here to do, and get it done before he lost the will to do it. He already felt like crying and that would ruin his lies. Lies that burned like acid in his throat.

"Lex, you have no idea how much I love you. You're on my mind the moment I wake up and you're the last thought I have before sleep takes me." He took her hands in his, pressing her palms against his chest. "But about next week—"

"Aidan? You're really doing this?" She let her hands fall to her lap, her shoulders slumped, and her eyes widened in surprise.

Of course, she'd seen this coming. She was clairvoyant. "You saw this?"

"Yes, but I never thought you'd actually do it." She shoved him back against the swing. "Why, Aidan? There were no signs you were even considering it." Tears of anger caught her in her lashes, each one like a hot knife ripping through his chest.

"How long have you known?" He could barely get the question out.

"Since you left, but it's never made any sense. Let's talk about this."

"Why did you let me go, Allie?" His throat tightened and he could barely speak. If she'd said something—anything about what she'd seen for them—he'd have never left. No matter how much Aidan had needed the escape then, he would have stayed, found a way to deal with her relationship with Darius, and the pain of knowing she was his Complement when she didn't. That pain was nothing compared to this. He'd take a thousand years of her not knowing over leaving her this way.

"I didn't want to hold you back from your dream, Aidan. You deserve this time—as much time as you want to take. I would never stand in your way. I ... I thought my gift was wrong. You've been blocking me so much lately. I just thought you were busy cramming for exams like I was."

She wasn't going to let him go without an explanation, and he couldn't tell her about the Initiative. She'd come in guns blazing to get him out of the mess he'd made of his life.

And then Allie would be caught up in the snare with him—not knowing she would be handing his enemy the biggest weapon they could use against him—both his Syntrophos and his Complement. The Initiative would manipulate Aidan for the rest of his life.

He was going to have to convince Allie he *wanted* to leave her, and it shattered something inside him to even consider it.

"You always said we would overwhelm each other," he began, but his mind whirled with every possible way he could get out of doing this. He came up with nothing. "You were right." The words tasted like ash in his mouth. It was the worst thing he could possibly say to her.

"You son of a bitch, don't you dare do this." She moved off his lap, settling in the swing beside him.

"I'm sorry, Allie." He turned to find their romantic setting gone. Lights vanished, blossoms faded, and Allie sat beside him in her jeans and t-shirt, like always. She was still lovely. Still the only girl he would ever love, but he had to protect her the only way he could. He had to leave her, block her from his mind in every possible way. He had the motivation to do it now—he just needed to rip the Band Aid off and make it quick.

"You're *sorry*?" She shook her head, too bewildered to let it sink in. "I thought there would be clues you were pulling away from us. I thought I would have time to change your mind. Where is all this coming from, Aidan?"

"I want you to have your own life, Allie. We're young. We both need time to figure out who we are without each other." It was the one thing he knew he could say to convince her. It was the reason she'd resisted loving him for so long. She'd never thought he'd understood that before but he always had. She fought falling in love with him because so much of her life she'd spent alone and lonely. He knew what that was like, too. Allie's greatest fear was going back to that life. She feared loving him meant she would lose him, and she'd never wanted to risk their friendship. But Aidan always knew what they had was worth the risk. It still was. He would be free of the Initiative. Someday. And then they would have the rest of their lives together.

"So that's just it, then? You're shutting me out without a single explanation?" Her tears trailed down her cheeks, but she wiped them away, letting her anger take precedence.

"I've already decided to stay in Germany to finish school. I think it will be easier this way. Easier for both of us if we make it a clean cut." Aidan wanted to take the words back. To scream from the mountaintops that he wanted to spend the rest of his life with her. But his life was no longer his own.

"Fine, stay. I understand you want to be there. You've always had my full support. Why does it have to be all or nothing? Have you met someone else?"

"God no, Allie. It's not like that at all, baby." He would not let her believe that. He would do this, but he couldn't let her think there would ever be anyone else. Aidan tried to pull her back into his arms, not ready to let her go just yet.

"No. You don't get to hold me and try to make this easier on yourself." She shoved him away. "I resisted this relationship for so long, Aidan. And I finally let us have this. Trusted you with my heart, and now you're leaving? Screw you, Aidan McBrien!" She shoved him again, beating her fists against his chest. Hard.

"Allie, please. Listen to me, baby." He slipped onto his knees in front of her, holding her hands in his. "I need you to trust me, Alexis Ann." His voice broke on a sob as he kissed her perfect hands, and pressed his forehead against her knees, his eyes swimming with tears of his own. "This is for the best.

I'm going to leave in a minute, and I'm not going to come back." He didn't know how he'd have the strength to actually do it. "And you're not going to hear my thoughts anymore."

"No." She shook her head stubbornly, swiping at the tears falling freely now. "Don't do this, Aidan," she whispered. "Don't you dare leave me alone."

"But you're not alone, Lex. You have Sasha and all our friends. You have Liam and Darius."

"Is that what this is about? My bond with Darius? I've told you a million times—"

"It's not him, Allie. We need time apart. And you and Darius need so much more time together."

"No." She shook her head again. "We're fine, Aidan." She clutched his hands like she'd never let go. "This is ridiculous."

Aidan stood, his knees shaking as he pulled her up with him. "I love you, Alexis Ann. That will *never* change." He drew her against his chest, leaning down to kiss her beautiful lips, searing the memory of this kiss into his mind forever. Allie's hands slid up his chest and around his neck, her fingers tangling in his hair. He slipped his arms around her, holding her tight as he kissed her, trying to convey the depth of his feelings for her through their kiss. Trying to say everything he couldn't say with words.

"No, Aidan. No," she cried as he stepped away. "Please stay with me. Don't do this." She sobbed, taking a step toward him.

He couldn't find his voice, and he was seconds away from taking it all back. Aidan couldn't stand to hear the pain in her voice. Allie was the strongest person he knew. She would be fine without him, but he would not be fine without her.

"You bastard!" she screamed. "Don't do this to us."

Staring at the ground like a coward, Aidan turned and walked away.

Chapter 17

Allie | Kelleys Island | December

"Allie, wake up!" As Darius shook her a desperate scream ripped from Allie's throat. She searched for Aidan's thoughts but he was gone. Her mind was an empty, lonely place without him. "No," she sobbed, unable to find the words to tell her Syntrophos what was wrong.

"Don't. You have to ease her out of the dream," Liam said, moving to the other side of the bed. "Shaking her like that's a good way to get punched."

"Did you hear her all the way across the street at your place?" Darius asked, as Allie shrieked Aidan's name. Her heart shattered in a million pieces but in that moment, she wanted to hate him. Hate him for making her love him. It would be so much easier than this soul crushing anguish he'd left her with.

"Yeah. She never screams like that. Something's wrong, she hasn't had a bad night like this in a long time," Liam said. "Not since we moved here."

"Not a dream," she gasped, wide awake now. "He's gone." Her eyes searched for Darius, not seeing him. "He left."

"Shhh, Allie. It's just a bad dream." Liam climbed into the bed next to her, holding her tight.

"This is more than a bad dream, Liam," Darius said, gathering Allie's hands in his. "I ... can't breathe ... it hurts so bad." He looked to his uncle for help. "She's devastated. Allie, what did you see?" Darius asked, he eyes wide with fright.

"Little one, you need to talk to us," Liam said, singing softly to calm her.

"Aidan left." She managed to get the words out, but they still didn't make any sense. He loved her. He wouldn't do this to her.

"He left months ago, Allie," Darius said.

"He left *me*." She slammed her fists against her head, unable to stand the silence there. Her heart raced, like it was trying to run away from this pain. This pain so intense she knew it would change her forever. "He ... cut me out. He's gone." She beat her fist against her head again until Liam pulled her hands away. The emptiness echoing in her mind was so foreign she couldn't comprehend it. Aidan had spent so much time in her thoughts. Without him there, her mind was a cold, dark place she didn't recognize anymore. She couldn't bear the loneliness of her solitary thoughts.

"That asshat broke up with you? In the dreamworld?" Darius growled. "Why?"

"I don't know. He just ... he wanted out." She sifted through their conversation and couldn't pull out a single logical reason for his rash decision.

"I'll kill him." Liam pulled her tight against his chest. "I'll make him rue the day he ever hurt you."

Allie shook her head, trying to stall the tears that kept flowing. Anger. She needed to cling to her anger now. Anger was better than whatever hell this helpless feeling was. *Over a boy. I am not going to fall apart over a boy. I am not that girl.* But it was too late for that. She already lay scattered in a million pieces, like a broken doll.

"He's always been an idiot, Allie," Darius said, his voice cold. "He'll come to his senses." He stared at her with narrowed eyes that said he would tear his brother limb from limb for hurting her like this.

"No." Allie bit her lip, sitting up against the headboard. She took a deep breath, wincing at the pain, like a knife in her chest where her heart used to be. "If he doesn't want to be with me, then it's over. I'm not doing this twice." Even if he came crawling back to her in a month or a year, she could not go through this again.

"What do you need?" Liam asked, clearly at a loss.

Allie gulped back her tears. Wiping her face with her sleeve. "I need coffee and breakfast. And then I need to get to school. I have a project due today, so I can't miss critique." She shrugged out of Liam's arms and got out of bed. Nausea threatened to send her running for the toilet, but she took a deep breath and refused to waste another thought on Aidan.

She didn't want to waste another thought on him ever again.

Allie charged down the tunnel to the underground, far ahead of Darius. She couldn't wait for Liam and Quinn to finish transforming the barn behind their cottage into a gym. Then she could avoid Kelleys Island as much as possible. Too many memories of Aidan haunted this place. It made it hard to stay angry.

"You want to talk or hit something?" Darius asked, as he followed her into the large gym off the common room. She refused to step foot in Aidan's office or the places where they trained together.

"Hit things. Definitely hit things." Allie searched through her gym bag for her gloves.

"Are you sure you don't want to talk about Aidan?"

"Nope." She strapped her fingerless gloves on. "I'm fine." She wasn't. She wasn't fine at all, but the moment she let herself talk about it or really feel it, she was going to lose it.

"All right, then, let's break in this new punching bag, shall we?"

Allie ran through a sequence of kicks and punches to warm up. Anger fueled her strength as much as her bond with Darius did. Soon, the bag was swinging so hard it nearly swept Darius off his feet. As it came sailing back toward her, she prepared to catch it. Palms outstretched and ready for it, but the bag never reached her. It came to a dead stop in mid swing.

"That was weird," Allie said. "What did you do?"

"That wasn't me," Darius said. "Try that again." He gave the punching bag a shove, sending it swinging around in an arc. "Wait, let me give it another good push."

As the bag circled around the room, Allie waited for it, paying attention this time. The warmth of her power rose to the surface, and she saw it then—a tiny tendril of something new branched away from her solar gift and she managed to grasp it before it vanished like smoke. This time as the bag came toward her, she followed her instincts and released a portion of her stored energy. The bag went limp, hanging from the ceiling like she'd never touched it.

"That's definitely new." Allie took a step back, looking to Darius for answers.

"I felt it that time, like a wall of energy. It's like you're moving the bag with your solar energy," Darius said.

"Is that even possible?"

"Well, you just did it, so yeah, I think it is."

"No, is it possible for solar energy—like the kind produced by regular solar panels, not a college freshman—to move things?"

"No idea." He shrugged. "We'll have to ask Graham. He would know. Try lifting the bag up this time and keep holding onto that righteous anger of yours. It has to have something to do with this."

Allie closed her eyes, focusing on her power, searching for the telltale heat of her solar gift. Once upon a time, it was almost impossible for her to split that thread of her gift, to grasp hold of such a small facet of her ability that ultimately allowed her to use it as a weapon. That thread had grown into a stronger branch now. Darius had taught her how to do it then, and now here they were again, searching for a third facet of this gift that might grow into its own sturdy branch someday.

"Focus," Darius coached. "Take your time and get a good grasp of it."

Allie's eyes snapped open as she felt the energy leave her this time. The bag trembled but didn't move.

"Almost."

"One more time." She blew a strand of hair out of her sweaty face. This time she focused on her anger right before she latched onto the growing thread of her gift and held it tight as the energy blasted from her body. The punching bag lifted straight up to the stone ceiling.

"You got it, Red, nice job." Darius clapped, just as eager to test this new toy as she was.

Allie grinned as she really grabbed hold of this new ability, tossing the heavy punching bag around the room until she ran out of steam.

"Whew!" She sank to the floor. "That really took it out of me." She lay sprawled across the mat.

"We haven't had much sunny weather lately; you're probably just low on fuel."

"I probably need to play around with this until I can do it without drying up the tank." She panted, wiping the sweat from her brow. "Pretty cool trick, right?" Beaming, she couldn't wait to tell Aidan.

And then she remembered she wouldn't be sharing anything with Aidan anymore.

"Just don't ever use that on me," Darius said.

"You think I could do that? Use it on people?"

"You just tossed around that two hundred pound bag like it was air. I think you could easily add that as a defensive weapon to your arsenal."

"Did you just do what I think you did?" Livia stuck her head in through the open doors.

The sight of her outside her cell always sent a chill down Allie's spine. She was getting to know her sister in the dreamworld and they were building a tentative relationship, but she still had trust issues with Livia. Allie relaxed when she noticed the metal collar around her throat that blocked Livia from her power. Allie knew she frequently visited the Yard, just down the hall from the gym.

"You mean did I just kick this punching bag's big butt? I sure did." Allie grinned at her sister from her spot on the floor. "Now, I'm a pile of goo down here, but I did it."

"That was the first time?" She leaned down to check Allie's eyes and felt her pulse.

"Yeah. I'm okay, though. I won't push it any more today."

"That really took it out of you. You're as weak as a kitten." She scowled at Darius like it was his fault Allie had pushed herself so hard. "This kind of training is dangerous, Allie. Not every ability needs to be explored and split time and again. You are powerful, but you have limits. I don't want to see you overwork yourself this way."

"It kind of just happened, Liv, but yeah, food might be an emergency situation." She tried to sit up, but her limbs felt like string cheese. "Uh oh." She swiped at the blood oozing from her nose. "I guess I did overdo it."

"Come on, Red, let's get you into the kitchen." Darius and Livia grabbed her under the arms and hauled her up.

"Good thing you stopped by," Allie said.

"I was just visiting Navid," Livia said. "Um, Liam's regular babysitter wasn't available, so I watched Kahlynn for him this morning."

"You babysat?" Allie wrinkled her nose.

"With Navid," Livia said. "The munchkin likes me."

"You didn't scare our niece to death did you?"

"She's your niece, Allie. Liam is not my brother."

"Oh right, I always forget that little detail." Allie sank down onto the barstool, hoping she had the strength to keep herself perched on the edge.

"You got it?" Darius asked.

"I'm good. Just need some protein and carbs. A pizza would be perfect."

"Nice try, kid. It's a clean diet for you. Especially now." Livia searched through the fridge and cabinets for ingredients. "You're getting plain chicken and left over quinoa."

"Put some Alfredo on there, and we might have a deal."

"That sounds disgusting and way too much fat. You can have avocado slices. And for now, you're getting a banana and peanut butter to hold you over while I cook." She set a plate in front of Allie for her snack.

"You're mean." Allie shoveled the banana in her mouth

just to get something in her stomach. She immediately felt better but still needed protein and lots of it.

"She's right, Allie," Naeemah said as she entered the kitchen. "I saw you carrying her from the gym. What happened?" Naeemah sat beside Allie, checking her vitals. Just the sight of Aidan's mother brought tears to Allie's eyes. She wanted to hurl herself into Naeemah's arms and tell her everything, but she choked it back, deciding to focus on her huge accomplishment instead of her failed relationship.

"New ability with my solar gift," Allie explained. "But I think I emptied the tank so I'm going to need a few bright sunny days before I try that again. And food?" Allie frowned at her sister. "Is food still happening?"

"I'm working on it," Livia said.

"You got this, Naeemah?" Darius asked. "I need to go pick up the paint and floor stuff for the barn. I promised Liam I'd get it today."

"I have training with Chloe soon." Naeemah glanced at the time on her phone. "But I'm just down the hall if you need me, Allie. I'll leave my door open."

"Sure, we've got this," Livia said. "There are enough of you coming and going in this place to keep multiple eyes on Allie while we have a sister chat."

"We're good." Allie nodded at their concerned looks.

"All right, you just call if you need anything. Both of you," she added for Livia's benefit. "Let me know if she doesn't perk up after a good meal."

"Behave." Darius leaned in, pressing a kiss to Allie's forehead. "Take it easy until I get back and then we'll head home early. I promise I'll feed you pizza later. Love you." He took a hesitant step toward the door.

"Love you, too. And I'm fine everyone, just go so I can eat." She shooed them out of the kitchen.

"Who knew you could cook?" Allie watched her sister buzz around the kitchen, putting different ingredients into a skillet.

"Just don't tell Santi. I used to make her do all the cooking back at my apartment in Atlanta. She made the best spaghetti and meatballs."

"That must be really strange being on the other side of the same situation with two of your former captives right here."

"We'll I must admit I have it easier than they ever did. Quinn has found a way to let it all go. I don't know how he can be so forgiving, but even before he and Santi escaped, he saw through all my walls and realized I was just as much a captive as he was. In his mind, I'm not to blame for the things I did. Santi on the other hand ... we'll get there. I put her through more than her fair share of pain and suffering."

"Quinn says you never had a choice." Allie scooped up the last of the peanut butter on her plate and licked her fingers clean.

"He's right. I had to do the things I did to protect everyone under my roof from a fate far worse. But it was still my choice to be there. For a long time I numbed myself to the things I did just so I could survive. I didn't let myself feel. Anything. And then Quinn and Santi came into my home and I just never understood those two. They were so kind, to the Soma kids, and to each other—even in the midst of their suffering. I'd never seen that before, and it made me uncomfortable. It made me feel things again. I lashed out at them for it."

"I guess you had to be hard, so you could do those things. I think you distanced yourself from the people around you to protect yourself. The woman who did those things ... she's not the same woman cooking me an emergency lunch right now." Allie might not trust her sister, but she could see the change in her now.

"You sound like Dad." She smiled. "I had a much harder time with Santi and Quinn because I actually liked and respected them." Livia tossed a mound of seasoned chicken into a hot skillet, focusing on cooking rather than meeting Allie's gaze. But they were really talking—like normal sisters. She didn't want to jinx it.

"It all worked out for the best in the end. And look at what you got. A fabulous little sister and a real father—a mother, too, if we can ever reach her."

Livia dropped her spatula, fumbling around on the floor for it.

"Okay, almost done." Her voice sounded too high. She quickly sliced a whole avocado and fanned it out over diced chicken breast on a bed of quinoa.

"That actually looks delicious." Allie shoveled a few bites in as fast as she could chew, oblivious of the temperature scorching her mouth.

"If you're still not feeling well when you're done with this, try a protein shake." Livia turned for the door.

"Wait." Allie used her new gift to slide the kitchen door shut. "What's wrong, Liv? Did I upset you with talk about our family? I know you have your own mother, just like I have Lily. I'm still trying to wrap my brain around having two fathers I love, but you can never have too much family. We'll find Kassandre some day."

"I don't deserve you." Livia's shoulders tensed, like she was terrified of this conversation.

"You've been through a lot, Liv. You deserve a chance at a new life. Don't be afraid of the good things happening to you now. You've made so much progress since you've been here. I'm ... proud of you."

"Dammit, Allie." Livia turned and leaned against the kitchen counter. "I didn't want to care about you. I didn't want a sister."

"Well, now you have one. I'm not going anywhere. I know we're still figuring things out, but we're family. We'll get there."

"What has Navid told you of our... of Kassandre?" Livia closed her eyes.

"Not much. He doesn't like to talk about her. But I remember her. Only vaguely."

"Me too," Livia whispered. "Just little snatches of memories."

"I remember the last time I saw her," Allie said. "I was just three years old. It was the day they left me with Lily and Carson for good. They visited me a lot before then, but I think they stopped once they thought I was old enough to remember them. It was only a few months later the Coalition attacked, and Navid and Kassandre faked their deaths. I don't know what happened to her after that. I've always thought maybe they got her that night but Navid escaped. I've never been sure how Navid would react if I ask him about it. Maybe we should both ask him, come up with a plan to get her back."

"Stop," Livia hissed, her eyes turning molten silver. "Just stop talking for once in your life."

"Okay. Sensitive subject? We can talk about it some other time." Allie instinctively leaned away from her sister afraid she'd pushed her too far.

"No." Livia did that thing where she seemed to turn to stone. Allie could almost see the concrete of her walls coming up to block her out. "Kassandre is dead," Livia said, her tone lifeless.

"Dead? She can't be dead if Dad is alive..." Allie's voice

died in her throat. There was only one way her father could survive if her mother was dead. "No." She shook her head stubbornly. It wasn't possible. Her sister would never use her gift against their parents.

"I killed our mother." Livia's icy voice was like a punch in the gut. After all this time, her own sister was the reason their family was torn apart.

The rage of Allie's judgment gift rose swiftly inside her, itching for her sister's immortality. For a single moment, she thought about releasing it. But Allie was not Livia. Her choices made her different.

"Go back to your cell," Allie whispered. "I never want to see you again."

Allie | Kelleys Island | January

Allie brushed a shimmery golden eye shadow across Chloe's eyelids. The same golden hue of her dragon's scales. The powerful sentry stood watch at Chloe's side. Her obsidian eyes so like Ming Lao's it brought a tear to Allie's eye whenever she saw the mesmerizing dragon.

"Ming would be so proud of you," Allie said.

"For what?" Chloe replied with a look of disdain. "Graduating high school before they could kick me out? You know I'm only graduating early because they want me gone." Chloe was constantly in trouble at school and even Graham couldn't seem to help her these days. None of them could. Allie was the only one Chloe even sort of got along with anymore.

Allie chose to ignore Chloe's venom. She'd gotten really good at it in recent months.

"Hurry up. I'm ready to get this farce of a graduation over with." Chloe's shoulders slumped as Allie worked on her makeup. Only a handful of Cliffton Academy seniors were lucky enough to graduate early, but no matter her behavior, Chloe's grades were outstanding.

"Have you picked a college yet?" Allie brushed a thin layer of blush across Chloe's cheeks. "You know you're welcome to come live at the cottage with us and wait to start school in the summer or fall."

"Thanks, that's just what I need, a house full of people trying to 'help' me get back to my stupid, happy Chloe self again."

Allie turned Chloe's chair closer to her and leaned in. "Look at me." She lifted Chloe's defiant chin to meet her gaze. "You're not that girl any more, Chlo. She died with your mother and that's okay. Losing a strong mother like Ming Lao changes a girl. We all know that and we just want you to find some peace with who you are now."

"Yeah, well tell that to Dad. All we do is fight about how I suck and he wishes I would go back to being the daughter he raised."

Jin Jing wasn't the same man either. Losing his Complement had shattered him and Allie didn't think he'd ever recover. Navid tried to help him. He knew what it was like after all. Allie's chest clenched with anger for Livia all over again. How had Navid ever survived Kassandre's death? It defied logic and nature for a Complement to die and leave their other half behind to live on without them. And it was all her sister's fault.

"Are you still thinking about majoring in fashion design?" Allie admired the white dress Chloe made for her graduation.

"I don't think college is for me." Chloe shrugged. "I just don't care."

Allie stared at her friend. She'd do anything to take her grief away. "Whatever you decide to do, you have my full support. I want you to find what makes you happy." She ran a brush through Chloe's long silky black hair. "You know, some people make it in the fashion industry on sheer talent alone.

Maybe you don't need college." Chloe desperately needed to get away and find a new start somewhere else but the adults in her life wouldn't hear of it. She was too young. "I know everyone expects you to be the same girl you always were," Allie said carefully. "You've been through a terrible tragedy that has changed you. You're about to begin a chapter of your life your mother will never be part of."

"Don't," Chloe whispered. "I can't cry any more, Allie. I just can't. It's been two years, and it still feels fresh because I'm stuck in this place where her presence is everywhere." She shot a dark look at her dragon curled on the floor beside her like a contented cat.

"Be brave, Chloe. You have the power to make the right choices for yourself. Listen to your gift, and you do what's best for you. If that means you go to school and stay here at home or you move into the cottage with us, then great. We will have so much fun together. But if that's not where you need to be, then go find your place and don't forget we're all here for you when you need us."

"I can't stand living so close to *her*." Allie didn't have to ask who she meant.

"You and me both," Allie murmured. "Livia remains in her cell. That's the best we can hope for now. If I had my way, she'd be in a real prison somewhere far away from here. She killed my mother, too." Allie continued brushing Chloe's hair, gripping the brush in her clenched fist.

"That kinda hurts, Allie."

"Sorry."

"I know you get it in a way," Chloe said.

"But I never had the chance to know my mother," Allie finished her sentence. "Livia took that away from me. But I still have Lily and she's my real mother."

"I hate being here, Allie, but I have no where else to go

and I'm afraid Dad will fall apart if I mention going away." She looked to Allie for help. "I can't with him anymore. I know he's never going to get over losing Mom. It's not fair. But I ... can't be the daughter he needs. All we do is fight."

"You both need time," Allie said. She didn't want to push her friend away, but she knew Chloe was standing on a precipice. She needed to mourn the loss of her mother in her own way. "It's okay, Chlo. You've got some tough choices to make right now." Allie knelt in front of her and took her hands. "I don't want to lose you. We love you and *always* will, no matter what, we are your family, and you are more my sister than Livia will ever be. But I don't want you to lose yourself, either. You know the right path for you, Chloe. Take it. And don't feel bad about it. We will take care of Jin so you can take care of yourself. He is your father, but he doesn't have to be your responsibility."

Chloe clutched her hands tightly. "I feel so useless here. I'm such a coward." She shot a glance at the shadowy dragon she'd created as a living monument to her mother.

"Chloe, my friend, you are one of the strongest women I know. You came from Ming Lao Long, you have the spirit of a warrior inside you."

"What do you mean, she's gone?" Jin Jing shouted, his voice echoing across the common room. His eyes were wild and frightened.

"I'm sorry, Jin," Allie said. "She left this for you." She handed him a letter. "I found it in the kitchen just now." It was similar to the one Chloe had left for her.

"No." Jin sank into the nearest chair like his legs couldn't hold him anymore. "I can't lose her, too." He ran his hands through his white hair, as he read his daughter's last words. He hadn't shown up for Chloe's graduation. It wasn't on purpose. He'd genuinely forgotten. He did that a lot since Ming's death. In some ways, he was like an elderly, feeble version of himself. Within a few weeks after Ming died, his hair had turned white. In other ways, Jin's behavior was more like an alcoholic struggling not to hit rock bottom.

"You haven't lost her, Jin." Allie crouched beside him. "She's taking care of herself right now. And that's exactly what you need to do."

"What the hell do you know?" Jin spat. "It's your fault this happened in the first place. We should have never taken you in. Then that sister of yours wouldn't be here, and my family would still be intact."

It wasn't the first time he'd lashed out at her. And it wouldn't be the last. His words hurt, but he was right, it was her fault. Allie's presence had disrupted this entire family.

"Jin Jing, don't you dare speak to Allie that way," Emma came to her defense.

"It's okay, Emma. He's right."

"It's not okay." Emma glared daggers at him. "And it is not your fault."

"Jin, I'm so sorry, but there is no changing the past; we can only hope to make the future a better one. Your daughter finally gathered the strength to do what was best for her. Let her mourn for her loss and find her path forward."

"Trust in Chloe's gift, Jin," Emma added. "She is young and she's hurting, but she is her mother made over. She will be okay."

"She has no protection." Jin crumpled the note against his forehead. "I have to go after her."

"We will keep a careful eye on her from afar," Emma said. "We won't let anything happen to her."

"I can't lose her," Jin muttered.

"Allie, I've got this." Emma draped her arm around Jin, helping him back to his office where he practically lived now.

Allie glanced down at the letter in her hand, reading it again.

Dear Allie,

Thank you for giving me the push I needed to follow my instincts. I love my father and our family, but I can't breathe here anymore. I know if I stay, I'm going to turn into someone I don't recognize, and I know Mom wouldn't want that.

So I'm leaving. I don't know where I'm going, or what I'll do when I get there, but I need this. In a weird way, I feel like I'm following in my mother's footsteps. She left home when she wasn't much older than I am now, so I think I'll be able to find her more this way than I ever will at home.

Tell Sasha and the others I'll miss them more than they could ever know and I'm sorry for being so hateful.

I love you, my friend. My sister.

This isn't goodbye forever. It's just a see you later,

Chloe

Allie wiped the tears from her eyes. She'd seen it coming since Ming Lao's funeral. The moment Chloe brought her dragons to life, representing the fallen of her family, Allie's mind had whirled with images. Random snatches of things to come, and things that might never be. In every instance, she'd seen Chloe, sometimes at her side, sometimes standing in opposition. Allie's gift had shown her how Chloe would grow into a formidable, powerful, and respected Immortal. The death of Ming Lao would have an extreme impact on Chloe's life. It would make her stronger, but if she didn't allow herself to fully mourn her loss and deal with her grief, it would send her down the wrong path.

Allie knew now that saying goodbye to Chloe—telling her it was okay for her to leave—to take care of herself had finally set Chloe on the path toward healing. She still had a long journey ahead of her, but Chloe would come back to her family. Some day.

Allie was just so tired of losing the people she loved.

PART III
ONE YEAR LATER

Chapter 19

Aidan | Milan, Italy | February

"Thirty seconds left," Aidan called, checking his stopwatch. "This one's going on your record, so pull it together, ladies."

"Ladies?" Neela wrinkled her nose in disgust.

"What? You don't like it when I call you girls, now ladies is out, too?" Aidan rolled his eyes. "What am I allowed to call you guys this week?"

"How about our names?" Ivy suggested, her face scrunched in concentration, as she worked to diffuse the last bomb to secure the perimeter of the test area and pass Aidan's latest attempt to stump them.

"I have to say Neela and Ivy every time?" Aidan leaned back against the brick wall. "Twenty seconds."

"How about Nivy or Ivyla."

"Ivyla?" Ivy shook her head. "That sounds stupid. Let's go with Nivy."

"Well you're going to be Nivy soup if you two don't get that bomb shut down." Aidan was sweating it this time, wondering if he'd made the challenge too difficult. He didn't want to hurt them, but if he interfered, Genevieve would just punish them and leave them to heal on their own. Otherwise, she'd let Aidan heal them if they were injured during training—but only if they tried their hardest.

"Is he saying he'd *actually* let us blow up?" Neela scoffed.

"I believe he is, Nivy."

"I'm serious, you have sixteen seconds left, and these are real bombs this time!" Aidan wiped his sweaty palms against his jeans. Neela and Ivy were two of his favorite students, but he would never tell them that. It would go straight to their egotistical heads. Nineteen years old, the girls hadn't met an explosive they couldn't conquer or a security system they couldn't penetrate. Cool in a crisis, they would be invaluable to the mortal world if he could just get them to their Proving without some outside force corrupting them. Aidan wanted to give them the freedom to forge their own way and actually make a difference in the world.

"Less than ten seconds. Come on, girls you can do this!"

"His voice is getting high," Neela said.

"Maybe we should tell him we've had this bomb diffused for at least three minutes?" Ivy pulled her hands out of the snarl of wires, a shit-eating grin on her face.

"You little assholes." Aidan ran a hand through his damp hair. "That's what I'm going to start calling you. And everyone will know exactly who I mean."

"Come on, you think this is hard for us? We've passed all your little tests without even trying. We're beyond this basic crap. Give us something real to work with; we're ready for legit mass destruction level stuff."

"No, you're not. But we'll see what Pilar says at your next review. We can try to step it up for next year."

"Next year?" Ivy sighed. "Will this Initiative crap ever end?" Her mouth turned down in a frown, and Aidan wanted to tell her she could leave whenever she wanted. But that wasn't true. They were stuck in this farce of a boarding school for however long their *benefactors* wanted to study them. It took Aidan a long time to come to terms with that. For months, he looked for a way out for himself and Naomi, but just as Cleo and Genevieve said he would, he eventually came willingly, for the kids. They needed him and he couldn't leave them behind anymore than he could Naomi.

"Initiative or not, I'll always be around to knock some sense into you guys. That you can count on. Now get out of here. Naomi will be ready for you by now."

"Later, sexy." Neela tugged her gloves off, patting him on the rear end on her way out.

"Look, his ears are totally red." Ivy giggled, following her Syntrophos from Aidan's training room.

"Those girls are trouble," Pilar's voice called from the open door that led to the training field at the center of the complex. "But you're so good with them."

"They're good kids." Aidan picked up all the loose wires and tools the girls had left behind. He would make them come back and get rid of the bomb casings later tonight. He'd learned the hard way not to touch them himself. They liked to surprise him with loud explosions wherever he least expected them.

"It's so weird, you're barely a year older than them."

"I feel like I've got at least a century on them." He swept a pile of debris to the center of the room. "This place hasn't sucked the life out of them yet, but it will some day; once they realize their lives will never be their own because of what they are."

"If it were up to me, I'd let them all go. Us included." Pilar grimaced. "But it's not my call."

"You aren't the one who dragged us into this mess."

"Maybe I'll be the one to get us out of it one day. Come on, Cleo's looking for you."

"She's back?"

"Yep, and she's in a mood."

"A throwing things at my head kind of mood or I'd better go armed kind of mood?"

"Worse. I've not seen this mood before. I think she's about to cry."

"Cleo does not cry."

"Which means the world as we know it must be ending."

"Lead the way." Aidan followed Pilar from his wing of the complex housing his and Naomi's private quarters, training rooms, classrooms, and even a walled in garden that sometimes reminded him of his mother's gardens at home.

Aidan moved to Milan six months ago. Cleo and Genevieve had been right. It didn't take Aidan long to decide for himself that his work for the Initiative was far more important than his musical education. Music could wait. These kids needed him. After his first few lessons with each pair, Aidan realized how very little they knew. Not just about being Syntrophos. Most of the kids knew precious little about their own abilities and their combat skills were pitiful. They came from average homes with limited resources, which forced Aidan to come to terms with his own privilege. Growing up, Aidan had the best of everything, including world class training—a thing he once thought every young Immortal had.

A few of them had parents who'd taught them well enough—if they were average Immortals. But none of them were just average. They were all talented and powerful young Immortals, largely due to the bond, which enhanced their natural, individual and collective abilities. They were all so ignorant they made Aidan look like a PhD candidate in Immortal studies. They needed him. Aidan's lifelong training had prepared him for this, and he owed it to these kids to teach them what they needed to know to survive what the Initiative would surely do to them. It was worth the sacrifice of his musical education, his freedom and his relationship with Allie. One day he would find a way to leave the Initiative—but he would take his students and Pilar with him when he did.

"Do you think the Senate is finally getting involved?" Aidan asked, as he followed Pilar to Cleo's office. Cleo was the official head of the Initiative, though it was clear she answered to someone higher up. Though Cleo and Genevieve were powerful Syntrophos, they were surprisingly ignorant about what that meant.

Pilar was the true teacher here. She'd studied the Syntrophos all her life. She knew the histories, the myths and the facts, but she shared those things judiciously—and not with their leaders. Aidan had learned so much from Pilar since his arrival, but they guarded their collective knowledge of the Syntrophos bond.

"It's not the Senate." Pilar rolled her eyes. "You're always on about that."

"One of these days, you're going to start listening to me. The Senate is always in the background pulling strings. And others stand behind the Senate pulling a different set of strings."

"You and your conspiracy theories." They walked down the long, cool corridor to Cleo's office, which faced Lake Maggiore and had the best views of the Italian Alps from her balcony.

"Come in." Cleo's clipped voice carried down the hall. "Hurry up and close the doors."

Aidan darted a last glance at Pilar. She looked worried.

"What's going on?" Aidan asked, as he stepped into the pristine office, taking the chair in front of Cleo's antique desk.

Cleo stood behind her desk, her back to them. She was tall and slim, her body made up of sharp angles and porcelain smooth skin.

Flipping through a stack of files, he could sense her distress. He recognized those files. There were five, one for each pair of Syntrophos, from Cleo and Genevieve, Aidan and Naomi, right down to Ivy and Neela.

"We're in trouble." Cleo tossed the files on her desk.

"What can we do to help?" Pilar asked, her tone indicating she meant the opposite. She never shied away from showing their leaders exactly what she thought of them and their tactics.

"Perform a miracle with these kids in the next twenty-four hours, or we're all going to wish we were never born." She flopped into her seat, tapping her fingertips against her full lips.

"How about we start with some answers, and then we'll go from there?" Aidan said. "What's the immediate issue?" For all of Pilar's bravado and courage, Aidan worried something far worse than Cleo and Genevieve was headed their way.

"Our benefactor is coming for a visit."

"Okay, we can deal with that," Pilar said. "It's probably a long overdue visit anyway. We'll get the kids ready."

"Who is the benefactor?" Aidan asked, although he could hazard a few guesses. This thing was always going to connect with someone bigger and badder than Cleo. "I've asked you before, and you've always been vague. If they're coming here tomorrow, now's the time to prepare us."

"You don't realize," Cleo said, running her hands through her long, dark hair. "She was never supposed to come here. Not for several more years anyway."

"Pull it together, Cleo. What are you saying?" Pilar asked.

"She's going to kill me." Cleo leaned her head back, barely keeping it together.

"Who is she?" Aidan said. "You've set up this entire operation on some benefactor's dime, and you didn't expect her to follow up on her investment?"

"I thought I had more time. I thought I could do it my way and still deliver what I promised."

"Who is it?" Pilar demanded.

"This cannot leave the room," Cleo said, her ebony eyes narrowed to slits.

"You have our word," Aidan said. "Just spill it, so we can help."

"Sarah and Charles Madison, the Chief Justice of the International Senate will be here tomorrow."

"Wow." Pilar's eyes rounded in surprise. "Looks like you were right." She turned to Aidan.

"You knew?" Cleo asked.

"Not them specifically, but I knew the Senate had to have their hands in this pie somewhere. It's what they do." Aidan shrugged.

"So they're coming here? Tomorrow? Okay." Pilar took a deep breath. "That's not terrifying at all. Can we reschedule?"

"Not an option. They're already on their way. And when the Chief Justice calls, you don't tell them to come back later."

"Cleo, what are they expecting to find when they get here?" Aidan asked.

"Not what they're going to see."

"What have you promised them?" Aidan's hand clenched into fists as his temper soared.

"They expect to find a team of Syntrophos, fully trained to a well-oiled machine."

"You promised them an *army*?" Aidan shot to his feet, the urge to strangle her had his hands itching to get around her throat.

"We'll, they're not going to get that," Pilar scoffed, grabbing a fistful of Aidan's shirt and shoving him back into his chair. "They do know we're training a bunch of kids, right? This takes time. We need at least a few more years before they'll be ready to function as a collective team."

"I've fought so hard to get us more time. Sarah gave me five years in the beginning but she's changed her mind. She believes eighteen months is more than enough. I don't know how to convince her we just aren't there yet."

"And where is *there*, Cleo? What does the Chief Justice of the International Senate expect to do with five Syntrophos pairs?" Aidan demanded.

"I don't know anymore. When we started this, the whole operation was meant to study the bond and train those who have it to be the best they can be. We wanted to create a refuge."

"You don't threaten and manipulate children to join a refuge, Cleo," Pilar said, her tone mocking. "That may have been what you originally wanted for the Initiative, but little by little you've compromised and cut corners, letting Sarah Madison push you until you couldn't even see your own intentions anymore." Pilar's entire body pulsed with indignation. "You lost your vision for this place a long time ago and all this time you've just been trying to please *her*? That woman is a lunatic. A lunatic building an army of children!" Pilar slammed her fist on Cleo's desk making her jump. "And it's your fault."

"What are Sarah's intentions?" Aidan asked.

"It wasn't supposed to be government related," Cleo said, her voice defeated. "When she first approached me, we discussed creating a school for these kids. I didn't realize it until it was too late, but she expects the Initiative to ultimately act as her personal Special Forces team."

"And what they're going to find is a group of spoiled rotten misfits, who get their kicks out of blowing things up," Pilar said.

"That's just Nivy," Aidan said. "I'll put the fear of God into them and stick them at the back. They'll behave."

"Our lives are on the line here. I will not lose Sarah's faith now." Cleo lifted her chin and propped her feet up on her desk. "We have to see it through. So what can we do to get through this visit? I will convince the Chief Justice we need more time. But we need to show them something."

"You're in trouble and you expect solidarity and support from the very people you've manipulated and controlled? We are prisoners here." Pilar shook her head. "Why should we help you? Why shouldn't we leave you and Genevieve holding the bag?"

"Because we are the lesser evil, I can promise you that." Cleo's miserable laughter was anything but funny. "You could all walk out of here today, but they will find you and they will drag every single one of you back here because we—all of us—belong to them. You think it's bad now? Imagine the shit storm the Senate would send your way? You want to spend the rest of your lives running? I certainly don't."

"We'll fake it," Aidan said, trying to dispel the tension in the room. Cleo was right, they just needed to survive this visit the best they could. "We can sit here arguing all day but that won't stop the leaders of the Immortal world from showing up on your doorstep tomorrow."

"Fake it?" Pilar looked at him like he was a fool. "You think Sarah Madison won't see right through it?"

"Listen, we can do this." Aidan sat on the edge of his seat. "I'll get everyone in line. They'll be perfect little soldiers, at least on the surface. They'll get a kick out of pulling one over on the big wigs. You guys figure out what we're going to show the Chief Justice. They'll expect to see a show of power, and we need to give it to them, but we cannot show all our cards yet." He didn't like it any more than Pilar, but they had to help Cleo through this visit. Once the Chief Justice left and their attention was elsewhere, then they could figure out a real plan. Hope swelled in his chest. Maybe after all of this, Cleo and Genevieve would work with him and Pilar to end the Initiative and give their students a chance to live their lives on their own terms.

"Our students are talented. I guess we could just show them the tip of the iceberg," Pilar said.

"Will they buy it?" Cleo asked.

"I've spent my life dodging the Senate and flying under the radar," Aidan said. They'll buy it if we distract them with something flashy. They're going to want to see our merged gifts, but we need to be careful not to show them our biggest guns."

"Right, we could show them things like how Naomi's ability to draw strength from the lunar cycle strengthens you as well," Pilar offered.

"And how you share your fire ability with Naomi. That's definitely flashy," Cleo added.

"But we won't show them how you can heal through Naomi even when you're miles apart," Pilar said.

"Exactly." Aidan stood to go. "You two handle that stuff, and I'll get the brats in line."

"Please," Cleo begged. "They have to understand this visit needs to be perfect. We *have* to impress them."

"We will, even if it does save your neck. But you probably should have checked your actions long before now. I hope you will in the future." Aidan left Cleo and Pilar to work out their part. He and Naomi had a group of Syntrophos to whip into shape. He would scare them if he had to. And bribe them if that didn't work, but one way or another, they would look like an army by the time the Chief Justice showed up. Just not enough to convince them they were ready for any kind of action. It chilled Aidan's blood to think of how the Chief Justice intended to use them. If he had his way, they'd never find out.

CHAPTER 20

Allie | Cleveland | February

"All right, Allie. You don't have to go home, but you can't stay here." Greyson towered over her with his hands on his hips.

"Are you quoting Semisonic lyrics at me?" Allie quirked a smile at him.

"Yes. Go *home*, Allie. Or am I going to have to pry you out of my house with a spoon?"

"I like it here." Allie sifted her hands through the rich, dark soil of Greyson's flowerbeds, placing tulip bulbs in neat little rows.

"It's *my* garden, kid." He crouched beside her. "I know it's peaceful here. I spent a good ten years hiding back here once because I wanted to escape my life. Don't make Darius come get you again."

"I just wanted to get these in the ground for you after I finished grading some papers. I'll go soon."

"How is it that my home has become your place of refuge?" Greyson started rearranging the bulbs farther apart. "It's not that I don't want you here, but it's not exactly fair to my daughter, you know. You two don't get along and I don't want to get mixed up in all of that, but she's my kid so I'm on her side. Always."

"And you should be. I'm just here a lot because I'm your intern."

"I've never had an intern try to move in with me."

"I'm not moving in, Greyson. It's just so beautiful here. A nice distraction."

"Away from all things McBrien?"

"That's not it. It's not about him anymore." After a year without Aidan, Allie had moved on with her life. She still missed him, but she had a lot of anger too. In the weeks after he pulled away, Aidan completely ghosted her. He changed his phone number and deleted all his social media accounts, but he was still in contact with his family, who refused to give Allie answers.

"I know you've moved on from Aidan, but you've pulled away from the family in the last year. And I'm the closest thing you have to a non-McBrien Immortal parent. I get it. Believe me. They are an intense lot, and being on the outskirts of that family is not always a fun place to be. They make you feel like you belong, but deep inside you know you don't." Greyson knocked the loose dirt from the tools Allie was using.

"Yep. And it's a blatant reminder when they stick to their own, keeping you in the dark."

"They're respecting his privacy, Allie."

"I know." She stood, taking the spade and shovel from Greyson to return it to the garden shed. "It's been a year. It's fine. I've moved on."

"Uh, no, you haven't. You've been hiding." He followed her to the shed.

"I've been dating Brigs for the last few months, how is that not moving on? I have a busy life with school, training,

Darius, Brigs and dreamworld stuff. It's not easy being around Aidan's family. There are just too many memories there."

"Aidan broke your heart, kid. He's not worth pining over."

"I am not pining. I'm building a life for myself that I happen to enjoy. I will never pin my happiness on a guy. Any guy. Right now, I like hanging out with Brigs. He's fun and he doesn't expect much. There's nothing wrong with that." It destroyed her when Aidan walked out of her life. It took Allie months to find the will to put herself back together, but she did it. Her clairvoyance had tried to warn her he would leave, and she chose not to listen. Allie was just so sick of everyone walking on eggshells around her. It was why she couldn't visit Naeemah and Gregg as much anymore. They looked at her like she was some kind of wounded, fragile thing their son discarded after he was done playing with it.

"Go home. Sleep in your own bed, and let me have my couch back," Greyson said. "Go do something fun with Darius and Brigs. Forget about homework for once, and maybe try skipping a class once in a while."

"Skip class? Are you nuts, I'm a double major. I can't skip anything."

"Allie, you need to get out more. Have fun, and don't take it so seriously."

"I think you just told me I need to rebel." Allie laughed. "I promise, I'd much rather work on art projects and college papers than hit the party scene. That's just not me."

"It's ironic." Greyson laughed, shaking his head. "Naomi keeps me on my toes, giving me heart attacks on a regular basis with the boys she brings home. You're the exact opposite. It's no wonder you two hate each other—you're like aliens from different planets."

"We don't speak the same language, that's for sure."

"Sometimes I think you two could be best friends if you'd take the time to really get to know each other. It sure would make my life easier, since I happen to like both of you."

"I doubt that's ever going to happen, Greyson." Allie shuddered at the thought.

"Honestly, I think Naomi's a little jealous of your connection with the family. She's always wanted that. Always wanted Naeemah's approval because she's the closest thing to a mother Naomi's ever had.

"How does that work?" Allie asked. "If your Complement, Isebeau, is still a captive of the Coalition and she's never met Naomi, does Naomi even have a mother?"

"That's the million dollar question." Greyson returned the gardening tools to their proper place before he headed back toward the house. "When I adopted Naomi, I knew the moment I laid eyes on her that she was our daughter and if Ise was free, Naomi would have bonded with her like all adopted Immortal children do. Theoretically, Isebeau is likely her true mother, but they've never had a chance to bond. That's left Naomi desperate for a real mom, but unable to have one. At least until Ise is finally free."

"No wonder she hates me." Allie felt a real pang of sympathy for Naomi. She knew what it was like to believe she had a mother somewhere out there in the world trying to get back to her. At least she did until she learned Livia murdered their biological mother. Allie reached for the coffee pot, refusing to give Livia another thought. "I have lots of mother figures. Lily's my mom, but Naeemah has always been like a second mom. But grandma Alísun can be very mom-like in the worst ways."

"You know, you and Naomi are more alike than you think."

"Take it back." Allie shoved the coffee filter in the machine.

"She's never known her true mother, just as you've never known yours."

"Okay, I'll give you that. We both might have mommy issues. But I still don't have to like her. I mean, when's the last time she's come home for a visit? Here she has a great dad, and she treats you like an afterthought. When's the last time she called?"

"Hey, that's my kid you're talking about." Greyson shot her a warning dad-glare.

"Sorry, that was rude. It's none of my business."

"No it's not. Naomi and I have a troubled relationship but we talk often. I've raised her to be a free spirit and I don't expect her to cling to her life here in Cleveland. Or to me. I want her to be brave and fearless."

"We'll she is definitely that." Allie said, letting a hint of admiration into her voice.

"She'll come home when she's ready. And when she does, you're going to have to find a different refuge."

"I promise, I'll do better respecting Naomi's turf."

"I guess we can call that progress."

"Tell me about Isebeau," Allie said. "If you don't mind talking about her."

"There's not much to tell." Greyson poured filtered water into the coffee pot and grabbed a carton of eggs to make breakfast.

Allie made herself useful, dicing veggies for their omelets. She was at home with Greyson in a way she wasn't with very many people these days. Somehow, her art teacher had become her safe harbor, almost like another mentor. It was nice, being with him. He didn't expect much from her beyond her intern duties and no matter what he said he liked having her around. Greyson desperately missed his daughter, but he refused to admit it.

"I met Isebeau in the fourteenth century, and we knew right away we were Complements. She was a princess of a small island kingdom in what became part of Portugal. Her father hated me. I had nothing to offer an Immortal princess."

"But you were Complements," Allie said, adding her mixture of veggies and cheese to the skillet.

"Didn't matter to the king. He was a controlling bastard." Greyson shook the pan like an expert chef, flipping the omelet like a pancake.

"Show off." Allie buttered several slices of toast and popped it in the toaster oven.

"Isebeau was young at the time. Not quite fifty and still Unproven. She'd never been allowed outside the castle grounds—officially—but she made frequent clandestine visits to the village beyond the walls of her palace."

"She must have been desperate to get out of there."

"Yes, she wanted us to run away, but I didn't want to take her away from her mother. We wanted to be together. We *would* be together eventually, whether her parents approved or not. I thought we should wait. At least let me try to gain her father's approval."

"Didn't work out for you?"

"Nope. He brought in all kinds of mortal suitors for her like she was Penelope straight out of the Odyssey. He wanted her to marry a mortal prince or king of another land to increase their fortune—many Immortal fathers used their daughters in such ways back then. He just saw her as something of value to trade for a lucrative marriage contract. Meeting her Complement at an early age didn't mesh with his plan. He tried to pay me to leave."

"Did you?"

"No, but I should have taken the money and run." Greyson looked pensive as he poured orange juice for them, and Allie set their plates on the breakfast bar. "It would have saved her life and a lot of heartache if I'd just disappeared for a while and been patient."

"So, you stayed and kept trying?"

"I stayed but we pretended I'd left, so we could sneak around seeing each other in secret. Apparently, our story became a local fairytale."

"Seriously? I want to hear it."

"The *Lagoa das Sete Cidades*, Lagoon of the seven cities. In Isebeau's kingdom, there were two lakes, separated by a narrow strip of land. One lake was green, the other blue. The legend says there was a lonely old king who lived with his beautiful daughter, an only child. He adored her, but kept her sequestered in the palace, only allowed to visit the gardens from time to time. The king feared to lose his precious daughter. The young princess was an adventurous girl and learned how to sneak out of the palace when her father wasn't looking. One day, she heard beautiful music coming from the hillside and followed. She found a young shepherd boy playing the violin, and they fell in love. Emboldened by his love for the beautiful princess, the boy asked the king for her hand. Enraged, the king refused and cast the boy from his kingdom. The two lovers met secretly for a time, but the young princess would not defy her father, and so she said goodbye to her one true love and the two cried all afternoon. Their sorrow was so great, their tears formed the twin lakes. Lagoa Azul, for the blue-eyed princess and Lagoa Verde, for the green-eyed shepherd boy. Far above the lakes, an angry volcano lay dormant, representing the king who kept the two lovers apart."

"What a beautiful, sad story," Allie said, picking at her omelet. "You play violin?"

"I did. Once. A very long time ago. I even made a good life for myself for a time, crafting the most beautiful stringed instruments, marrying my love for art with my love for music."

"Don't tell me you're Antonio Stradivari?" Allie teased.

"In the flesh." He shot her a boyish grin.

"Shut your face, I was joking!" Allie's jaw fell open at the thought of Aidan's beautiful Stradivarius violin with the intricate carved phoenix motif. She'd always thought those birds would make a great addition to her vine tattoo that followed the path of her scars from her jaw down to her throat and shoulder, all the way to her hip.

"I wasn't."

"Wow, okay, so what happened to Isebeau in the real life version of your fairytale?" Allie perched on the edge of her seat, digging into her omelet.

"We eventually ran away together after giving her family as many chances as we dared. But her father would not agree to a marriage that brought him nothing in trade for his daughter's hand."

"What a jerk." The story reminded Allie of Naeemah's time as Empress of the Mughal Empire of India after her own grandfather married her off to a mortal prince.

"That he was. We fled to Italy where we bonded our lives together and were married. We had four glorious days together before the Coalition came for us. I left her that morning to go find work and when I returned, she was gone. I believe her father preferred handing her over to those monsters to allowing us to live peacefully."

"You were married to your Complement for four days over six hundred years ago, and you haven't seen her since?"

Allie's eyes welled with tears; she couldn't fathom anything sadder than Greyson's story. But the last thing he would tolerate from her was pity. "You two got screwed, my friend."

"Yes, we did. It's been so long. Sometimes, I don't think I can remember what she looks like. And then other times, I remember her like it was yesterday."

"You tried making a deal with the Coalition for her back when Emma first met you." Allie remembered that part of his story from Emma's memories.

"I've tried everything, Allie. I worked for the Coalition for more than a century before I finally realized no amount of betraying my own kind would earn her freedom and if it did, she would never respect me for it. I've spent the better part of my life searching for her, but I still don't even know where she's held captive. She could be in one of those ancient prisons in some long forgotten cell where her mortal jailers don't even remember who she once was. I've stopped trying at least a dozen times, but every now and then I have to try again. Our bond still lives in here." He pressed his hand over his heart. "It will not rest until we are together again."

"I wish there was something I could do. I would totally help you break her out of prison if we could find out where she is."

"I had to come to terms with it a long time ago, Allie. We may never see each other again. Not until the entire world falls down around us, and the Coalition collapses. Then maybe we will find each other. Until then, I have to find happiness wherever I can. And that is exactly what you need to do, too, Allie."

"I'm working on it." She hopped up to refill their coffee mugs.

"I don't like Brigs for you, kid. He's kind of an asshole."

"Not to me." Allie poured Greyson's coffee. "And I'm not

looking for a commitment or anything serious. We're just casually dating and I'm cool with that."

"I just want you to find a way to be happy with yourself."

"Ding-ding-ding! He finally gets it, ladies and gentlemen." Allie slow clapped. "That's what I'm trying to do. Be happy with me, myself, and I. And Darius, of course. I like school. I like hanging out with you and working as your intern. I like Brigs but I don't need him or any guy to be happy. I *am* happy. I'm just not the same girl I used to be. But I'll find her again."

"Good girl. Now go home and do something fun with the rest of your Saturday."

"I have a sculpture I need to finish."

"No, you don't."

"Yes, I do."

"If it's the one for my class, it's not due for a month, so go do something fun."

"Fine, we'll go to a movie or something."

"I was thinking more like a kegger, but I guess a movie is better than nothing."

CHAPTER 21

Aidan | Milan, Italy | February

"All our lives depend on you guys pulling this off," Aidan said in his most authoritative tone. The one he hated using with his friends and family, but was grateful for now. "Do not let me down." His power reverberated in his voice.

"You got it, sexy," Neela said, her shoulders squared, her black uniform pristine. She was the image of a perfect student, until she opened her mouth.

"Just ... try not to speak if you don't have to. You either, Ivy," he said, before she could offer her two cents.

"We've got this, Aidan," Ezra said. "We promise we won't screw up."

"Yeah, we know what's riding on this," Wes added.

"All right, when we're called, we—"

"Run out in an orderly fashion, holding our weapons across our chests like you showed us," Bennett finished his sentence with an eye roll.

"Don't roll your eyes, Bennett. Samantha, help me out here." Aidan turned to face Ben's Syntrophos. Sam was a quiet, no nonsense kind of girl when it mattered. Aidan could trust her to help keep the others in check.

"He'll be good, promise." Sam gave a nervous smile, looking a little green herself.

"And when we're asked to display our abilities, we'll show something flashy and impressive, but not our greatest gifts," Ivy said.

"Pilar, are we ready for this?" Aidan sighed, running his hands through his hair. The kids were taking this too lightly. They had no idea what they were really facing. It gave him a panic attack every time one of them cracked a joke, but he couldn't let them see how scared he was.

"Look at me, kid." She turned him toward her, fixing his hair and straightening his uniform like he was four. They rarely wore their training uniforms. They were uncomfortable and itchy, and Cleo never made it a requirement. Unfortunately, that meant their clothes looked far too new.

"They're ready for us," Naomi said, as she stepped into the training room with Genevieve.

"How's it going out there?" Aidan asked.

"I can't really tell," was all Naomi would say. She was obviously tense, but he couldn't get a read on her emotions. "If we can get through this part, we're home free, at least until they decide to visit again."

Aidan and his students waited in his training room facing the massive field at the center of the complex. As the garage-style doors opened onto the field, Aidan and his students formed up in pairs.

Pilar and Genevieve led them across the field. Dressed similarly, their uniforms displayed their leadership status. Aidan had refused a promotion to field commander when he'd moved to Milan. He wanted to remain part of the team. His leadership within the group was through loyalty alone.

"Take a deep breath and get your head on straight," Naomi said. "I'm right beside you."

"Thank you. I couldn't do any of this without you." He gently squeezed her hand before he shifted his sword to rest against his shoulder. His dagger sheathed at his hip.

As a group, they jogged across the field in perfect sync. Naomi and Aidan followed Pilar and Genevieve with Ezra and Wes behind them. Samantha and Bennett brought up the rear with Neela and Ivy.

With a signal from Genevieve, they all stood at ease in front of a raised dais just below Cleo's office. Again in unison, they all sheathed their weapons, waiting for their orders. Cleo stood beside the Chief Justice, Sarah and Charles Madison on the dais, their armed entourage just behind them in the shade of the building.

"So few?" Sarah Madison frowned, taking a step forward to observe them.

"Our reports have always reflected five Syntrophos pairs live and train here," Cleo said.

"A special forces team of ten children." Sarah sighed. "They don't look like much do they, Charles?

"Not much at all, my dear," Charles said, like a parrot at his wife's side.

"With Syntrophos, the numbers aren't important." Cleo took a step closer to the Chief Justice. "It's what they can do together that makes them a force to be reckoned with—or will, once they are older. They are still very young."

"What are their ages?" Charles asked, like he was inspecting horseflesh.

"Our youngest is just seventeen, and they range up to twenty-nine. Most are in their late teens and still training hard to hone their emerging gifts. Genevieve and myself, of course, are much older and oversee their training along with Pilar."

"It's curious how so many young pairs are coming out of

this latest generation." Sarah's eyes swept through the group, like they were a huge disappointment. Disappointment could be good. It meant they still had a lot of work to do. But it was also unpredictable what the Chief Justice would do to remedy this situation. Aidan wouldn't rest easy until this was all over and the Chief Justice were on their way back to headquarters in Spain.

"They are a talented group, ma'am ... and sir," Cleo hastily added for Charles's benefit.

"You've prepared a demonstration?" Charles asked.

"Yes, Chief Justice, Sir," Pilar responded.

Aidan held his breath as Samantha and Bennett stepped from the group first. He felt helpless, like a momma bird shoving her babies out of the nest before they had the ability to fly on their own.

"Relax your face. They're watching." Naomi gestured at the entourage of Immortals standing behind the Chief Justice.

Aidan schooled his features. Naomi was right, they were all under a microscope and he needed to remain impassive.

"Samantha is twenty-two," Pilar began. "Her Syntrophos is Bennett, twenty." She nodded to Bennett to proceed.

A thick, viscous fog began to rise from the ground behind the Chief Justice. It rolled over them, swirling like smoke.

"A weather manipulation? That's what you're showing us?" Sarah snapped, waving the fog from her face.

"Pardon, Madame, but Bennett and Samantha are still developing and evolving their own abilities," Cleo said. "Bennett is a talented young Immortal on his own. The astonishing aspect comes from what Bennett and Samantha can do together." She nodded for Samantha to step forward.

Sam stood with her hands behind her back, staring at the

Chief Justice until Bennett's fog turned pink and the air smelled of strawberries.

"Ugh, what is this sticky sweet stench?" Charles fanned his face.

"I made a slight change to Ben's fog, Madame Chief Justice," Samantha said, her voice steady. "For the purposes of our demonstration, I made it harmless and pink with a sweet candy scent. But I could also make it a deadly toxin or a noxious deterrent."

"I can manipulate precipitation, Madame, but together we can make it rain acid, pristine, unpolluted water, or anything in between." Bennett dropped his head, stepping back in line with Samantha.

"Well, that is certainly more like it," Sarah said. "Please continue."

"Aidan and Naomi," Cleo called them forward. "Aidan is twenty and Naomi is twenty-nine."

Aidan stepped forward and lit a match tossing it into the stone brazier in front of the dais. Using his fire ability to enhance the flame into a raging pillar, he sent a stream of fire dancing around the Chief Justice, confining them within a burning circle. Part of him wished he had the nerve to put an end to this whole thing right here, right now. But assassination wasn't the pathway that would lead him back to Allie. It would only further alienate him from his normal life.

"What is the meaning of this?" Sarah's voice hit a high note as the fire raged around her and her husband.

Together, Aidan and Naomi stepped through the flames. Before their connection, Aidan was just as affected by fire as anyone. Now, they both could touch it briefly without harm.

With a sweep of her hand, Naomi sent the flames soaring higher and hotter. A moment later, she suppressed the flames, snuffing them out completely. Over the last year since they'd bonded, Naomi had adapted to his ability. Together, they could do a lot of damage, or a lot of good, depending on who was giving the orders. Aidan liked to think they might have a future putting out fires rather than starting them.

"Impressive." Sarah nodded. "But is that all? This young man is powerful in the extreme. What else can he do?"

"I am a healer, ma'am." Aidan gave her a curt nod. "And we are still experimenting with my developing abilities."

"I draw my strength from the lunar cycle," Naomi announced, pulling the attention away from Aidan with her rare ability. "Through our bond, my gift allows me to strengthen my Syntrophos as well."

"With no cost to your own strength?" Charles asked, impressed.

"That is correct, sir." Aidan and Naomi stepped back in line but he couldn't relax. Not until each of his students had their moment to share their abilities with the Chief Justice.

He watched as Ezra and Wes stepped forward for their turn. This one needed to go just right. Wes's most notable abilities needed to remain a secret. Aidan intended to get them all out of this situation some day, and when that opportunity came for them, they would need Wes's gift for evasion.

"Madame and Sir, Chief Justice," Wes greeted them with a charming smile. "I'm afraid I am not as talented as my fellow comrades, or my brilliant Syntrophos. I am a simple tracker with an ability to induce a sense of panic in those I pursue. If I may be so bold as to recommend myself as your personal bounty hunter. My Syntrophos, however, has much to offer." He gestured to Ezra who was holding a bouquet of flowers, looking terrified now that it was his turn.

Ezra shot forward to present Sarah with the flowers. Flowers that wilted and died as Ezra absorbed their vitality to enhance his own. "I never grow tired," he blurted. "I can keep going for days and days when necessary."

"I also reap the benefits of Ezra's gift," Wes added. "The vitality he takes from plant life bolsters me as well."

"A syphon? Very nice." Sarah nodded, looking pleased. "I wonder how he might respond after syphoning from the life source of a living person or beast, rather than taking it from plants?" She turned to Cleo. "You may find a deeper layer to this gift if you push him out of his comfort zone with simple plants."

Aidan clenched his mouth shut to keep himself in check. The absurd suggestion spoke volumes of what the Chief Justice intended for her Special Forces team. Aidan didn't care. He wouldn't force such a thing on Ezra if he could help it.

"I, um. I'm not sure ma'am," Ezra stuttered, glancing to Pilar for support. "I haven't made a habit of killing innocent things if I don't have to."

"I'd like him to experiment." Sarah spoke as if Ezra was not standing before her. "This gift has great potential. Be sure to explore its every facet—and don't be squeamish about it."

Cleo nodded, looking sick at the thought of her suggestion.

Only Ivy and Neela remained, and they managed to do as they were told for once in their lives. The girls were master thieves among their many skills. They demonstrated how Ivy could create an explosion, and Neela could enhance the range of her Syntrophos's explosion, but they really got the Chief Justice's attention as they were told to step back in line.

"Before we go, Chief Justice Charles, here is your wallet back." Ivy hesitantly approached him.

"And your pearls, Chief Justice Sarah," Neela added sheepishly.

"You dare to steal from us?" Charles blustered.

"They are skilled thieves?" Sarah asked, her tone one of interest as she accepted her pearls back from Neela.

"We don't get caught, Madame." Ivy took a step back.

"Ever," Neela added. "We're sorry, Chief Justice, Sir." Neela turned to Charles. "It was just for the demonstration." They returned to their place in line.

"Very interesting." Sarah stood, clutching her pearls.

"You have an excellent pool of talent here, Cleo," Charles said. "Excellent, indeed."

"It's unfortunate they are all so young," Sarah added. "We had hoped you might have progressed further in the last two years. Enough for them to be useful now, but I'm afraid we aren't there yet."

Aidan exhaled the breath he was holding. It was almost over and they'd managed to pull it off. So far, but the visit wasn't over yet.

"Perhaps in another year, darling?" Charles suggested. "With some proper motivation."

Aidan shared a worried glance with Naomi. He didn't like the sound of that, but he wasn't naive enough to think they would escape this day entirely unscathed.

"Perhaps." Sarah turned to one of her entourage waiting behind her and nodded before she turned back to Cleo. "You have created an incredible institution here. You should be proud."

"Thank you, Madame. We are very proud of our students." Cleo gave a hesitant smile.

"Ah, students. There you have stumbled onto the problem. Though they may be young, they are not students. Think of them as assets to their government. Their livelihoods depend on the work they do for us here. You are much too gentle with them, Cleo. They are a fine group of

Syntrophos, but my husband and I have funneled an enormous amount of money into this private Initiative. These Syntrophos need more discipline. Something to motivate them to the next level."

"You speak of them as property." Pilar's disgust showed on her face. "They are children."

"My dear, Pilar, you cannot think it prudent to allow these children to live freely among the Immortal population? The very nature of their bond makes them dangerous weapons. It is better their government care for them and train them, so in a sense, they are property," Sarah said. "They belong to us, dear. And we are not here to raise a horde of happy children. We are here to raise an army. My army. We will expect much more on our next visit." Sarah snapped her fingers, and her entourage opened a pair of doors behind the dais.

"I anticipated we would need to take it up a notch. Pilar, my dear, you are not the only one who has studied the Syntrophos carefully over the years. They are a curious sort. They not only bond with their partners, but they develop bonds as a group. Like a family. Even now, your more powerful pairs stand in front of the younger and weaker, shielding them from notice. This will not do for our future plans."

"Very well, how do you suggest we remedy this problem?" Cleo asked, her eyes closed in resignation.

"I'm glad you asked." Sarah Madison smiled. "A dear friend of ours has helped acquire three additional pairs."

Aidan and the others turned at the sound of boots pounding against concrete. Six new soldiers jogged in a line to join the Chief Justice.

This is not good. Sarah was right: the Syntrophos gravitated toward each other. They had their own family dynamics. This new group would, too, and they would not be loyal to Aidan. They would have their own sense of loyalty to each other. But as the new Syntrophos pairs settled into formation, Aidan did a double take. They were just kids. The youngest hadn't even experienced an Awakening yet.

"Rowan and Spencer, please step forward," Charles ordered. "Rowan is the field commander of her group. She will be in charge of discipline, and she will report to the Chief Justice office regularly. Her Syntrophos, Spencer, will be assisting Rowan in her duties."

Rowan and Spencer were both young women in their early twenties. Rowan was beautiful with dark wavy hair, shot with blue highlights. Spencer was petite with silvery blond hair down to her waist with blood red highlights, yet her countenance was disturbing. She stared with vacant eyes at Aidan and his team.

"The girls are joined by Gemma and Ruthie, and Lola and Ace," Sarah said. "I think you will all find Ruthie, Lola and Ace have not allowed their young ages to hold them back in the slightest. I have no doubt you will all learn a great deal from Rowan and her team."

"I would like to discuss all disciplinary action before anything new is implemented," Cleo said in a desperate attempt to regain her authority.

"It is simple," Rowan said, pacing in front of Aidan and his team members like a new drill sergeant. "There are rules you will obey. If you break my rules or fail to produce results, you will be disciplined. Period." She stopped in front of Aidan, her brow raised in surprise—the only outward reaction to accessing his power. He was stronger and more powerful than she was, and it bothered her. Aidan was in for a struggle for dominance with this one and he didn't intend to lose. If she expected to come in and scare everyone into submission, she was mistaken.

"And what kind of discipline do you intend to enact on my students?" Pilar asked.

"They are soldiers. And you will find out soon enough," Rowan said, dismissing Pilar.

Aidan had no illusions that they would all find out exactly what Rowan meant all too soon.

"We are not monsters," Sarah said. "We have sufficient reason to expect faster results than we originally planned. We do not expect more than these soldiers are capable of, but we have assignments for our Special Forces team. Dire assignments that need their attention soon."

"Anything you can share with us, Madame?" Cleo asked, her eyes glued to Ace and Lola, her gaze filled with pity. They couldn't be more than fourteen and Aidan couldn't fathom how they'd even bonded so young.

"When your training is complete, you all will leave Milan for a very special assignment that only you can accomplish. You will be going where only those Unproven are welcome. Soma. You will enroll as students and once inside, you will take over in the Senate's name. By your hands, the tyranny of Soma will end, and it will become a government institution for all young children to come and train without fear. There will be no more Immortal trafficking in the name of Soma. Not while we are your Chief Justice."

Chapter 22

Allie | Kelleys Island | March

"No! You are not letting her out of her cage." Allie slammed her fist against the stone wall of the crypt.

"Livia has proven she's not going to run," Gregg insisted. "She will stay in the underground, but we no longer feel it's necessary to confine her power."

"It's not your decision to make, Greggory McBrien. You don't get to decide these things for *my* family." Allie's hands shook with fury and probably fear as well. The idea of Livia roaming free terrified her.

"Aye, it is not my decision. It's the queen's. And we will abide by her wishes."

"Allie, dear," Alísun said. "I did not expect you to react this way."

"I don't have ice in my veins the way some people in this family do," Allie snapped and immediately regretted it. She didn't always see eye to eye with her grandmother, but she loved and respected both of her grandparents, and right now the look on Alexander's face shamed her.

Alexander began, "Allie-girl, we know you and Livia don't get along—"

"Don't get along?" Allie's chest tightened in anger, the rage of her gift swelling inside her. If she had it her way, she'd gladly use it on Livia to strip her of her immortality the way she'd stripped their mother of her life. "She's the reason my mother is dead. She's the reason we lost Ming Lao. She can't be trusted. The only things I know about my mother are the things you and Navid have told me about her, Gregg. That's the only way I'll ever know and love the woman who gave me life—through your memories. And you want to let her murderer walk free?"

"Alísun, I told you, Allie isn't ready for this, and I will not push her," Navid said. "We've all had the luxury of knowing and loving the woman we lost. We've each shared a lifetime with Kassandre. Allie and Livia will never know that. If Allie ever chooses to forgive her sister, she will do so on her own terms."

"Thank you, Navid." She was surprised to see her father agreed with her.

"I will never choose one daughter over the other," he replied. "Your mother and I knew there was a chance Livia would develop an ability she would eventually turn on her mother. Kassandre was prepared to make that sacrifice to give Livia a chance at redemption. It was the only path she saw for our eldest child. Your mother refused to abandon either of her children. We saw thousands of versions of your lives but we wouldn't sacrifice one child to save the other. For hundreds of years we worked to find a path where both of our children had a chance at a happy life. This is the life she chose for her children, Allie. The one where she didn't get to know either of you."

"Stop." Allie didn't want to hear any more excuses. She didn't care what drove Livia to make the decisions she had. She made the wrong choices. No one deserved to die the way

Kassandre and Ming Lao had. And no one deserved to endure a life without their love the way Navid and Jin Jing were forced to do every single day.

"Enough. You are not a child, Alexis. It's been long enough," Navid said firmly. "Your sister didn't have a choice the night she came for us. She never had a choice. And she only recently learned the woman she killed that night was her own mother. You can't imagine what using that ability costs her. You have no idea what Marcus has forced her to do with it, or how she is tormented by the souls of those she's taken. I will never ask you to forgive her. I will only ask that you allow her the chance at redemption your mother sacrificed her life for. We will release your sister soon, but I would rather do it with your blessing."

"She will not be allowed to leave the underground," Gregg added.

"Livia will stay of her own free will," Liam spoke, his eyes pleading with Allie to understand. She knew he was torn. He was falling for Livia. She was his Complement, and only Allie and Gregg shared that knowledge with him. Liam still hated the things Livia had done in her past, but he was convinced she could be a better person.

"I'll think about it." Allie nodded with reluctance. "I just don't trust her not to break her promises. She is manipulative. What happens if you wake up one morning and she's gone? Gone back to her father?"

"I am her father," Navid said, his voice weighted with the force of his power.

"She would die before she returned to Marcus," Liam said. "She loves Navid."

"And what if she's just playing you all for fools?" Allie shook her head. "I am so scared she will take someone else I love," she admitted, reaching for Navid's hands. "But I—I can do small steps. For you."

"Small steps? How?" Liam asked.

Allie took an uncertain breath. "For now, can she keep the magnetic collar on? Livia travels the dreamworld as she pleases and I am used to that now. We fight this war side by side but we are not friends. I do not trust her. Let me get used to seeing her roaming free before I can deal with a Livia with the full use of her power."

"I think that is a fair compromise," Alísun said. "You've faced a difficult situation and found the diplomatic solution. Well done, my granddaughter."

"I don't know if I'll ever be able to forgive her, grandma, but I will try to find a way to be okay with this."

"Thank you, Allie." Navid hugged her close to his side.

"Dreamworld, now." Quinn charged down the steps from the common room above. "We've got a location on the prisoners, but we need to move quickly."

Allie and Navid followed, jogging behind him to the Yard where Livia and Santi already waited.

Brecken and his inner circle had been guarding their prisoners for months, never allowing Quinn and his walkers to get close.

"What changed?" Allie asked. "How do we know it's not a trap?"

"We don't," Navid said. "But we have to try."

"Hurry," Santi said. "Sasha is on her way to come assist. We will monitor your time as usual, but if there is a chance..."

"We need to push our limits today, guys." Quinn sat in his usual spot under the shade of the trees in the Yard. "This is the closest we've come to liberating these walkers in a year. We need to get in there, hit them hard, and get out. We will meet the rest of the team at the keep and set out. You three are coming with me to do the liberating."

"Is that wise?" Navid asked. "They will have guards in place."

"Raina has been popping in and out for the last few hours, and they only have a few guards standing watch. Brecken has called his walkers in for strategizing. He's planning something big, but we need to move while we have a chance. We'll go in, but they won't expect us to send Allie and Livia."

"Sounds like a trap to me," Allie said. "But I'm game. It's not like they haven't tried to trap me in the dreamworld before. It never works, so you two just keep yourselves safe. I don't want to trade either of you for a bunch of crazies." Over the last year, Allie and Livia had participated in many battles with Quinn and his walkers. Quinn was stronger and he was going to win this war. Brecken often targeted Allie and Livia, even captured them a couple of times, but he couldn't touch them. Darius always called her back to the waking world, nullifying anything Brecken might have planned for them.

"Yes, please be careful, Dad. Quinn. You two are vital to the success of this war," Livia said, pretending not to notice how Allie always refused to acknowledge her in the waking world.

"If we play our cards right, there's a chance we can end this war soon," Quinn said eagerly.

"Then let's do it," Allie said, taking her seat to Navid's right. "Just give me the usual two minutes to puke, and I'll be ready to march."

"No marching today. You're going to have to travel like a walker and suck it up," Quinn said. "Brigs will be waiting for you near the towers."

"Great. Glad I had that big lunch 'cause we're all about

to revisit it." Allie closed her eyes, settling her hands on the top of her knees. She breathed deeply and exhaled, searching her mind for serenity. True to form, Allie stumbled, landing on her rear in the dreamworld. With a moan, she scrambled to her feet to retch behind the crumbling walls of the gates to the keep. Still aware of her physical body in the waking world, it always took Allie a moment to wrap her mind around the feeling of being in two places at once. For her, the dreamworld was every bit as real as the waking world.

"Every time." Raina's laughter still sounded crazy, but she was making great strides in her recovery. "Everyone's ready and waiting on the two wakers here."

"Allie, brace yourself." Quinn warned. "We're going now."

As they moved in together, Livia grabbed Allie's hand and gave a gentle squeeze of reassurance.

Allie wanted to snatch her hand back, but there was no time.

"Oh God," Allie groaned, as she landed on her butt again a moment later. The world whirled around her in a nauseating spin of colors and shapes. Clutching her stomach, she heaved again. Allie's pulse pounded in her ears, and she fell face forward into her own vomit. "Ugh, that's disgusting," she muttered, rolling onto her side. She just wanted to lie there for a minute. Just one minute before she would have to shake it off and go fight a war.

"Up." Quinn pulled her to her feet. "Carry her until she snaps out of it."

"I'm okay," Allie murmured, trying to clear the haze from her mind.

"Easy there, beautiful," Brigs said, reaching down to scoop her up. "I've got you."

"Hey." Allie managed a grimace of a smile as she wrapped her arms around his neck.

"Hey yourself." He winked.

Brigs was stupid hot. She generally lost the ability to speak whenever he was around, but he seemed to think she was hilarious.

"Drink." Brigs nodded toward the canteen at his belt. "It'll help you feel better."

"Thank you." Icy water passed her lips, refreshing her body, and clearing her mind. It tasted like ambrosia and sunshine. She could live on that water and nothing else for the rest of her life.

"That's better, I think you can put me down now."

"Nah." He kept walking. "Not while I have you held hostage."

"Hostage?" You know I could Kung Fu my way out of your arms, right?"

"Sweetheart, you could lay me out on the ground with those killer blades of yours. I'm no match for you. I'm just banking on the idea that you kinda like where you are at the moment."

I do love the dreamworld." Her flirty smile felt silly on her stupid face. She was never this uncertain of herself with Vince or Aidan. But Brigs was a little older ... and stupid hot. She liked their casual relationship because she knew it was going absolutely nowhere and that was just fine with her.

"How about dinner after we go kick some ass? Come over later and we'll grill some steaks. I say we, but I mean me. You're not going near my grill again after last time."

"Oh it wasn't that bad." Allie rolled her eyes. "You still ate a bunch of those ribs."

"Yeah but you destroyed my grill—"

"Not the time, Brigs. Put her down," Livia said.

"Where are we?" Allie asked when she was back on her feet.

"Deep in the redwood forest," Raina said. "The oldest part of the dreamworld outside the keep."

"We suspect Brecken has set up his own version of the keep in this area, attempting to pass it off as the original," Quinn said. "Like he can manufacture the dreamworld's recognition of him as its master."

"Some of the idiots that follow him actually believe it," Brigs said. "I don't know how they can resist the pull to Quinn."

"Brecken has to be masking it," Navid said. "The commander's lure is too strong now for them not to notice."

"Where are the rest of your walkers?" Livia asked.

"They're coming in toward the south of the prison world now, They'll wait until we strike the northwest corner before they launch their attack to confuse Brecken's walkers and split their forces."

"Raina, tell Danica we're moving in now. Give us a head start and launch your attack at the first sign of Brecken's walkers," Quinn commanded.

"Got it, boss." She winked out in an instant, gone to deliver her messages.

"Follow me." Quinn motioned them to move quickly. They kept low as they crept through the ancient forest of towering redwoods.

"This is where we need your help." Quinn turned to face Livia and Allie. "We can't go in there." He pointed to the lone black tower standing among the trees. "It's a horrifying prison world, but now that we know Brecken's towers don't affect you, we're going to distract the guards, so you can get inside."

For nearly a year they'd operated with the idea that Allie

and Livia could become trapped in Brecken's prison towers just like the walkers, but a few months ago, during a particularly nasty battle, Livia got too close to a tower and its gravitational pull dragged her inside. Allie tried to save her. She'd held on to Livia's hand as long as she could but Livia let go, shoving Allie away from the tower. Liam couldn't wake her and they thought they'd lost her, but a few hours later Livia walked out of the prison world looking rattled, but otherwise unharmed. Briggs escorted her back to the keep and she woke up in the Yard, refusing to talk about the experience other than to say it took her a long time to find the exit.

"We'll take care of the guards while you two go inside the tower and lead the prisoners out as quickly as you can. Raina will take them to the keep and then we'll figure out how to get them back to the waking world as best we can."

Allie and Livia watched as Quinn and Navid crept closer to the northwest corner of the tower, where Danica and her walkers would arrive any minute.

"Let's do this," Quinn gave the signal and the forest erupted into flames that didn't burn, a trick of Navid's. The guards would think it a threat and retaliate with water that wouldn't dampen the flames.

"Let's go, Brigs." Quinn crept forward with Navid to his left.

"Later, beautiful." Brigs winked and took off with Quinn.

"Wait, not yet," Livia whispered, holding Allie back. "Wait for the attack."

"Don't touch me." Allie pulled away. "We need to get closer."

"No, look." Livia pointed. Only one guard remained to inspect the fire. The other paced the perimeter nervously. "He'll run when Brigs makes his presence known."

"You're right." Allie ducked down beside Livia to wait.

"You don't ignore me in the dreamworld. Why is that?"

"We have a job to do here," Allie said. "I have to talk to you."

"I suppose that's something."

"Who knows, maybe we'll end this war today, and then I won't have to talk to you again."

"At least until the next war." Livia smirked.

"You can't say sarcasm doesn't run in the family," Allie muttered.

"There's our sign," Livia said, as the ground began to shake. An explosion of black stone darkened the sky.

"Now," Allie said as the second guard abandoned his post at the sound of screams coming from Brecken's castle in the distance.

Livia followed close behind. Allie ducked through an open archway into the tower, the pull of the tower flinging her to the ground once inside. The sounds of battle ceased and the stillness of the prison world weighed heavy in the air. Dusting off her hands and knees, Allie stood, taking a moment to get her bearings. A labyrinth of crumbling ruins and muddy roads sprawled out before her for miles. A dark and dreary sky loomed overhead providing little light to the world below. Allie shivered, calling forth images of warmer clothing to protect her from the freezing temperatures.

"Better than the last one," Livia said, her voice sounding like an alarm behind Allie.

"Jeez you scared me." Allie ran her hands over her arms.

"The last one was a fire world." Livia updated her own clothing to keep warm.

"This is awful," Allie murmured. A crude shed stood at the center of the ruins with a rusted tin roof to keep the prisoners sheltered from the elements. Filthy men and women wandered around aimlessly, lost in Brecken's special brand of nightmares designed specifically for walkers. Each dragged their feet, weighed down by some unseen force. Some of these walkers had spent years trapped here, well beyond their limitations. Allie wondered if it was even possible for a dream walker to recover from that kind of crazy. Raina had spent more than two years here, and she was still struggling.

"It's even worse for them," Livia said. "We'll never know what torture they're feeling. What they're seeing." Allie and Livia were lucky. Their cognizance of the dreamworld protected their minds from the horrors of Brecken's prison. They were here, but they were neither a dreamer nor a walker. Neither asleep nor awake.

"Let's free some walkers," Livia said, setting off down a path between crumbling walls. "Don't get lost," Livia called over her shoulder.

Allie set off in a different direction, keeping her back to the place where she entered the tower. She needed to exit the same way to meet Raina with the prisoners. Allie walked quickly, only stopping to spray paint markers along her path so she could find her way back.

The stench of unwashed bodies hit her first. Most of the prisoners were naked and exposed to the elements; their clothes long since rotted away. The dreamscape itself wasn't dangerous, but each was trapped within their minds. At least fifty walkers shuffled around the shed, screaming and crying from their madness and whatever pain this prison world brought them.

"Grab them by their leads." Livia darted ahead, taking up the leashes dragging behind the walkers. Livia had at least ten tethered behind her as she rushed back up the way she came to meet Raina. "Go, now, we don't have much time."

Allie raced into the midst of a crowd, gathering up as many leads as she could get her hands on. "Come on, follow me," she called, yanking on her group of prisoners. They screamed and pulled, but they were so weak, she easily managed seven on her own. But it was slow going back to the tower exit. Allie murmured in a soothing voice, cajoling the walkers to follow her out of their prison.

Daylight nearly blinded her when she stepped through the archway, back into the dreamworld proper. "Come, follow me. Feel the warmth? That's safety. That's it, let's go."

"I've got them," Navid said, coming up the path to help. "The guards are gone, and Brigs is keeping the rest occupied. We probably have about twenty minutes before they realize what's happening."

"I'll be back with more in a minute." Allie turned and raced back through the archway and into the toxic dreamscape, passing Livia with another bunch along the way.

This time Allie had to travel beyond the rusted shed, deeper into the labyrinth to collect more prisoners. The sky had grown darker, and it was harder to see. She had no control of this dreamscape, but she brought forth a lantern to light the way. The walkers seemed to respond to the light, like a beacon calling them home. "Yes, little darlings, come this way. I'll take you home now." She corralled five more and headed back. This was taking too long, and the remaining walkers were too far apart.

"How much time do we have now?" she asked Navid when she handed off her prisoners.

"Minutes, we need to move faster. The fight is coming to us. How many are left?"

"Not quite half."

Navid nodded. "Do what you can on this trip back but that's it; we'll have to leave the others for another time."

But there wouldn't be another time. Brecken wouldn't let

them have a second chance to save these people. They had one more chance to get the rest.

"Make this one count," Livia called, as she trotted past with her last group of prisoners, her smallest yet.

Allie darted back into the dreamscape, searching for the remaining walkers. With all the commotion, they were shuffling back toward the center, but they were still too far apart. Allie needed to get them to come to her. The lantern worked before—maybe she just needed a brighter light with a little warmth. It was so cold in here and they shivered violently.

Allie focused on a mental image of a bonfire burning tall and bright. It took her longer than usual, but fire wasn't always easy. "That's right," she screamed, "come to the warmth." These walkers emerged from the deepest part of the labyrinth. Dirty and battered, they resembled concentration camp survivors. There was no way she would leave any of them behind. The ground shook again. Brigs and the other walkers were busy battling Brecken's forces, but the fight was drawing closer and closer. She had to finish her part and get back to the keep with the others.

"Let's go, my littler walkers," she crooned softly, trying to set them at ease, grasping their leads as they wandered closer to the fire. As she headed toward the edge of the labyrinth, the walkers began to tug on the lines. They didn't want to leave the fire.

"Come on, it's warm and sunny where we're going." She tugged harder, digging her heels into the mud and slop at her feet. "We have clothes. Lots of clothes. A warm fireplace and food. Yes, that's it, keep moving with me guys. We're almost there." As she grasped the last tether, Allie turned to make her way out. If any remained, she couldn't help them now. "Want to go home, guys? We're going to wake you up and get you back to your families real soon, just keep following the sound of my voice." She didn't know if it was helping, but they slowly made their way out of the tower.

"Move it, Allie," Quinn shouted, his horse rearing back. The battle was here, and she had to get out of the way. She wasn't an asset in a walker battle.

The ground exploded at her feet, spraying a cloud of dust and rock around her. "Come on." She tugged on the lines. "We're going home." Allie charged through the forest, moving faster now that her walkers were away from the nightmare of the dreamscape.

"I've got them," Raina cried, wrenching the leads from her grasp and whisking them away to safety.

"That's it," Allie shouted over the din of the battle. "What now?"

"Where is Dad?" Livia asked, her eyes growing wide.

Allie glanced around, turning in circles. "He has to be with Quinn. They were handling the guards. I just saw him on the trail."

Allie and Livia charged back through the forest, searching for Navid. They moved fast, running to avoid the walkers locked in battle, their forms and weapons changing so fast, Allie and Livia couldn't even comprehend how the battle was playing out.

"You don't think he's ... in there?" Livia asked, as they arrived back at the black tower.

"Oh God, no."

Allie and Livia sprinted for the archway.

"Navid!" Allie screamed as she ran into the labyrinth.

"Dad!" Livia shrieked.

"There." Allie spotted him roaming the nightmare world with eyes locked on some horrific scene.

Allie and her sister ran together, focused on their father.

"No," Livia cried as the labyrinth began to fade and

crumble around them. The sky lightened and the ruins vanished. The mud dried around their feet, leaving Livia and Allie standing in an empty space where the tower once stood.

"Dad!" Both women screamed for their father, but he disappeared with a whisper of Brecken's voice.

"He's mine now."

"No!" Allie ran to where she'd seen her father last.

"I will end you," Livia screamed, falling in the dust on her knees, her wails echoing through the silent forest. "I will tear this world apart until I find you, Brecken!"

"No." Allie shook her head, fighting off the tears stinging her eyes. "No." Her voice faded to a choked whisper. Why did she always lose the ones she loved? *But no. Navid is safe in the waking world back in the underground.* "We have to go, Livia." Allie marched across the dusty clearing, the sounds of battle fading in the distance. Brecken was retreating, along with Navid as his newest captive.

"He's gone." Livia wiped the tears from her face. "We have to get him out of there." She lunged toward Brecken's castle.

"We will." Allie tugged Livia back. "We have to wake him up."

"Let's go." Livia was screaming for Santi to wake her up before Allie finished speaking.

"Darius, pull me back!" She hated this helpless feeling. "Get me out of here and wake Navid," she begged and in the next breath, Allie's eyes snapped open and she lunged for her father.

"Navid," she cried.

Livia was already trying to wake him with a rough slap of her palm across his face, but he remained locked in the dreamworld.

"We have to get back there," Livia demanded. "Take us

now." But the walkers were all still fighting in the dreamworld.

"Send someone after him," Allie begged Santi. "Call Raina. Where's Raina?"

"She isn't here, Allie. You're confused." Santi took a step toward her. "Raina is at the keep in the dreamworld, but her body is in the city with Brigs and the others."

"Allie?" Quinn's eyes flew open. "What happened?"

"Navid," Livia sobbed. "He's in the prison world."

"Are you sure?"

"Yes I'm sure. We saw him. Get me back there, now." Livia's eyes were wild with fury and fear.

"Please, take us back. We're wasting time," Allie said, grasping her sister's hand.

"I can't, Allie. I'm so sorry," Quinn said. "I love and respect Navid more than you could ever know. That man saved my life, but I cannot send my walkers after him. Brecken has retreated with his remaining few supporters. He's moved his fortress. The tower, too. We will have to search the dreamworld to find him again."

Aidan | Milan, Italy | April

Rowan must have taken lessons from Livia. She was just as bad as all the horror stories Aidan had heard from Quinn and Santi. Possibly worse. Some unseen force inspired her like a demon on her back, driving her to be as ruthless as she could possibly be. She was cold and clinical, showing no emotion despite the awful things she and her Syntrophos did to Aidan and his students since their arrival just weeks ago.

"Can I call in sick?" Ezra's pale face revealed how terrified he was. It was his turn in the spotlight today.

"Let's just get this done," Wes said, draping his arm around his Syntrophos. "You can do this."

"I don't think I can." Ezra shook his head, near tears.

Ezra was a strong kid. He'd been through a lot, but when it came to Wes, there was nothing he wouldn't do. Which meant Rowan would use that against him, as she had with all the other Syntrophos she'd tested so far in her brief time at the Milan Initiative.

"We'll be right there with you." Aidan gave his shoulder a gentle squeeze.

"I wish you wouldn't insist on standing with us when she

does this. It's bad enough I'm going to hurt Wes, but I don't want you to feel it, too."

"I can't sit back here like a coward and let her do this to you or any of the others. I'm with you because we are family. Don't worry about me, kid. I've been through this before. I may feel Wes's pain through my healing gift, but I have a high tolerance. I can take it."

"I wish you wouldn't be such a hero," Naomi said, her arms crossed over her chest. "Has it ever occurred to you that standing beside you while you're in that kind of pain kills me?"

"I'm sorry, Naomi, but I have to be there. You are free to stay behind."

"I guess I'm a damned hero, too, then because I'm not letting you go through that alone."

"Come on, guys, lets do this," Wes said. "I'm good to go. We know what she's likely going to do, and it's going to be way worse on Ezra than on me. I can take a little physical pain. But Spencer's going to up the anti with the emotional pain."

"Wes is right. Standing here talking about it is just making it worse," Neela said. "Just let the twisted sisters do what they do, and we'll get on about our day."

Aidan nodded and Naomi opened the garage doors. The twisted sisters were already waiting for them on the dais as they jogged out to the center of the field. The grass was still wet with early morning dew, and the sun just faintly painted the sky a rosy blush. It was a beautiful Italian dawn, but it was about to get ugly.

"She's a sadistic bitch." Naomi's voice caught on a sob.

The look on Ezra's face said it all. The poor kid was deathly pale. A ragged looking stray dog hopped around at his feet, her five fat little puppies waddling along behind her.

"Why did it have to be puppies?" Aidan's gut twisted with revulsion and he couldn't meet Ezra's horrified gaze. *I can't watch this.* His mouth went dry as his students looked to him, begging him with their eyes to stop this. He probably could. He was stronger and more powerful than Rowan but he couldn't take on her whole team by himself. His students would only get hurt in the process and they'd be right back here tomorrow, and it would be ten times worse.

"I know what you're thinking and now is not the time," Pilar said. "You have to let this happen."

"I know." Aidan's hands clenched into fists at his side, just the way Allie's did when she was furious and trying not to let it show. Thinking of her gave him strength in these moments.

"Can you get through this?" Naomi whispered softly.

"I'll have to." Aidan couldn't show a reaction to the pain Rowan was about to inflict on Wes. He did not want her or the Chief Justice to know the extent of his healing gift. Nor how easily it would be to inflict pain on him to manipulate his actions. They didn't need any help in that department. "I'm just glad Sasha isn't here. This would kill her."

"Poor kid." Naomi stood ramrod straight, watching Ezra absently pat the mamma dog to calm her exuberance. She thought she was here to play.

"Gemma, Ruthie." Rowan sent her minions to grab Wes.

"Ezra, don't pet the dogs," Wes said, his voice stiff. "It'll just make it worse." He shrugged Gemma and Ruthie off, walking back with them to stand between Rowan and Spencer. "Do whatever she says. I'll be fine."

Shrugging his shirt off, Wes stepped up to the dais, turning his back against a rough wooden beam. He stood, his feet shoulder width apart with his arms crossed in front of him like a seasoned soldier. "Do your worst."

Aidan was damned proud of him.

"We need a starting point," Rowan finally spoke after securing Wes's arms to the beam, raising them up over his head. "A way to measure the before and after. Tell me, Ezra, when you take vitality from the living, how does it effect you?"

"I-uh," Ezra stuttered.

Rowan drew a blade and sliced Wes's bicep open. Wes gasped, but Aidan barely flinched. The shallow cut was all her gift needed. The letting of blood allowed Rowan access to the nerves. All she had to do now was touch Wes's wound to cause him agony like he'd never felt before. Aidan would suffer right along with him today.

"Wait," Ezra shrieked.

"Take a breath, Ezra," Pilar said. "This will pass."

"Okay, okay. When I take vitality from plants and insects, it makes me more focused. A little stronger, faster, more accurate and decisive, and it spills over to Wes, too."

"Take a lap around the field and don't hold back," Rowan said. "Wes will thank you." She clapped a hand over Wes's bleeding arm and he screamed, his eyes rolling back in his head.

Ezra took off like a shot flying around the training field. Aidan couldn't watch: he could only breathe through the pain shooting up his arm and squeezing around his heart and lungs.

Ezra was fast, even when he wasn't pressured. He finished the half-mile lap in just under two minutes.

"We have a base line on speed. Now, take a shot." Rowan gestured at the array of weapons spread across a table beside the dais. A target stood at the ready at the end of the field. Rowan waited, still not releasing Wes or Aidan from her hold.

Ezra was a terrible shot on his own. Aidan prayed he could hit the target, so they wouldn't be here all day.

"Focus," Naomi said.

"Quiet." Spencer glared at her.

Ezra paced to the table, snatched up a bow and knocked an arrow. Still panting from his mad dash around the field, his hands shook.

Aidan closed his eyes, reaching out to Ezra with his healing gift. Thanks to his bond with Naomi, he no longer needed to physically touch for this kind of emotional healing. With a gentle nudge, his gift eased Ezra's shaking, slowed his heart, and brought him a sense of comfort.

With a deep breath, Ezra aimed and released his arrow.

The vise gripping Aidan's heart immediately relaxed at the loud thud that told him Ezra had at least hit the target. A collective sigh rang out among the group. It wasn't over yet. Not even close.

"Start with the mother," Spencer said, crossing the field to stand with Ezra. Her eyes blazed red, making the red streaks in her hair look like blood.

"Rowan's bad enough but this one is too much," Neela mumbled, her gaze on her feet.

"I can't watch." Ivy sniffed stepping closer to her Syntrophos.

"I can't. Please don't make me," Ezra pleaded. "Maybe a goat or pig instead? Something bound for the slaughterhouse anyway. Just not a dog. Anything but this."

Rowan didn't even bother responding before she drew her blade again and sliced Wes's abdomen open. Her cuts were never deep. They didn't need to be. With nothing more than her touch, she could make Wes feel like she'd disemboweled him.

Aidan braced himself for the worst. Naomi reached for

his hand, hers warm with her power. The moment Rowan's hand touched Wes's belly, he cried out and Aidan's vision blurred with the white-hot agony ripping through his lower half. Convinced his guts lay on the ground at his feet, Aidan almost fell to his knees. But Naomi held him up, her warmth snaking up his arm, lessening the pain.

A gasp of surprise left her lips, as her brow furrowed. This was dangerous. He wanted to throttle Naomi for trying something new out in the open like this, but Rowan was focused on Wes and Ezra now, her minions watching her with little reaction. Little Lola and Ace always stood by watching quietly with dead eyes.

"We've got this," Naomi whispered, her hand trembling in his.

"Careful you two." Pilar took a small step in front of them to shield them from notice. "Keep your eyes down."

Naomi was taking Aidan's pain. Sharing it with him so it was manageable.

Wes tried not to react to Rowan's torture, but he couldn't hold back his screams any longer.

"I'm sorry, Wes! I'm sorry. I'll do it. Just please, Rowan, please stop hurting him," Ezra begged. "Give me a minute, please?" But that was not how Rowan operated.

"Do it now." Spencer shoved him toward the dog.

"I'm so sorry," Ezra whispered, kneeling down to hold the mamma dog in his arms. He looked to Aidan for help, but there was nothing Aidan could do to ease the suffering of the dog. He could only help humans.

"It's okay, Ezra," Ivy said. "Do what you have to do for Wes."

Ezra nodded, wincing at Wes's screams of agony. The dog began to whine, pulling away from his strong arms. "I'm sorry, girl," his tone was soothing, but tears streamed down his face.

That was when Spencer touched him with her brand of torture. Ezra sobbed, clutching the dog to his chest, siphoning off her vitality and strength, as Spencer manipulated his emotions to make it that much worse. Where Rowan tore through layers of skin and flesh to expose every raw nerve of her victims to enhance their physical pain and suffering, Spencer reached into their minds, laying their emotions bare, making them feel more emotional pain than they could bear. For someone as kind and sensitive as Ezra, Spencer's torture was far worse than Rowan's.

"That's right," Spencer whispered in his ear. "Feel her fear. The way she fights for her life. The lives of her pups."

The mother growled and struggled in Ezra's arms but she was weakening. Her pups whined and cried, sensing their mother's distress.

"Please," Ezra cried. "I have taken enough. More than enough. Let me spare her life so she can recover. There is no need for death here."

"No." Rowan carved a path along Wes's chest, peeling his skin away to expose his raw nerve endings. "Finish it."

Wes's legs gave out and he sagged against the beam behind him, hanging from his restraints. "It's okay Ezra," he managed to gasp, his body covered in a sheen of sweat.

Aidan stood rock solid, measuring his breath and praying he could stay on his feet long enough to get through this.

"It's done. Let him go." Ezra stumbled away from the dead dog. Her pups cried and howled, sniffing their mother and finding no spark of life left. "It's done." Ezra's breath came out in a shaky gasp.

"Run," Rowan demanded, tearing the skin away from the left side of Wes's chest, eliciting an inhuman scream from her victim. Dark spots narrowed Aidan's vision and he clutched Naomi's hand, hating that she likely felt the same sensations.

"It's okay," she murmured. "We've got this."

Ezra finished the lap around the field seventeen seconds faster. He snatched up the bow and arrow with purpose, his eyes blazing with the heat of his power and laser sharp focus. As his arrow hit the heart of the paper target, the bull's eye flamed for a moment, curling the paper before it smoldered to ash.

"We are done," Ezra said, his voice stronger now with the life of the mother dog enhancing his natural abilities.

"The puppies." Rowan continued to carve up Wes's body, working on his back now.

Wes's breath came in labored, shallow pants. He was losing too much blood and Aidan wasn't sure he had much life left in him.

Fortified by the life of the mother, one by one, Ezra took the innocent lives of three puppies before Rowan was satisfied that with each life, his performance improved by a predictable fraction.

"We are done here," Pilar said. "I don't want you killing my student. It will just throw us all behind schedule waiting for Wes to regenerate. His recovery time will be slow enough as it is."

"You will keep the last two pups," Spencer said. "Raise them and learn to love them. They are to be with you wherever you go." Her voice had taken on a rasp of her power, making her appear insane as she leaned over Ezra. "Feed them. And watch them grow. And when you least expect it, you will end them just as you have their mother."

"He is holding back," Rowan said. "He wants us to believe just one life is enough."

"I'm not. I promise," Ezra said. "My gift. It works just fine if I syphon off a few moments of life from many things, so little they wouldn't even notice. I do not need to take a life to achieve more."

"We know that." Spencer laughed. "But you need to understand your place, darling. When you are given an order, you do not question it. Period."

"Yes ma'am." Ezra's face hardened. "Understood ... loud and clear." He took a step away from the crazy woman.

"Don't forget your puppies. They'll die without help." Spencer's maniacal laughter chilled Aidan's blood. He wanted to slay these crazy bitches where they stood, but he couldn't afford to display that kind of power. It wasn't the time.

Sam and Bennett stepped forward to take the pups, but Rowan shot them a look that sent them back in line. "Ezra will care for them. And only Ezra."

With a nod, he knelt to scoop up the puppies. They were terrified and snuggled into his arms. Their whimpers faded, but Ezra looked like he wanted to die.

"It's like watching *Old Yeller*," Neela whispered, clutching Ivy to her side.

"From now on, Ezra, you will begin your day just like today, taking a life to increase your own potential. It will get easier with time. And one day when it really matters, you will not hesitate to take a life when it becomes necessary." Without a word, Rowan and her team left the field, dropping Wes in a puddle of his own blood.

"Bastards," Neela fumed after their retreating forms. The only response was Spencer's peal of laughter.

Once the doors closed behind them, Aidan let out a strangled breath as he and Naomi collapsed.

CHAPTER 24

Allie | Kelleys Island | April

"You really love him, don't you?" Allie asked. She'd always thought Livia preyed on Navid's emotions. That by calling him "Dad," she was just buying his goodwill. Allie had been convinced her sister was playing on his sympathies to earn his trust and eventually her freedom. But Livia was a wreck since losing Navid.

"He is my father." Livia crossed her arms over her chest, her eyes red from lack of sleep. "And I am stuck in this god forsaken cell with this stupid collar around my neck, unable to do anything about it. When all I want to do is lay waste to the world of dreams until I find him."

"It's not really a cell anymore," Allie said. "You can leave whenever you want." She still couldn't bring herself to release Livia from her collar.

"It still feels like a cell."

"We will bring him back," Allie said, but she didn't know how. It had taken Quinn's team nearly two years to find the prison dreamscape. How long before they found it again?

"I didn't want to love him." Livia shook her head. "When he first came to visit me here in this cell, I didn't want to have anything to do with him or you. I've never had a true family. I love my mother, but we've spent more time apart than we have together. Marcus made sure of that. I hardly know her anymore."

"But he is Navid." Allie sighed. "You want to hate him for all the lies and manipulations."

"But you can't because he's our father, and his love is the most genuine I've ever known," Livia said. "God, I wanted to hate him for all the lies. For letting Marcus take me from my home when I was only four years old, knowing the next time I would see my parents would be the night Marcus ordered me to kill the Chief Justice." She hung her head in shame. "I vowed I would never forgive Navid for letting that happen."

Allie cringed at the mention of their mother's death. She hated Livia for what she'd done, but she saw it in her sister's eyes. Kassandre's death tormented her. In that moment, Allie realized what an immense burden that grief must be for her sister to carry all alone. Livia was just a tool, a weapon Marcus used to destroy his enemy. He was the true murderer. He was the reason Livia and Allie had lost their mother before they ever got a chance to know her.

"Navid is humble, and he has such a quiet strength," Allie said. "He never rushes you. He kind of just lets you find your way back to him. And before you know it, you love him like he was always your father, and you'd forgive him anything."

"It's kind of hard to stay mad at him when he and Kassandre were only trying to give us the best chance they could," Livia said. "He once told me the path they chose for me was the one life where you and I would be friends, working on the same side. I laughed in his face and told him it would never happen."

"I don't know, we're not exactly friends, but if we both

trust him and love him, maybe that's enough for now," Allie said.

"You still got the better life," Livia teased.

"I know." Allie gave a reluctant smile.

"But you got a crappy deal, too, kid."

"Same side of the fight?" Allie examined her sister with her gift, searching for any signs that she might not be as trustworthy as she seemed. Over the last two years of her captivity, Livia had changed. The woman before her now finally matched the things Allie's gift had always seen in her.

"You have nothing to fear from me, Allie. I want Marcus to pay for the terrible things he's done more than anyone."

"Our parents made the right choices for me. I forgave them for that a long time ago," Allie said. "It's difficult to see how their choices for you were the right ones, but I know we need to move on from our pasts. I can't forgive you for what you did to Ming Lao. Every time we speak, I feel like I am betraying Chloe. Even though she's gone now, pursuing a life of her own making, she will always be like a sister to me."

"If I could change it, I would," Livia's voice grew distant. "I thought I was trapped and I—"

"You protected yourself the only way you knew how." Allie interrupted. "Logically, I know that."

"I don't need you to forgive me, Allie. Hate me for the things I've done. Let Chloe hate me for as long as she needs to. What I did to her family is my shame. But if you can separate your hate of my past actions and terrible choices from the woman I am trying to become, I will never let you down again."

Allie nodded, overcome with a desire to know her sister. "One day at a time. That's all I can manage right now."

"I despise my gift," Livia said. "I always have. I would be

rid of it in an instant if there was a way to make sure the gift died rather than manifest in another."

"I can relate," Allie said carefully. Only three people knew what she was capable of. For the first time, she felt like she might be ready to trust Livia with her secrets. The green aura of her gift danced in her peripheral vision, telling her she needed to confide in her sister, that this moment of growth would set them on the right path forward.

"You think you can understand what it's like to rip Complements apart? To kill one and leave the other to survive?" Her tone wasn't filled with contempt like it once was. Hope shone in Livia's eyes at the thought that Allie might actually understand.

"Not in the way you do. But I do understand what it's like to have a gift you'd give anything not to have. A gift you can never relinquish to another for fear of what they might do with it. The sense of duty to keep such a gift simply because you know it's your destiny to bear the burden of it."

"You don't have to tell me," Livia said. "I can tell by the way you speak of it, you do understand." Livia reached for her hand, hesitating. Allie took her sister's hand, giving a gentle squeeze.

"I think I'd like you to know my secret. You could use it against me someday, but I'd like to think you wouldn't betray me like that."

"I will take your secrets to my grave, little sister."

"I can also kill with my gift."

"Lots of people can kill with their gifts, Allie."

"Kill Immortals?"

"Explain," Livia said, sitting on the edge of her seat.

"You know how Navid's judgment gift works?"

"He can weigh an Immortal's character and if his gift finds them guilty, he can send them into a deep sleep for a time to a place in the dreamworld similar to Brecken's towers. Like a prison sentence."

"I can also punish the guilty, but my gift strips the criminal of their immortality. So, in a way, I send one Immortal to a mortal death, leaving their Complement to a life of solitude. I do understand the gravity of what you can do and how it weighs on you."

Livia sat back in her seat, her leg bouncing.

"I can't hurt anyone," Allie rushed to explain. "Not without cause. I can't just go around taking immortality willy-nilly. It only works if my judgment gift finds them guilty of a heinous crime."

"Why they haven't put you in a cell down here next to me, I don't know."

"I know," Allie said softly. "It would be safer for every one if I did stay down here."

"No, Allie. Safer for you, silly girl. Do you know how many Immortals would hunt you if they knew what you could do? Do you have any idea what Marcus would do to you?"

"Believe me, I've had that lecture from Liam and Gregg often enough. I know how our world would react if they knew. But they don't. Only four people know. Including you."

"Do you remember seeing me in New Zealand just before your Awakening?" Livia asked.

"I'll never forget that day." Allie smiled. "It was the catalyst that changed my life forever. We moved to Sydney a few days later to be closer to Navid. I didn't know it at the time, but he was keeping watch over me."

"The moment I saw you with your mortal father, I knew you were special. I knew you were exactly the kind of young Immortal Marcus liked to collect and I felt a strange desire to protect you from him. For the first time, it struck me that someone like you could be the child of prophecy he sought. A girl. The perfect ruse because Marcus Servius would never anticipate the powerful child of prophecy could ever be a woman. Each time our paths crossed, little sister, I was trying to get to you before Marcus could. I was trying to protect you. Always."

Allie didn't know how to respond to that, but the ice around her heart, keeping her sister at bay, was finally thawing despite her best efforts to resist.

"Have you ever ... used that ability?" Livia asked.

Allie nodded. "Just once. The night of the Blood Moon when you came for us. One of your people attacked Aidan and tried to take his gift. I lost my shit when I saw it, and it just happened. It took me a while to figure out what I'd done."

"That's why I can sometimes sense Michael down here. He's in another cell?"

"We don't know what to do with him." Allie wiped the moisture from her eyes.

"Leave him there to rot. He deserves it and if you knew half of what he's done, you wouldn't feel bad about it. I ran Soma with an iron fist, and I did some awful things there, but there was one difference between me and those like Michael. He enjoyed torturing kids like Santi and Quinn, but I hated every minute of my life there. Every life I ruined will weigh on my conscience forever. Do not waste a single tear on that man, you hear me, Allie? He isn't worth your tears. You did the world a favor."

"But he has a Complement out there just waiting for him, not knowing he will die. That's a second life ruined who didn't deserve it."

"She'd likely thank you for it. The Complement bond is

not always a fairytale romance. There are times when two people who are madly in love just aren't good for each other. Marcus loves my mother but he abuses her. She let him for a long time. I was never so proud of her as I was when I learned she'd escaped him. I hope she never goes back to him. Michael's Complement might be just like him and they could do awful things together, or he or she might be a wonderful person he would have corrupted. You can't blame yourself for doing what you did to save Aidan from a terrible fate."

"Let's get out of here." Allie stood and crossed the room.

"What? I don't feel like going to the Yard."

"Grab your things for tonight. We're leaving this cell. You don't deserve to be here anymore and we're getting that collar off you tonight."

"Allie, we should talk to Gregg and Liam about this."

"I already have. They wanted to do this weeks ago, but I wasn't ready. I didn't trust you."

"And you trust me now?"

"I can see it in your eyes, and it's written all over your face. You love Navid and you love me. I convinced myself you were just playing him for a fool. But I was the fool. Let's go find you a new room. We're not sticking you in the Yard with the old people. It's turning into a retirement home out there. I think I have just the place for you."

"Let's go." Livia grabbed a few things and stuffed them in an overnight bag.

"We'll come back for the rest tomorrow," Allie said.

"I'm dying for a change of scenery."

Allie felt bad for leaving Livia in her cell for so long. She still wasn't ready to forgive her for the death of their mother or Ming Lao. But for now, she had to do the right thing and let her sister live in a proper apartment within the underground. She had to allow herself the chance to get to know

Livia and see if they could be friends—enough to work together as their parents intended. She wasn't there yet, but she knew she wanted to be.

"Where are we going?" Livia asked, following Allie up the stairs from the crypt and across the common room. "I've never been to this part of the underground." She glanced around, admiring the high fan-vaulted ceilings beyond the common room. "It's beautiful." She gazed up at the fine Gothic relief carvings that made the vaulted ceiling erupt in an array of fans.

"Naeemah?" Allie knocked on her office door.

"Come in, Allie," Naeemah called.

"I was wondering if you could help us," Allie said.

"Livia." Naeemah stood. "It's wonderful to finally see you out of that cell."

"Thank you," Livia said. "It's wonderful to be out."

"Can she stay here?" Allie asked. "Near your garden? And can we remove the collar?"

"Of course." Naeemah stood, taking a ring of keys from her desk drawer. "I am happy you've come to this decision on your own, Allie." She twisted the key in the lock at the base of Livia's neck.

"Thank you." Livia breathed a sigh of relief as Naeemah removed the heavy collar. "I feel lighter already."

"Well now, let's see about your rooms, shall we? Follow me, girls, we'll have your new place feeling like a home in no time."

Allie smiled, taking Livia's hand and tugging her down the hall after Naeemah.

"These rooms are perfect for you, Livia." Allie stepped through a pair of sliding barn doors into a huge living space, filled with sunlight from Naeemah's garden. "I've stayed here a few times. I think you'll enjoy the garden.

"It's beautiful, Naeemah." Livia crossed the room to the sliding glass doors opening to Naeemah's private garden.

"Feel free to spend as much time out there as you'd like. I can imagine you're starved for sunshine. The Yard is nice, but I find my terrarium a little more appealing."

"I love it." Livia took a deep breath, inhaling the floral fragrances from the garden.

"There is a nice sized bedroom back here." Naeemah opened a second set of barn doors. "And a lovely master bath, too. You can use the kitchen in the common room as much as you like. But we can set up a small kitchenette for you in here, too."

"And we'll bring up all your things tomorrow," Allie added. "All of your pretty white furnishings will look great in here against the dark wood flooring.

"There are toiletries in the bathroom, so make yourself at home tonight," Naeemah said. "And if there is anything else you need that we don't have here, just make a list, and we'll get it for you."

"Oh Naeemah, you and your family have done more than enough for ours. We'd be lost without you and Gregg." Livia seemed overwhelmed with her feels—not something she was accustomed to. "True kindness has been such a rare thing in my life. I never believed it existed until you people stuck me in a prison cell and forced me to see it for myself."

"We are honored to witness the real Livia coming back to herself," Naeemah said. "And I'm so glad to see you two getting along. There is nothing like the love of a sister."

Chapter 25

Aidan | Milan, Italy | April

"We've got to shut this down," Bennett said. Always a man of few words, his furious pacing across the back of the pub spoke volumes. "Can't we just leave?" He dropped his hands to his sides. "Before it gets any worse. We can't keep doing this."

They'd all spent the afternoon watching Ivy and Neela suffer for concealing a gift from Rowan and her team. Together, they could create an odd blue mist to protect them like a shield from their enemies. The girls held out as long as they could, but Rowan pulled it out of them. They had no secrets now. She'd made an example of them, making it clear that concealing anything from her was the best way to earn a bigger punishment.

Ivy was recovering from Rowan's blade and Neela refused to leave her side, suffering from her own stint with Spencer. The rest were laying low. But Aidan, Naomi, Sam, Bennett and Wes had left on the pretense of enjoying an *aperitivo*—an Italian happy hour—at the local cafe as a break from the intensity of the last few days. But they were really meeting with Pilar to discuss their options.

"Ben's right. We need to get out. Now," Sam said. "This is not what we signed up for."

Aidan shared a look with Naomi. With Rowan and Spencer breathing down their necks and the Chief Justice pulling the strings, their chances of escape were grimmer than ever. If they tried to leave now, they wouldn't make it far before Rowan hunted them down like dogs.

"They will just drag us back here and then it will be ten times worse," Naomi said. "If we're ever going to get out of here we need more than just a plan for escape."

"She's right. Running is not an option," Pilar said. Dressed in street clothes with her braids swept back from her face, she looked like one of the team. "I can't risk staying very long." She glanced over her shoulder out the window before she sat down beside Aidan in the secluded booth. "I wanted to warn you all while I had the chance. They expect you to run. They're waiting for it, so we all have to stay put for now. I have a plan. It's not a great one, but it's the only one that will get us out of this mess permanently."

"I like the sound of permanent. Whatever your plan is, we're on board," Ben said.

"It will take time, and you'll have to convince Rowan of your loyalty. Once she reports back that she has you all under her control, they will start sending you on assignments to prepare you for the takeover at Soma. That's their end game. Sarah wants it so bad she can taste it. So we all have to play their game for a little while. You've got to convince the Initiative you are lethal soldiers willing to do whatever they ask. You will perform whatever tasks they give you to perfection, but when they send you to Soma, you don't come back. You go in, infiltrate the system, and then you take over, but you don't hand the reins over to the Chief Justice. You keep it for yourselves. Convince those on the inside that you're the good guys who will actually put an end to the abuse they've experienced. Soma can give you the protection you're all going to need. It's your only way out."

"And what do we do when the Senate comes after us at Soma?" Naomi asked. "What's stopping them from blowing us off the map and sending us to prison for an eternity?"

"*You.*" Pilar said. "All of you. Your generation is so much stronger than you realize. You have the power to seize this world from the ancients and make it into something much greater than it has ever been. That terrifies the older generations. They don't want change. You have no idea how difficult the last three hundred years have been for Immortals. The world has evolved more in the last three centuries than in the previous millennia combined. The Senate wants to keep you under their thumb. They want to control you so you fear them, but they also hunger for your abilities to use for their own benefit. They'll never destroy you. You're too valuable."

"So if we used Soma to make a stand, you don't think they would retaliate?" Aidan asked, not sure he agreed with her.

"They would in time, of course, but if we plan this right, you'll have time to organize. Who knows what abilities you might have at your disposal to protect the building once you're inside? Ivy and Neela's blue mist gave me the idea. I know they would struggle to shield an entire building on their own, but what if they had help?"

"We could work with them to enhance that ability," Naomi said, her eyes brightening at the idea. "Once we're inside Soma, we could find abilities like theirs and set up shifts around the clock to keep the Senate out of Sterling Tower. We could shield ourselves from outside influence."

"It could work," Wes said. "If we spend every moment planning the takeover to our advantage."

"Can you get us plans of the building?" Aidan asked.

"I have a friend on the inside I can call. He is trustworthy and ready for a change," Pilar said. "Does this mean you're in?"

"I don't know, Pilar." Aidan sat back against the worn leather of the booth. "We could probably take the building by force, yeah, but keeping it? Inspiring all the people inside to stay and work with us? I don't know." Aidan glanced down at his hands. He didn't want to be a leader. Not like this. "Your plan is risky. What happens if we fail to recruit the Soma residents?"

"You inspire loyalty, Aidan," Pilar said gently. "It oozes from your ears. This group is a family, and you and Naomi are the glue that holds it together. If you step up and take over, the young people of your generation will follow you." Pilar gave him a level stare. "Hell, you inspire me, and I'm older than dirt."

"It has potential," Aidan relented. "But do you really think they will send all of us to Soma together? Even if they did trust us all to be there at the same time, Rowan and her team would be there too and she'll never go along with this."

"Once we're inside, we can deal with her," Pilar said. "But right now, escape is unlikely. The Chief Justice fears the strength your bond gives you. But with Aidan in particular ... they're obsessed. They believe you are some kind of answer to an old prophecy. They're practically giddy whenever your name comes up. There's no way they would allow you to escape their grasp."

"Prophecy?" Samantha scowled.

"Not the first time I've heard that." Aidan sighed. It was only a matter of time before someone higher up the chain made that connection. "Whatever they might think, it's not about me." But if Sarah and Charles Madison were eager to find the child of prophecy, then Aidan wanted them to believe it was him to keep Allie off their radar. And if he could get inside Soma and somehow start a mutiny ... and if he could find a way to protect the building and those inside, then the Senate couldn't touch them and they wouldn't have to hide. But it would all eventually come to a head. They couldn't stay behind the walls of Soma forever, but Aidan couldn't picture what that future looked like with him standing against the Senate as a criminal.

"Promise me, you will all consider the plan for Soma?" Pilar pleaded. "No matter what we do, we cannot let Soma fall into the Chief Justice's hands. Because what you're experiencing right now? They will do to every child inside Sterling Tower. And I promise you, those kids have already been through enough."

"I'm in," Samantha said. "I want out of the Initiative like yesterday, but Pilar is right, guys. We can't let this happen to anyone else. Just look at those poor kids on Rowan's team. It has to stop with us."

"I'm in," Bennett and Wes echoed.

"Aidan, I know I'm asking a lot of you and Naomi," Pilar said. "Take some time to think about it."

Aidan nodded, taking a sip of the watered down bourbon in his glass. She wasn't just asking a lot. She was asking him to head an army with the sole purpose of defying their government. What she was asking was suicide. Treason and pure insanity. And it might be their only way out.

"I've got to go. We don't want anyone seeing us all together like this. It's best if you all leave soon." Pilar slipped out of the booth and retreated to the back entrance through the kitchen.

"Do you know what we've just agreed to?" Naomi asked, swirling the contents of her drink with a straw.

"To staying here for at least another year?" Bennett sighed. "Yeah."

"I never wanted to be a damn hero." Naomi folded her arms across her chest. "Part of me just wants to go home and forget any of this is happening. And the other part of me wants to see Rowan part ways with her head."

"I'll drink to that." Aidan tossed the rest of his bourbon down in one gulp, wishing it would give him courage to keep fighting. Strength to get through another day without Allie. He was beginning to wonder if he'd ever see her again. That thought alone had him searching for answers at the bottom of a bottle most nights.

"Oh God." All the color drained from Naomi's face. Naomi, the feisty hellcat who wasn't scared of anything, was reduced to trembling hands and tear-filled eyes at the sight of Rowan making her way across the bar.

Their table fell silent as Rowan slid into the booth next to Wes, her face impossible to read.

"Who gave you all permission to leave the grounds?" Her voice sounded oddly normal.

"We come down here all the time," Bennett said. "We have permission to visit the village whenever we want.

"Not anymore. Cleo and Genevieve have been far too lax with their permissions. So, I'll say this once and only once. You are property, plain and simple. You belong to the Chief Justice, and you will abide by their rules. You are free to come and go as you please during your free time. Hell, I don't care if you want to drive to Paris for the weekend, but in the future, if you want to leave the grounds, you will ask my permission first. But you will *never ... ever* leave the grounds with your Syntrophos." She shot a glare at Aidan and Naomi, Sam and Bennett. "Your partner is our insurance policy. A guarantee you will return and not have thoughts about running away together. Are we clear?"

"Yes," Aidan and the others responded quickly. Any thought of escaping was out of the question now. Not for the first time, Aidan thought about taking her out. He and Naomi could handle Rowan and Spencer—if it was just them he had to worry about. But there was also Gemma and Ruthie, and Ace and Lola on her team, as well as Rowan's entourage of guards, not to mention Cleo and Genevieve. There were too many outside factors standing between Aidan and his team and their freedom.

"It doesn't have to be this difficult," Rowan said. "Fall in line and show me your loyalty and we'll all get along just fine." She waved to the waitress to get her attention, rattling off her order and a round for everyone else in perfect Italian. Rowan propped her feet on the empty seat in front of her. "So what are we drinking to?"

"I don't know about everyone else, but I'm drinking to forget the last couple of weeks," Aidan said. Never in his whole life had he ever felt like such a coward for wanting to escape. Not that he would ever leave anyone behind to save his own skin. He was just so homesick. He missed his family and the agony of missing Allie was with him every day. He spent his waking nights imagining what her life was like now. And every now and then, he had a weak moment when he spied on her through their link. He carefully guarded his presence in her mind so she would never know he was there. But he couldn't help himself. Sometimes she talked to him. Still, after more than a year of silence between them, when she said his name, he could hear it. She missed him but she'd moved on. She was happy. It killed him every time he drifted a little too close to her thoughts. But it was the most bittersweet heaven in the midst of his own hell.

"I'll drink to that," Bennett said. "And it'd be a whole lot easier to forget if you weren't here, Rowan," he added bravely.

The tension hung thick in the air between Bennett and Rowan, but he didn't back down.

The waitress brought their drinks and made herself scarce.

"It's all an act, you know." Rowan picked up her martini, plucking an olive from the plastic spear sitting in her glass. "A way to survive. You'll each find your own ways of surviving, too. In a few years, you'll be no different from me or any of my predecessors."

"I can't vouch for the others, but nothing could ever make me do what you did to Ivy just a few hours ago." Bennett's hands balled into fists like he was trying not to wrap his hands around her throat.

"You say that now. But they'll find what makes you tick and they'll use it. Right now, it's your Syntrophos. But what happens when they have your Complement, too?" She sipped her drink. "Believe it or not, I don't enjoy what I do. But doing what I do ... and doing it well, keeps the man I love safe. And eventually, I will earn his freedom. Right now, he's trapped inside Soma, experiencing the same horrors you're all facing now. So, I whip you all into shape, and he gets a light day, a good meal, and some much needed rest. I don't do it, and you can guess what that means."

"I've heard that same song and dance before," Aidan said. "I have a friend who struck the same deal once a few hundred years ago. He still hasn't reunited with his Complement." Greyson's deal was once with the Coalition, but in Aidan's mind they were all the same.

"Wait," Sam said. "That doesn't make any sense. The Chief Justice wants us to take over Soma, so they have you manipulating us to get us to do it. So, how can they also influence what happens to your Complement if he's *inside* Soma? The same Soma they want to control? You're lying."

"She's telling the truth," Aidan said. "The person behind Soma is the same person behind the Milan Initiative. He's playing both sides. The Chief Justice are in his pocket. Pawns like the rest of us." He knew very little about Livia's father, Marcus Servius. Just the few details Quinn and Santi had told him, but he knew enough to suspect he was likely the real benefactor behind the Milan Initiative. He'd built Soma into a powerhouse. A man like that would be on to the next bigger and better thing—an army of Syntrophos.

"And here I thought you were all mindless sheep." Rowan smiled. "Aidan pays attention."

"So, why stage this bullshit takeover at all?" Bennett asked. "Why waste time training us to take over Soma if they've already got it?"

"It's a coup for the Chief Justice. To our world, they will look like heroes," Rowan said. "Re-electable heroes. While behind the scenes, Soma just moves from his left hand to his right."

"Who are we talking about?" Wes demanded. "Who is this person making decisions for me and my Syntrophos?"

"You don't want to know," Aidan and Rowan said at the same time.

Aidan stared at Rowan as if seeing her for the first time. "What do you know of him?" He asked, not expecting an answer.

"Who do you think trained me?" she said in a hushed tone while the others continued to talk over them. "I have his ear. More than the fools who believe they are in charge of this venture."

"Why are you telling me this?" Aidan asked. "If you're

trying to gain my loyalty, it's not going to work."

"I don't need your loyalty. You can see me as a monster without a conscious, but I do what I must to take care of my own. They are my responsibility, and my loyalty lies with them and only them. Can't you imagine what I wouldn't give to be in the same room with my Syntrophos and my Complement? What I wouldn't give for the opportunity to keep them both safe? Until that miracle happens, I am a tool Marcus wields as he pleases." Rowan stood, tossing some *lira* on the table. "Order another round and then get back to your rooms. And remember the rules next time."

Aidan sat in silence, watching her leave. She was trying to tell him something without saying it. Whether she meant to or not, Rowan had just given him a great idea—if Naomi would go along with it.

If Aidan was going to sweep Soma beyond Marcus's reach, he needed to earn his trust. And if he played his cards right, Marcus would think he had the child of prophecy under his thumb at last. Aidan could use that to his advantage. When the time came for them to make a move against Soma, Marcus wouldn't think twice about sending the full army of Syntrophos to seize Sterling Tower for the Senate—including Rowan and her team. He would get her in the same room with her Syntrophos and her Complement. Aidan would give her the miracle she craved and when he did, she would cast her lot in with him. That was the only way Aidan could be sure no one was left behind.

"Who is this Marcus guy and what's he after?" Bennett asked, interrupting Aidan's thoughts.

"Power. Total control." Aidan shrugged. "It doesn't matter. He's on the wrong track anyway."

"How do you know all of this?" Wes asked.

"To be honest, I'm making a lot of guesses, but I know I'm

right. It's the prophecy." Aidan swirled the last of his drink around the bottom of the glass.

"So there *is* a prophecy about you?" Bennett asked.

"It's not about me," Aidan said. "Marcus will think it is. And that's fine, let him." As long as Marcus was fixated on him, he wouldn't spare a second thought for Allie.

"What does this prophecy say?" Wes asked.

"That a child will repair the damage our ancestors caused during the Great War. That he will lead us into an uncertain future filled with darkness." Naomi offered. "Many have thought Aidan is this child." She met his gaze. "And our family has had a few close calls with this Marcus guy."

"If it's not about Aidan, then who is it about?"

"We don't really know," Naomi explained. She still didn't know the prophecy was about Allie, though she might suspect it by now.

"It's about all of us," Aidan said. He would protect Allie no matter what, but her role in the prophecy was only one part. They were all in this together. "Our generation will rise up as one to stand against the corruption of our world—a corruption Marcus is responsible for. I'm beginning to wonder if Soma is where we make our stand. If we do this, I need everyone to trust me. Can I count on you all?"

Naomi gave him a worried look. "Of course."

"We're behind you a hundred percent," Samantha said.

"You can count on me and Ezra too." Wes added.

Aidan nodded, grateful for their loyalty. He just wished he could talk to his father. Gregg would talk him through this. But the moment Aidan reached out to his family, Cleo and Genevieve would be on Allie like a pack of wild dogs. If he risked it, he could end up just like Rowan and he wouldn't allow the two most important women in his life to be used against him like that.

Chapter 26

Allie | Cleveland | April

Allie paced the length of the barn gym back at her house. After nearly two months, Navid was still lost in the dreamworld, a captive within Brecken's prison tower and they still didn't have a plan to get him out. It killed her to watch his body waste away. He slept, ate, and shuffled around his home in the Yard. He mumbled and muttered when she tried to talk to him, but his mind was far away, locked in the world of dreams for as long as Brecken deigned to keep him prisoner. Everyone insisted she had to move on, but Allie and Livia spent every spare moment in the dreamworld searching for their father.

"Is there any change?" Allie blurted the moment her mentor walked through the door. She hadn't visited Navid in nearly a week and she was anxious for news of his condition.

"I'm sorry, no," Emma said. "Navid is resting comfortably at home. Raina is taking good care of him, making sure he eats and drinks and gets plenty of rest. His physical body is fine."

But he wasn't fine. Not in his mind. "I was just hoping for a change." Allie sank to the mat.

"Quinn and his walkers are working day and night to bring him home, Allie."

"I know. So what's on our agenda today?"

"Give me a second to catch my breath. I feel like I've been running a marathon today." She shrugged out of her jacket, her eyes sweeping up to the finished hayloft. "Our training room is ready?"

"It has walls, but we don't have any furniture up there yet. Or air conditioning."

"Oh. Bummer. I was hoping for a more comfortable space for our session today."

"We're not working out?"

"Not today."

"Want to hang out in the house? Everyone's at school, except Darius. We don't have class until this afternoon. I can tell him to make himself scarce."

"Let's do that. I don't relish sitting on the floor if we don't have to. These old bones are feeling their age today."

"We just need to find the time to furnish this place, and we'll be more comfortable here."

"You know, Livia has turned her new apartment into a beautiful space, and she's bored to death in the underground. I bet she'd be happy to order some things for the gym."

"Sounds good to me. I bet we could bring her here and let her go nuts. She'd love a field trip." Allie led her mentor through the barn doors and across the lawn to the little cottage she shared with her friends and Darius.

"Tea?" Allie offered. "I don't have coffee. It keeps disappearing when Naeemah visits."

"Yes, please, I'd love some tea and anything you have to eat. I'm starving." Emma climbed wearily onto a bar stool at the kitchen counter. "You know, one of these days, you're going to win that war with Naeemah." Emma laughed. "How do you even manage to buy coffee anymore? She's hit every grocery store in the city by now."

"You can't rat me out, Emma." Allie poured filtered water into the electric teakettle. "It's my secret weapon." She placed a hand on the kettle, heating the water with her solar gift. It was just faster than the old fashioned way.

"Your secret's safe with me."

"Well, it turns out, Naeemah can't work her magic mind mojo on a U Scan It machine so I sneak a few items into my shopping every week, coffee being the number one contraband item in this house. That and chocolate."

"But you're sticking to your clean diet most of the time, right? It's my duty to ask as your mentor."

"I actually don't mind the clean diet if I can have my vices every once in a while."

"Naeemah would likely agree with you and put an end to this nonsense."

"No way, man, we're having too much fun messing with each other."

Emma rolled her eyes. Eyes with dark circles.

"You sure you're okay, Emma? You look tired. Is everything okay at home?" Allie sorted through her tins of looseleaf tea searching for her favorite chamomile. She would deny it until the ends of the earth, but she'd recently discovered she actually loved tea. She wasn't about to turn her back on coffee, but she'd cut down on her caffeine intake since Naeemah strong-armed her into a clean diet. It wasn't so bad.

"I'm just so … exhausted with everything." Emma rubbed a palm across her brow.

"Any news of Chloe or Jin?" Allie asked.

"She doesn't want to be found and Jin won't rest until he brings her home. It's been a year." Emma's shoulders slumped. "I just worry about her. And Jin's not in his right mind. It's so heartbreaking to watch the way they use their abilities against each other. Jin follows her trail using his probabilities gift."

"And Chloe evades him with her version of that same gift." Allie sighed. "She can see his decisions before he even makes them."

"Chloe is capable. I know she can take care of herself and she'll come home when she's ready," Emma said. "I just wish Jin could see that for himself. If he would stop chasing her, she might settle down somewhere safe. For most of the last year, she's frequented the Boston area a lot. I can't help but think Chloe would stay with Graham near MIT if we'd just leave her alone."

"How is Graham?" Allie asked, trying to steer her mentor away from talk of Chloe.

Emma smiled. "He's doing great. I can't believe his freshman year of college is already behind him. He'll be home for the summer soon, and I can't wait to baby him a little. I love having Quinn so close to home, but he's all grown up now. He's still so young, but he doesn't need me as much anymore."

"He will always need you," Emma."

"I know, but it's not fair." Emma fumbled with her tea infuser. "Soma stole so much from him. He's only twenty-two but he's Commander of the Dreamworld and fully in charge of his own life. I completely missed the years between his adolescence and adulthood. He was my first baby boy. And my first child since Hélène. The world was different when she was young and I made so many mistakes with her. There are almost five hundred years between my two eldest children. Adopting Quinn was like starting over, and I so wanted to get it right with him in a way I never did with Hélène. I don't know, maybe I finally have it right with Graham." She sipped her tea. "All you kids have had such trials over the years. It's just not right. I want to protect all of you from this cruel world as long as I can but it never seems to work out that way."

Allie stirred honey into her tea, wishing she had the right words to make Emma feel better. "I think despite the crappy things we've all been through, we're stronger because of it. Because you've all prepared us for what's out there." Allie said.

Emma took a sip of her tea, closing her eyes and letting her shoulders slump.

"I know you're stressed, but are you sure you're okay, Emma?" Allie couldn't put her finger on it, but her mentor was not her normal self. Emma thrived on chaos and was always moving at a million miles an hour. There was nothing she couldn't handle.

"I don't know, Allie. I'm feeling a little run down and tired, I guess. I don't think I'm sleeping enough." She reached for her fourth vegan, whole grain "donut" that Allie normally left for Sasha to eat. In her opinion, they made better coasters than food. "But enough about me," Emma said. "We need to talk about evolving gifts. You're due for another spurt of progress."

But Allie wasn't listening to Emma's rambling thoughts. Something was wrong with Emma. She was in danger. Allie could see her future filled with blood and pain. Emma's screams of agony and terror reverberated in Allie's mind. Darkness. A perfect storm of unpredictable chaos. Allie couldn't see through the veil obscuring her visions, but she could hear the foreign cry. Emma was headed for a change—one she likely wasn't expecting.

"Are you even listening to me, Allie?"

"What? No, sorry." The aura around Emma had gone

green, telling Allie she was on to something with substance. The green visions always happened one way or another no matter how much or how little she meddled with the outcome.

"What did you see just now? You're looking at me weird."

Allie shook her head. "Something's ... strange here." She pulled her mentor up from her chair. "Just stay there. Let me get a good look at you."

"Allie, seriously. I'm fine."

"Oh, my God. No way," Allie gasped, staring at her mentor with wide eyes. A smile spread across her face. *She doesn't know!* But why would she? She was more than eight hundred years old. It probably never occurred to her.

"Why are you looking at me like that, Allie?"

"How long have you been feeling out of sorts, Emma?" Allie finally asked, hoping to lead her to the realization on her own.

"A while. I don't know, really. It's nothing."

"Emma, it's not nothing." Allie tried to hide her smile behind her hands, but she was losing this battle. All the screaming and blood made sense now. It wasn't exactly a dangerous vision, although it did seem like Emma might be in for a difficult night.

"Why are you acting like a goof? What are you smiling about?" Emma frowned. "You're making me nervous."

"Emma ... I think you're pregnant." Allie clapped her hands over her mouth, trying to contain her excitement. She couldn't wait to meet the baby. It was a boy but she waned to keep that knowledge to herself.

"What? No way." Emma shook her head, sinking back into her chair. "You're just nuts, lady. Totally nuts." Her face went pasty white, and Allie feared she was about to faint.

"Emma, you don't look so good there. Can Immortals pass out from shock?"

"I-I don't know." Her hands shook. "I don't know anything."

"Breathe, Emma." Allie snatched up a magazine from the pile of mail by the teapot, furiously fanning Emma's face.

"You've lost your mind, Allie." Emma shook her head again. "I can't be having a *baby*." She said baby like babies were aliens from another planet.

"Oh, but you are." Allie grinned.

"Oh, but I'm, not. I'm old! I'm so freaking *old*. I should be thinking about grandchildren soon. Not babies. Not *my* babies. Maybe Quinn's babies. But no, I'm not even ready for that yet. He certainly isn't."

"Ming Lao was about your age when she had Chloe," Allie said softly, hoping to find the right words to calm Emma down because she was totally cracking right now.

"Shut your face." Emma reached for Allie's hand, squeezing it like a lifeline. "I'm scared, Allie. Oh please, be wrong." She closed her eyes. "Please, dear God, please let my sweet, amazingly talented clairvoyant student be dead wrong."

"Should I call Daniel?" Allie asked.

"Nu-uh, he'll freak out, and right now *I'm* freaking. He doesn't get to freak. Oh my God! I'm going to kill him. My stupid husband knocked me up."

"Emma, you're a wonderful mother. You can do this."

"Nope, nope." She shook her head. "This is not fair. We're infertile for God's sake. We don't get to have babies. We're taught all our lives that it will probably never happen for us. We adopt the lost Immortal children and love them as our own. I don't want to do this, Allie. I can't grow a tiny human inside me! You know how crazy that sounds?"

"It's rare, but it happens; you know this, Emma."

"Well it's not supposed to happen to me! Oh, lord. I don't know anything about being pregnant. How long does it last?"

"Whoa, Emma, you've got to take some deep breaths with me. Let's concentrate on not freaking out so that brain of yours starts working again."

"How much time do I have?"

"Okay, we are going to take a deep breath in. Okay, Emma?

She nodded, turning her frantic eyes on Allie.

"One. Two. Three. Deep breath." Allie sucked in air along with Emma. "Hold it. And breathe out." Allie coached her through another few breaths. "You breathe and I'll talk."

Emma nodded again, taking another big breath, still clutching Allie's hand like a vise.

"When was your last period?" Allie asked.

"I don't remember."

"You need to try," Allie said.

"Allie, for God's sake, it was easily before your were born. I don't remember the exact dates."

"Really?"

"Once you get a few hundred years under your belt, your cycle gets erratic."

"Did not know that. That's something to look forward to, because this every month crap is for the birds."

"Allie, focus!"

"Right. So pregnancy lasts nine months. You know this—or you would if you ever watched TV." Allie blew a stray curl from her face, racking her brain for a way to talk Emma through this. "Right, you were there with Ming through her pregnancy with Chloe. It's all going to come back to you once you've had time to absorb the shock. My gift tells me you're a little more than four months along." Emma's grip on her hand tightened, but she kept breathing.

"You're going to be fine. We have at least four months to prepare for our new baby." Allie pressed on Emma's tummy, feeling the swell of a baby bump Emma should have noticed. "We're all going to be right here with you through the whole thing, and we're all going to spoil that little baby rotten, and he or she will grow up with Kahlynn and be best friends."

Emma's breathing broke on a sob. "I'm scared. I can handle the baby part, but it's the pregnancy and delivering part that I'm freaking out about. I don't wanna."

"I don't blame you. I can't imagine the shock after more than eight hundred years of believing it'll never happen. The idea of it actually happening seems insane. But I promise, Emma, you're going to be the best pregnant mom there ever was."

"Did you see the birth? You looked terrified during your vision. What did you see?"

"Oh it was nothing. Just confusing. Why don't we call Daniel now?" Allie poured Emma another cup of tea and reached for her phone.

"No! Um. I need something stronger than tea." Emma glanced around the kitchen.

"You can't drink alcohol, Emma," Allie reminded her.

"Oh! You're right. See, I don't know anything. How about water? Ice cold water, please." She nodded, setting the steaming cup of tea aside. "And then can you take me home?"

"Of course." Allie moved to make her mentor a tall glass of water.

"Can you tell him?" Emma asked. "I don't think I can do it."

"Tell Daniel he's going to be a father? No way. That's your job, momma bear."

Chapter 27

Aidan | Milan, Italy | May

"Aidan, I'm not sure I can do this." Naomi paced across their narrow living quarters, arms hugging her chest. "I know we have to get these kids out of here, but are you sure this is the best way?" She turned to face him; the moonlight streaming in through the floor to ceiling windows cast a sliver aura around her. He could almost see her growing stronger under the nearly full moon.

"I don't know." Aidan hung his head, feeling the same pressure and regret she did. "We're playing a long game here and we don't know all the moves yet, but I'm afraid this might be our only way out. Once we're inside Sterling Tower, we'll be safe." Aidan dropped onto the slate-gray suede sofa feeling much older than his twenty years. It didn't matter if they ran now or waited for the Soma takeover; whenever they fled the initiative, the Chief Justice would paint them as criminals rebelling against their government. It would be a Syntrophos witch-hunt. But they would at least be safe inside Sterling Tower where no one could touch them. They'd figure out their next move then.

"And when will that be?" She turned to face him. "And

what happens if your plan doesn't work? What if we get inside Soma and Rowan doesn't help us like you think she will? It's her job to make sure we actually hand Soma over to the Chief Justice."

"I don't know, Naomi. We'll just have to deal with Rowan when the time comes," Aidan said, thrusting his hand through his too-long hair. "Pilar has already set this in motion. She told Cleo I'm the child of prophecy just like we planned. There's no turning back, so I need you to be strong for whatever's coming next."

"I will." She sat down next to him on the sofa. "You know I will. Naomi's eyes filled with frustrated tears she wiped away with her palm.

Aidan pulled Naomi onto his lap, wrapping his arms around her. "We have to stay the course. This plan will work, we just need to be patient."

"I don't like what this place is doing to you." Naomi leaned her head against his shoulder. "It's making you harder. Angrier."

"I'm distancing myself from the pain. Trying not to feel it as much. I can't allow Neela's pain or Ezra's fear to affect me. I have to harden myself to it because it's not going anywhere anytime soon."

"I can't do that. I show off my tough facade, but it's only skin deep. I don't know how to distance myself from this when kids are involved—and it just never ends."

"We have to take it one day at a time and focus on how we'll get through the next hour or minute. And remember at the end of all of this, we have an amazing family who will do everything they can for all of our people."

"And remind me again why we can't just ask them for help? We're in over our heads, Aidan and it's about to get worse with your insane plan."

"Cleo and Genevieve have threatened Allie and our family more times than I can count. I know my father could handle them, but this is the Chief Justice we're really talking about here. They believe I'm the child of prophecy. They aren't just going to let me walk away because I called my parents to come get me, Naomi. They would destroy my entire family just to keep me here."

"But the prophecy isn't even about you, Aidan. Please help me understand why you want them to think it is."

Aidan caught Naomi's gaze. They had to watch what they said, even in their private quarters. They could never forget how, with just a touch of her hand, Cleo could see and hear through walls. He reached inside himself, searching for the bond that connected them as Syntrophos. He couldn't talk to her like he could with Allie, but he could use the bond to get her attention. "We cannot risk our family or anyone we love. It's too dangerous." The bond ignited between them as Aidan willed Naomi to understand what he couldn't say in words. Allie *was* the child of prophecy and she was his Complement, too. He could not allow anyone to use her against him. Too much was at stake.

"I understand." Naomi's eyes flashed in the moonlight, their bond humming between them. "She is important," she whispered softly in his ear.

"And so are you," he said. "I need you on my side." Aidan laced his fingers through hers. "I will never survive this without you. But if you need to go, I will help you leave."

"Shut your face. I'm not going anywhere until the day we all walk out of here together."

Aidan chuckled. "At least we have each other." He pressed his cheek on top of her head, grateful for her calming presence. In the midst of their stressful life, Naomi had transformed their home into a refuge using her gift for illusions.

The ceiling swirled like the night sky full of constellations and swirling galaxies from far off. Leaning back on the sofa, they stared into the depths of an endless universe much larger than their immediate problems. It was a comfort even on their worst days.

Naomi's heart thudded against Aidan's chest, an echo of his own. "You know tomorrow is going to be the hardest day of our lives, right?"

"Tell me about the prophecy," Rowan demanded, her eyes smoldering with the heat of her fury. She'd been at this for hours, torturing Naomi for information they would never divulge.

"You know as much as I do." Aidan's skin glistened with sweat in the afternoon sunlight. Rowan had no idea she was falling right into their plan.

"The prophecy is about you, Aidan. Your tough as nails Pilar already spilled the beans to save her own hide." She ran her knife across Naomi's arm, slicing open another cut, deeper this time.

Naomi's weak grunt barely passed her lips as she leaned against the wooden post at her back, her arms hanging above her head. She wouldn't give Rowan the satisfaction of her screams.

But this was the plan. As much as Aidan wanted to give in and free Naomi from her pain, they had a part to play, and they'd agreed neither would break no matter what Rowan did or threatened. To sell their plan, Aidan needed Rowan to believe she'd tortured him into spilling his guts. Still, all the lies he'd prepared to protect Allie were right on the tip of his tongue. He couldn't hold out much longer. Naomi was at her limit of what she could take. This was Aidan's point of no return.

"I told you, I don't know," Aidan said, letting the desperation he felt for Naomi seep into his tone.

"You're lying. You've spent your entire life hiding from the Senate, not because you're the most powerful Immortal most of us have ever seen, but because of that prophecy. Now tell me what you know. What does it mean?"

"Don't you think I'd tell you if I knew? You're killing her!" Aidan's scream held a savage edge to it. Naomi had lost so much blood she was bound to pass out any moment. "Please, let me help her."

"Tell me what you know and this all stops. Give me the truth, and no one else will suffer for your lies." Rowan was like a madwoman, so close to truth she wanted to see that she didn't even realize Aidan was playing her for a fool.

Aidan's gaze shifted to the silent onlookers. His students who had become more like family. Their faces reflected the fear and sadness that was their way of life now. He was doing this just as much for them as he was for Allie and Naomi. With the Initiative's attention fully on Aidan as the child of prophecy, Naomi and Pilar could plan for their takeover at Soma without detection.

"I don't know what the prophecy means." Aidan's voice came out in a rasp. "No one does."

"But the child it speaks of, it is you, isn't it?"

"Don't, Aidan." Naomi's voice was faint, and she struggled to play her part in this.

"We don't have a choice," Naomi." Aidan hung his head, his body weary from the severity of her pain.

"Answer the question," Rowan said, carving her knife down Naomi's back, eliciting one long pain-filled scream from Naomi before she passed out.

"I am the one the prophecy speaks of," Aidan shouted, spit flying from his mouth. "You will let her go. Now." His power surged along with his anger, causing Rowan to flinch at the authority in his voice.

"And what does it mean?" Rowan demanded, her own eyes blazing with triumph.

"I don't know, Rowan. I swear. There are so many interpretations, I can only guess." Aidan let his shoulders sag in defeat. "Only a true prophet could provide an accurate interpretation."

"It doesn't matter now," Rowan said, her voice hard as steel. "He will know what to do with you."

"Who?" Aidan asked, trying not to let his own triumph show.

"Marcus Servius. He is eagerly awaiting this news." Her vicious smile sent chills through Aidan's body. "The Master has been searching for you for thousands of years."

"Do you think she bought it?" Naomi asked as Aidan carried her back to their private quarters, a trail of blood flowing in their wake.

"Shhh, don't talk." Aidan shouldered through their front door and crossed the living room to the glass doors leading into the small garden. He laid Naomi on the stone dais in the center of the walled garden.

"That's better." A sigh escaped her lips the moment moonlight flooded her body. Naomi drew her strength from the lunar cycle. There was no better place for her after a full day under Rowan's knife—an experience she was all too familiar with.

Aidan left her there for a moment, returning with a first

aid kit and warm water to wash her wounds. Silently, Aidan clutched her hand, dabbing at her oozing wounds with a damp cloth. There were so many cuts. More than he could heal on his own. He focused on the worst of her injuries first, letting his healing power pool in his hands.

"I will heal on my own. S-stop fussing." Her breath came in an uneven rasp. She'd lost too much blood and her chest barely moved with each labored breath.

"Save your strength, Naomi. Don't die on me. We can't afford the time for you to regenerate."

"I have a decade on you, remember?" She attempted a smile. "I'll be out of the woods in a few hours."

"She took it further than I expected. I'm so sorry."

Naomi lifted a weary hand and clapped it against his face. "We got what we needed. Everyone here thinks you're the child of prophecy. So, now the spotlight is on you. And you-know-who is safe."

Aidan's laughter came out like a strangled sob. "She would make so many Harry Potter jokes about that." His eyes misted at the thought of Allie's laughter, a sound he couldn't even recall anymore. With each passing day, the pain of missing Allie was becoming more than he could bear.

"She's not ready for this yet. She needs to reach her Proving ..." Naomi erupted into a fit of coughing.

"Rest now." Aidan smoothed his hand over her hair. "You did an amazing job out there."

"Well, let's not make it a habit."

"I just hope our little act is going to be enough to get him here."

"And what are you going to do with Marcus once he's here?" Naomi asked.

"Don't worry about that right now. I just want to talk to

him." The lie tasted bitter on his lips. She would be furious with him when she found out. But it was for the best.

Naomi's breath rattled in her chest as she took a deep breath. "We're playing a dangerous game with this guy, Aidan. I hope she's worth it."

"She is, but this isn't just about her. It's about all of us. We need to buy her the time to come into her own so when she *is* ready, she can face Marcus with confidence."

Aidan's thoughts weighed heavily on his mind as he left Naomi to raid the dining hall. She was resting now, but she was going to need a good meal before breakfast. He walked on bare feet down the wide stone colonnade. The cool mountain breeze flowed through the open arches bordering the training field and the dim light of the gas lamps lit his way.

"What are you doing out past curfew?" Aidan jumped at the sound of Rowan's hateful voice, echoing behind him.

"I'm not out past curfew." He blinked at her in surprise. "I'm on the grounds. I was just getting Naomi some food. She's had a rough day. Or are we not allowed out of our rooms at all now?"

"Just go." Rowan waved him away. She was jumpy and her eyes were hollow. Her normal porcelain skin was the color of ash. She reminded Aidan of an addict in withdrawal. Her hands shook and her eyes twitched.

"Are you okay?" Not that he really cared, but Aidan needed Rowan on his side and if showing her a little kindness would make that happen, he could set aside his feelings about the woman.

"I'm fine." She returned to her nervous pacing along the

open corridor, inhaling in the fresh summer breeze like a healing tonic.

"You don't look fine." Aidan watched the way her power flickered in her dark eyes. She was battling with her gift and she was losing. "You overdid it."

"Nothing I can't handle." She continued to pace.

"Has your gift always worked this way? Or has it evolved since your bond with Spencer?"

"Are you really trying to mentor me right now?" She gave him a scowl, her dark eyes somber.

"Looks like you could use another perspective. Tell me what's got you so off balance?" Aidan stood, arms crossed over his chest.

"It's nothing I haven't dealt with before. I just need to focus on something else until the chaos settles down."

"This isn't the first time you've struggled. You're losing control, and it's slipping farther away from you each time, isn't it?"

"What are you, psychic?"

"No, but I know what it feels like so I recognize the signs."

"I've always had the ability to cause pain, but with Spencer, it's more ... intense and difficult to control."

"Have you worked with her to find a balance? If she exacerbates your gift, amplifying it so it's more powerful, then she should also be able to temper it with a little focused training."

"How do you know so much about Syntrophos?" She leaned against the stone wall beneath the gas lights, focusing on her breathing.

"Lean over and keep breathing," Aidan instructed. "It'll help."

To Aidan's surprise, she actually followed his suggestion, which meant she was truly struggling.

"I just happened to study about the Syntrophos in a history lesson once, and I found it fascinating." He shrugged. No need for her to know the truth. "I believe Spencer could help you."

"No." Rowan shook her head. "Spencer has enough to deal with on her own. I can handle this."

"Sure you can. Until you can't. And if you lose the battle you're fighting now, then what good will you be to Spencer and your Complement?"

"All right. Let's say I take your advice? How could Spencer help with this?"

"Can you tell me what you're feeling when your gift spirals out of control?" Aidan sat on the cold floor opposite her.

"Anger. Lots and lots of anger." She shoved her hands through her hair in frustration. "Like I want to make things burn kind of angry."

"Well, it might do us all a favor if you get that under control," Aidan muttered.

"You're not funny."

"You trust Spencer, right?"

"With my life."

"Then take her somewhere private where you don't have to keep up your pretenses and meditate."

"Meditate? Seriously? That's your sage advice?"

"It will work. I promise. Both of you need to find a quiet sense of peace within your minds, and then open yourself up to each other. Let your power mingle with hers."

"She struggles so much with her own abilities. Her own demons. I don't want to put more on her than she can take."

"You might find the simplest solution is to let your bond take care of both of you. Syntrophos are a natural balance to each other. By taking care of yourself, you'll take care of Spencer, too."

"Why are you helping me?" Confusion clouded her eyes. "You have no reason to show me kindness. Especially after today."

Aidan shrugged. "You're no good to me if you lose control."

"You using me, McBrien?" She frowned at him.

"No more than you're using us. Maybe I do you a favor today, and you'll owe me one."

"I don't like being indebted to my enemies."

"Then maybe we should be friends." Aidan set off down the hallway toward the kitchens. "Night, Ro."

Chapter 28

Allie | Cleveland | June

"You're here again." Greyson's deadpan voice rose above the din of classical music. "And you're making a mess of my kitchen. Didn't we learn anything from the fried chicken fiasco last month? You almost burned my kitchen down."

"Don't worry, Greyson," Santi's voice drifted from Allie's iPad. "I'm walking her through a simple spaghetti meal she can't possibly screw up."

"Oh, you'd be surprised," Allie said. "That's why you're on FaceTime, so you can supervise me."

"And why did you break into my house—again—to cook spaghetti?" Greyson set his messenger bag on the marble countertop.

"I didn't break in. I used the key."

"I hide it for a reason, Allie. How did you even find it in the garden shed?"

"Really?" Allie gave him a blank stare.

"You can't hide a spare key from a clairvoyant, Greyson," Santi said. "She's going to walk right to it every time."

"Right." He sighed. "I'm going to have to resign myself to the redheaded bandit forever, aren't I?"

"Sounds like a private conversation," Santi said. "Can you take it from here?"

"I've got it under control," Allie said.

"I was talking to Greyson."

"Funny." Allie lifted her iPad. "See you at home later."

"Later." Santi waved, ending the call.

Greyson nudged Allie away from the stove, removing the pasta from a roiling boil. "It's overcooking."

"How can you tell?" Allie frowned at the pot. "You haven't even thrown it against the wall yet."

"I lived in Italy for more than a century. I know how to cook pasta."

"Right. I'll just make some garlic bread." She reached for the box in the freezer.

"If you're going to be here, using my kitchen, you're going to learn how to cook."

"Lily's been trying for years. I don't think I got that whole cooking gene thing. But I can manage the bread."

"That box of crap is not food." Greyson reached for a loaf of french bread. "Cut this lengthways down the middle."

"Well, the sauce is homemade. Santi wouldn't let me use the jar stuff."

Greyson sampled the sauce and nodded his approval. "Tastes good. Next time, I'll show you how to use only stuff from the garden to make it."

"Sounds like a lot of work." She wrinkled her nose. "What's wrong with the jar stuff?"

"It's in a jar." He drained the pasta and tasted it. "It's edible, but well done."

"See, I don't even know what that means."

"Just work on chopping the garlic." He handed her a huge bulb of the stuff.

"This is garlic? What do I do with it?" She scowled at the

garlic like it was an alien.

"Oh, dear lord, how have you never seen garlic?" He took the thing away from her and showed her how to peel the cloves.

"It comes in jars already chopped, you know."

"Do you have something against *fresh* ingredients? This is from my garden. It tastes better."

"You do realize we bicker like siblings?"

"Why me?" Greyson rubbed his hand across his face."

"You love having me here, admit it. You'd be lonely if I left."

Greyson clamped his mouth shut. Grumbling something about "a homeless daughter he didn't ask for."

"I'm not homeless. I like my house. I just don't like it when it's empty." The silence was far too loud when Darius wasn't home. Greyson was a distraction. She enjoyed his company and he didn't treat her like a child ... most of the time.

"And where is Darius? Don't you two hate it when you're not together?"

"We don't like it, but Gregg makes it part of our training to spend time apart, so we aren't so dependent on each other. We have to spend several hours each day pursuing different things."

"So, what? I'm your hobby?"

"No." Allie smiled. "Working as your intern is my hobby, and we have work to do tonight. You're doing a guest lecture at Cleveland State on modern art next week, and they're presenting you with an award. You need to work on your lecture and your speech."

"You know, I've been writing speeches and lectures longer than you've been alive. I think I can handle it. And I can dig up an old lecture."

"An old lecture on modern art? Come on, you can do better than that. The Cleveland State art program is decent, but they have nothing on CIA. Give them something they aren't getting from textbooks. Give them something cutting edge."

"Fine, we'll work on it after dinner. You know, I pity your Complement, kid." He winked. "Poor guy's never going to win an argument."

"You aren't funny." Allie finally managed to get the last of the garlic cloves free from their confinement.

"You've managed to mangle those poor things. Give it here. I'll finish up. You go set the table outside. It's a nice night. We'll eat in the garden and talk ideas for my lecture."

Allie's phone blared with an alarming ringtone. "That's Quinn!" She darted to the phone, desperate for any news on Navid.

"Did you find him?" She breathed into the phone. "Tell me you found him!"

"We did, but we have to move fast. Where are you?"

"Greyson's."

"I'll be there in five. Does he have a safe place for you?"

"Yes, meet us in the garden out back."

"I can't stay with you. Once I get you there, I'll hand you off to Brigs, then I have to get to Livia; have you seen her?"

"Livia's at Liam's tonight." She'd recently started spending time there as a break from the monotony of the underground. "Don't worry about me. Greyson can watch over me while I'm under. I'll catch him up to speed. Just hurry." Allie shoved her phone back in her pocket.

"What's going on?" Greyson turned off the oven and burners, wiping his hands on a dishtowel. "How can I help?"

"They've found Navid. Quinn's on his way here. He's

going to escort me to the dreamworld. Can you watch over me?"

"Watch over you?"

"I'll be sort of asleep, but not really. I just need protection here in the waking world in case I have trouble leaving the dreamworld."

"And how do I wake you up and force you back here?"

"Slap me. Throw water on me, whatever works. If I start freaking out, you have to wake me up by any means."

"Why can't we just do that with Navid?"

"Doesn't work like that in his situation. Brecken has him trapped. He can't do that to me since I'm not a walker, so you can force me out if something goes wrong."

"Anything else I need to know?"

"Call Santi if something happens and you don't know what to do. Just FaceTime her on my iPad. She's the last person I called."

"Got it. Let's get you settled and ready before Quinn gets here. I imagine you need to relax." Greyson pulled his phone out of his pocket, typing a quick text as he followed Allie to the garden.

Allie dragged her yoga mat from the garden shed and tossed it across the grass. Sitting with her legs crisscrossed and her back to the rear garden wall, she placed her palms on her knees, taking slow, deep breaths.

Calming white noise rushed from the garden speakers, driving the frantic thoughts from her mind.

"Thanks Greyson, that helps." She counted her slow, deep breaths until she was only taking a breath a few times per minute. By the time Quinn arrived, she was focused and ready. Allie didn't even greet him: she stayed in her relaxed position, grasping Quinn's hand as he settled beside her.

The garden twisted and swirled around her until she felt

solid ground beneath her feet. This time she didn't fall upon entering the dreamworld, but she still ran for the bushes, tossing the contents of her stomach on the ground.

"Where is he?" she demanded of Brigs, wiping the vomit from her face. Quinn had already left her and was back in the waking world, racing to get to Livia.

"Follow me, Beautiful. We have another leap to make before this ride stops spinning." He took her hand, and Allie insides twisted and turned like ingredients in a food processor.

"Drink." Brigs shoved a bottle of sweet dreamworld water into her hands. She chugged it before she had a chance to puke, and her mind cleared and her stomach stopped churning. "Thank you," she managed to whisper through trembling lips. This was the closest they'd come to finding Navid in months, but finding him was only half the battle. Actually getting him out might prove impossible.

"Don't overthink it, Allie." Brigs wrapped his long arms around her, pressing a kiss to her forehead. "We all love him and we're going to bring him home. *Tonight*. And then you and I are going to celebrate. Deal?"

"Deal. Catch me up to speed."

"We're waiting here for the others. The prison dreamscape is just up the pathway through the woods." He pointed in the distance. She could just make out the tower at the top of the hill. "We're going to give you as much time as we can in there."

"Let's go now. Livia can catch up when she gets here."

"You know that's a dumb idea, Allie. We stay put until the Commander tells us otherwise so I'm afraid you're stuck with me, sweet cheeks."

"Your nicknames need work." Allie shook her head at him. "You're not as smooth as you think you are."

"Admit it, you find me and my nicknames irresistible." His lips quirked into a half smile that never failed to get her attention. Over the last year, Brigs had asked her out so many times she finally caved a few months ago just to shut him up. To her surprise, she enjoyed their first date, which had turned into a dozen or more since then. He was a fun—irresistible—distraction and it was good for her to move on. But, he wasn't Aidan. And the fact that he was so very un-Aidan made it easier to enjoy his company. But when they weren't together, the guilt consumed her. No matter how much she liked Brigs and no matter how long it had been since she last spoke to Aidan, the truth was, she felt like she was cheating on him. And that just pissed her off.

"Well you are a dream walker. I suppose that at least makes you interesting." Allie's gaze fell to his lips. He had such pretty, kissable lips.

"If you'd let me into your dreamscape, I could show you just how interesting I can be." He leaned in close, his breath warm on her face. "Think of all the oh-so-interesting dreams I could give you."

Allie's face flushed pink under his scrutiny. Brigs was hot and he knew it. He was cocky, but not always confident, which gave him an adorable quality she quite liked. He was just a few inches taller than Allie with short blond hair and sky blue eyes. He also had full tattoo sleeves covering his muscular arms and wide shoulders. He probably had many more tattoos she hadn't even seen. His angular jaw was covered in a perpetual five o'clock shadow and he dressed casually, always in ripped jeans, t-shirts and boots. Brigs also made Allie laugh. And it didn't hurt that Darius didn't hate him. But he wasn't coming anywhere near her dreamscape. That was sacred Aidan territory and she just couldn't do it.

"You stay out of my dreams, mister." She let a teasing

tone into her voice, but she was also dead serious.

"We could have so much fun, Allie." He took a step forward, tilting her chin up. "Just imagine what a date in the dreamworld would be like."

"I am not going on a date with you in the dreamworld," Allie said, forcing her attention back on what was truly important.

"Fine, come to my house when this is over. I'll make you dinner and I'll up the ante with a cupcake bribe." Brigs gazed down into her eyes, giving off hella sexy vibes.

"Chocolate?" she asked nervously.

"Gooey chocolate cake and frosting for miles."

"You're on. But I want sprinkles too." Allie said, taking a step back to put some distance between them.

"It's a date. You know, after we rescue your father from Brecken's prison world and the threat of madness."

"You think we can pull this off?" Allie asked, pacing the narrow pathway through the forest. She could see the tower through the trees. Several guards patrolled the area and they were the only reason she didn't make a run for the tower right this minute.

"Orders are to stay put, Allie. Don't even think about it." Brigs came up behind her.

"I know. It's just ... he's right there and we might not have an opportunity like this again."

"It's a trap, Beautiful," Brigs said. "But if Quinn is our commander, then Navid is our commander's mentor. We will fight for his freedom, as we would for Quinn."

"Thank you, Brigs. My family appreciates all you have done to help find my father."

"And we appreciate all you and Livia have done to help us fight this war and free our walkers."

"How are they all doing since waking?"

"Better. Some of them were trapped here for a really long time. It will be years before most of them will recover. But they will, thanks to you two." He nodded behind Allie where Livia and Quinn now stood.

"Let's do this," Livia said, her jaw set in a firm line.

"What's the plan? Same as last time?" Allie asked, eager to get inside the tower.

"Sort of," Quinn said. "But this time, we're bringing every able-bodied walker to stand sentry around the prison while you're in there."

"What about Brecken's warriors?" Livia asked.

"We're going to have to fight to get you inside. It's what they want. They're drawing us out so it's going to be a dirty fight. You guys need to do this quickly. In and out. Raina will take Navid home the second you have him."

"And then I'll get you two back home safe and sound," Brigs added.

"I wish we were with Navid's body now," Livia said, shaking her head. "I should have stayed home."

"Santi and Sasha are with him now," Quinn said. "They've done this before with other walkers we've returned to the waking world. They'll know what to do for him when he wakes up."

"Can you pick me up at Greyson's?" Allie asked her sister. "We'll get to the underground together?"

Livia nodded. "Liam is ready to go as soon as I get back. I should have never let him talk me into leaving Dad alone tonight."

"We'll get to Dad soon, Liv," Allie said. "And we'll help him get better."

"Damn right we will. Let's go."

Allie and Livia followed Quinn's growing team into the barren landscape surrounding the new prison tower. At the top of the hill, Allie got her first glimpse of the black tower. It was worse than the last place, and at least ten walkers patrolled the perimeter.

"When we get down there, Brigs is going to get you close to the tower." Quinn nodded. "Try to get inside before you puke, Allie."

"Just like last time," Brigs said. "You'll be fine."

"I swear, I'll drag you in there while you're puking if I have to," Livia almost growled.

"Just be safe, Quinn, please? Don't let anyone else end up inside that thing," Allie said.

Quinn nodded and his walkers vanished, reappearing at the top of the hill amidst the guards. All hell broke lose as Livia and Allie grasped hands with Brigs and followed suit.

Allie stumbled this time, but Brigs wrapped his arms around her and poured water down her throat before he shoved her toward the open tower archways. She barely had a moment to absorb the intensity of the battle before she was inside the prison world.

Allie's feet moved the instant she felt solid ground beneath her. "Navid!" she called, sprinting in the opposite direction of her sister.

"Dad!" Livia shouted.

This world was different. It was a desert with no end in sight.

"How are we going to find him?" Allie shouted across the barren landscape after Livia's retreating form. She shielded her face from the blistering hot sun, gazing in every direction. Miles and miles of cracked earth stretched out before her.

"We aren't leaving until we find him," Livia called.

But Allie feared only a walker could search this dreamscape in the time they had. That was Brecken's doing. He knew Allie and Livia would never find Navid in such a large prison world. And no walker could step foot in here and not be affected by the nightmares surely haunting this place.

Allie ran, pumping her arms and legs, stumbling across the rocky ground, but she never saw a single landmark. Nothing but wasteland.

"Allie!" She turned to see Livia in the distance, running toward her, shouting something. Allie hurried to meet her, but something was wrong. Her limbs didn't want to obey her.

"Come this way," Livia panted, dragging Allie behind her. "There's a small lake over that ridge. He'll likely stick close to a water source.

Allie's limbs grew heavy, and her cheeks stung like someone slapped her.

"No." Allie gasped, clinging to her sister's hand.

"What's wrong?" Livia demanded. "Are you waking up? No, Allie, stay with me!"

But Allie no longer felt the hot desert air against her skin. The evening breeze of Greyson's garden chased the heat away, cooling her face and the sticky perspiration on the back of her neck. But something else was there. Something wrong and unnatural. Allie felt weak. So weak, she struggled to open her eyes. "Greyson," she slurred her words. "I wasn't ready." She was so tired. She'd felt like this only once before. Allie's eyes snapped open and she clawed at the collar around her throat. She sat in the garden, but she wasn't alone. Three strange men stood between her and Greyson.

She glanced between his guilty face to the stone cold looks of disgust from the men—their magnetic weapons trained on her.

Coalition.

"Greyson, what have you done?" Anger, panic and heartbreak swelled in her chest as the gravity of his betrayal hit her.

CHAPTER 29

Aidan | Milan, Italy | June

"You sure about this, man?" Samantha asked. "My tatts are permanent." She eyed Aidan's existing tattoos his cousin Erin had given him.

Aidan nodded. "Completely sure." He'd thought long and hard about these tattoos. They were reminders of the people he loved. Reminders he desperately needed.

"Your cousin can really remove these and make changes?" She ran her hands over the tattoos covering Aidan's biceps, studying Erin's intricate work. "Wonder what I could do with a partner like that?" she murmured.

"You guys would make a great team; you're both crazy talented. She can even make her tattoos visible to mortals or leave them only for Immortal eyes."

"I would kill for that," Sam said. "But really, Aidan? You don't want anything fancier than this?" She eyed the rough sketches Aidan had made. "I could work up some designs for you based on these drawings."

"Nope, nothing fussy for these. It's more about what they represent than how they look."

"You're sure?"

"How many times you going to ask me?" He grinned.

"All right, lay back on the table and we'll get started with the Sanskrit forms, and we'll move on to the Egyptian stuff later, but like it or not, I'm making the Eyes of Ra fancy." Sam leaned forward, sketching the letters on his chest, right over his heart.

"All right, you ready for this?" she asked, her needle humming at the ready.

"Don't you need ink?" Aidan asked. "Your inkwell is empty."

"Nope." Samantha gave him a satisfied smirk. "I just need the needle and a little Sam mojo and we're good to go." She leaned over Aidan's bare chest. "What does the Sanskrit mean?"

"Love, friendship, loyalty and compassion."

"She'll love it." Sam smiled.

"Not too cheesy I hope?" He'd searched for just the right way to represent Naomi in his ink. The fact that Sam's tattoos were permanent added something more to the gesture.

"Totally cheesy, but I'm so jealous. I'm not sure it would even occur to Ben to do something like this for me. But you guys are a little move lovey dovey than we are."

"We are not lovey dovey," Aidan insisted. He loved Naomi and he craved her presence, but he wasn't in love with her.

"Yeah, you are. It's adorable."

"I have a girlfriend."

"Sure you do, bro. But you also have a Naomi."

"And for the foreseeable future, we are separated from my girlfriend." Aidan sighed. He hated calling Allie his girlfriend when she was so much more than that. Even after all this time apart, she was his whole world. "I guess we'll figure out the messy stuff some day."

Aidan flinched at the first touch of Sam's needle to his skin, not from pain, but from surprise. A trickle of her power flowed into his skin. He watched, fascinated as a thin ribbon of light poured from the tip of her needle.

"That's so freaking cool." He stared in the mirror positioned above him so he could watch.

Sam was fast and finished the Sanskrit tatts quickly, moving on to the Eyes of Ra representing Aidan's mother and her Egyptian heritage. Sam spent a lot more time on those, not letting Aidan watch in the mirror. When she finally let him look, her work took his breath away. She'd placed the Eyes of Ra beneath his collarbones. The one above his heart seemed to leap off his chest with an array of sunbeams behind it with two birds flying together toward the sun. The other eye was identical, but instead of a sun behind it, she'd drawn a moon.

"It's perfect. More perfect than you could even realize." Sam didn't know Allie drew her strength from the sun the way Naomi drew hers from the moon. With all four elements, this one tattoo represented the most important women in Aidan's life. "What made you include the birds?" It was a small but subtle representation of Sasha.

"I went with my instinct there," Sam said. "Sometimes my gift reveals the tattoo to me as I work."

"It's beautiful."

"Okay, so what are these?" Sam returned to Aidan's sketches. "Cuneiform?"

"Yes." He turned on his side to go over the sketches with her one more time. "The first ones are Cuneiform symbols for sun. And these other three mean strength, love and divine light.

"These tree symbols are terrible. Can I jazz them up a little bit?"

"As long as they match the Cuneiform style of the others, do what you want, but I want those and that last one over my heart."

"What's it mean?"

"The trees are the symbol for orchard and the last one means brave hero."

"The one that looks like a bunch of squiggles?"

"Yes."

"These are for your girlfriend? You sure you want this to be permanent?"

"Positive." Aidan lay back on the table. He needed these reminders more than all the others.

"Okay, but I have another one I'm going to add because my gift tells me you need it."

"Go for it." Aidan relaxed as she set back to work, moving quickly through the simple forms.

"Whoa, whatcha doing there, Sam?" Aidan glanced down at his chest. "That hurts."

"Suck it up you big baby, I'm almost done."

"I don't think I requested a nipple tattoo. Ouch, that's sensitive skin there."

"Would you sit still? I'm almost done. This is my contribution to your chest of reminders."

"What is it?" Aidan craned his neck trying to see what she was drawing. "If you mark me with something ridiculous, I will kill you."

"Oh relax. It looks cool." She sat back and handed him a mirror.

"Hey, that's kind of sexy." Aidan admired the unexpected ring around his nipple. "What's it mean?"

"It's an Egyptian Shen. It means eternity."

"Fitting."

"It's a reminder to you from me. No matter what you're

facing right now, it's only temporary. You have an eternity to look forward to with your girl."

"How'd you know?" Aidan's shoulders slumped. He didn't want anyone to know Allie was his Complement, not that Sam even knew her name. It was just safer for everyone involved if no one knew.

"The red tatts." She tapped his chest where Allie's symbols still shimmered with Sam's power. Unlike the other tattoos that were all black, Allie's were intensely red, like blood. "To everyone else, it's just ink, but my gift knows when a tattoo is connected to something as powerful as a Complement bond," she said in a hushed whisper. "And don't worry, your secret will never pass these lips. I wouldn't even tell Bennett."

"Thanks, Sam." Aidan stood to put his shirt back on.

"Hey, guys." Bennett shoved through the door to the suite he shared with Sam. "They're calling us in." He darted into his bedroom for a clean shirt. "Hurry up Samantha, this doesn't look good."

"At this hour? It's after midnight." Sam scooted her chair back and secured her needle and supplies. "I want to touch those up later. Keep them clean and dry." She gestured at Aidan's chest before she twisted her glossy black hair up into a high ponytail and followed Bennett from their quarters, Aidan right behind them.

"What's going on?" Aidan asked as he spotted Naomi down the hall.

"Surprise visit." Her eyes widened. "The Chief Justice are here for an inspection, so I'm guessing they've had that report from Rowan by now."

"And they've brought that guest we've been expecting," Pilar added in hushed tones. "You two need to lie low and not call attention to yourselves. It's what they'd expect, so if we're going with Aidan's crazy plan, we need to sell it. Tonight."

"I'm ready." Aidan took a deep breath. This was what he wanted, but now that it was here, he wished time would stop long enough for him to get his head on straight.

"You sure about this?" Naomi asked.

"No, but we're about to find out if this is going to work." Aidan and Naomi continued following the crowd down the long corridors to the library where Cleo and Genevieve waited with the Chief Justice and their distinguished guest.

Marcus Servius was an unremarkable, average looking man. He was so boring and beige, Aidan's eyes wanted to slip right past him.

Just as they had the first time the Chief Justice visited, the Syntrophos of the Milan Initiative were trotted out for inspection. But this time their owner was present and he looked delighted.

"Eight pairs?" He beamed a fatherly smile at them. "All under the age of thirty, you said?"

"Cleo and Genevieve are much older, but the remaining seven pairs are quite young, but powerful," Sarah Madison spoke like a proud momma.

Cleo and Genevieve stood just behind the Chief Justice, clearly uncomfortable at being lumped in with the other Syntrophos.

"Judging the reports you've sent, their collective abilities are just astounding," Marcus said, walking among them like a rich and powerful man at a slave market. "These will do well. Very well, indeed."

"You are pleased, sir?" Sarah couldn't contain her relieved smile.

"You've outdone yourselves, Sarah. Charles." He gave an absent nod in Charles's direction.

"May I ask, sir," Cleo said, stepping forward, "what are your plans for these children?"

"No, you may not." Marcus ignored her. "For now all you need to know is what you've been tasked with. Get them ready to take over Soma."

It didn't make any sense. Aidan knew for a fact this man owned Soma, had built it from the ground up with Livia. But what was his end game? It couldn't just be about giving the Chief Justice a coup to get them reelected. That had to be the motivation he gave to Charles and Sarah but a man like Marcus would have something much bigger in mind.

"Would you like a demonstration, sir?" Cleo asked. "The children would be happy to show you their unique skills."

"Another time." Marcus dismissed her with a wave of his hand. "Ah, here he is. The man of the hour." Marcus came to a stop in front of Aidan, studying him from head to toe. "I've heard much about you, young man." He held his hand out and Aidan made a show of shaking his hand with an eagerness he didn't feel.

"An honor to meet you, sir." Aidan returned to his stance, hands behind his back like he'd been taught. This was it. The moment he'd been working toward for months. Marcus was Aidan's means to an end. He would convince the evil son of a bitch that he was the child of prophecy and his new best friend. "May I have a private word with you before you leave, sir?" Aidan asked.

Marcus raised his eyes in surprise. "Getting down to brass tacks already?" He gave a friendly chuckle. "Not yet, son. Let's meet your Syntrophos first, shall we?"

Aidan nodded. "Of course. This is Naomi." Aidan lifted a hand to his right where Naomi stood ramrod straight, appearing as fierce as he'd ever seen her.

"Lovely." Marcus strolled around her. "And what do you do, my dear?"

"I am an illusionist, sir," Naomi said with a respectful nod. The ambience of the room immediately changed from one charged with tension to one filled with the cheery warmth of the crackling fire and the scent of hot cocoa and fresh baked cookies. Everyone collectively exhaled in relief.

"Quite the talent, young lady," Marcus said, patting her shoulder in appreciation. "There is something to be said for experiencing such a gift first hand rather than reading about it in a report." His chuckle made him sound like a kind old grandfather, but Aidan would never be fooled by Marcus's witty charm and casual banter.

"Thank you sir." Naomi took a step back to join the others. She still wasn't sure about this, but she'd reluctantly agreed to kiss some ass to help Aidan sell this ruse.

"A fine partnership. Nearly equals, some might say." His gaze drifted around the room, as if to say they were all Aidan's equals like the prophecy claimed. "Tell me, Aidan, why haven't you taken the field commander's position offered to you?" Marcus asked.

"I prefer to be one of the team, sir. Any leadership role I take on happens naturally through their loyalty to me. I don't need a title to show my superiority." Aidan nearly choked on that last part. But he needed Marcus to think him arrogant and power hungry—a kindred spirit. The other Syntrophos held their reactions in check, but Aidan knew they didn't like what they were hearing. Naomi would explain his actions later and he hoped they would understand in time.

"Leave us," Marcus called to the room. "The other Syntrophos may retire. Aidan and I will have a private word here, and we will send for you when we are ready." He turned to Cleo and Genevieve. "Ladies, Chief Justice, you're dismissed."

"I believe we should be present for this interview, sir," Sarah said, her tone respectful but her eyes betrayed her outrage at his blatant dismissal.

"Leave us." Marcus said again, this time his tone held a hint of his power and authority over her.

"Very well." Sarah tilted her head back and marched out of the room with whatever was left of her dignity.

"I'll see you at home soon," Aidan said, as Naomi gave him a worried look.

"Be careful," she murmured, closing the library door behind her and the others.

"Aidan McBrien." Marcus sized him up again. "Tell me, what makes you think you're the child of prophecy?" Marcus took a seat in the leather armchair in front of the fireplace, gesturing for Aidan to take the chair opposite him.

"What makes you think I'm not?" Aidan said with an arrogant smirk. He sat with his ankle propped against his knee in a casual manner. Aidan's gift told him Marcus was excited to meet him. The man's heart rate was through the roof, though he played it as casual as Aidan. "My father suspected it when he adopted me. As I grew up, the strength of my power increased with every passing year. I am likely the most powerful Immortal of my generation. The fact that I have a Syntrophos kind of sealed the deal for me. Watching so many other Syntrophos pairing up around me also fits with the prophecy. My healing gift is mentioned as well. If it's not me, then I'd like to meet the guy who fits the description better. And let's be frank, you wouldn't be here if you didn't believe it too."

"What of your lineage?" Marcus sat across from Aidan, seemingly at ease, though Aidan's gift told him he was anything but. "Can you prove you are the second child of the seventh daughter of your line?"

"No, but who could possibly prove that these days? I was adopted when I was a baby, but that doesn't mean my lineage is weak."

"You seem to think you know me, young Aidan. Just exactly who do you think I am?"

"I have no idea, really, but I recognize power when I see it. Cleo and Genevieve are the babysitters. Sarah and Charles Madison may be the Chief Justice but I knew they were not driving this bus. So, I've been waiting patiently for the true benefactor behind the Milan Initiative to show up, and here you are." Aidan shifted in his seat, letting his hands fall on the armrests as Marcus continued to size him up.

"And what did you wish to speak to me about?" Marcus finally asked.

"Get. Me. Out of here," Aidan said, giving his words a sense of urgency.

"You expect me to send you home? Come now, Aidan, you're not that stupid."

"I don't want to go home, but this place is for children. You're wasting my time and my talents here in this boarding school."

"And what do you suggest I do with you?"

"Take me with you. Train me to lead this army against Soma. I already have their loyalty and they respect my Syntrophos just as much. Let her train here as my field commander and give me the training someone of my stature deserves. You're an ancient and your power is unlike anything I've ever sensed." That wasn't exactly true. He'd met Allie's grandparents before he left for school and they were scary powerful, but the man sitting before him now was off the charts. Marcus was the great Lord Teigan, a relic of

Indriell from before the Great War, before the power was corrupted. His power was pure and that made him dangerous and unpredictable.

Marcus threw his head back and laughed. "You don't pull any punches, do you, my boy?"

"No, sir." Aidan smiled, relieved Marcus seemed more relaxed now.

"And why do you think I'd waste my time training you?"

Aidan shrugged. "You're the one who came all this way to meet the child of prophecy. I guess it's up to you if you want to use me to your advantage or hold me back. Either way, I'm still your prisoner. The question remains will we be allies or enemies?"

A delighted smile spread across Marcus's face. "You have my attention. Sell me on the idea and we will see if you're worth my time."

"I think you've been looking for me for a very long time," Aidan began. "My family suspected I was the child of prophecy and they protected me. In some ways, they smothered me." Aidan hated himself for the lie. "The Milan initiative has given me the chance to break away from my family's plans to hide me until I'm Proven."

"They wanted to coddle you because you are young." Marcus shook his head in disgust. "A surefire way to see you never reach your true potential. A boy of your talent needs to be pushed to his limits."

"And leaving me among a bunch of women and children is any better?" Aidan's brow lifted, though the words disgusted him. Aidan knew from the way Marcus spoke with Cleo and Sarah that he had little confidence in women.

"Touché. But training is not all you're after, is it, Aidan? Go ahead, speak your mind." Marcus's face revealed nothing as his hands formed a steeple against his lips.

"Dissolve the Milan Initiative. The Syntrophos are trained and they are loyal to me. Let them return to their lives. When we have need of them, they will answer my call."

"You are confident, I'll give you that." Marcus considered his offer. "I find cages work better than loyalty."

"Maybe for you." Aidan shrugged. "You can leave me in a cage, and I'll be here waiting for you when you have need of me. But you won't have my loyalty or cooperation. That offer expires once we leave this room."

"I see," Marcus murmured with an amused smile. "Go on."

"Once we leave this room, you and I will either be friends, working together and learning from each other, or we will be enemies. If I have to break out of this prison, I will, but if I do, I'm taking my army with me. So, you have to decide if you want the son of prophecy and his army of equals in your pocket or standing against you?"

"You ask for too much trust," Marcus said. "How do I know the Syntrophos are so blindly loyal to you?"

"You put a viper in our midst to sew dissension among us. It didn't work. Rowan's Syntrophos might be loyal to her ... for now, but it is only a matter of time before I win them over. Rowan herself is already indebted to me." Aidan sat back against the smooth leather of his chair. "We are an army of Syntrophos, how long do you think cages will hold us? Eventually we will have the power to fight whatever force you or the Senate sends against us."

"You aren't there yet, my boy. I am not convinced you have as much to offer as you think."

"Very well, you want us to take Soma for you, we will. But what will that earn us?"

"Your lives." Marcus sneered.

"Then I guess we are done here." Aidan stood to leave.

"Sit down, son. We're not done negotiating, and I have not dismissed you. I will not release my Syntrophos. You're asking too much and offering too little. Shall I counter your offer? Or do you have any other little surprises for me?"

"Proceed," Aidan said, returning to his seat, anxious to close his deal with the devil.

"I will not release the Syntrophos, but I can make their lives somewhat easier."

"I'm listening." It wasn't what he wanted, but Aidan knew from the beginning he wouldn't get everything he asked for.

"They will remain here at the Initiative where they will continue training. You will come with me for your own training, leaving Naomi behind as a gesture of good faith. The Syntrophos will resume training under Cleo's direction for another eighteen months, in which you will return often enough to continue your training with your Syntrophos. They will be treated well. Rowan and Spencer's gifts will only be used for punishment in the most severe cases. The Syntrophos will all live separately. Your bond gives you immense power but your dependency on each other is your greatest weakness. From now on, the Syntrophos will only be together during training. That gives me the confidence they will continue to experience a life of discipline and they will be at the ready when I have need of them."

"And what will my training entail?" Aidan asked, not sure he really wanted to know. He was opening himself up to a world of hurt with Marcus, but if it kept the others safe and Marcus distracted from Allie, then it was worth whatever time he could buy her.

"I will push your limits to the edge and you will pursue every shred of potential you possess. This will not be easy."

"I wouldn't expect otherwise." Aidan swallowed back the last of his fears. The deal was all but done.

"Don't think for a moment that I don't realize you're soft, McBrien. You've presented a good front. Arrogant, ambitious and confident in the extreme. But you've also willingly sacrificed yourself for the comfort of others." Marcus sneered, showing Aidan just what he thought of that.

"I trade myself to give my Syntrophos a better life, ensuring their undying loyalty in the process. In exchange, I get the kind of training someone of my stature truly deserves from someone who knows where I am going. It's a win-win for me." Aidan tried to convey his lack of sympathy for his students through his stony expression and flat tone. "Do we have a deal?" Aidan asked, confident that as long as Marcus believed Aidan was the child of prophecy, he wouldn't let him walk out of this room without a deal.

"For now, Mr. McBrien, we have a deal. We leave in an hour."

"You played me." Rowan pushed off the wall when Aidan stepped through the doors into the colonnade. "You wanted to bring him here."

"Come with me." Aidan charged down the open stone corridor and through the archway onto the dark training field.

"I'm such an idiot." Rowan shook her head. "You wanted to usurp my position here and you played me."

"You're still in charge here, Rowan. And you're not going to have to torture anyone. For a while at least."

"What did you do?" She lowered her voice and glanced back over her shoulder.

"I traded myself to make it easier on everyone here."

"You're going with him, aren't you?" She gave him an incredulous look.

"Yes."

"You have no idea what he's capable of." Her eyes filled with worry. Worry for him. Underneath her hard exterior, Rowan was probably a decent human being. He just wondered how much he could trust her. Before this was over, he was going to need her on his side.

"I know I'm probably going to regret it but I have other people to think about."

"You really think you can save everyone, don't you?" She shook her head in disgust. "He's going to see right through you."

"I don't have much time so I'm going to ask you one thing and then I'm going to leave you and Naomi to take care of everyone while I'm gone. I don't know if I can trust you, but I don't have much of a choice, so here goes nothing. If I can get you the impossible—if I can get you in the same room with your Syntrophos and your Complement—if I can give you freedom, where would your loyalties lie? With Marcus? Or with me? You don't even have to answer now. Just think about it."

"I don't have to think about it, McBrien." She looked over her shoulder again. "You make that happen and I'm on team Aidan."

CHAPTER 30

Allie | Cleveland | June

Someone close to you will betray you. Navid's warning from years ago rang out in Allie's mind. She'd thought it was Livia. When her sister confessed her part in their mother's death, it broke Allie's heart. The betrayal of Livia's confession had shattered whatever fragile bond they were building. That bond was only just now growing again. But all this time, it was Greyson—her rock during the difficult time of the last two years. Her friend. Her refuge. How had she not seen it?

"I'm so sorry, Allie." He couldn't even look at her.

"Sorry?" She hissed as angry tears blurred her vision. She wanted to lash out at him, but the magnetic collar severed Allie's connection with her power. "I trusted you!" A stab of despair shot through her. "You were like family to me, Greyson. Why?" she demanded. She deserved that much.

Another Immortal presence brought Allie out of her shock. A once beautiful woman sat immobile on a picnic bench. "Isebeau?" Allie stared at the woman. "You traded me? To free your wife?" Her voice sounded like gravel in her throat.

"I can't do this." Greyson turned to the three men in

desperation. "She's just a kid." He tried to cross the lawn between them, but the Coalition agents stood in his way. He might feel remorse for his betrayal, but it was done. These agents wouldn't let him go back on his deal now.

"And an Immortal with unspeakable powers if you've been telling the truth," one of the agents said.

"I thought he was lying," another said, shaking his head. "The Margrave will want her. They'll put her gift to good use."

"No, Greyson, how could you?" Isebeau cried, shaking her head. "Not like this. He wouldn't do such a heinous thing." Her frail shoulders trembled and her wide eyes seemed not to trust what she saw.

"I'm sorry. I couldn't live without you anymore," Greyson's voice broke on a sob.

"You wouldn't sentence a child to a life like mine." Isebeau's cold voice was garbled and harsh, like she hadn't used it in an age. "My husband wouldn't do such a dishonorable thing."

Allie searched the walled garden, desperate for a way out of this mess.

"Get the girl," one of the agents barked. "You have what you bargained for." He cast a disgusted sneer at Isebeau. "Worthless pile of nothing that she is."

Greyson charged the agents, putting himself between them and Allie. "She will understand everything before you take her or we have no deal."

"The deal is done. Make your point and do it quickly." The man waved his gun in Greyson's face. "Or we'll just take all of you."

Greyson whirled around to face Allie. "I've fought this for years," Greyson said, a note of desperation in his voice, like he could possibly offer an acceptable excuse for his betrayal. "Since the day I met you, I knew this was coming. I knew I wouldn't be strong enough to resist this when you were right there—the key to bringing my Isebeau back."

Allie managed to get to her feet, rage burning inside her. "And it took you three years to find the balls to do it?" She took an unsteady step toward him, desperate to get her hands around his throat. "Of course, you knew everything." Allie's eyes filled with tears. Greyson's gift told him exactly what she could do from the first moment he'd laid eyes on her. He knew before she did that she would have the power to strip Immortals of their immortality. He knew all her secrets and he'd traded on them. All this time, she'd believed only a select few knew of her gift. She'd forgotten all about Greyson. But Gregg would have realized.

"Gregg swore you to secrecy, didn't he?" she said, connecting all the missing pieces. "He trusted you with my life and you betrayed that trust."

"I can't expect you to understand." Greyson hung his head in shame.

"You were my friend." Allie tried to find the strength to fight for her life, but her limbs wouldn't work. She'd experienced the effects of a magnetic collar before, and she knew it was futile to resist the influence of the cold, harsh metal. "I would have helped you get your wife back. I *offered* to help." Allie would have been on board with the plan to use her as bait to lure these Coalition assholes here with Isebeau. It could have been so easy to dupe them and get her back without all the lies and betrayal.

"I ... I let myself think this was the way you could help. I really thought you'd see it coming. That we could get through this together and free Isebeau in the process."

"Enough," the lead agent said. "We're leaving with the girl." He gestured for his two subordinates to subdue Allie, but she wasn't about to let them touch her. She took a step back and something about her must have scared the agents because they gaped at her with terror filled eyes.

"She's weak and cut off from her power, she can't touch you," the one in charge reminded them.

"It doesn't look like she's cut off. Not completely." The second agent took a step away from Allie, his hands shaking as he pointed a magnetized knife at her. "You sure that collar is strong enough to hold her?"

That's when she saw it. The collar around her throat glowed hot with the light of her power. It was doing its job, but Allie wondered if her will was strong enough to overcome the magnetic influence of the collar. Whatever it meant, it was clear these agents had never seen the like before.

"You think I can't take you with that silly little thing?" Allie sneered at the agent with the knife, showing off her tattooed battle scars from the last time she faced a magnetized weapon. "Go ahead, come at me, bro." Allie crouched in a defensive pose. She was so full of shit right now, but she was counting on the weird glow of her collar and her false bravado to get her out of this mess. But Allie barely had the strength to remain on her feet.

"Enough with the drama," the lead agent said again. "The deal is done and we're leaving. Greyson, enjoy that bag of bones you call a wife. She was a tough one to find. Buried in the bowels of an old prison and long forgotten. I'm sure she's bat shit crazy by now."

Isebeau still sat at the picnic table with her head down, weeping into her arms. She didn't seem to have the strength to hold her head up.

The agents managed to get over their fear of Allie as they advanced on her together.

"No." She lashed out at them, but they had her arms

bound with heavy zip ties behind her back before she could protest further. She desperately searched for a way out of this and saw none. "Greyson, don't let them do this!" She cried, her voice shaking with fury. "Help me, goddammit!"

"I'm sorry, Allie." Tears of humiliation tracked down his face as he turned away from her to go to his wife's side.

"You bastard!" She kicked and struggled between the two agents, grasping onto the rush of adrenaline for whatever strength she had remaining.

"Release her." Liam and Gregg came charging around to the backyard with Livia leading the way. Darius and Naeemah burst through the back door with Vince and Kayla right behind them. Each Immortal trained their weapons on the mortal Coalition agents and Greyson with his weeping wife.

"You son of a bitch!" Naeemah punched Greyson so hard he dropped like a dead weight.

"You don't think we've prepared for this?" The Coalition man laughed. "You Immortals are powerful and gifted, but you're also predictable creatures of habit. We have backup."

"You mean that vanload of Coalition waiting in the driveway?" Vince asked. "Yeah, they're all passed out. Seems they got a little dose of carbon monoxide poisoning. Not enough to kill them, but they won't be waking up any time soon." The short length of garden hose in his hand and the running van out front explained everything. Allie was never so happy to see her ex-boyfriend and his girlfriend as she was in that moment. *How do they always know when I need them?* She couldn't fathom what brought them here to save her ass, but she was grateful. Vince knew more about her world than any of her Immortal friends realized and he'd just blown his cover tonight.

"Your grandfather will hear about this, young man," the

lead agent said as he stumbled to the ground, his hands bound by the force of Gregg's electromagnetic gift.

"The old man's not my biggest fan anyway." Vince shrugged. "Lucky for me your son is a loud mouthed idiot. He told me about your "career making" raid tonight so here I am, Uncle Will." Vince crouched beside the furious man. "Making sure that doesn't happen."

"You're just like your father. Always on the wrong side of the fight," Will said. "Always consorting with the wrong people." He shot a hateful glare at Kayla.

"We can choose for ourselves who and what we fight for," Kayla said, her voice strong and confident.

"And my money's always going to be on the redhead," Vince added.

"Darius! Get this collar off me," Allie sobbed once Gregg had all three agents restrained.

"I swear, Allie, you're going to be the death of me." Darius came toward her with the magnetic release for the collar he'd pilfered from Will's pocket. It fell away with a thud against the ground as Liam cut the zip ties binding her hands behind her back.

Allie threw her arms around her Syntrophos, the warm tendrils of their bond entwined, humming with satisfaction. "Never again, Allie." Darius cupped her face between his palms. "I don't care what's at stake, if you need to enter the dreamworld, you have to wait for me to protect you while you're gone."

Allie nodded, sniffing back her tears.

"I'm the only one we trust with your life, got it?" Darius hugged her tight.

"Got it." Allie stood on shaky legs, turning to search for her sister. "Livia." She rubbed her chafed wrists, crossing the lawn to Livia's side. "Thank you." She wrapped her arms around her sister. "You saved my life. How did you know?"

"I knew someone was going to betray you. Navid prepared me for it months ago. When you disappeared from the dreamworld at the worst possible moment, I knew something was wrong, and you weren't protected."

"And Navid?"

"Is home." Her face lit up with a beautiful smile. "I found him near the lake. He seems to have had enough sense not to wander too far from the tower entrance. I think he's been traveling in circles around that lake for months, just waiting for us to come get him."

"I hate to break up the reunion, but we need to get out of here before the other assholes wake up," Vince said. "We're the most fragile ones here, so we're going to go lay low somewhere until this blows over." He took his girlfriend's hand.

"Wait." Allie walked toward them. "How can I thank you?"

"Take care of that niece of yours." Vince whispered. "And it wouldn't hurt if these guys could forget about us, if you know what I mean."

"Consider it done." Allie would have to convince Daniel to work his memory mojo on all those who'd witnessed Vince's assistance tonight, but she was certain he would do whatever he could to protect Vince and Kayla for proving their loyalty to Allie tonight. "Thank you. Both of you." Allie took each of their hands in hers. "You risked too much coming here. You're like my freaking guardian angels."

"Time to go, little one," Liam said. "We'll talk about *this* situation you've managed to get your self into later." He eyed Vince and Kayla with suspicion.

"Sure, Liam." Hopefully Daniel could work his memory magic before Liam wanted to have that conversation.

"Come on, Allie." Livia draped her arm around her sister. "Let's get you out of here."

"Yeah," Allie said. "Let's go get our dad."

"Dad!" Allie and Livia darted across the Yard back in the underground. Navid stood with Alísun and Santi on the edge of the small underground lake near his cottage.

"Give him a minute," Santi cautioned them as they approached. "Let him see you first. After almost four months in Brecken's prison world, he's disoriented. Navid believes he is still captive in the dreamworld."

"What should we do?" Livia asked, her eyes glued to her father.

"Stay calm and just talk to him like you normally would. Don't try to touch him. Let him come to you."

"How long will it take him to recover?" Allie asked.

"It's different for everyone but he is in good hands and in a safe place with people who love him. He will recover in time."

"My girls?" Navid caught sight of them. "It's not safe here." It shattered Allie's heart to watch him shuffle across the Yard like an old man. Allie and Livia walked slowly, trying not to startle him.

"It's okay, Dad," Livia said. "You're safe now."

"You can't stay long, my girls." Navid cast a nervous glance around him. "The landscape is always changing, but the lake is the constant. I stay here, waiting and watching, but I'm not sure why." He grasped his daughter's hands with a sense of urgency. "You have to go, please. Take care of each other." He shoved them away, growing more and more agitated.

"You're okay, Navid," Allie said. "We'll go." She took a step back, resisting the urge to fling herself into her father's arms.

"Run, girls. He's coming. You don't understand. He kills you every time." Navid's bloodshot eyes filled with tears. "After all the sacrifices we've made, it can't come to this." He stumbled to his knees. "You're all I have left."

Allie and Livia both rushed to his side, helping him back to his feet. Livia threw her arms around him and whispered something in his ear.

"We love you, Dad." Allie wiped the tears from her eyes, feeling helpless.

"Come now, my girls" Alísun said. "Gregg and Alexander are waiting for us." Their grandmother draped her arms around Allie and Livia. "It's okay my darlings, we will keep trying until Navid comes back to us."

Allie just wondered how long that might be.

"How is Navid?" Gregg asked the moment Allie and Livia stepped into his office with their grandmother.

"Not lucid yet." Allie sighed, pausing to hug her grandfather. "But it's good to have him home. I'm just so grateful Livia was able to get him out before she came for me."

"I'm grateful she was able to save you too, Allie-girl." Alexander squeezed her shoulders.

"I'm afraid we need to decide what to do with this traitor." Liam gestured to Greyson sitting quietly in the corner. They had him restrained with magnetic cuffs around his wrists. He sat with a vacant stare, waiting for whatever came next.

"Tell me why I shouldn't kill you where you sit," Livia

said, her voice cold and menacing. "You've conveniently brought your Complement along with you, it can be arranged."

Allie didn't like seeing this version of her sister again. She didn't like anything about this whole situation.

"I would see him punished for this," Gregg said, "but we will leave that to you and your family." He couldn't even look at his long time friend.

"We cannot let this attempt on Alexis pass without severe punishment," the queen agreed. "Perhaps when Navid is well again he can pass judgment for a sentence fitting the crime?"

"Alísun, dear, we should let Allie decide his punishment," Alexander said. "It's her call to make."

Allie crossed the room to Greyson's side, unable to fathom a punishment severe enough for what he'd done.

"Look at me," Allie demanded.

His green eyes lifted, misery and shame etched across his face. "I am so sorry, Allie. I—"

Allie's fist slammed into his face before he could finish his sentence. Blood spurted from his crushed nose, giving her the sense of satisfaction she desperately needed in that moment.

"You almost destroyed our chance to bring my father home. You were willing to trade not only me, but Navid as well. You would leave him to an eternity in a torture world?"

"I wasn't thinking clearly. I can't ever—"

I know." She lifted her hand to stop another apology from tumbling from his mouth. "You were desperate. I can't imagine what it must be like to live so long separated from your Complement."

"I was weak." He cast his gaze back down to his hands resting in his lap. "It happened so fast and I just didn't think it through."

"You know all my secrets, Greyson. All the dangerous things about my power, my family. Darius. The prophecy ... you know it all. I was stupid to forget what your ability knows of me, but even if had remembered, I still would have trusted you with my life."

"I will never be able to atone for what I've done." He shook his head, his eyes dazed and glassy like the last few hours didn't feel real. "I deserve whatever punishment you decide. Just please don't punish Ise for my mistakes? She's so fragile. If ... if you choose to end my life." He glanced at Livia. "Or take my immortality, please take care of my wife and our daughter." He sent a pleading look to Gregg. "You are Naomi's only family. She will need you."

"I would never ask my sister to use her ability on anyone —for her sake," Allie said. "And as angry as I am, as much as I might want to lash out at you right now, my judgment gift doesn't thirst for your immortality."

"Well, that's more than I deserve." Greyson fumbled to wipe the blood trickling from his nose.

"You took advantage of the situation. I trusted you to protect me in a vulnerable moment—didn't even think twice about it, and you jumped at the chance to ruin me. I will choose to believe that is a decision you made in a moment of weakness."

"It was, Allie. Isebeau would never want this—I never wanted it this way. It was just a constant temptation I succumbed to in a moment of insanity."

Gregg slammed his fist against the wooden surface of his desk. "Then you should have talked to me about that temptation, Greyson. We would have dealt with it. But you didn't because you knew you wanted to act on it and you wanted her there when you finally had the balls to do it." Gregg's voice was like acid, full of disappointment and regret. "I don't know, maybe I should have seen it." Gregg shook his head.

"Where is Isebeau?" Allie looked to Liam.

"Resting for now. It will be a long time before she's ready to join the modern world. It will be far worse for her than it has been for Daniel. She's spent the bulk of her life in captivity."

"Please just get on with your punishment," Greyson said. "I'm ready."

"Punishment? You think I have any idea what to do with you? I'm heartbroken, Greyson. I'm angry. I want to strangle you with my bare hands, but even after all this, I still care about you. Isebeau needs you. She's been through enough."

"I never deserved your friendship." Greyson turned his head away, refusing to meet her eyes.

"She is a wise young woman with a capacity to forgive that I will never understand," Livia said. "If she isn't ready to punish you, I am more than ready to accept the challenge."

"No, Livia. I won't sit here and watch you revert to the woman you used to be. I will punish Greyson my way." Allie looked to her grandparents for their approval. The queen nodded her consent.

"You will take Isebeau to a safe place," Allie said. "Somewhere far from society where she can recover in peace. And you will stay there in a prison of your own making."

"You're letting me go?" Greyson asked, incredulous.

Allie nodded. "And don't ever come back. I won't ever think of you again after tonight but my brother will monitor your movement."

"And I will," Liam said, crossing his arms over his chest. "Though my sister is much too lenient."

"And what about our daughter?" Greyson's voice shook

with emotion. "Will you allow Naomi to visit us? Or will you ban her from her friends and family too?"

"Naomi will always be welcome here among those who love her and she is free to visit her parents as much or as little as she wants. But if you ever betray my secrets again, Liam will find you and then Livia and I will come for you, and you won't like what we'll do to you and your Complement then."

Chapter 31

Allie | Cleveland | July

"Wait *how* much were these chairs?" Allie gawked at her sister.

"I think six thousand." Livia shrugged, placing the beautiful white leather chairs at the center of the hayloft room.

"Each?"

"They're Barcelona chairs," Emma said, holding up paint samples against the finished walls.

"Does that mean they lay golden eggs?"

"No, silly. It means they're as comfortable as they are beautiful. Try them out," Emma said. "I'll never make it back up from those things with this twelve month pregnant belly."

"It's nine months, isn't it?" Livia frowned.

"She's being factious. She's only eight months along." Allie sat opposite her sister, and she suddenly found herself looking up at the new skylight, watching the rain come down in torrents. Her feet dangled a good four inches from the floor. "Comfortable you said?" Allie struggled to sit up straight.

"We'll get you a little stool to put your feet on," Emma offered.

"This leather does feel like butter." Allie smoothed her hand over the divine material. "But what's with the dead cow on the floor?" she asked as thunder and lighting boomed and crashed outside.

"It's a leather rug," Livia said.

"It still has its hair." She wrinkled her nose. "How much did that cost?"

"Don't ask." Livia rolled her eyes.

"Who's paying for all this? I thought we'd just pick up some used furniture at a yard sale or something. It's a *barn,* guys. A barn that's now a gym. It doesn't need to be fancy."

"Uh, yes it does," Livia said. "And don't worry about the cost. Consider it a lifetime of birthday presents and a special something extra for your twentieth birthday in a few months." She sat in the chair opposite Allie, somehow making the chair look like the perfect throne.

"You did this? The twelve grand on two chairs was your idea?"

"You don't like it?" Livia's face fell.

"It's beautiful, but it's awfully grand for a place where we're all going to sweat and bleed ... a lot."

"It's my gift to you. Just don't bleed on the furniture."

Allie turned around in her seat, draping her legs over the back, her hair brushing the floor. "Are we rich, Liv?"

"I am. I don't know about you." Livia smirked. "But that mortal mother of yours downstairs hanging the artwork has likely taken care of your future already. At least your immediate future. And Liam will spoil you rotten for the rest of your life."

"People do tend to just buy things for me. I used to complain about it a lot. But I never won those arguments, so I stopped trying."

"You have such a weird life, kid." Livia laughed.

"Tell me about it." A loud splatter hit the floor, and Allie stared up at the ceiling. "I think we have a leak. We'll have to get Liam in here to fix it. I don't want my new leather stuff to get ruined."

"That wasn't a roof leak." Emma stood by the door, frozen like a statue. "Was that my water breaking?" She peered down at the puddle between her feet. "You have another month. You stay in there little girl." She stroked her stomach.

"No, no, no." Livia stood up, a look of utter terror on her face. "She's supposed to have another month." She shot an accusing glare at Allie.

"Babies come early sometimes." Allie shrugged. "Maybe I was off by a few weeks."

"A few weeks? Allie, I'm not ready for this." Emma's voice went up a few octaves.

"Hold your legs together, woman." Livia's eyes widened in terror. "We are not equipped to handle this. We need an adult."

"It doesn't work like that, Liv." Allie rolled her eyes and slid out of her chair.

"It's the storm of the century out there." Livia turned wide eyes on Allie. "And it's just us and Lily here with *her*." She stuck her finger out at Emma like she was a bomb about to explode. "And Lily is probably going to notice weird things about this birth."

"We'll just call an ambulance," Allie said. "These things take time, and she's just gone into labor. It'll be hours, plenty of time for help to arrive."

"Nope." Emma shook her head. "I am Immortal. I will just hold this baby inside until the storm passes. We'll just reschedule it." Emma clamped her legs together, rubbing her belly like she could stop the labor pains.

"Allie, we can't call an ambulance!" Livia's voice barely concealed her panic. "They're going to notice she heals."

"What? Heals?" Allie started to panic with her sister. "What's to heal? It's a baby, not a knife wound."

"I think things tear. Down there," Livia said.

"Tear?" Emma's eyes widened. "Nobody said anything about tearing."

Allie crossed the little soundproofed room to open the door, slamming it shut behind her. "MOM!" Allie shouted. "Emma's in labor." She rushed down the steps to where Lily was hanging the artwork on the lower level. Allie told her Immortal family that her mother thought this was just a run-of-the-mill workout gymnasium, and that Lily wanted to help decorate the space.

"Can you pretend this is a normal thing?" Allie whispered. "We can't really call an ambulance."

"Allie, it's the most normal thing in the world." Lily laughed. "No sense in freaking out. "

"Do you know what to do? We are the stupidest group of women ever when it comes to this stuff."

"I delivered you." Lily laughed. "And your mother was just as freaked out as Emma probably is."

"You did?" Allie's eyebrows shot up in surprise.

"I was there from the moment you took your first breath. And I'll tell you a big secret," she said, lowering her voice. "I delivered Graham, too, and now I get to deliver his little brother or sister."

"Graham? What? How?" Allie stood, completely thunderstruck.

"Oh, come on, Allie. You've seen Kahlynn with Vince and Kayla. Haven't you figured it out yet? Your niece looks just like Kayla, and she's got Vince's nose and smile."

"But ... Graham isn't a natural born." Allie shook her head in confusion.

"Did you think the stork brought him?" Lily teased. "Of course, he was born the old fashioned way. You all were."

"But who was his—"

"Birth mom? Your sister, Josceline. You never noticed how much he looks like her?"

"Wait, when did that happen?" Graham is my nephew? Sort of? I'm so confused." Allie hadn't seen her mortal sister in ages, but she thought she would have remembered if Josceline had ever had a baby—even it happened when Allie was just a kid.

"You look exactly like you did the first time I told you where babies come from."

"Mom." Allie groaned, following her mother back up the stairs to the loft. "We're talking about this later," she hissed. "I'm going to need you to explain everything you just said. In detail."

"Oh, come on, we have a baby to deliver. I'll play the dumb mortal. I've been doing that for most of my life."

"I love you, Ma." Allie rushed into the room behind her.

"Deep breaths, Emma," Lily crooned. "We'll get through this together. I'm afraid the storm has us stranded here. But I've done this before, believe it or not."

"Oh, thank God," Emma said, still rubbing her belly. "I've read all the books, but I hadn't ever planned to do this, you know. And I'm not a young woman," she rambled. "So I don't know how prepared I am for this."

"When did the pain start?"

"I don't know. I've been a walrus for months. Everything aches all the time."

"Little cramps all day maybe?" Lily asked. "Like a back ache but a bit stronger."

"Well, yes. All afternoon actually, but I thought labor pains would be more obvious."

"Not always. It can sneak up on you. When was the last pain?"

"Maybe about five minutes ago. But it wasn't bad."

"All right, I think this is going to be a long night. Let's get you in the house and more comfortable."

"Comfortable is good." Emma nodded. "And I'm a barge, I can just float us there."

"That sense of humor is going to come in handy." Lily laughed. "Livia and I are going to get you downstairs and if you need to rest at all, just tell us."

"Got it." Emma grabbed Lily's hand. "I'm so glad you're here."

"I've got you." Lily smiled. "Allie, run ahead to the house and call Daniel. Tell him Emma is fine, but she's gone into labor. He is *not* to try to get here in this storm. Got it?"

"Yes, ma'am." Allie rushed down the steps ahead of them. A loud pop sounded, and sparks flew from the power lines between the house and the barn. The lights went out a second later. "Trees are down in the yard, but we can still get to the house if we hurry." Allie peered out the windows, worried about getting Emma to a safe dry place.

"Go, Allie. Call Daniel and then clean off your bed down to the sheets and gather up all your clean towels."

"My bed?" Allie wrinkled her nose.

"Go!" All three women yelled at her. Allie darted through the downpour. Her hair was plastered to her head by the time she made it through the back door of the cottage. They were going to need lots of towels.

"Come on, pick up," she murmured into her phone. She finally heard his voice. "Daniel? She's in labor."

"I'm coming. Where are you?"

"The cottage. I'm supposed to tell you not to try to get here. It's too dangerous in this storm."

"I'm not missing the birth of my child. I'm on my way." The line went dead before she could tell him to be careful. She had no idea how he intended to get across the lake, but she had bigger things to worry about.

Allie raced around her house, doing as her mother said. She was ready with towels and blankets when they finally made it inside.

"Let's get her into some pajamas," Allie said, holding up a clean pair of fleece pants and shirt.

"Not conducive to delivering a baby, kiddo. You have a night gown anywhere?"

"Right, sorry. I have some long t-shirts." Allie grabbed a clean shirt, and together they helped Emma strip off her wet clothes. Livia helped her dry off, and Allie tugged the shirt over her head.

"Now, we're going to move her to the bedroom," Lily instructed. "Allie, do you have any hand sanitizer?"

"Uh. No, sorry." She never needed it. Germs didn't affect her or anyone who lived in this house.

"How about alcohol? This is pretty much a frat house, right? You kids must have some booze here somewhere."

"Uh, yeah. I think Darius has a stash."

"Bring a basin with you."

Allie ran for the kitchen and returned with a bottle of vodka from the freezer and a plastic container.

"Pour it over my hands," Lily instructed, playing the part of the clueless mortal worried about germs that didn't even matter. "Livia, get her on the bed. Keep her calm and her breath slow and deep."

Allie sat next to Emma on her bed, grabbing her hand. "You're going to be okay, Emma."

"That's right," Lily said. "I'm just going to check you over and see how things are progressing." Lily lifted the hem of Emma's t-shirt.

"Deep breath, Emma," Allie said. "Inhale nice and slow. Exhale slow. Good."

"Okay, relax, little momma." Lily moved to cover Emma with a blanket. "It's going to be a while before this kid's ready to be born."

"You're sure?" Emma asked.

"Positive. Allie, I'll sit with Emma. Can you and Livia find some flashlights and candles? It's going to get really dark in here soon."

"Anything else we need? Hot water? A knife?" Allie asked.

"Bring some protein bars, some bottled water and a really sharp knife."

"Got it." Allie was pretty sure pregnant women didn't eat during labor, but Lily had to know Emma would need it to keep up her stamina, especially if this was going to be a long delivery.

After scrambling around the dark house, gathering everything they could possibly need—including some things Lily sent them for that Allie didn't think they'd ever need—the baby still wasn't coming.

"He's a slow chap, isn't he?" Allie sank into the armchair by the gas fireplace in the living room. She dunked her tea bag into the hot water she'd heated with her solar gift.

"You know it's a boy?" Livia asked in a soft tone.

"Oh crap. I hope she didn't hear me. I've been so careful the last few months not to let it slip."

"Boys are easier." Livia took a long gulp from the vodka bottle.

"I hope Daniel makes it in time," Allie said.

"The rate this kid is traveling he'll be here in plenty of time." The storm still raged all around the little cottage, rattling the windows and filling the house with flickers of lightening.

A sudden shriek echoed in the silence between bouts of thunder, and Allie and Livia ran for the bedroom.

"Is it time?" Allie asked.

"Almost," Lily said, examining Emma's progress again. "Yep. It's time to start pushing, Emma."

Emma looked exhausted already. A sheen of sweat glistened on her brow, and her eyes were bloodshot, a simmer of power pulsing with every labored breath.

"You ready for this?" Allie brushed a damp cloth over her mentor's brow.

Emma nodded. "As ready as I'll ever be."

"Allie, I want you to sit behind her and prop her up," Lily instructed. "Hold her hands when she has a contraction and help her breathe through it until I say push."

"Got it." Allie kicked off her shoes and climbed on the bed behind Emma. Sitting on her knees, Allie leaned Emma back against her, taking her hands and giving her a reassuring squeeze. "We've got this, Ems. You just squeeze as hard as you need to."

"Come on, Emma, I know you're tired, but you can do this." Allie winced as Emma screamed and dug her nails into her arms, pushing for all she was worth. She'd been at it for hours. Allie had seen more of her mentor than she'd ever wanted to. And she'd seen more gross things in the last few hours than she had in her entire life, and that included the time Gregg took Jin's head off with a sword to teach her a lesson.

"Why won't she come out?" Emma sobbed. "What's wrong with her?" Emma was convinced she was having a girl, but Allie knew she would be just as happy when she met her little son.

"Nothing's wrong," Lily said calmly. She was often the only calm one in the room—and Livia was absolutely no help at all. She'd noped right out of the room at the first sign of blood. "It's just taking her a little longer than most. She'll come out when she's ready."

Emma's contractions were right on top of each other now, and Allie braced herself for another push. Emma gripped Allie's forearms, as her hands were pretty well crushed after hours of Emma's pushing to no avail. Lily pretended like she didn't notice the odd way Allie's hands and fingers swelled and bruised.

A loud crash at the back door startled them.

"Daniel?" Emma rasped. "Is he here?"

"Emma?" Daniel's footsteps pounded down the hallway just before he burst into the room. Soaking wet, his eyes wide and crazy, Allie was pretty sure he just took a really long swim to get here in time for the birth of his child. "I'm here." Daniel scrambled to take Allie's place behind his Complement. "We've got this, Emma."

"All right, Mom, now that Dad is here, let's have a big push, now," Lily coached.

Emma gripped Daniel's hands; letting out a string of what Allie was sure was a lot of French swear words.

"That's it. Good job, Emma," Lily said. "The head's out, and this baby has a full head of dark hair just like Mom."

Thunder boomed and lightening crashed as candlelight

filled the room. Emma's screams of pain and frustration nearly burst Allie's eardrums. The blood. The darkness. The screams. Allie finally realized why her visions of Emma's child coming into the world had been so violent and terrifying.

"That's it, keep pushing," Lily said. "He's almost out."

"He?" Emma gasped, clamping down on Daniel's arms once more as she made a final push.

"It's a boy!" Lily cried. "And he's beautiful." Allie watched in awe as her mother swept the baby's mouth clean, clipped the cord, and smacked him on the butt. He was so tiny, but he gave a healthy wail right along with his mom.

"He's so little," Emma cried, reaching for him as Lily laid him on her chest.

"Ten fingers, ten toes. He's perfect." Daniel beamed.

"And he looks a bit like Graham, don't you think?" Lily said.

"He does," Emma laughed, tears of joy running down her face. "He has his brother's nose, thank God. I was afraid the baby would get Daniel's nose."

"Hey, I have a perfectly fine nose," Daniel laughed. "But I think this little one looks just like his beautiful mother.

"Is it over?" Livia peeked her head in through the open door.

"Come see him, Liv." Allie couldn't contain her huge smile. "He's so beautiful."

"He's all red and wrinkly," Livia said, looking over Lily's shoulder. "Is that normal?"

"Perfectly normal," Lily assured her. "Once the storm has cleared, we can get you two to the hospital if you want to, Emma, but it's perfectly natural to have a baby at home and then follow up with your regular doctor in a few days and file for a birth certificate."

That was a load of c.r.a.p., if Allie had ever heard it. But

Emma didn't know any better, and Lily provided the perfect excuse not to go to the hospital. An Immortal mother and child would never need things like doctors and Darius would handle a forged birth certificate. Fake documents were his specialty.

"Thank you, Lily." Emma reached for her hand, cradling her son with her other. "I can never thank you enough for guiding me through this. We would have made a mess of it without you."

"I'm just glad I was here." Lily stood to bathe the baby and wrap him in a warm, clean towel before she gave him back to his mother.

"What are you going to name him?" Allie asked while her mother got Emma cleaned up.

"We thought he'd be a girl, so we were going to name her Parker Alexis Loukas," Daniel said, unable to take his eyes off his son.

"But since he's a beautiful boy, his name is Alex Parker Loukas," Emma said.

"After me?" Allie almost started bawling.

"Of course, you're my favorite student," she whispered.

"I'm your only student." Allie sniffed.

"Will you be Parker's godmother?" Emma and Daniel smiled at her.

"Me?" Allie was shocked at their level of trust. For Immortals, godparents took on a different role than the traditional mortal one. They were asking her to be their child's mentor.

Emma nodded. "There's no one better for the job.

"I'd be honored."

CHAPTER 32

Allie | Kelleys Island | August

"Emma?" Darius shouted, his voice echoing across the empty common room in the underground. "We need you!"

"Darius, I'm fine now." Allie tried to shrug off his death grip around her shoulders.

"You are not fine." His voice sounded harsh in the dark. It was nice having someone care so much about her. Most of the time. But sometimes having a Darius was like having another mom and Allie had plenty of those.

A sword flicked against Darius's throat. "I will slice your carotid open right here if you yell one more time," Emma's voice was tinged with a little crazy.

"We just got Parker to sleep," Daniel said in a whisper. "If you wake him up, I will kill you with my bare hands, if my wife doesn't get to you first."

"Not much sleeping happening with a newborn, huh?" Darius took a careful step back.

"We're too old for this." Emma's shoulders slumped, letting her sword down at her side. "He won't sleep in his perfectly lovely crib at home. No, my son prefers the underground like some kind of goblin baby."

"I told you this could have waited for tomorrow," Allie said. She knew something new was emerging and she needed her mentor, but the whole thing just reminded her of all the times when Aidan was the one insisting she seek out Emma's help. And Allie spent a great deal of effort avoiding anything that made her think about Aidan. She missed him too much. And missing him made her angry.

"What's wrong?" Emma finally looked at Allie. "You need me, too?" She sounded like she wanted to cry.

"Nope. I'm good."

"We're already here. Tell her," Darius insisted.

Allie rolled her eyes. "I kind of freaked out in a public place." She shrugged. "I saw a bunch of stuff that wasn't actually there. And then I sorta went blind for about an hour. But I'm perfectly fine now."

"Get her in my office." Emma pointed down the hall with her sword. "Daniel, coffee? Lots of it."

"I don't think you can have coffee if you're still nursing," Allie said, and then wished she could swallow her tongue.

"You want to fight with me, too, Red?"

"Nope. Bring on the coffee."

"Could be why the kid doesn't sleep," Darius muttered. "Can caffeine pass from her to the baby? I mean she could be feeding him a steady diet of cappuccinos."

"I have no idea, but shut up and keep walking. Remember she has a sword." Allie grabbed his hand and speed-walked toward Emma's office.

"Define freak out?" Emma flopped onto her sofa a moment later, setting the baby monitor on the coffee table. Parker made the cutest gurgling noises from his crib in the room at the back of her office.

"Well, we were out at this school thing earlier tonight, and I saw a bunch of ... stuff that no one else saw."

"Stuff?"

"That's all she'll say," Darius offered. "I'm still trying to figure out that part."

"Giant people-sized blobs of ... stuff just moving around like everyone else. There was sound, too—lots of it—but I couldn't make out words. It was scary, and I guess I screamed over the noise, thinking everyone could see and hear it. And now everyone at school thinks I'm even more weird."

"And the blindness?" Emma sighed, resting her hand against her temple.

"I've been having trouble with blurry vision for months, but I just thought it was dry eyes from all the late night studying. I didn't even think to mention it before. But the blurry part happened earlier today, worse than usual. And when I saw the ... stuff, everything went blurry again and then nothing. For like an hour, I just couldn't see anything. And now I'm fine."

"Scared the hell out of me," Darius said. "So I brought her straight here."

"I've been waiting for something like this to happen to one of you," Emma said. "Figures it's Allie."

"I'm not sure how to take that." Allie sat up straighter.

"Everything happens to you, Allie." Emma smiled. "It's just a given."

"What does it mean?"

"It sounds like a Syntrophos thing. We know you balance each other. You're stronger and faster because of the bond, but in my studies, I've learned some Syntrophos can experience a sort of merging of abilities. I suspect it happens more so for younger pairs who are still evolving and more susceptible to the change."

"So, this is some sort of hybrid gift?" Allie asked.

"I think you just had a vision, Allie. A simple vision like

you've had thousands of times. But instead of it happening in your head where your mind's eye can see it, it happened right in front of you, like a three-dimensional vision."

"How is that a Syntrophos thing?"

"Oh. I get it," Darius said. "It's like what I see when I visit a crime scene."

"A reanimation?" Allie frowned.

"For me it's a replay of the crime. I can see it similar to the way mom tells a story and shows her animations, so you can see her stories. Kind of like that, but a little less cute when it's murder, blood and violence. For me, the reanimations are fairly crude, so maybe that's why you're not seeing anything discernable yet."

"That's a great analysis, Darius," Daniel said, setting a tray of coffee cups on the table in front of his wife. "I'm not sure I would have made that connection to your gift so quickly."

"Okay, so my visions are getting a three-D makeover? Is that it?" Allie accepted the steaming mug from Emma, taking a sip of the rich, dark Greek coffee Daniel preferred.

"We'll have to wait and see." Emma sipped from her mug. "And we'll deal with it as it comes."

"But what about the blindness?" Darius asked.

"Probably just a symptom of the change," Daniel said.

"It shouldn't happen again," Emma added.

"I told you. Easy peasy," Allie said. "Next time, I won't shout, and eventually maybe those blob things will actually look like something."

Chapter 33

Allie | The Dreamworld | September

"I don't like you going back to the dreamworld, Allie." Darius stubbornly crossed his arms over his chest. "Not after last time."

"Last time was a fluke. You're here to watch over me this time. It wasn't the dreamworld's fault someone decided to betray me." Allie refused to say Greyson's name out loud. It just hurt too much and reminded her how much she missed him. Since Greyson and Isebeau left for the remote areas of Northern Ontario along the Hudson Bay, Gregg had changed his approach to Allie and Darius's Syntrophos training. They no longer had to spend forced time apart. Gregg decided that had ultimately done more harm than good, driving Allie to spend more time with Greyson.

Now that they were together more often, their relationship felt more balanced and natural. Except when Darius threw a hissy fit about her safety.

"At least wait until we can get to the Yard. I'd rather you do this somewhere safe."

"I am somewhere safe, Dare. Our home is perfectly safe and Liam is just across the street with Kahlynn."

"Let me at least call Brigs to come over."

"No." Allie's voice was sharper than she intended.

Darius's eyebrows shot up. "Trouble in paradise?"

"Paradise?" Allie snorted a laugh. "It was never that."

"Was?"

"Brigs doesn't know it yet, but my gift tells me he's leaving soon. If I can ever get to the dreamworld to help win this war."

"Fine. Just please be careful," Darius relented.

"Yes, Mother." Allie rolled her eyes, taking a seat on their living room floor.

"Let's get this over with so Brigs can leave. The sooner the better."

"I thought you didn't hate him?" Allie frowned, placing her hands on her knees.

"Then I've done my job well. That guy's not good enough for you and he knows it."

"I swear if you had it your way, I'd be a freaking nun." Allie muttered as she quickly found the calm state she needed to enter the dreamworld, hopefully one last time to win the war against Brecken.

Allie face planted in the grass, the dreamworld sun warm at her back. The nausea was old hat by now, but the others swarmed around her to give her a minute to adjust.

A familiar hand helped her up, but she quickly tugged it away. She liked Brigs, but it occurred to her she wasn't all that sad that he would be moving on soon.

"Alright, she's here, now what's the plan?" Livia demanded. She was with Darius. Livia didn't want Allie in the dreamworld either.

Quinn cleared his throat as he turned to address his walkers. "The night we brought Navid home, we were able to free the last of the walkers held captive in the towers."

A roar of approval swept through the dream walkers, along with a lot of back-slapping and fists in the air.

"Well done, my friends. We couldn't have done any of this without your help, but it's time we officially end this war. Over the past few days, even Brecken's most faithful have left his side, seeking my protection and pledging their loyalty to the true commander."

"Why now, after all this time?" Allie asked. "What changed?"

"Good question." Quinn nodded. "We've always known Brecken preys on the fear of our dreamers to strengthen himself and those beneath him, but I could never figure out how he could also promise his followers more time in the dreamworld. He made grand promises to those who supported him, vowing to double their thresholds. It was how he was able to inspire such loyalty. Now we know how he accomplished such a feat."

"The prisoners?" Brigs asked, a horrified look on his face.

"Exactly," Quinn said, his voice grew harsh with determination. "Brecken has been syphoning enormous levels of power from his prison towers, using it to give his supporters what they craved. Now that the source of his power is gone, the loyalty he purchased has also vanished, leaving him alone and vulnerable."

"What of those who have left him?" Raina asked. "Will they be punished?"

"Most have defected to our side in fear of the repercussions it is my right to deliver," Quinn said. "And I will punish them as I see fit, but first, we must deal with Brecken himself. He is holed up in his castle, afraid to face me. He's surrounded himself with dreamers to protect him and I will not stand for it."

"Then let's go get the bastard." Danica took a menacing step forward. "What's the plan?"

"I will fight Brecken alone," Quinn said. "But I need your help to get to him first. We will have to fight through the dreamers, but I would prefer we not hurt them if we can avoid it. That's where you two come in." He turned to face Allie and Livia. "You've been able to lure large quantities of dreamers back to their dreamscapes with fire. Can you teach the others to help?"

"Of course," Allie said. After helping the first prisoner's escape, Allie discovered the walkers responded to the warmth of fire even when they were locked in the nightmares of the prison world. She'd discovered the dreamers were similar. After some trial and error, Livia and Allie had learned to create a source of fire imbued with all the safety of home and warmth and good things so the fire acted like a beacon to the battle weary dreamers who were nothing more than scared children.

"How do you make the fire blue?" Quinn asked.

"And it smells like fresh baked cookies and reminds me of my mom," Brigs added.

"Yeah, you should bottle that stuff," Danica said. "We're all pretty much in love with it."

"We'll teach you how to make Allie's nauseating fantasy fire, but when is this happening?" Livia asked.

Quinn's eyes hardened and he lifted his chin in defiance. "We leave in half an hour so make it quick."

Allie waved her twin torches like flags, blue fire dancing at the tips. A swarm of dreamers followed her through the carnage of Brecken's failing dreamscape.

"That's right, kiddos. Follow Auntie Allie and her magic fire. The nightmare is almost over. You're going to wake up, warm in your beds and you're only going to have good dreams from now on." One by one, she lured the battle weary soldiers beyond Brecken's reach. She knew they would be okay when their identical hardened exteriors melted away, revealing the frightened children underneath. Most of them were so young she hoped the memory of the dreams would completely fade from their minds in time. As the last girl drifted back to her own dreamscape, Allie raced back to the castle to round up another group.

The ground shook with a massive quake and Allie tumbled head first down the hill, landing at Brigs's feet.

"Sometimes I wonder how you manage to fall so much." He crouched down beside her.

"The world likes to trip me." Allie rolled onto her back with a groan.

Brigs offered his hand and pulled her back to her feet.

"How's it going in there?" Allie worried about Quinn facing Brecken alone.

"Judging by the state of Brecken's castle, not good for him. I think this war is all but won."

"Alright then, let's go catch the end of it." Allie jogged across the rocky landscape, mostly free of the roaming soldiers that had filled the space when they arrived. Brigs and the other walkers had managed to escort most of the dreamers from the war zone.

"Over there." Brigs pointed to the collapsed bridge where the other walkers and Livia had gathered.

"What's going on?" Allie asked as she joined her sister.

"I don't know. Lots of destruction, but they move so fast, I can't tell what's happening."

"Quinn is bringing the castle down around Brecken's

head, but Brecken is putting up a good fight," Brigs said. "I don't know why he doesn't just surrender. It's clear who the master of the dreamworld is."

"Clear to everyone but Brecken," Allie muttered. She watched in awe as the castle battlements collapsed, fading to fine dust before they hit the ground. The remnants of the castle stood in a pile of rubble where the two men fought for dominance. Quinn's sword blocked Brecken's as he countered his opponent, pushing him back. A sheen of sweat covered Quinn's bare back, his dark skin like obsidian against the stark white stone of the castle.

"Surrender." Quinn's voice echoed across the sky, his authority and power over this world clear to everyone present.

"So you can banish me from this world?" Brecken raged, his massive chest heaving with the effort to fight the Commander of the dreamworld.

"Drop your sword and end this war now and I will not banish you, but I will only make the offer once."

"Why should I believe you?" Brecken spat in Quinn's face.

"Because I am your commander. Now, end this." Quinn's voice grew dangerous, like the sharp edge of a blade.

Brecken swore and threw his sword down. "I suppose you want me to kneel too?"

"I am no king. Your surrender is all I require."

"Quinn, you have to banish him," Brigs said. "He'll just rise up again."

"No he won't." Quinn said, dismissing Brigs's concern. The ground began to shake as trees and grass sprouted from the barren landscape. A lake burst forth from the ground like a geyser and the land where the castle once stood lifted beneath their feet, morphing into a butte at the center of

Brecken's dreamscape. The rubble of the castle retreated, reforming walls and rooms within.

Quinn stepped away from the much smaller castle, joining his walkers near the newly repaired gates where a bridge once stood. "Brecken, for your crimes against the dreamworld, you will never be accepted among the walkers of this realm. But I will not banish you from this world, nor will I trap you inside it. You may come and go as you please between the waking world and your own dreamscape. You may bend this small corner of the dreamworld to your will, but you may never leave this place. No dreamer will ever enter this remote corner. And no walker will join you to rise again. You will remain a part of the dreamworld, but you will never again have fellowship with your own kind.

"For how long?" Brecken asked. His shoulder slumped, resigned to his punishment.

Quinn tilted his head. "Forever." He turned to join his people.

"Quinn, wait," Brecken called. "You may as well trap me in this prison of my own making. I'm as good as dead once I return to the waking world."

"Then may God and whatever master you serve have mercy on your soul."

Chapter 34

Aidan | Atlanta | September

The others have it so much worse than I do. Over the last three months, Aidan had constantly reminded himself he was lucky compared to everyone else living on Marcus's estate. If you could call it living. He never saw them. Marcus kept his prisoners secured beneath the estate. Some never saw the light of day. Most were ancients, important Immortals their contemporaries had long forgotten. Allie's grandmother was once one of them. She'd managed to escape with the help of Marcus's wife, Porcia. But Porcia was long gone and there was no one here to help Aidan now.

Marcus treated him like a son—a prince even—at least in Marcus's estimation. He'd tried to insert himself as a father figure into Aidan's life, but Aidan had an amazing father. One that could never be replaced. If anything, Greggory McBrien had prepared his son for this. At the end of the day, Aidan would have a comfortable bed to sleep in and enough food to keep him strong. He had a world of luxury at his disposal, but Marcus could never buy his loyalty. Aidan's loyalty belonged to the people he loved. They gave him strength. So Aidan let Marcus call him "son" and pretend to be a father, while Aidan kept those he loved in a part of his mind Marcus would never penetrate. His thoughts and memories were his lifeline in those moments when Aidan thought he would lose control. Sometimes he forgot why he'd chosen this difficult path and then he remembered his family. Allie. Naomi. His Syntrophos family. He was doing this for them, but Aidan often wondered if he'd known what he was getting himself into if he'd have had the strength to make the same decisions again.

"Again," Marcus demanded. "And focus this time, son. I want you to be strong. Strong men push themselves."

"Strong men do not back down in the face of their power." Aidan picked himself up off the ground, wiping the blood from his nose.

"That's right, son. Be a man and own your power. Keep pushing."

Aidan's power raged inside him like a storm he knew he couldn't contain much longer. Already, he felt like his power would rip him apart, but Marcus had barely begun.

"This is where your weak father failed you." Marcus stormed across the training ring. "You fear your power will overrule you, so you pull back when you need to push. You will conquer your power, Aidan. You are strong, and you have it within you to push past the confines of the corruption to touch the pure power the way our kind was meant to."

"I will keep trying, sir." Aidan's voice rasped like sandpaper against his raw throat. Raw from his screams. Aidan swayed on his feet, closing his eyes, he focused on the sounds beyond the walled estate. Sounds of the city surrounded his prison. Like Aidan could just climb the brick wall and escape among the streets of Atlanta. Freedom was just yards away, but impossible to reach. And just another way Marcus liked to torture those inside his gilded cage.

Aidan dusted the red Georgia dirt from his clothes, pacing to the center of the training ring, a clearing beneath the ancient oaks that bordered the estate. Marcus's home was a mixture of an antebellum southern plantation with a splash of the luxury of Versailles.

Aidan's newest prison existed behind an impenetrable shield from the rest of the world. The only way through that shield was with Marcus's permission. Aidan still hadn't figured out how both the queen and Porcia had managed to escape and he probably never would.

"You haven't explored the endless possibilities of your power, Aidan. Every ability is multifaceted and has at least one opposite. If one can tell the skies to flood the earth, they also have the potential to cause a drought. If one can heal, they also have the potential to destroy. One only needs to find the right branch of their gift. Once found, we nourish that branch until it becomes a mighty oak." Marcus held his hands up to the giant trees surrounding them to illustrate his point.

This was what Aidan had volunteered for. He had the role of a lifetime to play and he intended to play it well. Without waiting for Marcus to push him, Aidan reached for his healing gift. He knew it better than Marcus realized. Of course Greggory McBrien had taught his son how to explore his gift. Aidan had studied every potential use of his healing ability, pursuing those he wanted to cultivate, and pruning those, he never wanted to touch. Like a healthy sapling, his gift flourished, growing toward the light, shying away from darkness. Marcus wanted him to explore that darkness.

I am still in control. It doesn't matter what abilities Marcus pulls out of me, my choices will always define me. Not my abilities. Aidan had watched Quinn struggle with the nature of his gifts. Aidan would follow Quinn's lead. He would embrace his darkness but he would always choose light and goodness over evil. He knew he had the strength to follow Marcus into hell and still find his way back. Allie waited for him at the end of this journey and he'd gladly walk through fire to see her again. *I just hope I'm still me when I get there.*

Aidan probed his gift among the darkness, feeling for a handhold. A sliver of a branch he could cling to. He saw several possibilities, but looked for the one with the most light among the darkness.

"That's better," Marcus encouraged him. "Keep going. One breath at a time, Aidan."

Aidan's legs gave out and he fell to his knees. Blood poured from his nose and eyes, but he kept searching. Reaching. Fighting for control of his power, pushing himself to ignore his instincts that told him to end this madness.

"Do not stop," Marcus shouted through the chaos of Aidan's mind. "You will own your power. You will not cower in fear of it as you've been taught."

Only fools pushed themselves this far. Fools and madmen. As Aidan's lungs threatened to burst, he passed the point of no return. His power crashed through him, a perfect storm of anarchy he had no business confronting. Staring into the eyes of a monster of his own making, fear unlike any he'd ever known engulfed him. Aidan's screams ripped from his throat as tears of blood streamed down his face.

"Focus!" Marcus demanded. "Do not falter now or you will lose this battle and you'll be useless to me."

Eyes wide with fright and his sight clouded with blood, Aidan recoiled from the beast he faced. If he failed now, it was all over. His power would consume him and he'd never recover.

"No. You will conquer your fear, Aidan." Marcus slid to his knees in the dirt beside him. "You are the master of this power." Marcus grasped Aidan by his hair and pulled him back to his feet. "That abyss you're staring into right now, that is you. Never fear yourself or the things you can do. Own it. It's yours. Take it now or let it have you. The choice is yours."

Choice. That was what it all came down to. Aidan grasped the miniscule thread of his healing gift, latching onto it with a strength he didn't know he possessed. The strand felt awkward and unnatural, but he powered through the revulsion.

"That's it, son," Marcus praised. "Take it."

"I am not your son," Aidan hissed through clenched teeth. Clinging to the tainted thread of his gift like a lifeline, Aidan clawed his way back. He would take it all. He would soak up everything Marcus had to teach him.

And then he'd use it to destroy him.

PART IV
18 MONTHS LATER

Chapter 35

Aidan | Milan, Italy | March

Aidan stared out the dark, tinted windows of the limousine, watching the now familiar Italian countryside sweep past as they left the chaos of Milan behind. After more than a year of traveling with Marcus, Aidan was used to their frequent visits to the Initiative. He was desperate for the first sight of Lake Maggiore—the first sight of home.

Funny how I think of this place as home now. But home was wherever Naomi was. *Or Allie.* He dreamed of the day when the two most important people in his life could be in the same place at the same time. *And that day could be soon. Please God, let it be soon.* Aidan lost a little more of himself to Marcus each day. There was a cold darkness inside him now. A version of himself he feared. Too many times, Aidan found himself agreeing with Marcus and seeing the sense of his plans for the Immortal world. Not that Marcus shared much with him.

Thoughts of Allie and Naomi kept Aidan sane. They existed somewhere deep inside his soul in a place Marcus could never reach. Aidan protected them there, shielding them from Marcus. And in turn, they protected Aidan, reminding him of who he was and the man he wanted to be. When this was all over, Aidan still needed to be worthy of his Syntrophos and his Complement.

"That woman is as much a weakness as a strength," Marcus said, annoyed. "Settle down. Aidan. You'll see your Syntrophos soon enough." He continued reading through his reports, not sparing Aidan a glance.

"Sorry, sir, just anxious to see her." That man wouldn't know what love was if it slapped him in the face. Marcus saw nothing beyond power.

"What is it about her that makes you so irritating? I swear, you're worse than a couple of lovesick, newlywed Complements."

"She is my Syntrophos, sir. I can't explain it, but if she's not with me, it's physically painful. And after a separation this long, the reunion is all I can think about."

"You saw her two weeks ago. We've been traveling for over a year now, and you see her often enough. I need you to adjust. The constant need you have for her is a weakness."

"Sorry, sir, I will keep working on it." Marcus would never understand the connection he shared with Naomi. He couldn't see how Aidan's need for his Syntrophos wasn't just about the love he had for her, but the power that brought them together and made them stronger.

"See that you do."

"How long will this visit be?" Aidan asked, hoping for more than their usual two days.

"Not a visit this time. I need you to work with your Syntrophos, bring her up to your level and together, you will take charge of my army."

Aidan rubbed his chin to hide the smile he couldn't contain. There was a time when Marcus would have Rowan and her Syntrophos lead his army, but over the last year, Aidan had usurped her position.

Aidan allowed himself to relax the tension in his shoulders. He wouldn't have to say another heartbreaking goodbye to Naomi. But his happiness was short lived. Marcus wanted Naomi performing at Aidan's level and he wanted Aidan to train her. He should have seen this coming.

"How shall I train her?" Aidan asked, afraid to hear the answer.

"The same way I've trained you. Teach her to push herself. Teach them all the lessons I have taught you. I want to see progress when I return next month.

A month? A whole month without Marcus was music to Aidan's ears. But how did he expect Aidan to teach his students the lessons it had taken Aidan and year and a half to learn?

"I don't expect a miracle," Marcus added as if he could see Aidan's thoughts. "Do what you can with them. Rowan and her girl will help you motivate them."

"Of course, sir," Aidan said miserably.

"Don't go soft on me again, Aidan. You know how that angers me."

"You can count on me, sir." Aidan forced a confident tone. He would have to do it. There was no way around it. "Will we be making a move on Soma soon?"

"That is why we are here. You'll be leading my army against Soma very soon."

"May I ask, sir, what is the point when you already own Soma?"

Marcus sat his papers aside, removing his reading glasses to give Aidan one of his meaningful stares. He wanted Aidan to answer his own question.

"Right." Aidan glanced down at his hands. "Well, you

already have the Chief Justice in your pocket so staging a coup that could get them reelected would benefit you. But it can't be about just that."

"That's the obvious agenda. Keep digging," Marcus said.

Aidan thought about the man before him, wondering what could possibly motivate him to spend so much energy on what amounted to a PR stunt.

"There's the matter of the next election." Aidan struggled to swallow. "It's coming up in just a few years and a second Chief Justice will be elected at that time to fill Ashar and Kassandre's seat." Since their assassination eighteen years ago, the Immortal government had operated with just Sarah and Charles Madison occupying two of the four seats meant for the Chief Justice branch of their government.

"Very good, Aidan."

"You want to fill that position," Aidan said.

"It's the only way to ensure I have complete control of the International Senate."

"What about your wife, sir? Voters will expect her to sit beside you to complete the role of the Chief Justice."

"I will bring Porcia home soon. She deserves to enjoy her perceived freedom for a little while longer."

"And when you have taken the Senate, what will you do with it, sir?" Aidan didn't expect an answer. He liked to think he'd earned Marcus's trust over the last year but the man was judicial with his secrets.

"Do you really want to know?" Marcus gave him a level stare.

No.

"Of course. I want to help," Aidan said, leaning forward to convince Marcus of his sincerity as much as his interest.

"Once I have the Senate, I will occupy a place within every stronghold of our world. As the child of prophecy, you are one of those strongholds, Aidan. The Senate is the last piece of the puzzle."

"And then you intend to make a move against the mortal world?" Aidan had suspected that was Marcus's ultimate goal, but he'd never come right out and said it.

The mad glint Aidan recognized all too well returned to Marcus's eyes. "I intend to destroy it."

Aidan's pulse quickened as the limousine eased down the long drive toward the Milan Initiative. He leaned forward, his hand on the door handle, waiting for the car to stop, so he could escape into the arms of his Syntrophos.

A heavy hand pushed him back into the seat.

"You will see her later. We will address the team first. You may see the girl when I am done with you."

"Of course, sir. Whatever you wish." Aidan suppressed his anger seething just below the surface. Marcus never used Naomi's name. He had no respect for the woman who made Aidan more valuable to him. Marcus believed Aidan was the child he'd sought for millennia, and on top of that, he was the most powerful of his generation *and* a Syntrophos. Marcus had turned Aidan into a weapon and his pride and joy, yet he despised Naomi simply because she was a woman. Marcus had very little respect for the female gender. He blamed Queen Alísun for the fall of Indriell and the rise of the mortal population, and seemed to fault all women for her weakness.

Let him hate Naomi. Let him underestimate her. She was safer that way. Aidan wanted her left unscathed by the evil sitting beside him. Yet, what of himself? So many times, Aidan found himself wanting to please Marcus. Not to keep him happy or to keep him from questioning Aidan's motives, but because on some sick, twisted level, the darkness inside Aidan craved Marcus's approval. It was time Aidan distanced himself from this cruel man. If Aidan was going to salvage the man he wanted to be, then he could not let Marcus continue to mold him. This reprieve from Marcus could not have come at a better time.

Aidan waited patiently as the driver came to a halt in front of the massive building. He waited for permission to leave the car, like the well-trained dog he was. But he wasn't, really. With a nod from Marcus, Aidan stepped out of the car, buttoning his tailored suit jacket. Marcus Servius might think he'd trained the perfect loyal lapdog, but Aidan intended to bite the master where it hurt the most.

"And Mr. McBrien." Marcus took a step toward the entrance. "Do not disappoint me."

Aidan's gaze lingered on Naomi as the Syntrophos pairs lined up on the training field. She looked so lost, standing there alone. He wanted to close the distance between them so badly he could barely restrain himself. But that would only anger Marcus. To him, the constant need to be near his Syntrophos was Aidan's greatest weakness.

But Marcus equated any show of love as weakness. He even refused to complete the Complement bond with his own wife, claiming it was an unnatural flaw that kept the Immortal race from flourishing. He was from a time before the Great War when the most powerful Immortals married their equals to produce even more powerful offspring. In his time, Complement bonds were for the lower class. The one thing they had to make their lives bearable.

So Aidan stood on the dais, mimicking the cold, arrogant

look on his mentor's face, and ignoring the other part of himself standing just across the field, begging him with her eyes to come to her side.

"Greetings." Marcus pasted on his fake diplomat smile, raising his hands as if to envelop them all in a warm embrace. Aidan had seen this transformation more times than he could count. On the short walk up the front steps, Marcus changed from the indomitable, dark and mysterious man Aidan knew all too well, to the bland, harmless and forgetful version of himself he presented to others.

"I am pleased with your collective progress. Each of you has proven his loyalty to the Milan Initiative this last year. It pleases me to say that not one of you has failed in his assignments."

It rankled Aidan how Marcus, a relic of the past, still used the collective male pronoun for every situation. He had little use for women in his endeavors and constantly underestimated them. Wherever there was a strong woman, Marcus begrudgingly saw her, but inevitably attributed her success to the men around her. It was going to bite him in the ass someday, and Aidan couldn't wait to be there to see it happen.

"I am both excited and remorseful to tell you the task you all have been training for these last years is finally at hand. Excited because I know you are all prepared to support the Senate in this endeavor, remorseful because it has to be done at all."

Marcus, the supreme bullshitter, ladies and gentlemen.

"The entity known as Soma is a threat to our government and the future of our great race. Our children are precious and deserve a safe place to train and hone their gifts. Soma is not that place. It is a corrupt slave market, and it must be stopped."

That's rich coming from the guy who created it.

"This has been our dream since the inception of the Milan Initiative and the rediscovery of the Syntrophos bond. Yet someone threatens that dream, has gone so far as to seize Sterling Tower from its leaders in the name of some long forgotten branch of Indriell nobility. I am here today to ask you to put a stop to this once and for all. I humbly ask those of you who are willing to step forward and march against Sterling Tower to negotiate the surrender of this *terrorist* cell and bring them to heel."

Aidan was the first to step forward. Marcus would expect it. But Aidan trembled with fear. *In the name of some long forgotten branch of Indriell nobility?* It screamed Allie. But she wouldn't. She'd never reach for that kind of power. Not the woman he loved. But nearly four years had passed since he'd last seen Allie. Aidan liked to envision her life as a happy college student, but it was silly of him to think that time had stood still for her. Allie was no longer the girl he remembered, but he couldn't fathom a version of her that would seek any kind of recognition or authority. It must be her family leading this endeavor with Soma.

One by one, Naomi and all the other Syntrophos pairs stepped forward. They all knew this was the pinnacle of their plan. Taking Soma was their way out of the Initiative and out of Marcus's reach. Once they were safely inside, Aidan intended to seize Soma for himself and his students, and damn the consequences.

Marcus beamed a fatherly smile at the children before him. "I am proud, so proud to see you all stand at the ready to do your duty, but we have enemies within the walls of Sterling Tower, so we must proceed with caution. Half of you will go, and half of you will remain."

Aidan's blood ran cold. He should have anticipated this.

"A Syntrophos pair is a rare and valuable thing. We must

protect it from those who would use it against you. The safest course of action will be to split the pairs, ensuring the enemy cannot be tempted to use your most trusted partner against you. For the moment, we seek to parley with these usurpers. We will strike soon, but first we must attempt the diplomatic approach. And if the usurper refuses, we will seize Soma by force, in the Senate's name."

Aidan saw through the fancy speech. Marcus wasn't ready to fully trust him yet. This parley was a test. A test Aidan intended to pass. Marcus didn't want a peaceful surrender. He wanted a battle. And as long as Marcus and the Chief Justice were in control, Aidan had to play along. But for the first time, he saw a light at the end of the tunnel.

Aidan ran along the empty corridors to the rooms he shared with Naomi, desperate to see her. After hours in a private meeting with Marcus, Cleo and Genevieve, Aidan was finally free. At least for a time. Marcus left without a backward glance, and Aidan wasn't sad to see him go. He hoped he'd never see him again.

"What are we going to do?" Naomi blurted the moment he stepped into their living room. It appeared as if she'd spent the last hours pacing a hole in the floor.

Aidan crossed the room and pulled his Syntrophos into his arms, desperate for the closeness they shared only with each other. She clung to him as tightly as he did to her. For once, their bond settled, rooting them to the spot and calming the chaos of their minds.

"That's better." Aidan pressed his lips to her forehead, breathing in the floral scent of her hair.

"I hate this." She murmured into his chest. "I hate the separation."

"I have to leave for Soma soon, but when I return, we'll have at least a month together," Aidan whispered, their bond practically purring with contentment.

"And what does he want from you during that month?" Naomi asked, leaning back to search his face for answers.

Aidan took Naomi's hand and led her outside to their private garden. He wasn't certain how private it was, but it was better to talk outside. Less of a chance for Cleo to overhear them.

"I have to train you, Naomi." He pulled her down to sit on a bench beside him. "I'm supposed to bring you up to my level."

"In a month?" Naomi ran a hand through her curly hair. "He wants you to hurt me, doesn't he?"

Aidan nodded. "It will hurt. But there are some benefits." Aidan took her hand. "You'll be more powerful."

"Do any of us really need to be more powerful, Aidan? When is enough, enough?"

"If it helps us get out of here."

"We need a new plan," Naomi whispered, hanging her head. "We can't keep waiting for Marcus to send us to Soma together. It's never going to happen."

"After I meet with this usurper person in a show of diplomacy, we will *all* be marching on Soma. I promise."

"I'm scared about this takeover, Aidan. And frankly, I'm scared of what he's done to you."

"Why? This has been our plan all along. Please just stick this out with me for a few more weeks. We're almost at the finish line."

"This last eighteen months, I've watched you change. I can see a darkness in you that was never there before. I can feel it in our bond like a taint." She clutched her chest. "I can feel *him* in our bond and inside you, and I don't like it. You've been with him for so long, I don't think you're seeing clearly anymore."

"What do you want from me, Naomi?" Aidan stood to pace the length of the narrow garden. "I'm just trying to survive this, trying to get our people out of this nightmare."

"We need another way, Aidan. One that doesn't involve you taking over Soma. I'm worried you'll take it too far."

"You're worried I'm going to turn into *him*?" He could see it in her eyes, that was exactly what she feared, and it gutted him to think she worried he could be anything like Marcus.

Naomi nodded. "I don't feel like I even know you anymore and it scares me."

"Naomi." Aidan knelt in the grass in front of her. "I'm still me. I've had to do some terrible things. Things I never want to talk about. But it's all a means to an end." He took her hands. "I've taken measure to protect my mind from his influence. I know where my line in the sand is and I'm still miles away from it. Marcus has trained me to be his most ruthless weapon and I've let him do it. Marcus can teach me all his tricks, but at the end of the day, it's my choices that make me the better man. I am still Greggory McBrien's son. I'm still Naeemah El Sadawii's momma's boy, and I'm still Naomi Hauser's Syntrophos. *And Alexis Carmichael's Complement.* I've held on to those truths every day of the last eighteen months. I may be different, but I am *not* broken."

"Then let's end this and let's do it soon, Aidan." Naomi pulled him back onto the seat beside her. "Before Marcus has a chance to push you across that line."

CHAPTER 36

Aidan | Atlanta | March

"What's the real plan, bossman?" Neela asked, staring at Aidan for direction.

"Well, we're not taking over Soma today," Bennett said. "Right? I mean, we're not leaving the others in Italy."

"Not without our Syntrophos here." Rowan looked to Aidan with a scowl. "This is just another of Marcus's games." She still wasn't Aidan's most loyal student, but Naomi assured him Rowan was on board for the takeover as long as she came out the other side with both her Syntrophos and her Complement, who still resided within Sterling Tower.

"No, we're not making any big moves today," Aidan said, still unsure exactly what they were doing, standing in Piedmont Park, gazing up at Sterling Tower. He had an army behind him. His students—half of them anyway—but he also had a troop of Senate soldiers with him to increase their numbers and create a bigger show of power. They were currently busy chasing mortals out of the area, sending out vibes that would tell them this park was the last place they wanted to be today. Hell, it was the last place Aidan wanted to be. This negotiation was looking a lot more like a battlefield before the battle.

"Who do you think it is?" Pilar asked. Genevieve was supposed to accompany Aidan to Atlanta, but she'd conveniently excused herself and sent Pilar instead. Aidan was grateful for the presence of someone he trusted.

"Marcus claims a relic of some noble house of Indriell has taken Soma, but I don't think we're dealing with just a claim here. I think we're about to face the last Queen of Indriell herself."

"Queen Alísun?" Pilar gave him a surprised look. "She died ages ago."

"No, she's alive. I've met her." Allie's grandparents sought refuge on Kelleys Island right before Aidan left for Germany. Both were intimidating, to say the least, but they were kind and reasonable people. He had no delusions that someone like Alísun would ever back down from her claim on Soma. But Marcus didn't want a total surrender—not today. He was testing Aidan one last time, but Aidan was confident he would pass. And then next time Marcus would send Aidan with his full army of Syntrophos.

"A real, live *queen*?" Pilar shuddered. "I find that prospect terrifying."

"So what exactly are we looking at right now?" Wes asked, frowning at the bizarre gelatinous shield surrounding Sterling Tower.

"I've seen it before," Aidan said. "I visited a compound in South America with Marcus last year. He had some dealings with Valkyrie Enterprise, and the whole place was protected by this stuff. It's the dreamworld pulled into the waking world. We can't cross it. Not without a dreamwalker."

"So even if we were all here we'd never make it inside." A look of defeat settled into Pilar's eyes.

"Oh, we could get in," Aidan said. "If we were prepared to defect to the other side right now. I know the man who likely made this barrier. He would give us refuge, but we aren't ready for that today." Aidan wasn't sure he could even face Navid after all this time, much less ask him for asylum.

"Will we ever be ready?" Wes asked. "I've got to get Ezra out of the Initiative but if we're never allowed out on assignment together, we're screwed."

"I need you all to trust me. Our chance for escape is coming and it's going to be soon. But for now, we have other business to handle. Come on, they're opening up." Aidan and his soldiers lined up in front of the barrier opening. The familiar faces lurking inside sent Aidan's heart racing.

Navid and Quinn were the first to appear beyond the barrier, protecting Sterling Tower from Marcus. The years had changed the young man who was so like a brother to Aidan. He wanted to go to Quinn's side, but Aidan had a job to do first.

"The First Princess will see you now," Navid said, his tone solemn and his eyes sad.

First Princess? Why would the last Queen of Indriell take a lesser title? That title belonged to ... someone else.

"Are you okay?" Pilar whispered. "You look like you're about to vomit."

Aidan shook his head. "No, I am not okay." He saw her before she saw him. He couldn't breathe or move for fear he would charge across this park and never look back. Aidan had expected the queen. Never in a million years would he have guessed Allie was the one behind the Soma takeover. She'd beaten him to the punch and in the process, she'd stolen his only means of escape right out from under him. A hopeless rage ripped through Aidan's body. The darkness within him wanted to throttle Allie almost as much as the other half of him wanted to take her in his arms and never let go.

She was even more beautiful than the last time he'd seen her—more mature and regal. Confident, but guarded. His arms ached to hold her.

"They are devoted to her. Like full on, drank the Kool Aid, legit followers," Neela said. "They love her."

One look at the sea of adoring faces surrounding Allie as she made her way through the barrier told Aidan she had their trust and their devotion. "She is worth following."

"That's your girlfriend?" Rowan gaped. "Man ... she scares the bejesus out of me."

"And we're about to go piss her off." Aidan stood ramrod straight, too angry and frustrated to let himself feel the joy the sight of her should bring him. After all this time, this wasn't the reunion he'd dreamed of. *She doesn't know she just destroyed our only chance of escape.* His rage wasn't for Allie. The moment he saw her, Aidan sank into a deep well of despair. Marcus knew about her. But had he connected all the dots yet? Did he know she was the child of prophecy? Aidan's only recourse now was to continue with this farce of a meeting and return to Marcus for his next orders. Aidan studied the faces among the Senate soldiers, knowing some, if not all would report to Marcus with the details of this "parley."

"Yeah, let's try not to piss off the scary princess girl," Bennett said.

"Just follow my lead." Aidan's jaw creaked with tension. Four years had changed them. He hardly recognized himself. He couldn't expect Allie to be the same girl she was, but this ... this just wasn't her. She would never want this.

"You heard the man," Pilar said, "let's do this."

"Dad." Aidan hid his shock behind his stony facade when

Gregg and Liam marched down the lines of soldiers pouring from the barrier entrance behind Allie. His father barked instructions, yet his eyes never wavered from his son. In that moment, it gutted Aidan to see his father and his uncle preparing to battle him. Shame bloomed in his chest and he couldn't bear the look of sadness on Greggory McBrien's face.

But Aidan saw a glimmer of hope. Marcus knew he'd sent Aidan into the midst of his family. This was a test of his loyalty. This was the key to earning Marcus's trust and his permission to lead the whole Syntrophos army right to Soma's doorstep. Aidan just hoped his family would forgive him someday.

"I know this is your family, but don't waver on me now," Pilar said.

"I've got this," Aidan said, though he wished the earth would open up and swallow him.

Aidan waved his soldiers forward to approach Allie and her gathering at the mouth of the barrier. Aidan's numbers were equal to hers, though hers were a rag-tag group of students and teachers come to stand behind her. *How did we get here?* Aidan's thoughts pressed against a different barrier. The one in his mind that kept him isolated from Allie. *How did we end up on opposite sides?*

Aidan reached deep within himself, touching the warmth of his power and the darkness Marcus had awakened inside him. Pulling on that darkness now, Aidan embraced his anger. It was the only way he would survive this encounter with his Complement and convince those watching that he was Marcus's man through and through. Allie had cut him off at the knees, doing the very thing he'd spent years planning to do for himself and his students. Whatever led her to this, she'd done the right thing for those inside Sterling Tower, but in doing so, she'd called attention to herself. After everything he'd done to protect her—to buy her more time—she'd annihilated the house of cards Aidan had so carefully built.

"Alexis." Aidan's voice sounded like broken glass, but he schooled his emotions behind a calm facade. Just for today, Aidan needed to be her enemy. "Or should I say, *princess*?" He gave a mockery of a bow, showing as much disdain as he could. The look on her face wounded him. He'd cut her too deeply.

"Aidan, don't be a dick." Sasha took a step forward, but Quinn held her back. It was nice to see some things never changed.

Aidan raised his hand to bring his Senate troops to a halt behind him. They lined up like experienced soldiers on a battlefield, putting her show of force to shame.

"Aidan." Gregg came to stand beside Allie, his arms crossed behind him, as if waiting for her orders.

"Dad." Aidan nodded at his father, wanting to say so much more, but now was not the time.

Allie closed her eyes for a brief moment, and Aidan could feel her hammering at the barrier in his mind.

"You know me better than this." Her voice was so strong, and it was like music to his ears. If it weren't for Naomi, trapped an ocean away back at the Initiative, Aidan would fall on his knees in front of Allie and beg her forgiveness.

"Do I? You've made some serious claims against the Senate," he said. "The Chief Justice calls you an imposter, and I'm inclined to agree. The Allie I knew would never reach for this kind of power." It was true. The woman he loved was not power hungry, but Aidan wanted to understand her motivations.

"I am no imposter." She lifted her chin in defiance. "I am

the named heir of Alísun, the last queen of Indriell, and you damn well know it."

Of course, he knew it. She'd confessed her fears about her family lineage years ago. He'd known she was a princess then, even if she wasn't ready to accept it. The naming, however, that was news to him. He found himself wondering how that went over.

"How can we know your claim is anything more than words?" he asked, standing stiffly with his hands behind his back. "The queens died ages ago without naming an heir. Indriell carries no weight with the Senate or the Immortal population. How can an unknown girl expect to take the name of Indriell without any proof?"

"I see my idiot brother has reached an entirely new level of stupid." Darius gave Aidan a hostile glare. "You know who she is, Aidan."

"I thought I did." Aidan's hand drifted to the hilt of his sword when what he really wanted to do was hug his brother and tell him how much he'd missed his stupid face.

"We are her proof." Alísun and Alexander stepped forward. "She has been named." The ancient queen gave off an aura that demanded those near her take notice of her authority. There was no mistaking Alísun for the queen she was.

"I've got this, Grandmother," Allie said with respect. Her face took on a serene look, and a mantle of power just like the queen's settled over Allie's shoulders. Aidan was in awe of this beautiful creature he no longer recognized. She was the First Princess, and he wanted nothing more than to kneel and pledge his loyalty to her this instant.

"Indriell carries no weight with the people?" Allie tilted her head, her eyes blazing with power. "I'm sure the Senate would like to think so. Yet look at all the Immortals standing behind me." She gestured over her shoulder.

"I see," Aidan said, his mouth dry and his skin burning with awareness of her, and the Complement bond she still did not recognize. That alone shattered the last vestiges of his spirit. He used to think after so many years apart that Allie would only have to take one look at him when he returned and she would know.

"You are supposed to be dead, Alísun." His eyes burned with the threat of tears as he forced his attention away from Allie to the queen. "The history books tell us you died thousands of years ago." He knew the books contained false records. He'd met the queen before, but witnesses needed to corroborate his ignorance.

"I am the Scholar. I wrote the history books, son," the ancient man beside the queen said. "To protect our family, I recorded our death."

"Now that we're here face to face, I can sense you are who you claim to be," Aidan said with a hint of regret in his voice. "But the Chief Justice would ask you, what right have you to return, seeking power after all this time? Why use this girl to make such a claim?" He leveled an accusing glare at Allie, knowing she would likely get stabby at the idea that he would think she'd ever let anyone use her.

"We have not—" Alísun began, but Allie held up her hand to silence her grandmother.

"Use?" Allie arched a brow at Aidan. "I am no puppet. The queen has named me her heir, and it is my place to decide what's to be done in my name."

"Our lineage gives Alexis the right to stake a claim in the leadership of this world," Alísun said. "The people here today have chosen to follow her. And more will come in time. Alexis has the authority of the ancient queens coursing through her blood. The people recognize that, and they will follow her. She will be heard. She will be respected. But she will *never* be controlled."

I like this queen. Aidan could see so much of Alísun in her granddaughter. For years, Aidan had been surrounded by people he didn't trust. Fighting for causes he didn't believe in. He wanted so badly to change sides and finally have something worth fighting for. Just the idea that he might have that chance soon lifted the darkness clouding his mind. Allie would bring him back to himself. He could be the man his father raised him to be. *That* was the choice he would make to set himself free of Marcus's influence.

"What do you expect to accomplish by standing in the way of the Senate, Allie?" Aidan asked, returning his gaze to her. His voice wavered as he spoke her name. She deserved reverence and love, not disdain.

"Soma belongs to the royal family," Allie said in a firm voice. "I do not wish to rule anyone, and I have no thirst for power. You know that better than anyone, Aidan McBrien. But Soma will *not* fall under the Senate's thumb as long as I am the heir."

Aidan shivered at the power and authority radiating from her. *She is glorious.* He wasn't sure about the other people standing around watching this insanity, but he would follow her to the ends of the earth and back again.

"The Senate demands you cease and desist. You will remove this barrier and allow us entry. Soma belongs to the Immortal government now."

"I'm afraid we aren't moving, Aidan."

She couldn't tear her eyes away from him any more than he could. She was different, yes. She had changed and grown into an amazing woman, but the girl he loved was still there, too.

What have you been through? Her thoughts hammered at the mental barrier standing between them. He fought her, determined to keep her out, but he wanted it too much. Aidan's resolve crumbled as her thoughts filled his mind.

I could ask you the same question, Lex. The touch of her thoughts was like home. His hands shook, and he wasn't sure he could keep this up any longer. She still loved him, and it was breaking her heart all over again to see him like this.

"The royal family intends to disobey a direct order from the Senate?" he asked. "Do you have any idea of the consequences you will face if you do not yield to me now?"

"I will not yield and damn the consequences. The Senate has proven time and again that they have as little regard for young Immortals as Soma had." Her voice shook with rage. "I've watched them use and abuse those I love. The royals will not stand aside any longer. Soma *will* be a safe haven for our generation and those that come after us. I will not tolerate the abuse any more." *Least of all what they have done to you.*

"The Senate holds the same desire. There is no need for you to oppose us. We are all on the same side here. Stand down, Alexis. While you have the chance." *Please. You don't know what you're doing. I can imagine you must be thrilled to have your true family with you finally, but I fear they have led you astray.* Aidan kept his real opinions from her. Witnesses needed to see her anger. He could not risk telling her too much.

In case you forgot, I have a mind of my own.

He could never forget her beautiful mind.

"Shall I ask your team if they feel confident in the Senate's desire to protect them?" Her hands rested on the hilts of her weapons sheathed at her side. "You stand here with half an army of Syntrophos soldiers behind you, yet their other half is missing. I stand beside my own

Syntrophos," Allie said. "I'd sooner come to you unarmed than to leave Darius behind for such a meeting as this. I can only assume the Senate has used the bond to manipulate you and your soldiers' allegiance."

Of course, they had. It was the only thing standing between him and a reunion with the woman he loved. Naomi was just as important to him as Darius was to Allie. He would not leave her behind.

"Our allegiance is to our government," Aidan said, the words tasting like ash in his mouth. "Not to a long dead nation or a queen who abandoned us to extinction thousands of years ago. We leave our Syntrophos behind to protect ourselves from those who would think to use us for our collective power."

"Like the Milan Initiative uses you?" she asked. "You are never allowed to leave with your Syntrophos unless you are escorted. Doesn't that sound familiar? A trick straight from the Coalition's rulebook—manipulating one Complement with the safety and wellbeing of the other. Or does it sound like Soma? Did you know that's what they did to Dean? For the last four years, your cousin has been a slave, Aidan. Bought and paid for through Soma. He managed to earn a certain level of freedom, but he and Tessa were never allowed to leave together. They love each other, and their *owners* used it against them. Sound familiar, Aidan?" Allie's voice rose in anger, as she clenched her fists at her side.

"Things need to change. The Senate sees that," Aidan said. *But you don't have to be the one to do it, Allie.* He knew she could do it, he just didn't want her to have to. But right now, he needed her to think he didn't have faith in her.

"I don't care for their methods." This is my choice. We can stand here arguing all day about how much you believe I am being manipulated, since you clearly don't think I'm capable

of making sound decisions. Or you can come with me now. You and your Syntrophos soldiers. We will liberate your partners as a top priority.

"That is not for you to decide. Stand aside now, and you will not be charged for your crimes against the Senate. They will take your position into consideration." *Leaving is not an option, Allie. Would you leave Darius if the situation were reversed? I know you think you are doing the right thing, but trust me, you're in way over your head.* There was just so much about this she didn't know. She was throwing herself at Marcus's feet and it was only a matter of time before he realized he had the wrong child of prophecy. Aidan just wanted to buy her more time. Time to reach her Proving.

"Then we truly are against each other." Allie's face hardened at his words. Like he'd shattered something inside her. He prayed he would have the chance to explain his motives someday soon.

"I will not allow you access to Soma."

"We will act by force if necessary. Your barrier can't keep us out forever." I have a job to do. Please stand down. I don't think you have the full story.

"As long as you stand with the Senate, you will not find entrance to Sterling Tower today or any other day. But if you seek refuge..." Her voice lifted to address his soldiers. "If you seek asylum, then we can talk."

Do you have any idea how much I've missed you? How much your complete lack of faith is killing me right now? Her thoughts were a jumble of chaos in his mind. She was torn between her duty to her position and her heart. This whole thing started as one in the same, and somehow things had taken a drastic turn for the unexpected, for both of them.

I've been with you everyday, Lex. Just because you haven't been able to hear me, doesn't mean I left you. I'm afraid this will not end well for either of us, Aidan said. *I've tried like hell to protect you from all of this. And here you are, despite all my best efforts, right in the middle of it.*

Aidan, when will you ever learn? I don't need your protection. I don't need you making decisions for me. I just need you ... I need my equal standing here beside me. Not over there, standing against me.

That was all Aidan ever wanted.

"Stand down, Alexis," Aidan said again. "Or you will endanger everyone you're so eager to protect."

"I cannot." Not even for you.

Then we are at an impasse. "The Chief Justice will be in contact. The Senate intends to end the exploitation of young Immortals by entities such as Soma, including any *royal* who stands in our way."

"An admirable vow, but considering the Senate's involvement in the Soma slave market, I don't believe you," Allie said.

"The Senate has no official involvement with Soma. Any Senate representatives participating in the Soma slave market have been punished."

"My answer hasn't changed. I don't believe you. I have personally seen the slave market in action. I've seen Senate members purchasing young Immortals without batting an eye. Pardon me if I don't trust the government at their word. And quite frankly, I can't believe you would either. The Chief Justice will have to do much better than half-hearted promises if they expect us to work together. I am no threat to them or their administration. I have no wish to rule our world. I simply want to protect those who need it." *I need you to trust me, Aidan. Please, come with me now, and we will figure this out.*

I can't do that. I won't. "We have only the best of intentions," Aidan said. He wanted to say so much more, but now was not the time.

I don't think I know you anymore. "I don't trust the Senate's intentions. We are done here," Allie said. "You should go."

"Those are daring words," Aidan said. "Are you quite certain you understand what you're doing?" *You are crossing a line here. One I can't help you uncross. This could mean war.*

I don't need you to fix anything, Aidan. I need you to trust me. Allie stood ramrod straight, her anger blazing in her eyes. "I am Alexis Carmichael, the named heir of Indriell." Her voice took on a commanding tone even he didn't recognize. "Second natural daughter of the ancients, Ashar and Kassandre, former Chief of Justice. I am the child of prophecy, First Princess and granddaughter of Queen Alísun and Alexander, the Scholar. I know *exactly* what I am doing, and you would do well to recognize my power, if not my authority. I am no child playing at war here. I am not the naive girl you met all those years ago, Aidan. I haven't been her in a very long time. I am the leader of Soma. You will be the one to back down today. Return to the Chief Justice and tell them the ball is in their court now. The Senate must cede the fate of Soma to the royals. If they choose war instead, so be it."

Chapter 37

Aidan | Barcelona, Spain | March

"Who is this girl claiming to be the child of prophecy?" Marcus sat behind his desk, his hands steepled beneath his chin.

Aidan stood in front of the desk of Senator Robert Sinclair, yet another of Marcus's many aliases. Aidan and Pilar were surprised to find themselves in Barcelona, Spain when the plane landed on their return trip from Atlanta. Marcus had Aidan and his team brought to the Senate headquarters upon their arrival. Naomi and the others were already there.

"She's just a girl, sir." Aidan shrugged. "An ex-girlfriend of mine from ages ago."

"And why have you never told me of this ex-girlfriend?"

"I have lots of ex-girlfriends, sir."

"And are they all such powerful Immortals?" Anger flickered in Marcus's eyes.

"May I be brutally honest, sir?"

"Please." Marcus took a breath, struggling to maintain his patience.

"Most average Immortal girls fear me and I don't find that

very attractive, so to answer your question, sir, yes most of my ex-girlfriends are quite powerful. It's not something that ever occurred to me to share with you."

"Very well. Perhaps you can tell my why she's made such a serious claim?"

"She knows things about me, sir. Things she's used to place herself in a position of power. She's just after some attention." Aidan shrugged. "I apologize if I failed you, sir. I wasn't prepared for the barrier."

"Or the presence of your family?"

"No sir."

"Sit down, son." Marcus relaxed his posture, reaching for the cut glass decanter of brandy on his desk. Aidan took his seat, watching as Marcus poured them each a tumbler of the amber liquid.

"You proved your loyalty to me despite the failure of your mission." Marcus set Aidan's glass in front of him and raised his own. "We will try again soon, once my sources have more information on this girl and her supporters. I believe the queen is just grasping at straws, using this girl to gain a following."

"I will need a larger show of strength next time," Aidan said, sipping from his glass. "With the barrier in place there was simply no way to take the tower this time; and negotiating with this girl was pointless. She is nothing but a figurehead."

"My thoughts exactly." Marcus downed his drink in one gulp. "Next time you will have what you need to breach that barrier and take Soma back for me."

"I won't fail you again, sir." Aidan tossed the rest of his drink back. This was exactly what he needed to get back on track.

"I know, son. I trust you."

"Shall I return to Initiative to work with Naomi and the others like we planned?"

"Yes and no." Marcus leaned back in his leather chair. "I need you here with me while the Senate is in session. It's the perfect time to introduce the Chief Justice's Special Forces to the Senate. They need to grow accustomed to your presence."

"Of course, sir. How shall we serve the court?"

"For now you will sit in on the proceedings. Watch and observe our government at work."

"That's it?" Aidan frowned. That sounded almost boring.

"In the evenings you will work with your team to bring them up to your level. Especially the girl. I want your Syntrophos to be as disciplined and dependable as you are. If you can bring them up to scratch, you may take the full team with you to Soma next time."

Aidan hid his smile behind his empty glass. "You can count on us, sir."

"Your girlfriend is legit scary, dude," Wes said.

"Yeah, and she legit screwed us over," Pilar added.

"She didn't know," Aidan said. "But we will have another chance soon. And this time, all of us are going."

"What's the new plan, Aidan?" Naomi rested her fingertips against her temples. "How do we know Marcus will let us all go next time?"

"Gather around everyone." Aidan leaned forward in his chair. They were all staying in a large suite at the Senate headquarters, but Aidan wasn't sure how safe it was to talk honestly with his team. "I know we all want a chance to fight together to prove to the Initiative how much more effective we can be as a full army. We will soon get that chance, but before that can happen, we have to crank our training into high gear."

"And what does that entail?" Naomi asked.

"For the next few weeks we will spend our days observing the Senate proceedings, learning more about how our government operates and responding when the Chief Justice have need of us. We will spend our evenings and every other waking moment training. I'm going to be teaching you some of the lessons I've learned over the past eighteen months. This kind of training will be brutal, but it will push you all to the next level. And if we are successful, it will also earn us the right to work together as a team to take over Soma for the Senate."

Aidan met the gaze of each of his students to ensure they heard everything he wasn't saying. "Now everyone get some good rest. We're due in court early tomorrow, so let's prepare for a long day."

Chapter 38

Aidan | Barcelona, Spain | April

"Have I mentioned I hate our new job?" Ezra yawned.

"Only about a million times, bro," Wes said.

"Well, it sucks." Ezra sat back against the hard bench below the Hall of the Senate. "I mean, don't get me wrong, it's way better than killing puppies, but it's so boring."

Aidan and his team of Syntrophos waited here every day at the beck and call of the Chief Justice. They listened to tedious trials and judiciary rulings all day long and trained for hours each evening.

They were exhausted and cranky.

"Should we run through it again?" Samantha asked.

"No," Aidan said. "We each have our own connections and knowledge of the building. I think we could navigate this place in our sleep. Let's not risk getting caught snooping around just because we're bored out of our minds." For weeks, Aidan and his team had spent every possible moment scoping out the Senate headquarters, finding the likeliest exits, and making friends with the guards. It was the beginnings of Aidan's Plan B. They needed a backup in case Marcus didn't keep his promise. If he left half of the team behind when the other half went to Atlanta again, Naomi would lead them on an escape from the Senate building and they would meet Aidan in Atlanta as soon as possible. It was a desperate plan, but one he hoped they would never need.

"We could totally walk out right now, and no one would miss us for at least an hour," Bennett grumbled to himself.

"What are we waiting on? I mean, what's really stopping us?" Gemma asked.

"Some of us have other people to consider," Rowan said, shooting her field commander a hateful glare.

"If we walked out right now, within an hour the Chief Justice would be on our trail, alerting the Immortal world to our existence," Aidan explained. "If we ever want to enjoy our lives, free of the Initiative, Marcus and the Senate, we need the safety Soma can give us. It'll still be a witch-hunt, but I'd rather wait until Allie can help us."

"That's if your girlfriend will even let us in," Pilar said. "She's more likely to punch you in the nuts than open her home to you after that mansplaining display of testosterone you threw at her back in Atlanta."

"She knows that was an act," Naomi said. "We need to be patient and follow Aidan's lead."

But Aidan wasn't as confident as Naomi. He was tempted to let his walls down and contact Allie through their mental link. They could work out a plan together, but he wasn't sure she would trust him. And he was holding onto the last threads of her anonymity. For the moment, Marcus believed her to be a silly girl with lofty ambitions. Aidan needed him to continue to think that for as long as possible.

"Ezra?" Aidan took a hesitant step toward his favorite student. "You can do this, Ez." Ezra's eyes were black as night as blood oozed from his nose and ears. "I won't let you lose control, but I need you to trust me." It was asking a lot to trust the person torturing him. "I've been right where you are. I know how terrifying it is, but I also know you can do this. Now find it!" Aidan pushed him. "Think of the team, Ez. We all have to push ourselves to earn the right to fight together. I need you to latch onto the branch, Ezra."

"I don't know what that means!" Ezra cried out, lost in the nightmare of his mind.

"Reach for your power, but don't embrace it. Not yet. I need you to examine what you see. Identify your gift for syphoning from the life around you. Study that branch of your power. We're looking for a new handhold, Ez. Something new you can grab hold of."

"I don't want to!" Ezra hissed through clenched teeth as he sank to the floor on his knees. "This gift has caused me enough pain." Tears leaked from his eyes to mix with the blood pouring from his nose. "It's too much."

"We're looking for the opposite." Aidan approached Ezra, crouching beside him, his voice gentle and soothing. "You have to ability to restore the life you've taken, Ez. We just need to find it."

Ezra's eyes snapped open, his irises blazing with his power.

"Yes. That's it. Keep pushing." He was so close, Aidan felt like he could reach out and take the branch for his student. He was almost there. But Ezra was at his breaking point. If he didn't take the upper hand now, it wasn't going to happen today and they'd be right back at it tomorrow.

"Do it now, Ezra and you get tomorrow off. The pain ends and we can move on."

Ezra panted, on his knees curling into himself, he screamed, pushing himself one more time.

"That's it! Now, just like we did with your evasive talent. Grab hold and fight for control." Aidan placed his hand on Ezra's trembling shoulders, wishing he had Allie's gift for lending strength.

They'd started small just a few weeks ago. Ezra had a talent for sneaking up on unsuspecting Immortals. In the short time he'd trained with Aidan, Ezra had cultivated that gift, enhancing it so he could be standing right behind Marcus himself without giving away his presence. Marcus was quite pleased with Ezra's progress.

All of Aidan's students were progressing quickly. But they all looked at Aidan with a sense of fear and doubt. They still trusted him, but they didn't like him very much at the moment.

"I got it." Ezra panted.

"Very good. Just catch your breath and try to relax, but don't let go. We need to test this potential facet of your ability. See if it's worth cultivating."

"It's a tiny thread. But I've got it under control." Ezra clenched his fists against his chest like he needed his whole body to hold that one tiny thread of power.

"Let's start with a plant." Aidan placed a healthy green houseplant in front of Ezra. "Take what you can, but leave it with just a hint of life."

Ezra nodded, placing one hand into the soil. The large leaves began to shrivel as the life faded from the plant.

"That's enough," Aidan coached. "Now take a deep breath and focus on that little thread of your gift, and let's see what happens."

It took him a few tries, but as the color began to return to the leaves, Ezra's spirit lifted and his focus grew.

"Yes, you've got this, buddy." The plant wasn't exactly healthy, but it wasn't dead either.

"Aidan, does this mean what I think it means?" Ezra sobbed.

"We have some work to do, but in time, you should be able to return the life you've borrowed. There will always be a deficit, but this is huge progress. Our superiors might not see it that way, but this is much more important for your moral." And the fact that they would be leaving soon and Ezra would need to focus on this positive aspect of his gift to help him deal with all the terrible things the Initiative made him do.

"Thanks, Aidan." Ezra grasped his hand and pulled himself up.

"Let's call it a night. I still need to meet with Naomi." Aidan clapped Ezra on his shoulder.

"I know that must be really hard, working with your own Syntrophos this way."

"It's one of the hardest things I've ever done." And that was saying a lot.

"Knock-knock?" Wes peeked into the room. "I take it we're done for the day?" Wes bent to help Ezra off the floor.

Aidan nodded. "Make him give those dogs names. They're his to keep for as long as he wants them."

"Really? Wes's eyes widened. "Despite everything he loves those damn dogs. Don't say it if you don't mean it."

"I mean it." Caring for the last two puppies from the litter Rowan had made him kill that first day was supposed to be a punishment. A way to torture Ezra with the anticipation of their death, but he'd earned the right to keep them. They followed him everywhere he went. Even during their long days in court, the loyal dogs waited outside for him.

"Night, Aidan," Wes said, guiding Ezra back to their rooms.

Aidan sank down into the soft leather chair beside the fireplace in the common room they all shared.

"My turn?" Naomi said, closing the door softly behind her.

"I'm sorry." Aidan stood, not ready to force this on her again.

"I have a surprise." She smiled. "Sit. I don't think we'll need a full session tonight."

"That would be wonderful." Aidan dropped back into his chair.

"I found it." She sat on the leather ottoman beside him, beaming like a proud student. "Last time we were so close. I managed to grasp hold of a new aspect of my lunar gift, but we couldn't figure out what it does. I've been practicing on my own since then."

"Naomi." Aidan took her hand. "You shouldn't push yourself like that without help."

"Sam's been helping me. We know how important this is. You have to succeed in this training, which means we all have to show progress."

"What have you found?"

"This branch of my gift is stronger now so I can take hold of it at will. It's a subtle gift though, but Marcus will appreciate it. I think."

"Spit it out, Naomi." Aidan gave her hand a gentle squeeze.

"I can manipulate the lunar cycle to affect moods."

"Give me an example."

"Alright. Let's say I wanted to create tension among a group of people, I could call on the full moon to cause emotions to run high and chaos to rein—even when it's not the full moon—and I think my reach will be quite impressive with a little more practice. But *during* the full moon, I can enhance the natural effects of that lunar phase and make it even stronger. With this aspect of my gift I can tap into each phase of the lunar cycle at will, but during a particular lunar phase I'll have even more control of that one phase—in addition to the added strength I gain from my natural gift."

"This is great progress, Naomi." Aidan leaned forward eagerly. "Marcus will definitely be impressed. He is drawn to subtle gifts like yours. He believes this kind of gift has more range of use than more obviously powerful gifts.

"I think manipulation of the tides might also be possible but I need you to pull it out of me."

"I don't like pushing you so hard. You were right before, we're powerful enough. This endless pursuit of even more power feels wrong."

"I know, but we have to keep working at this if we want our plan to work."

"I just hope the end is near. I can't keep this up much longer."

Chapter 39

Aidan | Barcelona, Spain | May

"You're like clockwork, Mr. McBrien," the security officer waved Aidan through the crowd waiting at the security desk. "Coffee break?"

"Long day." Aidan smiled. "Can I get you anything, Julian?"

"I'm good, I just topped off a few minutes ago." Julian held the gate open for him.

Aidan nodded and continued down the familiar corridor beneath the Hall of the Senate. His routine was clockwork for a reason. Aidan's need for coffee didn't equal his need for the security guards to see him coming and going frequently. He and the others had done their best to make as many friends in the building as possible. It was looking less and less like Marcus would send them to handle Soma, and more and more like they would have to act on Plan B. The plan would leave them fugitives in Europe and make it nearly impossible for them to reach Atlanta to beg Allie for asylum, but it was likely the only option they would ever have.

Aidan ducked into the break room to make himself a cup of coffee. He'd developed a taste for it over the years. He couldn't seem to pour the stuff without smiling, thinking of Allie and her caffeine obsession. He frequently wondered if the battle between his mother and his Complement still waged. Knowing both women, he wouldn't be surprised if neither of them had given up yet.

"Ugh, you always have a smile on your face, McBrien." Kathy Rhodes rushed into the break room with a stack of documents clutched in her hands. "You're too damn chipper." She paused to make herself a cup of coffee. Kathy clerked for Senator Robert Sinclair, AKA, Marcus Servius. Aidan still wasn't certain if she knew his true identity, but she loathed the Senator and that made her an ally.

"It's my nature." Aidan smiled and leaned against the counter. "How's the Senator treating you today?"

"He's in a horrible mood." She sipped from her cup.

"That's not unusual from what I hear."

"I swear, one of these days I'm going to quit. Or do something to completely screw him over just for the hell of it."

"Who knows, maybe that day will come sooner than you think." Aidan patted her shoulder and made his way back to the courtroom vestibule where he and his fellow Syntrophos spent their days waiting for the Chief Justice to call them upstairs.

Sarah and Charles Madison called their "Special Forces" team into the courtroom several times a day to deal with unruly prisoners. They were glorified bailiffs and it was a complete waste of their time and talent. They lived for the times Sarah sent them out to bring in a reluctant witness or track down important evidence, but that was a rare occurrence these days. *If I don't get out of here soon, I'm going to lose my damn mind.*

Aidan continued to wait and watch. Marcus hinted they would be on to bigger and better things once the Senate closed session for the season. He had a feeling Marcus stuck them here to bore them all to tears so they wouldn't complain when the real assignments finally came their way.

"Aidan, I'm sorry, they just brought her in," Naomi said as he approached the rest of his team.

Aidan raised his hand to silence her. Not to be a dick, but because his eyes were playing tricks on him.

"Mom?" Aidan watched the line of prisoners waiting with the court bailiffs for their trials. Naeemah stood regally, wearing a magnetic collar around her throat and bands around her wrists. His mother stood with the worst of the criminals. "Mom?" he said louder, crossing the room until she shook her head for him to stop. But Aidan knew his bailiff friends would look the other way, at least for a moment.

"What happened?" Aidan wanted to hug his mother and rest his head on her shoulder like he did when he was little. Just seeing her brought everything raging to the surface.

"It's a trap," she whispered, fighting with the cuffs around her wrists. Her eyes filled with longing at the sight of her son. "They arrested me for shielding Allie from the Senate. They have issued a summons for her, but they seem to believe she's going to come quietly."

Aidan resisted the urge to fold his mother into his arms and never let go. It wouldn't do to put that kind of emotion on display here. "That's probably my fault. I've met with the Chief Justice frequently since our visit to Soma. I've let them believe she's not a threat. I figure it's best they wildly underestimate her."

"They think she will trade herself for me." Naeemah took his hand, her eyes bright with tears.

"She wouldn't be stupid enough to come here. I'll get you out of this, Mom." He lifted her hands, pressing a quick kiss against her fingers.

"You don't know Allie anymore, Aidan." Naeemah shook her head. "She is not the girl you left behind."

"And I'm not the boy who left her." Aidan hung his head, a sudden sense of shame swept over him in the face of his mother.

"Naeemah?" Naomi approached.

"Naomi, dear, we were so afraid you got caught up in all of this with Aidan. I'm happy to see you both look well enough, but I'd be much happier if we were all at home right now."

"I've missed you, Mom," Aidan said, fighting back the tears that burned his eyes. The words felt empty, like he couldn't possibly tell his mother how much she meant to him.

"We've both missed you," Naomi said, clenching her hands, resisting the urge to fling herself at Naeemah.

"Then it's time for you both to come home. You know your father is going to show up to get me out of this. I've told him to leave me to whatever happens."

"But he's Dad." Aidan smiled.

"So you will come with us when whatever happens, happens. Be ready."

"We're ready." He spoke softly, but anger burned in his blood. He wanted to punch something, preferably someone, for putting his mother in this position. Instead, Aidan kissed Naeemah's forehead and turned, leaving her to face the court on her own. He had work to do.

"It's time." He and Naomi returned to their team. "We're doing this today."

"Finally," Ezra leaned forward. "What's the plan?"

"Gemma, we're going to need transportation for all of us and I'm guessing quite a few of my family members," Aidan began. There was no way the McBrien boys wouldn't show up in full force for Naeemah. "When I give you the signal, you and Spencer leave to get the cars ready." Gemma acted as their chauffeur. The guards and officers of the court were used to seeing her come and go. They wouldn't take a second glance at her leaving with Spencer.

When they first started working here, Aidan quickly realized the security teams knew to watch for them in certain pairs. He and Naomi would attract attention together, where he and Neela flew under the radar. Moving around the building without their Syntrophos gave them the freedom to roam farther and explore more. They were ready for this.

"Rowan, I need you to wait outside the court room. When we come out, if anyone tries to stop us, you know what to do. When Gemma gets back, she's to wait for you."

"Got it." She turned to leave for the main entrance.

"Ruthie." Aidan began.

"I know, stay here with Ace and Lola and keep Gemma informed about what's going on." Ruthie could share the things she saw and heard with her Syntrophos, so Gemma would know what was happening in the courtroom and be ready to react when the time was right. Ace and Lola were barely sixteen and still too young to participate at this level.

"And when it's time, you get Ace and Lola out the back where Spencer is waiting." Aidan gave Ruthie's shoulder a gentle squeeze. "Everyone, get your heads on straight and follow my lead."

In that moment, Aidan knew as sure as if she stood beside him right now, Allie was indeed stupid enough to come here. She was going to trade herself for Naeemah. If he ever got his hands on his Complement again, he was going to kiss her like there was no tomorrow, and then he was going to wring her redheaded neck. She was too important to sacrifice.

"Gather your weapons, Special Forces, you're wanted in the main courtroom," the bailiff announced.

"It's about time," Aidan muttered. Hours had passed since he'd seen his mother led like a criminal to the gallows. He was on edge and ready for a fight.

"You're not going to believe this either," the bailiff said, shaking his head with a smile as he unlocked the cabinet behind his desk where their weapons were kept. They were only allowed to arm themselves when the Chief Justice wanted a show of force. "Some redheaded nutcase is up there raking the Chief Justice over the coals. She's going to get herself locked up for a good long time if she doesn't shut up."

Aidan's heart seemed to want to climb out of his throat. "That's our cue guys." Aidan could hear Allie's voice drifting down the stairs, and he was one hundred percent certain she had lost her mind.

"You don't know me," Allie's words were directed at the Chief Justice. "You accuse me of having *questionable* abilities, but you don't know me or my gifts. What right have you to take me into custody based on that alone? What right have you to find Naeemah and Gregg guilty without the benefit of an actual trial?"

"Dude, your girl is either brilliant or crazy," Wes said.

"Both. Definitely both." Aidan shook his head.

"It is the court's prerogative to punish you for your crimes," Sarah Madison all but shrieked across the courtroom.

"Crimes worthy of the International Senate's time?" Allie fired back.

"Let's go," Aidan said, charging up the stairs behind the courtroom dais, Naomi right behind him.

He felt her before he saw her. What would she think to find him here, on the wrong side once again?

Allie stared at him as Aidan and his team of armed Syntrophos filed into the room. Aidan's eyes wouldn't leave hers, his hand gripping the hilt of his sword. Part of him wanted to charge across the room and kiss her, but the rational part of his mind knew they needed to tread carefully if they were going to get out of this alive.

Allie tore her eyes away from him, returning her attention to the courtroom.

Aidan groaned when he caught sight of his entire family waiting in the witness seats behind Allie. Why did she have to do everything the hard way? This was going to be impossible.

Aidan couldn't keep her out. Not now. *Why did you come, Allie?* He opened his mind to hers.

You expect me to leave your mother here, alone?

I had hoped you'd let me handle this.

How was I supposed to know you'd even be here? That you'd even know what was happening?

"Guards, take this young woman into custody immediately," Sarah ordered.

Aidan moved to stand between Allie and anyone stupid enough to try to take her away from him. Naomi stepped forward with him.

"That won't be necessary." Allie marched toward the podium. "You won't be arresting me today."

Allie don't. You don't know what she's capable of. Sarah was one of Marcus's puppets, but she was an evil, power hungry puppet.

I think I do. Please, for once in your life, trust me?

Aidan nodded. He was behind her all the way. But Sarah Madison was going to destroy Allie with her bare hands in front of this courtroom if he didn't think of a way to get them all out of here soon.

"We should follow her lead," Naomi whispered. "She knows what she's doing."

"Who are you to presume so much?" Sarah demanded of Allie.

"You know exactly who I am, Sarah." Allie mocked the Chief Justice. "Let's dispense with the pretenses."

Yeah, my Complement's going to jail. For a really long time.

"Very well, Alexis Carmichael, by showing yourself here today, you have agreed to the terms outlined in your summons." Sarah stood. "Your presence is an admission of guilt. We are done."

"You misunderstand, Sarah. I am not here admitting guilt for anything. I am here to negotiate the release of Naeemah El Sadawii and Greggory McBrien, Governor of the Great Lakes Region of North America."

Aidan followed Allie's gaze across the courtroom where his father now sat beside his mother. Both wore magnetic collars. This whole thing was spiraling beyond his control, but Allie seemed to have it well in hand.

"Negotiate?" Sarah smirked. "That is not an option, my dear. We were told you wouldn't show," she muttered in irritation. "And if you did, you'd come quietly."

My bad, Aidan said. At least that part of his plan worked. Sarah had underestimated Allie and wasn't at all prepared for the spitfire who boldly addressed the full court without an ounce of fear.

"We don't negotiate with children," Sarah said. "Besides, their case has been decided. And you will address me as Chief Justice Sarah Madison."

"Come now, you and my parents were good friends once," Allie said disdainfully. "Surely, we are all on a first name basis here."

"I do not know your parents, child. Stop wasting the court's time," Sarah said.

Come on, Allie. Don't give it all away. But Allie exuded confidence. Naomi was right, she knew what she was doing. Aidan relaxed as he watched the way she spoke with such conviction. Allie was definitely not the same girl he remembered. She was so much more.

Alright, babe, I'm with you. Let's do this together.

"My parents once sat right beside you, ruling as the Senate was meant to be ruled with proper checks and balances."

"You dare to speak of the dead with such lies?"

Allie turned to address the Senate. "How dare you allow this government to become a dictatorship? My parents died *eighteen* years ago, and you still haven't elected a Chief Justice to replace them? You all are so careless with time. You see it as an endless commodity. No need to act now, we'll have another election in a few decades. Yet, how can you not see how much damage can be done in that time? You've lost control of our government and in your complacency, you don't even realize it."

Allie and her mortal brain. She didn't think like any Immortal he knew. In her mind, she wasn't mortal, but she wasn't entirely Immortal either. She considered both sides in everything. It was one of the many quirks that made her special.

"Who are you, young lady?" a senator seated to Allie's left asked.

"I am Alexis Carmichael. Don't I look like my mother, Kassandre?" She turned, smiling with confidence. "It's the hair." She brushed her long locks over her shoulder. "But I have my father's eyes."

Who is this strong, gorgeous, confident woman? Aidan

could hardly focus on what was happening. She was breathtaking, and not because she was the most beautiful woman he'd ever seen, but because she was such a complete badass right now. Aidan's instincts always told him to protect her, but she didn't need it. He'd sold his soul to the devil to buy her more time, but she hadn't needed that either.

"Kassandre and Ashar had a natural child more than two centuries ago," Charles Madison spoke for the first time. "She was the image of her father, with her mother's eyes. Do you expect us to believe you are their second natural child?" he snarled.

"Yes," Allie said simply, her gaze drifting through the crowd of senators.

Aidan cringed. *Not the prophecy.* His eyes swept the room, looking for Marcus, but he was too difficult to find in a crowd. Aidan had no choice but to escape with his Syntrophos now. Allie was about to blow up the lie he'd spent the last several years cultivating. If Marcus was in the room, his cover was blown. Anger surged from that dark place inside Aidan. It was no small thing to realize everything he'd worked for over the last three years no longer mattered. It was all a waste of time and so much energy. He couldn't help his anger at the way circumstances had played out. It wasn't anyone's fault. Allie was on her side doing the best she could and he was over here doing the best he could. The only thing that mattered anymore was getting them all out of this building alive.

As Aidan watched her, he realized Allie was trying to distract the Chief Justice while she searched the crowd for something. Or someone.

"We have heard enough of this nonsense," Charles said.

"I don't think we have," Aidan blurted. "She has done nothing wrong."

Well we're in it together now, babe.

A collective gasp swept the courtroom. All eyes turned to Aidan.

"Who are you to question this court?" Sarah said. "I have been told your training is complete, but I will not tolerate this kind of insubordination in my courtroom, young man."

Aidan opened his mind to Allie once again. *I'm stalling here. Keep looking for whatever it is you're looking for.* "See something, say something." Aidan shrugged. "Our trainers have taught us to seek justice. That is our job as Special Forces to the Chief Justice, isn't it? I am no one, but I am not seeing justice in this courtroom today."

With all eyes on Aidan, Allie continued her search of the crowd.

What are you looking for? Aidan asked.

An empty seat that shouldn't be empty.

She was looking for Marcus. She'd never find him in this crowd. But he must be here somewhere, masquerading as a Senator. The Senators were grouped in twos. *Brilliant, Lex.* Don't look for Marcus, look for his wife. Porcia wouldn't be here to occupy her seat.

"I apologize, Madame," Aidan said. "Perhaps I have overstepped in my desire to serve this court." *Left center, about midway down.* There sat Marcus Servius, smiling at Allie like he'd just won the lottery. He knew who she was now. But he didn't seem surprised. As Marcus's gaze turned to Aidan, his smile faded. Rage burned behind his eyes. He would take his revenge for wasting time on the wrong young Immortal. Aidan would have to worry about that later. Right now, they needed to get out of here. And fast.

"I am afraid we agree with the head of your Special Forces." The Chairman of the Senate stood from his seat on the lower dais. "Has this young woman committed a crime so heinous that she does not deserve a trial? As Chairman of the Senate, we must remind you, once again, to follow protocol." Chairman Edward Thomas was a decent man. Aidan had observed enough of the Senate to know that he and his Complement frequently reminded the Chief Justice that they must follow the law.

"We ask that her formal charges be read for the court's approval, since they are not recorded on today's docket."

"She was raised as an unknown and has failed to register with the Senate," Sarah said simply. "We have received multiple reports that she possesses questionable abilities."

"That is all?" the Chairman asked. "That does not sound like a crime that would interest the International Senate, much less the Chief Justice. Alexis's local authorities should be handling her case. As I see, they are in custody." He gestured at Naeemah and Gregg. "I must ask the court to be more specific concerning their crimes of neglect."

"Their case has been closed," Charles Madison said.

"Perhaps we were too hasty. Please, tell us what specific crimes the governor has committed."

"They have harbored this young woman, in full knowledge that she was an unknown."

"The governor adopted Alexis then?"

"No, but they took on the responsibility of training her," Sarah Madison said. "Which is why this court has charged them with neglect of their official duties."

"I see." The Chairman nodded. "That is a huge oversight on their part, but does the crime warrant sentencing when a fine would be more appropriate?"

"The Chief Justice does not believe a fine is severe enough punishment for this crime and asks the court to support their decision."

"Very well. The Chair requests permission to question the girl."

Sarah looked like she wanted to deny the request, but she had little choice but to comply. With a nod, she gave her permission.

"The Chief Justice has failed to inform you that I have also taken over the institution known as Soma," Allie said. "My summons claims charges of treason have been filed against me, but perhaps the Chief Justice wishes that aspect of my *crimes* to remain secret."

Shocked whispers swept the room, and Aidan had a mild stroke. *Treason?* This was getting worse by the minute.

"What is she doing?" Naomi whispered. "I thought we were supposed to be getting out of here?"

"Give her time. She's just getting started. Tell everyone to stay alert. When I give the order, I want Sam and Bennett at the doors."

"It'll be a miracle if we make it."

"My granddaughter speaks the truth." Alísun's voice pulled Aidan back to the trial. "You can surely sense the mantle of authority she now wears. She is my named heir and first princess. You would do well to listen to her. She is wise beyond her years."

"This farce of a trial has gone far enough," Sarah Madison said. "Guards, take the girl into custody as I have commanded, or face charges for your insubordination."

Aidan held his breath as each of his Syntrophos looked to him for direction. This was the moment of truth. The moment Marcus and Sarah finally realized their army was actually his. He had earned their loyalty. With a slight nod from him, his soldiers settled back to attention.

"Respectfully, we will not," Aidan said.

"She is guilty of treason, and I will charge you all with

accessory to her high crimes if you do not follow orders now!" Sarah was a madwoman, her eyes wild with fury.

"High crimes? Treason? I have not finished questioning the accused." Chairman Thomas raised his hand. "I find little evidence of treason, despite her claims to Indriell, or what amounts to a corporate takeover of Soma. If anything, we should be thanking her for dealing with that accursed institution. Soma was never under our jurisdiction, and she has not made a bid for the power of the Senate. So I ask you, how can her actions amount to treason? If this woman is to face punishment, she will have a fair trial first."

Thank God someone in this room has a backbone and some honor.

"We have heard quite enough," Charles said. "The girl is guilty of treason for daring to call herself first princess."

"The court has not yet decided what that means," Chairman Thomas said. "The Chief Justice will remember they work for the Senate, who represent the people of this democracy. They do not have supreme authority to sentence anyone for their crimes without evidence of those crimes. The Chair asks the court to reevaluate the charges against Ms. Alexis Carmichael. I move that the court disregard her failure to register with the Senate in light of who she is. She was obviously trying to protect her identity and her privacy. Any further accusations against Ms. Carmichael will come *after* the court has questioned her. What say you?" The Chairman turned to the Senate for a vote.

Aidan breathed a sigh of relief at the overwhelming response of "Aye" from the court.

"The court wishes to understand the identity of Ms. Carmichael as the named heir of Indriell, as well as her intentions," Chairman Thomas addressed the court.

"Queen Alísun, you stand here today, a relic of the

ancient world come to life again." Chairwoman Thomas stood, speaking for the first time. "I can hardly believe it, but clearly the last queen of Indriell we all thought to be dead stands before us again with the Scholar at her side. This is an unprecedented moment in our history. You claim this child, your granddaughter, is the second natural daughter of the ancients, Kassandre and Ashar?"

The queen nodded. "We do."

"Then by default, you also claim she is the child of prophecy? The *son* we've waited and wondered about for millennia?"

Aidan chanced a glance at Marcus. His stone cold glare chilled him to the bone. Marcus would find a way to kill him for this. Aidan returned his glare in kind. If he walked out of here today, Aidan and his family would make it their mission to end Marcus.

"I am the one who foretold of Alexis's birth. I recorded the original prophecy with a false interpretation to protect her," Alísun said.

"Then how can we know for certain what the true prophecy means?" Chairman Thomas asked.

"It is a sad day when the nature of prophecy is no longer understood by those who profess to lead us." Alísun stepped forward. "Do you not realize what you have standing before you? I am a prophetess. The knowledge of every prophecy I've ever spoken lies within my gift. If the court wishes to see the original prophecy concerning Alexis, I am prepared to share that knowledge with everyone present."

The volume in the courtroom rose as court officials talked over one another. No one saw Gemma and Spencer step through the ancient doors far above the dais. They were ready. It was up to Allie now.

Chapter 40

Aidan | Barcelona, Spain | May

Aidan's blood ran cold as he met Marcus's steely gaze across the courtroom. Queen Alísun was about to show the true prophecy about Allie for the whole courtroom to see. Overwhelmed with the gravity of his failure, he didn't know how to move forward from here. He'd spent the last years of his life fighting to protect everyone he loved and it all came to nothing. In the end, he hadn't even been able to protect himself. Marcus destroyed something inside of him and awakened a darkness Aidan struggled to control. His Syntrophos suffered every day of the last few years because of him. And Allie stood across the room, a total stranger, risking it all to take care of herself.

Aidan shared a look with Naomi.

"She's a big girl now, Aidan. She can handle her own shit."

Aidan hung his head. "I know. I just thought ... I thought I was helping her."

"Maybe that was your first mistake?" She arched a brow at him. "Maybe you don't need to kill yourself protecting the people you love."

"You're right." Aidan watched the chaos happening in the courtroom. Sarah Madison was like a rabid dog ready to tear Allie's throat out. Yet, Aidan was the reason it had all come to this. In his desire to keep everyone safe, he never accepted the help he needed to handle the situation before it escalated beyond his control. He wished he could go back to the night of his arrest and make different choices. Though, at the time, few choices were available to him.

"The court wishes to get to the bottom of this," Chairman Thomas said. "We will hear the whole story. Including the original prophecy as given by the queen."

"The queen?" Sarah harrumphed, leaning back in her seat.

Alísun ignored Sarah's remark as she approached the podium to stand beside Allie. "Please take your seats and try to relax as I share the prophecy. This will not be comfortable." She raised her eyes toward the oculus above them, the fading light of evening casting them all in shadow.

The silver of her eyes grew opaque, like opals. A cool breeze flew in from the oculus causing those inside to shiver. Alísun held out her hands for Allie and Livia. "Stand with me, my girls. I am sorry to have to show you this."

Allie and Livia quickly took their grandmother's hands, standing solemnly beside her. Aidan and his soldiers sank down onto the bench beside the dais. A blast of power shot through the room, snapping Aidan's head back. Tightness coiled in his chest, and a sense of doom settled all around them like a mist. Murmurs of distress rose from concerned voices but were silenced as a shadow, thick as night, fell upon the room. No one could move. No one could speak. Terrified eyes gazed above.

Silvery swirling figures took shape, dancing across the domed ceiling. The sound of the queen's otherworldly voice echoed across the chamber as she quoted the prophecy Aidan knew by heart. But something was lost in the translation from Alísun's original prophetic vision and the simple words she ultimately recorded on paper.

The ethereal figures took on the forms of the ancient queens: Allie's ancestors. Queens Ashlynn, Celyn, Alyvia, Fáelynn, Eiselynn and a younger Alísun with a baby Kassandre in her arms, all looked down on the Senate with disappointment and anger—anger for their laziness and complacency.

The queens faded, leaving only Alísun and her young daughter, Kassandre, standing beside her father, Alexander the Scholar.

Alexander chased his young daughter with a spark of laughter in his eyes. A shadow of his voice called out for his "Kassie-girl."

Kassandre grew into a strong woman with her Complement, Ashar, by her side. Aidan heard Allie's strangled sob and wanted to go to her. Allie cried out in anguish when an innocent young Livia joined their parents. Her sister was a beautiful child, surrounded by a family who adored her. But a moment later, a faceless man ripped Livia from her parent's arms and disappeared with her in a puff of smoke. Several lifetimes would pass before they saw their daughter again.

"Livia," Allie sobbed her sister's name.

More than two hundred years later, Kassandre and Ashar grew strong again as the only daughter of Indriell to never be queen, became Chief Justice of the modern Immortal world alongside her Complement.

The figure of Kassandre drifted away from Ashar as she grew heavy with her second pregnancy, hiding it from the Senate. Kassandre removed herself from her duties for a short while until after the birth of her secret child. Kassandre sobbed in agony as she kissed the redheaded child on her head and left her with Lily and Carson Carmichael.

"Allie-girl!" The ghost of Kassandre's voice echoed across the domed ceiling. Kassandre and Ashar raced down the beach toward a toddler-Allie, sweeping her up in a tight embrace. "How we've missed you, my love." She buried her nose in Allie's hair, turning to greet Lily and Carson, thanking them for caring for their daughter.

Allie's shoulders shook as she sobbed at the sight of both of her mothers and fathers.

"Stay strong for our girls," Kassandre spoke softly to her Complement. "Watch over Allie. She will be lonely. She'll need you more than she knows. And help Alivia forgive herself. She is a fighter. She will survive it all and come out stronger for it, but she will be hard on herself. And promise me, if you can ever learn to love again, my darling Ashar, find whatever happiness you can." The life in Kassandre's eyes grew dim as blood bloomed across her chest. Kassandre and Ashar vanished like smoke on the wind.

A young Allie stood alone and lonely as the years went by until Ashar returned for her, taking her to a safe place to become the woman she was destined to be.

An ominous darkness lay behind Allie, an oppressive void representing an uncertain future that no other prophecy had ever foretold. A faceless man grew strong in the darkness. He moved with stealth through the years, seeking to destroy everything the modern Immortal world had built. This faceless man *was* the great darkness and Aidan understood he was watching Marcus destroy the world.

But Allie shone as a beacon of light in that void. Shadowed young Immortals came to stand with her. Strong and powerful, they were united with the strength of their ancestors. They shielded Allie with an aura of power and protection. *They* were the pathway through the abyss. They would find the light of the future together. The uncertainty frightened the older generations, but it excited these brave, young warriors.

Only they would have the strength and power to fight the darkness and move their people forward. Their biggest obstacle wasn't the unknown: it was their parents and grandparents. It was their leaders and teachers who told them time and again that they didn't matter because they were too young. Allie stood as their champion. To stop her was to let the darkness win—a darkness that already held sway within the world.

Aidan's head fell forward as the prophetic moment faded into nothing. Silence echoed across the ancient chamber. He took a deep breath as the sound of movement returned. Quiet murmured conversation hummed all around the courtroom, but Aidan only had eyes for Allie. She sat beside her grandmother, lacking the strength to stand.

Aidan couldn't fathom why he'd ever doubted her. His instincts told him to protect her for as long as he could, but he should have known she didn't need that. Allie was strong. She would weather the storm ahead of them and *she* would be the one to lead them all. Not him. Aidan wasn't meant to fight this battle alone. He should have been fighting beside her this whole time. His biggest mistake wasn't trying to protect her; it was leaving her in the first place.

Aidan ached to go to her. Allie's tearstained cheeks did nothing to dispel her authority. For surely everyone in the room who just witnessed the queen's prophecy would never dispute Allie's claim to the throne of Indriell ever again. Seeing the prophecy for herself was probably more than she could bear in this moment. It damn near broke his heart to watch it.

Silence echoed across the ancient chamber before murmured conversation rose in a din around him. But Allie's deep, shuddering breath was the only sound he could hear.

Stand up, Alexis Ann. You're the strongest person I know. The prophecy isn't just about you; it's about all of us. Get up and show them who you are.

Allie nodded, settling her eyes on Aidan. Reaching for her grandmother's hand, she got back on her feet.

"Seeing is believing," Allie said, her voice a soft echo, commanding their attention.

"I think we can all agree that Alexis Carmichael is the undisputed heir of Indriell and the child of prophecy," Chairwoman Thomas said with an unsteady voice. "Yet the court needs to determine what that means in terms of her authority in the modern world."

"Really, Chairwoman Thomas?" Sarah scoffed. "That is quite a leap."

"Have you ever witnessed a prophet speak, Sarah?" she asked. "I have. My father was a prophet with nothing resembling the talent the queen possesses, but I know a true prophecy when I see one. No one here can deny what we just witnessed was indeed the original prophecy. Not even you."

"Are you prepared for what comes next?" Chief Justice Sarah Madison asked the Senate. "It is Soma today, but what happens when this girl desires more power? We cannot allow her the kind of authority the royals are suggesting."

"Do not put words in my mouth," Allie said. "I have no desire to rule. Perhaps the court should ask me why I seized Soma in the first place?"

"You have the floor," Chairman Thomas said.

"I never wanted anything from you," Allie said. "I just wanted to be left alone to run Soma as an independent safe haven for young students to come and learn without the threat of being used for their talents."

"While you train your students to support your bid for power wherever you can?" Charles Madison accused.

"No more interruptions," Chairman Thomas said. "Let the heir speak."

"I initiated the takeover of Soma before Chief Justice Sarah and Charles Madison could do so," Allie announced to the wild murmurs spreading across the room. "I couldn't allow Soma to become a government institution. We must provide a place for our children that has no ties to any government."

Aidan finally saw her game, and he couldn't believe he hadn't thought of it himself. *My girl is freaking brilliant.* He fought the grin tugging his lips. Allie wasn't going to let Sarah or Charles walk away from this. She was going to take them down, right here, right now.

"How do you know the Chief Justice meant to seize Soma?" Chairman Thomas asked.

"Move to strike the question," Charles said. "This child is skating on thin ice with her accusations."

"Denied. The Chair would like to hear her answer," the chairman said. "Please continue, Alexis."

"The Milan Initiative," Allie said. "A top secret organization meant to take over Soma with the aid of a Syntrophos army Sarah and Charles have built."

"Syntrophos?" Outraged cries rang out among the Senate.

"What do you mean, Syntrophos?" Chairman Thomas asked.

Allie glanced at Aidan and his team. *Will you show them?*

Hell, yes, we will. "She means us. The Special Forces

team," Aidan said. He turned and nodded to his soldiers. "Show them."

Aidan and Naomi were the first to drop the protective facade shielding their bond from the Senate. The others followed, one by one, until all five Syntrophos couples stood proudly, allowing the Senate to experience the bond for themselves. Allie and Darius followed suit, as did Sasha and Quinn. Collectively, their power surged together. Their bonds ignited among all the Syntrophos, feeding off one another, leaving no doubt in the minds of those who witnessed it that a Syntrophos army was something to be feared.

"The Syntrophos bond is alive and well among our generation. I suppose you can thank me for that," Allie said sadly. "You just saw my grandmother's prophecy of how I would 'gather my equals.' This bond unites us all. But my fellow Syntrophos here today have been hunted and drafted into the Milan Initiative. Aidan McBrien's family was threatened unless he agreed to enter the Initiative. They also threatened him with my safety." Allie turned her gaze to him. "We believe he agreed, so he could protect his family. To protect me, at first. But as time passed, he also took on the responsibility for the others. He stayed with the Initiative for them."

Aidan's heart swelled with love for her. *I knew you would get it.* She understood him in a way no one else ever would. He only wished he understood her half as well. One of these days, he would figure out all the intricacies of Alexis Carmichael. And he would love every single one of them.

"Aidan and the others have been trained for the sole purpose of seizing control of Sterling Tower on the orders of the Chief Justice."

"She lies," Charles said, furious.

"I can prove it." Allie raised her voice over Charles's blustering.

"How?" the chairman asked, darting a glare at the dais.

"If the Senate would allow my mentor, Emma Renard, to question the Chief Justice, all will be revealed."

"Emma Renard? She is an officer of this court, is she not? Lieutenant governor of the Great Lakes Region of North America, I believe," Chairwoman Thomas said.

"And a powerful truth seeker," Allie added.

Aidan cast a glance back at his team, letting a small smile light his face. This was going better than he could have dreams. He wanted them to know this was working—trusting in Allie would see them freed from the chains that bound them to the Initiative. "Be ready," he whispered, giving them a reassuring nod.

As Emma questioned the Chief Justice, who were starting to freak out now that this was blowing up in their faces, Aidan studied the exits. Marcus would slip out undetected. He wasn't going down with his puppets. But that worked for Aidan's plans. They were going to make it out of here, and they would survive to fight Marcus another day. And if they played their cards right, they wouldn't be fugitives either, thanks to Allie.

"Did you ever intend to inform the Senate of this army or of this Soma takeover?" Emma demanded.

"No. We do not need their approval for matters of security." Charles's eyes grew wide with fright. He was putty in Emma's hands.

Cries of indignation arose from the Senate body.

Emma consulted the paper Allie had handed her before she continued with her questions. "You routinely disregard the Senate's permissions for such endeavors," Emma continued, ignoring the outrage of the court. "Who orchestrated the capture of Alivia, first born of the ancients, Kassandre and Ashar?

"The Coalition," Charles said. "Everyone knows that; it was two hundred years ago."

"But it wasn't the Coalition, was it? Alivia was taken by one Marcus Servius when she was just four years old, and you helped him do it, didn't you?"

"Yes." Charles stared down at his hands, unable to resist Emma.

Aidan turned his attention back on Marcus, expecting him to be long gone by now. Still, he sat, observing the goings on like one of the crowd. He refused to meet Aidan's gaze. He had eyes only for Allie now. Aidan knew that look. Marcus would not stop until he possessed Allie for himself. Aidan had spent the better part of four years working his ass off to keep this from happening, yet here they were. But as he regarded his team of Syntrophos a surge of confidence hit him. Maybe not all was for naught. He had a loyal army now. And his family. Together with Allie, they would shield the world from the man who threatened their way of life.

"And the assassination of Chief Justice Kassandre and Ashar? Who is responsible for their deaths?" Emma asked.

"The Coalition," Sarah forced herself to say.

"They are an easy scapegoat. But let's try that again," Emma said. "The truth this time."

"W-we gave the order," Sarah said through gritted teeth.

Aidan jerked his head toward Allie expecting to see shock, but she clearly already knew the answer before Emma asked the question.

"And who do you work for?" Allie asked, her voice laced with acid.

"Answer the heir," Emma demanded.

"The ancient, Lord Teigan, betrothed to Queen Eiselynn

before she ruined the Immortal world forever." Sarah's voice rang out like a death knell. Her own. "He will claim what is his by right!" she screamed. "And we will be by his side when he brings the Immortal world into the light of day once more, banishing the mortals to death by fire, as she should have ordered thousands of years ago." She shot Queen Alísun a hateful glare, collapsing in her seat.

"We will not have this." Charles stood. "I demand this entire testimony be stricken from the record."

"Denied," Chairman Thomas said.

"And where is this Lord Teigan now?" Emma asked.

"I do not know," Sarah said, though she struggled to speak the lie.

"Rephrase the question," Emma said. "Where is Marcus Servius? Charles?" She turned to the more susceptible of the two.

"He sits there." Charles Madison stood and pointed at the man in question. "He is Senator Robert Sinclair."

Loud murmuring rose to a roar as Emma continued, "Senator Robert Sinclair, also known as Marcus Servius, the man who abducted the young Alivia. Among his many other aliases, this man is also known as the ancient, Lord Teigan, correct?"

"That is correct," Charles said.

It was too late: Marcus had already slipped away. Aidan stared at the two empty seats where Marcus had just sat only moments before.

"Bailiffs, search the building for him," Chairwoman Thomas ordered.

Three uniformed men ran from the chamber, issuing orders to the guards outside the room.

"You won't find him," Allie said. "He disappears as fast a

smoke in the wind. With his common features and extraordinary gift for evasion, he is already gone."

Aidan's heart raced in his chest. Had she already had dealings with Marcus, or was this her clairvoyance speaking?

"Madame Under Secretary, please issue a warrant for the arrest of the man known as Senator Robert Sinclair, Marcus Servius and the ancient Lord Teigan," Chairman Thomas said. "I put forth a vote to the Senate," he continued, turning to face the courtroom, "to remove the Chief Justice Sarah Madison and Charles Madison from office and charge them with high crimes of treason against the International Senate they have sworn to serve. What say you?"

Aidan breathed a sigh of relief at the unanimous sounds of agreement from the Senate body. *She pulled it off.* And God help him, she did it the old fashioned way, through the law. Just like a mortal would. He wanted to laugh. Allie's mortal brain saved the day. He had to stop thinking of that as her handicap—clearly it was an asset.

"Bailiff, take Sarah and Charles Madison into custody to await their trial," Chairwoman Thomas said with formality.

"You cannot do this. You don't have the power to remove the only seated Chief Justice," Charles snarled.

"That is for the Senate to decide. You have been stripped of your office and will receive a formal trial," Chairwoman Thomas said, as the remaining bailiffs rushed to arrest the Chief Justice, leading them from the room.

Allie rushed forward. "I ask the court to release the Governor Naeemah El Sadawii and Greggory McBrien immediately and dismiss the charges brought against them. They have no ties to the royal family and should not be held accountable today, or any time in the future, for my actions. Please allow them to continue to loyally serve this government as they always have."

When this was all done, Aidan was going to crawl on his knees over broken glass to thank her for keeping his family safe.

"In light of today's events, your requests are granted," Chairman Thomas said.

Aidan didn't wait for direction. He crossed the room and stripped his parents of their restraints.

"We're getting out of here," Aidan said.

"All of us." Naeemah took his hand. Her look said she would end him if he didn't come with her.

"All of us." He nodded.

We need to get out of here, Allie. I still don't trust any of them. Aidan escorted his parents across the chamber to sit with the rest of their family.

Agreed. Get all of our people behind me.

Aidan lifted a hand to call his Syntrophos to his side. "Time to go," he murmured instructions to each of them, as they took their places between Allie and their family and the rest of the courtroom.

"The court apologizes to you and your family," Chairman Thomas said. "But it seems we find ourselves leaderless. We cannot adjourn until we have appointed a temporary Chief Justice today. For the first time ever, we have a queen in our midst." He turned to Alísun. "Will you and the Scholar step in to lead us until arrangements can be made for an election?"

"We will not," Alísun said. "It is not our decision to make. It has been a very long time since the queens ruled our people. But when a queen names her heir, the heir becomes the highest authority of the Immortal world. This decision falls to Alexis."

"I am afraid we cannot allow an Unproven child to make such a decision," the Chairman said.

"You mistakenly discredit youth." Alísun shook her head

sadly. "In my day, we revered it. Respected the voice of our children, for they would be the ones leading us when we grew old. Alexis is more than capable of appointing a trusted substitute. Her gift will guide her. She is the highest authority in this room, and the decision should fall to her."

"We cannot accept your recommendation," the Chairman said. "The Senate will decide."

"I will decide." Allie's authority swirled around her like a cloak as she stepped forward. "You will do as I say, and you will respect my authority." She paced in front of the Senate, her eyes blazing with fury and the strength of her power. "I do not wish to govern, but I will if you continue to push me."

That's my girl. Aidan put himself as close to her side as he could get.

"Chairman Thomas." Allie approached Edward and his wife. "May I take your hand?"

"Of-of course." Both the Thomas's extended their hands to her, wary of Allie's show of strength.

Allie studied them with her gift, determining if they were suitable candidates to replace the previous Chief Justice. "You will take on the role of *temporary* Chief Justice."

"If the court agrees, it would be our honor to serve," he said with a respectful nod.

Allie turned to the raised dais where the under secretaries sat. Darius, Livia, Aidan and Naomi followed her. She studied the Madison's secretary, finding something she didn't like. "You are dismissed from your post," Allie said. "They will stand trial as well."

Aidan gestured for Ezra and Wes to arrest the under secretary and send them down to the waiting cells beneath the courtroom. "Hand them off to the bailiffs downstairs and come right back."

"Who shall take the remaining seats?" Chairwoman Thomas asked.

"The people must choose." Allie turned to face the Senate. "I ask the court to make arrangements for public elections to be held within the year. The people deserve the right to elect two new Chiefs of Justice who will then appoint a new Chairman of the assembly."

"That is not enough time," the secretary insisted. "We will need at least a year to plan the election and a year for the candidates to campaign."

"You people drag your feet when you need to take action." Allie slammed her fist down on the dais railing. "I don't care what you have to do to make it happen. Make the announcements, and give the candidates four months to campaign, and then we will have an election *this* year. If you fail to take action, then I will return and take action for you."

"And what do you intend to do as first princess?" Chairman Thomas asked. "What authority are you assuming here?"

"I have no desire to participate in the Senate unless I have to. Don't make me have to." Allie glared at the silent senators. "Take your positions seriously, or I will clean house. Otherwise, I will remain in my position as the leader of Soma, free of government interference." Allie stepped up to the podium, turning to address the assembly. "I ask that every member of this Senate, from the high-ranking officials seated here today right down to the lieutenant governors who police the cities, to set their slaves free. Any person who has been purchased from Soma will be freed one way or another. I will be following up, and if I find you have not complied with this simple request, I will remove the slave from your home, and you will be charged with crimes of human trafficking." Allie stood silently for a moment to let her words resonate. "I will not tolerate corruption."

"While you and the royal family have the full support of the Senate as well as our respect," the Chairman said, "we simply must determine the legal extent of your authority in the modern world." He took a step toward her. "We would like nothing more than to foster a positive relationship with the royals, but the parameters of your authority and ours must be clear in the eyes of the law."

"That matter has already been decided," Alísun said. "My heir has stepped forward, and everyone in this chamber has already accepted her authority, whether you realize it or not. The matter is closed."

"It is not closed," Chairwoman Thomas said. "While we believe the heir deserves a voice in this chamber, the weight of that voice must be discussed at length."

"The royal family will decide the extent of my authority," Allie announced. "No one else has that right. The queen has never abdicated. Her sovereignty remains, just as it was when she was named queen thousands of years ago. You are here today in your positions of power because she allowed it. And we are here, displaying the mantle of our authority, because you have allowed yourselves to become corrupt in your thirst for more power."

"Perhaps you are right," the Chairman said. "But I am confident we will reach an agreement both parties can be happy with." He stepped down from the dais. "We invite you to stay here in the city. We can reconvene later this week to make the necessary decisions. You and your family are more than welcome to stay in the hotel suites here for our distinguished guests."

That's our cue to leave, Lex. Aidan stepped between Allie

and the Chairman, as his soldiers fell into a V formation around Allie and her family.

"That won't be necessary," Allie said, backing away from the Chairman. "We will be leaving now."

"I'm afraid we cannot allow you to leave until these matters have been decided." The Chairman raised his hand, causing all the doors to the chamber to slam shut, their locks clicking into place.

Time to go. Aidan and his team started backing up. "Samantha. Bennett." Aidan nodded for them to break formation.

The two raced to the top of the chamber. Raising their hands together, Samantha and Bennett demolished the locked door. Splinters and debris rained down where the door once stood.

"Stop them," Chairman Thomas called.

Senators rose from their seats to intercept, but they were too slow to react.

"Now." Naomi nodded at Neela and Ivy.

The two grasped hands, and an icy blue mist formed a wall around Allie and her people, closing them off from the Senate's reach.

"Quinn, Darius," Aidan said. "A little help?"

Quinn and Sasha joined hands, cloaking everyone under the veil of mist with Quinn's invisibility, and Darius threw up his soundproofing barrier, so they could no longer be heard or seen.

"All right, everyone, we're walking out of here now," Aidan said. "Go, quickly."

The Senate erupted in chaos when Allie and all of the Syntrophos disappeared.

"Seal the building," the Chairman cried. "Do not let

them leave. Especially the Syntrophos. They cannot be trusted."

How are we getting out of here if the building is on lock-down? Allie asked.

Same way we're walking through this doorway. Aidan ushered her through the crumbling debris of the chamber doors and into the lobby. Relieved, he saw Gemma and Spencer standing outside, waiting by the cars they'd acquired with Ruthie, Ace and Lola behind the wheel, waiting to drive them far away from this place.

Is everyone with us? Allie asked, frantically looking over her shoulder.

My team will get us all out of here.

Samantha and Bennett charged across the lobby, using their gift to demolish the glass facade of the building at street level.

Shards of glass no bigger than grains of sand exploded out of the building, causing the guards to panic, desperately searching for a threat they couldn't see or hear. Mortal men and women on the sidewalks screamed at the explosion, cowering behind cars, searching for a source of the violence.

Allie and Aidan shot from the building with their hands clasped.

"Where will we go?" Allie asked, searching up and down the street for a way out.

"This way." Aidan turned, dragging her to the cars waiting along the curb. Gemma and Spencer rushed to meet him.

"You planned this?" Allie asked.

"I had a feeling we'd end up on the same page at some point." Aidan skidded to a stop beside a white delivery van. Pilar was behind the wheel.

"Get in." Aidan shoved Darius and Livia into the back of the van. Alísun and Alex were right behind them.

Allie tugged Aidan's hand as she stepped into the van, but he pulled her back.

"You were amazing." With one arm around her waist and his other hand splayed across her back, Aidan kissed her. And then he shoved her into the back of the van and slammed the door in her face.

"Get her out of here," he barked orders to Pilar and Neela, who'd jumped into the front seat with Ivy. "My family will take care of you. You two," he said, leaning into the front seat to speak with Neela and Ivy. "You stay with Allie. You hear me? She is your full-time job now. Guard and protect her."

"You got it, sexy," Neela said.

"Now go." He still had some work to do before he could go home.

Chapter 41

Aidan | Kelleys Island | June
Two Weeks Later

"Mr. McBrien, Ms. Hauser, we can't thank you enough for bringing our daughter home." Lola's mother clutched her daughter's hand. "And for taking the time to teach us how to understand her bond with Ace."

"And thank you for opening your home to Ace," Naomi said. "I know if his parents were still with us, they would be grateful to know their son is settled with a nice family."

Aidan just prayed they would take his advice and bring Ace and Lola to Soma soon.

"We will see you in a few weeks," Lola said. "At Soma, right?" She glanced back at her mother. She was just fourteen when she'd left home for the Milan Initiative, but she was almost seventeen now and mature far beyond her years. She would never fit into her old life now. None of them would.

"We will talk about it, darling," her mother said.

"I can't stress it enough," Aidan said. "Lola and Ace will never be safe on their own. The Syntrophos must stick together. You will all be welcome at Sterling Tower in Atlanta."

"I'm just afraid that's not safe, either." Lola's father said. "We've heard such awful things about that place, but we will discuss it as a family."

"Perhaps we should just go somewhere off grid? Maybe that's the safest thing for all of us." Her mother twisted her hands in her lap.

"Mom, you're going to have to be okay with this," Lola said. "After everything we've been through, Aidan and Naomi are my family, and I trust him with my life. We are going to Soma."

"Lola, we need to take some time to chill," Ace said. "To put the Initiative behind us. But we will come." He turned to Aidan.

"Take care of yourselves." Aidan pulled them both into his arms. "See you soon."

"You call us if you need anything," Naomi added. Each time they left one of their own with their families, they took a little piece of Naomi's soul with them. She wouldn't feel whole again until they were all back together.

"Are you going back now?" Lola asked. "To Allie?"

"We have one more stop to make, and then we're going home." Aidan smiled as he left his youngest soldiers with a mother and father who would probably never get it. He and Naomi had escorted each of his Syntrophos back to their homes with an invitation to come to Soma within the month. He had no doubt they would all reunite there soon, but he gave them all an out. They would never be held against their will again. But they were family now, and they would stick together.

Aidan drove away from the Kelleys Island ferry dock and turned his motorcycle east toward home. Naomi clutched his waist, her tension mounting the closer they came to their long anticipated reunion.

Home? It was surreal after all this time away, so odd and yet so familiar. This place was in his blood. But he wasn't sure he would ever call it home again. His home was wherever Allie was—Allie and Naomi.

He left his bike in the driveway of his parents' home. The home he grew up in. He would see them all later. Right now, he only had eyes for Allie.

"I'll let myself in," Naomi said. "Go find her."

"I love you," he reminded her.

"Love you too." Naomi left him where he stood.

Aidan made his way up the grassy slopes behind the house. He found Allie sitting at the base of the old laurel tree along the cliff side where they'd spent so much time when they were young. Her arms rested on her knees, and she looked so lost.

Neela and Ivy waved to him from their vantage point on the hillside, waiting and watching for any harm that might come to her.

Allie smiled when she saw him, but it wasn't the reaction he'd hoped for. She sat watching him with a wistful look on her face. He wasn't sure where they stood now, but he'd expected some excitement ... or at least anger.

He paused on the hillside near the laurel tree where she sat, uncertain how to approach her after all this time. He was both nervous and afraid. Nervous because he couldn't think of what to say and afraid because she might reject him.

Suddenly, Allie sat up straighter, a look of confusion puckering her brow.

"Allie?" He finally found his voice.

Allie closed her eyes tight like she was willing him away. She gasped when his shadow fell over her.

"Open your eyes, Alexis Ann," he said, crouching before her. "I want to see those weird green eyes again."

"You're not here," she whispered, shaking her head. "You can't be."

"But I am." He sat beside her just as he had when they met here as teenagers a lifetime ago. "Why don't you trust what you see?"

Allie opened her eyes, stilled filled with confusion.

"I'm really here." He took her hand. "Tell me why you think I'm not."

"The visions." She waved her hand in the direction of the hillside. "They're everywhere."

"All the time?" He frowned, realizing she really didn't trust anything she saw.

"Are you back?" Her voice was a strangled whisper.

"I'm home." His smile was hesitant, but then she flew into his arms.

"You're really here?" She leaned back, running her hands up the length of his arms. "For how long?"

"I'm not leaving again." It felt so good to say it. So good to hold her, knowing he didn't have to leave—would never leave her again if he could help it.

Allie hugged him tighter. "I swear, Aidan Loukas McBrien, if you ever slam a car door in my face like that again, I will tear your face off." Her words came out garbled but they were like music to his ears.

"I'm sorry about that." His smile spread wide across his face. Here she was, the girl he fell in love with ages ago. His fingertips brushed the hair back from her face. "You have no idea how much I wanted to come home with you after the trial." He held her at arms' length, his hands cupping her face, and his thumb caressing the length of the tattoo along her throat. "But I had to take care of my people first. They depend on me."

"You brought them with you?"

"Not all of them. Not yet. I gave them the choice to return to their lives, but they all chose to take a brief visit home to take care of their families. They will make their way to us in time. It's the way of the Syntrophos. We need each other." Aidan's hands wandered down her arms, grasping her hands again. "To set the record straight, when we came for you at Soma, I never once questioned your position as First Princess and the named heir of Indriell. But I was so angry. I had a plan I'd been working toward for a long time, and I had to rethink things when you beat me to the punch. I convinced myself you were being used and manipulated. It was just so unlike you to reach for that kind of power. Then you told me off right before you turned away, leaving me and my soldiers gaping like morons. That was when I knew you really were the mastermind behind everything happening at Soma."

"I was doing it for you, you big dummy." She sniffed.

"I didn't think you'd still ... that you'd put yourself out there just for me."

"It wasn't just for you. I did this for all of us. But bringing you home was my main motivation. It wasn't until much later —when Darius pointed it out to me—that I realized all along I was telling myself I was going to rescue you when I'd never even considered that might not be what you wanted. Not like I could have asked, but I shouldn't have made that decision for you."

"We have to stop doing that to each other." Aidan smiled.

"Yeah." Allie sighed. "It's a lot harder than it sounds."

"I would get down on one knee, but I'm pretty sure you'd kick me in the nuts if I did." Aidan gave a wry grin. "Alexis

Ann." He reached to brush a stray curl from her face. "You have my loyalty and my fealty."

"Aidan, don't." She squeezed his hand. "You are my equal. You don't have—"

"Of course, I do. I pledge my life and my service—and that of my army, no matter how big or small it may prove to be—to the heir and future queen of Indriell, however she chooses to reign. I will be her equal and her confidant. If she'll have me?"

"Why did you leave, Aidan? Before all of this madness started."

"Lots of reasons. None you'll like."

"Try me?"

"At first it was the Darius thing. I knew that was going to be hard on you and even harder with me here. So, I planned to take myself out of the picture for a few months." That wasn't all of it, but he couldn't tell her the real reason. She needed to see him as her Complement when she was ready. He wouldn't rush her.

"And then?"

"And then Naomi happened." He shrugged. "And it became even more complicated and more clear to me that we needed the time apart. But in the end, she needed me more than you did. You had Darius. She didn't have anyone."

"I wish you would have discussed it with me first." Allie stared down at their entwined hands.

"I know. It was stupid and selfish. I only hope that one day you can understand what my eighteen-year-old head was thinking when I made those choices—not just for us, but for myself. I hope you'll understand that I was doing what I thought was best for Naomi and me. And the time apart ... that wasn't just about you."

"The time apart was never the issue. I came to understand just how much we needed it, too. It was your silence that killed me."

"I never really left you, Lex. I was always right here." He tapped her forehead. "For the last four years, whenever you've thought of me or spoke to me, I heard you."

Allie's eyes filled with tears. "One of these days, I'm going to kick your ass for that." She managed a watery smile.

"You never answered my question," Aidan said, brushing the tears from her eyes with his thumb. "Will you have me, my queen ... to be? It would be my honor to serve the royal family."

She titled her head back, meeting his gaze. "Aidan, I don't want you in my service. I want you as my equal and my friend. Besides, you have an army." She flashed him a wide grin.

"There's the smartass I remember." Aidan pulled her into his arms. Inhaling the familiar scent of his Complement, the darkness inside him faded just a little. He was finally home.

Aidan almost fell out of his seat when the doors to Allie's council chambers nearly splintered off their hinges.

"Just who the hell do you think you are?" Naomi raged, baring her teeth at Allie.

Oh, shit. Aidan rubbed a hand over his tired face. *What now?* In the days since joining Allie at Sterling Tower, the thinly veiled hostility between his Syntrophos and his Complement was a constant bubble of tension hanging between them. And judging by the look on Naomi's face, it had finally burst.

"Excuse me? Who do you think *you* are barging into my council like a deranged lunatic?" Allie raged right back.

Naomi didn't hesitate before she snatched a white marble statue from the entry table and launched it at Allie's head.

Allie ducked and the statue crashed against the thick windowpane behind her, sending an array of cracks across the surface.

"Naomi!" Aidan stood, his chair thudding against the wall behind him. "What are you doing?"

"Indeed," Queen Alísun said, calmly rising to her feet. "Explain yourself, young woman. This is First Princess's private council.

Naomi ignored the queen, stalking across the room toward Allie. "You *banished* my father?" Her voice hard as steel. "I repeat. Who the hell do you think you are?"

"Stand down," Livia said, putting herself between Allie and Naomi. "Before I put you down."

"Allie, can you please call off your guard dog? That's my Syntrophos she's threatening." Aidan's heart thumped in his chest, not sure which woman he needed to defend in this situation.

"Stay out of it, son." Gregg murmured, shoving Aidan back into his seat. "They need to deal with this without you."

"Greyson betrayed me, Naomi." Allie stood her ground.

"Wait, you sent Greyson away? From Sterling Tower?" Aidan asked, trying to keep the accusation out of his voice.

"Seriously, don't pick sides." Gregg thumped him on the back of the head. "You'll live to regret it."

"No," Naomi snapped. "She sent him away from his *home.* The home where I grew up. She just tossed him aside like garbage." Naomi's hands clenched into fists. "What could he have possibly done to deserve that?" Angry tears gleamed in her eyes. "He was never anything but kind to you."

"He tried to sell me to the Coalition," Allie said.

"You're lying. He wouldn't do something so dishonorable."

"I'm afraid he did, Naomi," Gregg said gently. "Your father made a desperate choice to sacrifice Allie to save Isebeau. Luckily, Livia intervened and we managed to avoid a terrible outcome. But we can no longer trust Greyson. If it were up to me, his punishment would have been far worse. Allie showed great restraint when she sent him away. Your father took Isebeau to a remote community in Ontario where she can recover in peace."

"I'm afraid we cannot allow Greyson to return, Naomi," Allie said. "But, of course, you are free to visit him as much as you'd like."

"He's with Isebeau?" Naomi's eyes glazed. "They're together? Finally?"

"I would have helped him," Allie said, her shoulders slumped. "I loved Greyson like another father. I would have done anything to help him find his Complement, but he betrayed me and I can't have that around me during these trying times."

Naomi turned her ashen face toward Aidan. "You don't think..." Her tears broke free, falling down her face as her knees gave out.

Aidan lunged to catch her before she fell. "I don't know, but we'll go find him." Aidan guided Naomi to his seat. "If it was him, he didn't know about our bond," Aidan murmured, crouching beside her. "He'd never hurt you." But Aidan felt sick at the idea because he knew she was right.

"It had to be him." Naomi shook her head. "He betrayed us?"

"No. He betrayed me."

"What is she talking about, son?" Gregg asked.

Aidan stood on shaky legs, running a hand through his

hair. “When the Initiative first came looking for me, they knew everything about me. I mean everything. They knew things only someone who’d known me my whole life would have known.”

“He betrayed both of you?” Naomi frowned. “And me.”

“Naomi.” Allie crouched in front of her. “Your father loves you more than anything in this world. If he knew Aidan was your Syntrophos and his actions led to what you’ve experienced with the Initiative, he would have died before betraying you like that.”

“But he sacrificed Aidan.” Naomi turned her wide eyes on him. “He’s the reason you’ve suffered.” She shook her head. “I can’t ever forgive him for that.”

EPILOGUE

Aidan | Sterling Tower | December
Six Months Later

Aidan's smile wasn't forced, but it still felt foreign on his face. The last six months at Sterling Tower with Allie, Naomi and everyone he loved finally together in one place should have been easy.

I should be happy. He sat beside the bonfire, watching his Complement and his Syntrophos playing in the snow with the youngest Soma kids. Allie and Naomi would probably never love each other, but they were trying, for his sake.

Allie had planned an end of term holiday party for all her students at Sterling Tower. She even got the old Immortal who lived in the Warehouse to transform the huge landscape under his roof into a winter wonderland. Kids were ice-skating on the lake and sledding down the hills, basking in the brisk winter sunshine. The whole place looked like a holiday card.

But Aidan still felt absent. Maybe he'd changed too much. He hadn't expected to pick up where he left off, but he hadn't expected it to be this hard either.

"She's an amazing person." Brigs came to sit on the log beside Aidan in front of the warm fire. "You're a lucky man."

"The luckiest." Aidan's jaw creaked with tension. He hated the idea that Allie was ever with this dream walker douche-bag. Unfortunately, Brigs was an integral part of the protection that separated Sterling Tower from those who opposed the royal family—and he wasn't going anywhere any time soon.

"So are you ever going to get your head out of your ass and be the guy she needs or are you going to spend the next century brooding about your difficult past?"

"Excuse me?" Aidan turned a menacing glare on the man sitting next to him. "You might want to leave, now."

"You're a scary dude, Aidan. You could probably hand me my own ass without moving from your seat, but you're also kind of a dick." Brigs lifted a flask from his coat pocket, pouring the contents into his coffee. Without a word, he offered the flask to Aidan.

Aidan held his cup out, watching as Brigs tipped the clear liquid into his steaming coffee.

"That woman loves you. Even when you left and broke her heart, she tried her best to move on with yours truly, but she still loved you. Even when she didn't want to. You can hate me, but both of us know I never really had a chance."

"I'll agree with you there." Aidan lifted his mug to toast Brigs before he took a long sip of his coffee.

"Allie has lots of secrets and I don't pretend to know half of what's going on around her." Brigs stood to leave. "But you're in it right there with her, so man up and get your shit together, bro. She needs an equal, not a hero."

"Do I need to stage an intervention here?" Darius asked as he joined them by the fire. "The last thing I need is more boy drama hovering around my Syntrophos." Darius took a seat beside Aidan, stretching his legs toward the fire. "Honestly, I could use a little female drama if you know what I mean." Darius stared at Pilar gathering up a group of older students for a hike up the mountain.

"Pilar's a little old for you, brother," Aidan said, sipping his drink, wishing it was a little more vodka and a lot less coffee.

"But she's so hot in an I'll-cut-your-throat-with-my-sword-if-you-don't-stop-staring kind of way."

"Definitely," Brigs agreed. "Not to mention she's a lot too tall for you, bro."

"I can climb," Darius said without missing a beat, making Brigs and Aidan laugh.

The laughter felt good. It felt real.

"Brigs! Come sled with me?" Raina called across the wide expanse of undisturbed snow. A healthy pink glow flushed her cheeks.

"That's my cue to leave, gentlemen." Brigs made a show of fixing his perfect hair before he set off to join Raina.

"Are you here to yell at me too?" Aidan asked, letting his gaze drift back to Allie.

"Nah." Darius lifted his arms over his head arching his back in a lazy cat-like stretch. "You've always been a broody son of a bitch. I'd worry if you weren't moping around about something."

"Asshole." Aidan punched his brother in the shoulder.

"You know she's basically turned this school into Hogwarts, right?" Darius laughed. "I haven't seen her this happy in a long time. Just don't hurt her again or I'll have to end you."

"If I can help it, I'm never leaving her side again." Aidan watched Allie divide the youngest students into groups. "What's she doing now?"

"She's sorting all the eleven-year-olds into their houses." Darius snorted. "She's got them all watching the Potter movies and reading a book about some Percy Jackson kid. She keeps telling everyone the theme of this party is *Camp Half-Blood* but no one knows what she's talking about."

"I freaking love that crazy girl." Aidan shook his head. "She's going to be our next queen, but she's such a dork."

"And the people adore her for it." Darius smiled. "Our girl is something, isn't she?" Darius gave Aidan a playful shove. "I just hope you're a patient man, my brother, because you are in for a long wait with that one."

"What, does everyone know but her?" Aidan groaned.

"Mark my words, Allie will be the last one to figure out what's staring her right in the face."

"How did you figure it out?"

"What can I say, sometimes I know her better than she knows herself. Allie is stubborn and strong-willed. She will come to you when she's ready and not a minute before then. So do what you have to do to keep her happy, but I'm going to need you to figure out a way to be happy with your relationship as it is. She's worried about you and she has the world on her shoulders right now. So like Brigs said, get your shit together, man."

"I'm trying," Aidan said with a sigh. But that was easier said than done.

"If I have to share her with anyone, I'm glad it's you," Darius said, wrinkling his nose. "That sounded all sorts of disgusting."

"I know what you meant." Aidan laughed. "I feel better just knowing you have her back."

"You know, one thing I learned from Allie might actually help you." Darius stood, staring down at his younger brother. "In the weeks after you cut her out, she clawed her way out of a deep depression she never let anyone else see. She fought for her happiness and she found it within herself. Take a page out of Allie's book, Aidan. Figure out what makes *you* happy and stop sacrificing yourself to protect the people you love, and just ... be you, bro. We missed you."

"I missed your stupid face too, Dare." Aidan forced a smile he still didn't feel. Darius was right, he had a lot of work to do on himself. And when Allie was ready to see him, he intended to be worthy of her.

"Now, if you'll excuse me, I have to go hand out some magic wands." Darius lowered his sunglasses onto his face and left Aidan alone by the fire.

Aidan's stomach growled as he stepped off the elevator to the penthouse apartment he shared with Allie, Darius and Naomi. It was a strange living arrangement, but it seemed to work for them. For most Syntrophos pairs, one stood at the center of the relationship between their Syntrophos and their Complement as the anchor. Aidan and Allie were both anchors, which complicated their already confusing relationships.

Aidan paused in the hallway outside their apartment, his shoulders slumping. "Oh no, she's cooking again." Black smoke billowed under the door and Aidan thought about getting back on the elevator down to the dining hall. After a long day of training with his Syntrophos students, he needed a good meal, but Allie was nothing short of a disaster in the kitchen.

Peals of laughter reached him, easing the tension in his shoulders as he opened the door.

"Do my ears deceive me or are you two laughing? Together?" Aidan jumped back at the kitchen doorway when towering flames greeted him.

"Sorry!" Naomi's eyes blazed as she smothered the fire.

"I don't know what it says about us that you're more surprised by the laughter coming from the apartment than the billowing black smoke." Darius stood in the living room waving a towel like a flag toward the open balcony doors.

"I'm used to the smoke." Aidan eyed the charcoal briquettes on a sooty sheet pan he was pretty sure was brand new before Allie got her hands on it. "What was that supposed to be?"

"Cookies." Allie giggled when Naomi fanned the smoke out of her face, smearing a line of soot across her cheek.

"You guys really suck at this." Aidan shook his head.

"We'll we finally found something we have in common." Allie elbowed Naomi playfully. "One of these days I'll master the art of making chocolate chip cookies. Last time I tried, I mixed up the salt and the sugar so they were awful. My boyfriend at the time tried so hard to choke one down, bless him."

"Boyfriend?" Aidan reached for Allie, tugging her into his arms. "When was this?"

"Long before you." She smiled, resting her arms around his neck. "Hey," she whispered.

"Missed you this morning." Aidan rested his forehead against Allie's, brushing his nose against hers. "I don't like waking up without you next to me—or draped over me like a blanket to be more accurate." He captured her mouth in a warm kiss, pulling back much too soon.

Allie's face heated as she chewed on her bottom lip and he very much wanted to whisk her away somewhere private.

"Sorry, I had early meetings, but I'll be sure to tell my assistant to never mess with my mornings again."

"What did you burn?" Pilar stomped into the foyer with a bag of groceries on her hip. "Girls, you had *one* job."

"You might not want to leave them unsupervised in the kitchen," Aidan said, trying not to laugh at Pilar's look of confusion.

"Many have tried to teach the princess to cook, sweetheart." Darius hopped on the step up to the dining room and leaned in to kiss Pilar—a sight Aidan could not get used to. "And many have failed."

"I wish we could just go out for sushi," Naomi said.

"We won't be stuck here forever," Darius said, standing behind Pilar with his arms draped around her shoulders. "Once the election happens, we should have a much better relationship with the Senate and then we can actually leave Sterling Tower."

"About that." Allie's shoulders immediately tensed. "I've received some disturbing intel. I could use some advice."

"Can we discuss that out on the balcony before I choke to death?" Darius coughed.

"This might call for a liquid dinner." Pilar grabbed two bottles of wine from the fridge and Naomi gathered glasses from the cabinet.

"Should we call Livia?" Aidan asked, taking Allie's hand.

"She's with Liam tonight. Let's not disturb them. I'll call the council together in the morning but I'm not sure how I want to deal with this yet." Allie flopped onto the sofa outside on the wide balcony, accepting a glass of wine from Naomi. "I'd like a chance to discuss this with family before I take it to the council."

They were a strange family, but every person here was loyal to Allie—even Naomi. In a way, they were the future queen's closest advisors, including Livia and Liam.

"What's the deal, Red?" Darius asked, sitting on the armrest beside Pilar.

"The Senate has canceled the election for this year." Allie sipped her drink.

"The one you gave them no choice about?" Aidan frowned. He didn't like where this was going.

"The very one," Allie said. "They've decided I do not have the authority to change the election laws, so they will proceed with the next election on schedule."

"In three years?" Darius cursed under his breath. "Haven't they learned anything? We can't go another three years with a temporary Chief Justice. All four seats must be filled for our government to function properly."

"Exactly. But that's the least of our worries." Allie drained her glass and sat back. "The Senate is about to publish their official statement regarding the authority of the royal family. Specifically, my authority as First Princess. They have decided I am to be a figurehead and nothing more. I will have no legal authority in the modern Immortal world and no voice in the International Senate."

"They can't do that," Pilar said. "The people will not stand for it. Your approval ratings are through the roof."

"Which scares them." Naomi stood to pour them another round. "But we can deal with this, Allie. They're just pushing back to see what you'll do."

"The thing is, I don't want a voice in the Senate." Allie sighed. "I don't want any legal authority, I just want them to do their damn jobs and be honorable about it."

"There's more, isn't there?" Aidan took her hand in his.

"The International Senate has passed some new laws. Laws we will have to acknowledge if we want to keep our side of the bargain and maintain peace with our government. After the first of the year, any child preparing for an Awakening will have to work with a Senate official and only that official can be present during the Awakening."

"That's bullshit," Pilar gasped. "That completely undermines the mentor relationship."

"Allie, we have at least thirty students who will have an Awakening next year," Darius said.

Allie nodded. "So that means each one of those students will have a court appointed "mentor" in residence here at Sterling Tower—if we comply and let them in. But it doesn't stop there. The same rule applies for those who will reach their Proving, too. Except when then the time comes, the young adult must present themselves before the Senate to undergo their Proving with court supervision."

"You're not doing it, Allie." Aidan shook his head, his heart thundering in his chest. "You're Proving soon and they know it. They did this so they could get you alone and cut off from your council."

Allie took a long gulp of her wine, swallowing slowly, her eyes burning with the fire of her power. "And they just started a war."

DON'T FORGET YOUR FREE BOOK!

In Betrayal, find out what happened during the time Allie and Aidan were apart. And then download your free copy of Scholar to discover everything there is to know about the Immortals of Indriell. **Loyal subscribers will also receive bonus chapters and a short story.**

Visit **bit.ly/ScholarOffer** to download now

Also by Melissa A. Craven

Immortals of Indriell Series:

Emerge (Book 1) | Catalyst (An Immortals of Indriell Short Story) | Edge (Book 0) | Judgment (Book 2) | Scholar (An Immortals of Indriell Series Companion) | Volunteer (An Immortals of Indriell Short Story) | Captive (Book 3) |Assignment: An Immortals of Indriell Novella | Heir (Book 4) Betrayal (Book 5) | Runaway (Book 6) | Proving (Book 7)

Queens of the Fae Series

Fae's Deception (Book 1)

Fae's Defiance (Book 2)

Fae's Destruction (Book 3)

Fae's Prisoner (Book 4)

Fae's Power (Book 5)

Fae's Promise (Book 6)

About Melissa A. Craven

Melissa A. Craven (the "A" stands for Ann—in case you were wondering) writes Young Adult Fantasy with crossover appeal to other genres and audiences of all ages. She believes in stories that make you think and she loves twisty plots, and playing with foreshadowing, leaving clues and hints for the careful reader. She draws inspiration from her background in architecture and interior design to help her with the small details in world building and scene settings.

And if you love Sweet Romance and Contemporary Fiction too, you can find Melissa's books in those genres under her pen name, Ann Maree Craven.

Join Melissa's Facebook Group, Fantasy Book Warriors
Follow Melissa at Melissaacraven.com
TikTok: @ATaleOfTwoAuthors

facebook.com/MelissaACravenAuthor
twitter.com/melissaacraven
instagram.com/melissaacraven
bookbub.com/authors/melissa-a-craven
amazon.com/Melissa-A-Craven/e/B00VSPF86W

Acknowledgments

Y'all, this book tried to kill me.

The longest of the series, Betrayal wraps up so many timelines and plot points—and begins new ones—I think I've had a migraine for the last eight months. But, once again, I think it's my favorite of the series. (I know I say that with every new book.)

I have to thank my patient editor, Rebecca Jaycox for her mad skills. I'm pretty sure I ugly cried when I handed her the manuscript and asked her to please find my book in the mess I'd made of it. She's amazing.

Another huge thank you to my sister, Angela for putting up with another round of "Let me just finish this book and then I'll do (insert whatever task Melissa has been putting off), I promise."

And, as always for helping me talk out ideas. You guys can thank her for the ending of this book ;)

And to Michelle Lynn, my author bestie for always being there for venting, crying and freaking out—and most recently, for co-authoring a new series with me.

To my family, I could literally never do this without you. A special thanks to my mother, Debby for her hilarious text messages of "I need more chapters" and "are you done yet?" and "WHY are you so mean to Aidan?" To my Dad, thank you for constantly showing me and my sister that we'll *never* know what it's like to have one of those fathers who just doesn't care. And for teaching me the subtle art of sarcasm ;)

To Jenny, you are the best, best friend I could ask for.

Thank you for your encouragement, and for the way we will always pick up right where we left off, no matter how much time has passed or how busy life gets. And for game night. Game night is important.

To Daqri Combs at Covers by Combs for the very special redesign on all the Emerge covers and the purple! I love the purple theme for Betrayal. I love your work and appreciate your guidance.

A big thank you to the city of Cleveland and to Kelleys Island especially. The island as it is portrayed in the book is purely fictional, but is based on the real Kelleys Island near Sandusky, Ohio. To all of my author friends across the world, thank you for your constant support, encouragement and sense of community. The indie community is an amazing place and it is such a comfort knowing I am not doing this alone. To C.J. Redwine, Author of The Shadow Queen and leader of YA Books Central, thank you for bringing me on as the site indie manager and for providing ALL the books. The experience has been invaluable and I look forward to the future of YABooksCentral.com

And most importantly, to my ever growing audience of readers who have waited patiently for each Emerge book, thank you from the bottom of my heart for your enthusiasm and loyalty. I promise there will be much more to look forward to in the years to come.

Finally, I thank God for the constant reminder that I am doing what I'm supposed to be doing. Over the past years, circumstances *always* bring me back to writing—my favorite thing to do in the whole world.

www.ingramcontent.com/pod-product-compliance
Lightning Source LLC
Chambersburg PA
CBHW030524310726
48979CB00010B/1786/J

* 9 7 8 1 9 7 0 0 5 2 1 6 9 *